W9-BGM-528

Di Morrissey is one of Australia's most successful writers. She began writing as a young woman, training and working as a journalist for Australian Consolidated Press in Sydney and Northcliffe Newspapers in London. She has worked in television in Australia and in the USA as a presenter, reporter, producer and actress. After her marriage to a US diplomat, Peter Morrissey, she lived in Singapore, Japan, Thailand, South America and Washington. Returning to Australia, Di continued to work in television before publishing her first novel in 1991.

Di has a daughter, Dr Gabrielle Morrissey Hansen, a human sexuality and relationship expert and academic. Di's son, Dr Nicolas Morrissey, is a lecturer in South East Asian Art History and Buddhist Studies at the University of Georgia, USA. Di has three grandchildren: Sonoma Grace and Everton Peter Hansen and William James Bodhi Morrissey.

Di and her partner, Boris Janjic, live in the Manning Valley in New South Wales when not travelling to research her novels, which are all inspired by a particular landscape.

www.dimorrissey.com

Di Morrissey

Barra Creek

PAN
Pan Macmillan Australia

Dedicated to . . .
a special friend

First published 2003 by Pan Macmillan Australia Pty Limited
1 Market Street, Sydney

978-1-250-05326-8

Barra Creek is a work of fiction. The story, events and most of
the characters in it are fictitious, although some people have
kindly allowed their names to be used in the book.

Acknowledgments

As ALWAYS MY DEAR family, who are such good sounding boards and always mightily supportive . . . my mother Kay Warbrook, my children, Dr Gabrielle Morrissey and Nick Morrissey, Uncle Jim, Rosemary, David and Damien Revitt. Ron Revitt Jonach and his family with thanks for Ron's sketches.

And in the USA . . . Leila, Julie, Emma and Sherry. Happy ninetieth to darling Dottie (Dorothy Morrissey). To Mollie and the gang, all the Hutchinson clan and Aunt Edith Morrey.

Darling Boris and little Bunya who make every day precious.

Thanks to all my friends in Normanton, especially the Gallagher family. My thanks as well to Kevin Miles.

Thanks to Anne and Bill Meyer for their New Zealand input.

Thanks to Dr Kate Irving for her advice on Alzheimer's disease. And also thanks to Susan Bradley.

Bernadette Foley, my editor, for her calm patience, sensitive advice, hand holding and always being cheerful and protective.

EVERYONE at Pan Macmillan, in particular, James Fraser, Ross Gibb, Roxarne Burns and Jane Novak.

And not forgetting Ian Robertson from Holding Redlich with a promise to write the you-know-what-book before too long.

Prologue

New South Wales, 2003

SHE WAS STRAIGHT-BACKED, hands folded in her lap, feet together flat on the floor, her head turned towards the window that framed the rain wet garden. In the grey light the woman in dark clothes looked like a black and white photograph, the caption possibly titled: 'A woman alone.'

The words 'sad', 'lonely', 'abandoned' came to Kate's mind as she paused in the doorway of the small room that was now this woman's world. A single bed with a table beside it, a shelf, a small cupboard, functional carpet, a table and two chairs. She had pulled one over so she could sit by the window.

She was one of the lucky ones, they told her, having a window to look out onto the garden. But it didn't open. There was no breeze, no smell of flowers to relieve the antiseptic air. The view only reminded her of that other world, now lost to her. How had she come to this? The shame and embarrassment ate at her. It wasn't paranoia. She didn't feel safe and secure here. She longed for all that was familiar; a place where she could feel valued and accepted with the knowledge of the distressing journey ahead of her.

'Lorna?' Kate spoke gently so as not to startle her. It was a greeting and a question, unspoken: Are you here at the moment? Or are you back among old friends, past enemies, other days, other places?

The woman turned in response to the soft, warm voice. Kate looked far too young to be the Director of Nursing, Lorna thought. A sweet, caring girl, not yet thirty. How long before she would become brisk, bitter and frustrated in a job where she was always battling for funding, drowning in bureaucracy, shouting in the face of disinterest and discomfort at the business of aged care? What would a pretty blue-eyed brunette, so slim and tiny she didn't look fully grown, know about how it felt to be old? To know you were losing your faculties, your grasp of reality, that soon enough you would forget even the habits of a lifetime – how to dress, brush your teeth. Why would this little girl want to study this thing they called Alzheimer's disease?

'What are you thinking, Lorna?' Kate pulled up the other chair and sat facing Lorna, diagnosed by two doctors and a psychologist in a swift and efficient interview as being in early stage dementia.

The woman's face softened and her shoulders relaxed slightly as she smiled. 'I was thinking how long would it be before you start to hate your job, before the system beats you, before you get out and get a life? Before it's too late.'

Relief flashed across Kate's face as she realised Lorna was here today. She'd lost a few hours last week, the staff had told her. Though often Kate felt that may have been by choice; Lorna would rather be anywhere but here. Apparently the family were well off. Her sons, no doubt dutiful, but living far away, didn't visit. An English daughter-in-law had brought some grandchildren in once but Lorna had sent them away after a short while. It was depressing for them all and anyway the children didn't know her, Lorna had told Kate.

Before Kate could speak, Lorna asked, 'Why do you do this?'

'Because I care. I want to make a difference, make a change. It's a challenge, Lorna.'

'You can say that again.' She gave another faint smile. 'How am I doing?'

'You tell me.' Kate reached over and took her hand. 'Do you want some more library books?'

'Yes, please.' She paused. 'Would it be too much trouble to find some older books – about Queensland, about the Gulf country?'

'You've been thinking about those days again, have you?'

'I never stop remembering.' Lorna looked back at the wintry garden. 'I never thought I'd miss it, the red earth, the dryness.'

'What else do you remember?' Kate leaned forward. Some of the people she cared for at the home remembered the past so vividly, while the day before or an hour ago could be a problem. It was a professional question but she was unprepared for the vehemence of Lorna's reaction.

'I wish I could forget it. All of it. Except her, she's the only one . . .' her voice trailed off. 'It doesn't matter. It's too late now.'

'What is? What's upsetting you, Lorna? Who are you talking about?'

'I wish I could see her. She's the only one who'd understand.'

'Tell me about her.'

The woman's agitation had subsided and Kate wondered if Lorna had retreated from the present. Although it was healthy that she showed this frustration and spirit. So often people with dementia lost their sense of excitement, adventure, interest in the world around them. They could be impulsive, though, suddenly selling possessions they've cherished, giving money away, buying expensive things when they'd always been frugal before. But lifting her shoulders, Lorna sighed, 'The governess.'

Then in a stronger voice she said, 'I must see her, Kate. While I'm sane and sensible enough to tell her. I must talk with her.' She turned her stricken eyes to the young woman. It appeared desperately important to her.

'Where is this governess now?' Kate recalled anecdotes and rambling stories about Lorna's days on a cattle station far up in the Gulf country of North Queensland. She imagined it from books, photos and TV shows as a place of vast emptiness, blue sky, red dirt tracks through scattered gums, a wide river and a homestead with lots of lattice and shade. For a girl who had grown up in the damp lushness of a Victorian dairy farm, outback Queensland – the Gulf country – seemed to Kate to be a romantic place, unchanged since Lorna's days there in the 1960s and seventies.

'Can we phone her?'

'No, I must see her.' She rose and went to the drawer in the bedside table and took out an envelope and handed it to Kate. Inside was a Christmas card and under the printed greeting was written:

Dear Lorna,
I hope this reaches you and that you are keeping well. Fond wishes and regards to the boys. I'm now running a small art gallery down on the south coast

and I am a grandmother! Can you believe it? I think of you often.
Love Sally.

Kate looked at the envelope. The postmark showed it had been sent two years before from Kiama, New South Wales. 'I don't suppose Kiama is a very big place.'

'Take me there, Kate. Please, I'll have no peace until I talk to her.'

'What could be so important, Lorna? Besides, I can't kidnap you from here.'

The older woman ignored her hint of levity and said calmly but with resigned seriousness, 'Then kill me.'

It wasn't the first time a patient, in pain and afraid, had asked Kate to relieve them of their anguish, to release them from a lingering death. But Lorna's request, her demand, shocked Kate. She was spry and quite fit and healthy for her age – apart from the periodic misfiring of her brain that caused blanks or haziness in her thinking. She suffered a little from arthritis but otherwise she was doing exceptionally well. The disease was only in its early days, but Lorna would continue to decline over the following months and years. Alzheimer's had a trajectory of five to fifteen years. Now, though, she was fit enough to be living on her own, Kate thought, as long as someone checked on her each day, even by phone. But the family and the local authorities along with her doctor thought otherwise. Lorna had had a few 'turns'; several lapses at times of stress. She'd had one on the day she was examined and had floundered when they had asked her a series of routine questions, and was therefore diagnosed as being of 'diminished capacity'.

Kate had always argued that this judgement of capacity was relative; that it didn't account for fluctuations in behaviour and state of mind. Nevertheless, the papers had been signed and Lorna Monroe was declared incapable of running her home or her life.

Lorna was one of the few in the nursing home who had clung on to who they were. She took care of herself and maintained order in her life. Her grey hair was neatly smoothed into a French roll, she wore powder and lipstick. Her nails were manicured. She wore jewellery – earrings, her watch and a double strand of pearls; and dressed smartly in sweaters and blouses, pressed slacks or skirts. She chose not to wear the formless floral frocks favoured by most of the women in the home.

It hurt Kate to see her here. If only on the day of her medical assessment Lorna had been fully present and alert, aware of the importance of the occasion. Maybe it was nerves that had sent her retreating to whatever safe place she went to in her mind.

The silence had lengthened since Lorna's shocking request and now she said firmly, 'I'm serious, Kate. I'm not asking you to take any action. Just give me the means to do it. I'll decide when.'

'To kill yourself? Lorna, you aren't in any danger of falling apart yet. From what we know it will be a long time before the full loss of awareness sets in.'

'Then why am I here?'

Kate had no good answer to this. Lorna would probably do much better in familiar surroundings, stimulated by some social life, looking after her house, her garden, a pet. 'I believe it was your family's decision,' she said quietly.

It always was, thought Kate. Few came willingly to a place like this, even though it was an expensive aged-care home. Home! Facility more like it. Kate had her own ideas about how to make these places less institutionalised. She'd just finished her PhD on nursing care of patients with dementia. At twenty-nine she was leading a small group at the Department of Health as well as teaching aged-care nurses new methods for looking after the frail and elderly.

Kate was vibrant, a party girl, popular at university. Her friends wondered why she had decided to bury herself in smelly, old-aged homes with infantile, spoon-fed, wandering patients. But they didn't know how Kate had come to this field or why she found it stimulating and challenging. People like Lorna made it special.

So now as she looked at Lorna's hurt expression, she knew a platitude wouldn't suffice. 'Your sons think it's best for you.'

'My sons!' She turned back to the window and Kate waited for what she heard so often – *After all I've done for them!*

Instead Lorna spoke to her reflection in the glass. 'It's my fault. I brought this on myself. It's what I deserve, though I never thought it would come to this.' She shrugged and turned back to Kate. 'One never anticipates or plans one's last days on earth very well, I suppose.'

'Lorna! You're eighty-two but you still have years ahead of you.'

'In here? And in what state of mind?' She raised an eyebrow. 'Please, Kate, help me find her.'

'The governess?'

'Yes. Sally Mitchell, as she was then. She might not want to see me, though.'

'She sent you a Christmas card.'

'She always had good manners. She was well brought up, came from a good New Zealand family.' She paused. 'We went through some hard times. She might not want to remember them. But I must, she must. I need her help.'

'Write her a letter.'

'What I have to tell her cannot be written down.'

Kate stood up and placed the chair back at the table,

then crouched down in front of the woman and rested her hands on the laced fingers.

'Unfinished business, Lorna?' Kate knew that the elderly often needed to make amends, achieve resolution, extract retribution – reach closure.

Lorna nodded. 'I must see her. Please, please help me. I'm trapped in here.' She waved vaguely around her, then tapped her head. 'And in here.'

Kate stood up. 'I'll try to find where she is. No promises beyond that.'

Lorna's face softened and her body relaxed slightly. 'That's a start. Thank you.'

Kate left the room knowing she'd have to make good on her offer. Lorna might have periodic lapses but she wouldn't forget what Kate had promised her – to find her governess from the 1960s, Sally Mitchell. She must have been a special young woman. And what had she and Lorna shared that was now so important?

'Got your handbag, dearie?'

The woman shepherding the group onto the minibus patted Lorna's arm as the driver helped his elderly passengers aboard. Lorna nodded, thinking she needn't have bothered taking her good lizard-skin bag as they only allowed them five dollars each in cash. They weren't considered responsible with money, matches, valuables or sharp instruments like nail scissors. But the women clutched their empty, bulky handbags as if they were life preservers.

Lorna hadn't wanted to go on this enforced outing. Most of her companions were only vaguely aware of where they were, though the lure of ice-creams penetrated some foggy minds.

'This'll be good for you,' said Mrs Jackson. But Lorna felt it was Mrs Jackson who was looking forward to it.

Even with six women and three men in her charge, going for a 'scenic' drive around the suburbs then stopping for ice-cream and drinks at the Park Cafe was preferable to looking after them in the home.

Lorna sat at the rear of the bus, distancing herself from the excited childlike chatter of the two women in front of her. She paid little attention to the 'sights' – manicured lawns and gardens, homes like the ones they may have lived in once – followed by a slow twirl through a big park until they stopped outside the Park Cafe, a simple tea room with tables outside. Across the road was a squat square bank building.

'I'd like to sit outside, please.' Lorna put her handbag on a table.

The waitress assisting Mrs Jackson frowned. 'You're not going to smoke, are you?'

'This *is* outdoors,' snapped Lorna.

'Don't worry, dear,' said Mrs Jackson to the waitress. 'They're not allowed ciggies.'

Lorna sat down. She'd asked a friendly nursing assistant with a smoking habit to bring her a packet of cigarettes, but then realised she was jeopardising her job by asking her to break the rules. She almost smiled to herself. It'd probably be easier for the young woman to slip her excess medication than cigarettes.

Mr Thompson sat beside her. He was a gruff, withdrawn chap. Half the time Lorna wasn't sure if he was unaware of his surroundings or just being sulky.

'Better out here. You can hear the birds,' he said.

'Fresh air, sunshine. I miss that. Being able to wander outside whenever you want,' Lorna replied.

'It's bloody dreadful being told what to do all the time. Bossy bloody women.' He fell silent, looking morose.

A glass of orange juice with a straw was put in front of him; a cup of tea with a biscuit for Lorna.

'You can manage all right, Mr T? Don't spill any on that nice jumper.'

He didn't answer, but held his shaking hand with his good one, guiding it to the glass as he leaned over and took a sip.

Lorna stirred her tea, gazing across the road. 'There's a bank over there. I have an account with them.'

'Rare species these days, a regular bank. My kids closed my account. Buggered if I know how they got control of my cheque book.'

Lorna stared at him. He'd never talked so much in all the time she'd seen him around the home. 'Would you mind waiting here for a bit longer? I have to go to the ladies room.'

'I'm not going to run away. Nowhere to go.' He looked morose again.

'I am.' Lorna was flushed. She pushed her cup away and tucked her handbag under her arm and got to her feet.

'Run away? You won't get far. But good luck to you. I'll tell 'em you're in the loo.' He was not surprised at her impulsive decision.

He watched her walk steadily and quite quickly across the grass towards the block of public toilets, veer around it and head to the pedestrian crossing and push the button to change the lights.

'Want a sandwich, Mr T? Now where's Lorna?'

'She's allowed to go to the blessed lavatory, isn't she?' he said, shifting his weight in his chair to block the view of the street.

'Now don't be like that, Mr T, or you won't come out on these nice trips.' Mrs Jackson hurried back inside to the group of women who were busy stuffing muffins, pepper, salt and sugar sachets along with plastic cutlery and paper napkins into their cavernous handbags.

He glanced up again and saw that Lorna was across the road and going into the bank.

'Morning. How can I help you?' The teller gave her a bright smile.

'I'd like you to call Mr Stephen Benson at the head office, please.'

'Excuse me?' The smile grew tighter.

'I want to take money out of my account. He can arrange it.'

'Oh dear. Don't you have your card? Your passbook, cheque book?'

'No, it's been taken away from me. Please telephone him. He knows me.'

'Sorry, madam, I can't help you if you haven't got identification or means to make a withdrawal.' The smile disappeared.

'Could I see your manager, please?'

'I'm afraid he's busy at the moment.'

'Then I'll wait. Tell him Mrs Lorna Monroe is here to see him.'

'Do you have an account with us?'

'Not with this branch, but Mr Benson knows me.'

'Is there a problem?' The supervisor appeared at the teller's shoulder.

'This lady has no documents and wants to withdraw money. She says some Mr Benson knows her. She wants to see our manager but I explained he was busy.' She was signalling with her eyes that she wanted the supervisor to help her move on this troublesome customer. There were others in line.

'Did you say you know Mr Benson?' asked the supervisor.

'That's right. Mr Stephen Benson. He looked after my account.'

'He's the Managing Director in head office.'

'That's right. Would you please tell him Mrs Lorna Monroe needs to speak to him. It's quite urgent.'

The supervisor asked Lorna to step through the swing door and ushered her into a small office. She returned a short time later and Lorna detected a change in her manner. She picked up the phone on the desk and handed it to Lorna.

The call was brief, the expression on the supervisor's face showing surprise, slight shock, then sympathy as she listened to Lorna's side of the conversation.

Lorna hung up. 'He says I can have five hundred dollars in cash until he sorts matters out for me.'

She left the bank, holding onto her handbag more tightly. The teller had told her there was a taxi rank just down the road.

The car pulled up outside 28 Kavanagh Street, in a neat, respectable Sydney suburb. Lorna sat looking at the overgrown front garden, annoyance, happiness, relief and trepidation welling up in her. The driver turned around and repeated the fare.

'Oh, sorry. Here you are.' She handed him the cash.

He looked at her and back at the house. 'You'll be all right, lady? Doesn't look like there's anyone home.'

'It's all right. It's my home.'

The taxi turned around in the street then stopped as the driver watched the woman walk slowly to the front door and fumble in her handbag. He wanted to be sure she was safe. She had no luggage, the blinds were drawn and the place looked like it had been empty a long time.

Lorna unzipped the small compartment in her bag and took out a front door key. No one knew she'd kept it. She'd also written her address on a piece of paper. Praying her son hadn't changed the locks, she slipped the key into the deadlock and sighed as it clicked. She opened the door and stepped inside.

As she walked through the house, anger slowly replaced her initial trepidation at returning to her home of twenty years. It had been stripped of everything she'd owned and loved. Only a shell with basic furniture remained. In every room she imagined how it once looked – the pictures, the cushions, the furniture, the curtains, the knick-knacks, the lovely rugs. All gone.

Why had they done this? She wasn't in her grave and she wasn't an imbecile. Yet.

Her growing fury fuelled her energy. She began to plan. There was electricity, the fridge and stove were still there, as was a bare bed, and table and chairs in the family room. The phone was still connected. She would call a taxi and go to the shops, stock up on some necessities and telephone Kate. She'd kept Kate's card in her bag too.

'Lorna! What are you saying? I don't believe this.'

'Kate, I don't want to get you into trouble. Please don't tell my family or the home where I am. Just ring them and tell them you know I'm all right, I'm with friends. Not to worry about me.'

'My God, the staff at the home have probably got the police searching the streets around the park right now. Okay, I'll ring them. Give me your address and I'll be right over. Do you need anything?'

'Not really. I've been out and bought a few things. I caught a taxi home. It was just a few blocks away. Promise me you won't tell them anything. Don't break a confidence, you know what I mean.'

Kate sighed. 'I shouldn't do this. I'll tell them I'm dealing with your case and I'll bring you back.'

'We have to talk about that. I'm not going back there.'

'We definitely need to talk. Put the kettle on and

make yourself a cup of tea, I'll be there within an hour. I have a bit of re-scheduling to do.'

'Thank you, Kate.'

'Don't thank me, Lorna. I'm not agreeing to any of this. I'm just buying you a little time.'

Lorna smiled as she hung up. Time. That's what she needed. Time to find, and talk to, the governess. Eventually time would run out . . . for all of them.

The small blue car travelled out of the town through light rain showers, past farm gates into a lush valley with thickly wooded ranges on either side. They passed a tea room and some shops before seeing the white gate with its sign saying 'Art Gallery'.

'Very rustic. Pretty. She must have quite a big acreage,' said Kate as she turned into the gravel driveway lined with Japanese maples.

'Horses too, I'm sure,' Lorna said, looking across at the white-fenced paddocks.

'That must be the gallery at the side there. Where it's glassed in, with the lights on,' said Kate. 'This is the address on the Christmas card.'

They sat in silence staring at the house. Lorna twisted her hands as she did when she was agitated.

'Are you sure about this, Lorna?'

'I'd better be after all the drama getting here.'

'You're not wrong.' Kate didn't want to think about the machinations involved in getting Lorna temporarily released from the home into her care. They said it was an urgent family matter that had driven Lorna to rush away. If Kate hadn't been a qualified geriatric nurse the managers at the home would never have agreed to it. And she still had to face the return, even though Lorna was adamant she wasn't going back. But there was no way she could stay in her old home, her oldest son had arranged its sale. It was going up for auction in a month's time. Lorna was lucky that she had made her escape from the nursing home when she did. Kate undid her seatbelt. 'Do you want me to go in first?'

'No. I'd rather go in alone. Would you mind waiting here?'

Kate was surprised. 'Are you sure?'

'It's probably best. Just for a bit. I'll see how she reacts. If she offers me some tea and has the time to talk, or rather listen, then come in.' Lorna wondered how Sally would react to this surprise visit.

'All right. I'd like to meet her and then I'll go into the town and get a coffee or something. If you're sure you'll be okay?' Kate was curious.

Lorna nodded and opened the car door, then she stepped into the damp air, pulling her coat around her.

She rang the bell beside the door with the coloured leadlight inserts and through the wavy pink and blue glass saw a melting figure coming up the hall.

The door was opened by a smiling young man in his twenties. 'Can I help you?'

'The gallery . . . I was wondering if Mrs –'

'The gallery is only open on weekends, but as you're here and it's so miserable in the rain, come on in.' He glanced out at the car. 'Does your friend want to come in too?'

'No. Thank you. Actually, I was wondering if Sally still ran this place?'

'Yes, she does. Are you a friend of hers? Would you like to see her?'

'Yes. If she's not busy. We knew each other once.'

'I'll go and get her. Are you interested in art?'

'A little.' Lorna's eyes darted around the hallway and her attention was caught by a series of framed family photographs. She recognised one large shot in particular. It was of a young woman on a stunning white Arabian horse galloping over a paddock. She sat well in the saddle, her hair flying, the horse's plumed tail arched.

The young man followed her gaze. 'Great photo, isn't it? That's Sally when she was young, in New Zealand. She loves horses.'

'You're related?'

'Oh no, I just help out in the studio and I'm teaching her how to use her computer. My name's Julian. I'll go and get her.'

Lorna heard a muted conversation, shoes tapping on the polished floorboards, then silence as the woman walked onto the Persian runner and came down the hall. Lorna turned back to the photograph.

The woman was slim, wiry almost, her burnished auburn hair cut stylishly short, glasses on the tip of her nose, a welcoming smile.

'Good afternoon. Julian told me I had an old friend visiting.'

Lorna turned around and pointed at the photo. 'You always rode well. Though the horses at Barra Creek weren't as nice as that one.'

Sally's smile changed to shock, surprise, then pleasure. 'My God, Lorna. Is it you?'

'Hello, Sally. I hope you don't mind me dropping in unannounced?'

'Of course not, though it is a bolt out of the blue.' She was trying to add up the years since they'd last seen each other. 'Come into the sitting room, thank goodness I was here. You should have let me know. Are you passing through . . .' Sally knew she was babbling and Julian was looking at her with an amused expression. 'Jules, put the tea on, would you?' Her mind was racing and she was surprised at how rattled she felt. How unusual of Lorna, who was always so terribly correct and polite, to drop in unannounced. 'My goodness, after all these years. I sent you a card a couple of Christmases ago, I wasn't sure if you got it.' She didn't need to add she'd never received a reply.

'Is your friend joining us?' asked Julian.

'You have someone with you? One of the boys?'

'No. A . . . friend, Kate. She kindly drove me here. She'll just say hello, then she wanted to go into town. Do you have a few minutes, Sally?'

'After all these years? I should say so.'

After Julian left the women studied each other.

'I needed to talk to you. There's something I have to tell you before I slip off the perch.' Lorna tried a small laugh.

'You look like you're going to be around for a long time yet,' said Sally, leading the way into a small sunroom. 'We won't be disturbed in here. Sit there, in the comfy chair.' She sat at one end of the sofa and watched Lorna ease herself into the armchair. 'I suppose this has something to do with the old days?' Sally said in a quiet voice.

Lorna adjusted the folds of her skirt, avoiding Sally's eyes. 'I often wondered if you thought about . . . what happened. If you ever had any concerns, any conclusions about anything that happened at Barra Creek.'

'Why would I want to rehash unhappy memories? It was so long ago. We've moved on. I like to remember the happy times.'

Lorna's lip trembled. 'I haven't. The older I get the more I re-live it all. I'm tired of carrying it around inside myself.'

Sally didn't answer but she was thinking, You haven't changed, have you? Always needing someone else to deal with the uncomfortable stuff, despite being so capable yourself.

Involuntarily Sally straightened in her chair then

sighed. 'I'm not sure how I can help you. But I'm pre-pared to listen. Let's wait till we've got our tea. Oh, this must be your friend, Kate.' She rose in some relief as Julian ushered Kate through the door.

They introduced themselves and Sally was startled to see how young Kate was and she suddenly saw herself again – bright-eyed, eager, energetic, sympathetic. Sally had to hand it to Lorna, the old devil, she hadn't lost her touch. She could frighten a bunch of rough stockmen, berate the Aboriginal house girls to re-do a task for the fifth time, and charm the birds from the trees. Everyone did Lorna's bidding.

They chatted over their tea, filling Sally in on Lorna's circumstances and Kate's role in her temporary 'escape'.

'Lorna,' said Kate, 'do you mind if I tell Sally a little about why we came here and how you are feeling?'

'No, that's fine. She should know.'

'I hope this is not an imposition,' said Kate politely. 'I suggested to Lorna that she could call or write to you, but she insisted she had to tell you – whatever it is – face to face.'

Sally nodded but didn't say anything.

'She can lose the thread of what she's saying, but she's been good lately, very focused. Seeing you means a lot to her,' Kate explained.

'We shared a lot, even though it was over forty years ago,' said Sally.

'After this visit, I think Lorna will feel more settled. Then we can tackle the problem of her future,' said Kate with more assurance than she felt.

Sally couldn't see Lorna feeling settled. She may be frailer and older, but Sally knew that behind the pale and wan face, the wringing hands and mournful eyes, Lorna was as fiercely determined as a buffalo.

What could be so important, after all this time?

Chapter One

Ashford Lodge, South Island, New Zealand, 1963

THE REFLECTION IN THE mirror showed a determined young woman wrestling with the ends of her stock tie. A second figure appeared behind her, taller, heavier set, but with the same hazel eyes and auburn hair.

'Sally, aren't you ready? You can't be late. Mother wants us downstairs.'

'I'm just having trouble with my stock, it's got too much starch in it.' She swung the long tie around her neck, folding it in front, and began to pull on her beige britches, laced the legs up to the knee then sat on her bed and pulled on the long black leather riding boots.

'What about your hair? You know Dad doesn't like wisps sticking out under your bowler.'

'Yvonne, why don't you go down and eat breakfast? I'll be ready in a minute.' Sally glared at her sister, got up and went to the window to look out at the manicured front lawn.

In the crisp cold morning long trestle tables, covered in starched white cloths dotted with silver serving dishes, had been set up for the formal breakfast that followed the Hunt, although it would be hours before the riders sat down to eat. The Rangiora Hunt had become well-known and was a tribute to her father's years of effort. He'd started breeding steeplechasers and the bloodline was carried on in the fine animals in the lush paddocks enclosed by white rail fences that Sally could see in the distance. Her father, Garth Mitchell, had imported the sire of the foxhounds from England, and the pack of hounds was now a formidable line. The dream of this hunt had begun when the girls were little and Mitchell had set up a paper chase for Yvonne and her friends on their ponies, pinning paper on a long trail they could ride around their home, Ashford Lodge. He had ridden behind, watching in amusement as the children followed the paper trail.

At their mother's insistence Sally and Yvonne ate bowls of porridge sprinkled with brown sugar, a nob of butter and fresh cream. Yvonne sat at the dining table, but Sally preferred to pull up an armchair close to the large open fire in the adjoining drawing room. Placed around the rooms were beautiful pieces of antique furniture. The two rooms were separated by folding doors, and when the family was entertaining, they opened the doors to make one large room.

She took her empty plate into the kitchen and after downing a cup of tea with her mother she ran up the stairs to finish dressing. She loved riding, even though her father's involvement – being Master of the Hunt – dominated the family's social life. Sally couldn't imagine not being part of this ritual, which had started in Britain and now flourished and had evolved its own customs in New Zealand.

Her father drummed it into Sally and Yvonne that they were to carry on this tradition from the 'old country'. Sally did sometimes rail against the strict rules and regulations of the Hunt and was happiest riding on her own across the paddocks and through the outlying district of the local town. But being the younger daughter of the Master she knew that her position in the social hierarchy of this island world, which was even more British than the British, was one of honour and privilege.

Garth was proud of the fact that he had bred one of the best packs of foxhounds in New Zealand. He'd also trained a huntsman and two whips – keen young men who controlled the hounds in the field and who hoped to follow in the Master's footsteps one day.

In her room Sally reached for the gold stock pin her father had presented to her on her eighteenth birthday, centred it on her stock, then folded the ends of the stock into her check waistcoat. Next she put on her black hunting jacket with its royal-blue velvet collar – the colours of this hunt – then pinned a gold hunt button onto the lapel. She much preferred to wear her tweed hacking jacket, jodhpurs and riding boots, which were the more relaxed dress for the Tuesday Hunts. Her attire today was traditional, subdued and appropriate. One was never to draw attention to oneself and modern accessories such as sunglasses, jewellery or unnecessary tack were forbidden. Anyone less than correctly turned out was sent to the rear of the field by the Deputy Master.

Sometimes Sally wanted to rebel and do something outrageous just to shock the whole lot of them. Especially her supercilious and righteous older sister. She loved her family dearly, and never wanted to hurt her father or mother, but Sally recognised within herself a longing to one day do something totally disgraceful – and fun.

Garth Mitchell sat on his seventeen-hand grey mare and watched with pride as fifteen couples came down the drive from the kennels under the watchful eye of the huntsman and whips. The hounds were taken to the front paddock and kept in a tight group; now that they were out of the kennels they were raring to go.

A field of one hundred and twenty were riding in this opening hunt of the season, and they gathered at the front of the house where the lawn was encircled by a white gravel driveway and neatly clipped hedge. The two girls rode up beside their father to watch him being presented with the traditional stirrup cup by the local farmer, who doffed his cap as the Master returned the small silver goblet to him, acknowledging permission for the Hunt to ride across his land.

They rode out the front gate, the girls behind Garth, the hounds a long way ahead, the gravel road crunching beneath the horses' hooves. Twenty minutes later they turned right to a clearing and a ricker, where the first strand of wire on the fence had been pulled down and a rail placed on top, and jumped into a lush paddock. The Master and the field stayed at a distance as the huntsman and whips assembled the pack. With a flick of the whips to the lead hound, the huntsman cast the hounds and silence fell over the field. Noses to the ground the hounds ran feverishly, looking for the scent as the field waited. In fifteen minutes the lead hound took up the scent of the hare and gave tongue and immediately the rest of the pack started to speak.

Sally felt her adrenalin surge as her big strong mare stretched into a full gallop. To her left was her father, on her right Yvonne, and close by Lachlan, the Head Cadet who was in charge of the Master's horses. Behind them streamed the rest of the field. Yvonne always thought being at the fore, taking the fences in the lead and following the hounds, was thrilling. Sally, while an excellent rider, was only too conscious of the hundred odd horses pounding behind her and the unpredictable line the hare might take ahead of them. It often meant jumping thick gorse hedges, rickers and the occasional barbed-wire fence. She concentrated on the blurring ground in front of her, hearing only the thud of hooves, but then the field took a check.

Sally found she had dropped back but decided to stay there as the field waited. She thought she knew everyone in their Hunt but a strange horse, a black gelding ridden by a slight man she didn't recognise, was beside her.

'Seems we've got a smart one,' said Sally softly.

'Trying to outfox us, eh?' He smiled at her as the horses stood, breathing heavily.

At these times while they waited, Sally preferred to be back in the field. Yvonne always accused her of flirting, even if only with eye contact. Sally thought her sister took the Hunt too seriously. Yvonne saw their participation as being part of a great and grand tradition, and was a stickler for the pomp and ceremony. Sally thought of it as sport and fun. She was in it for the thrills, speed and social interaction.

'I haven't seen you here before,' whispered Sally, hoping no one would overhear their subdued conversation. The Master frowned on chatter when the field was on check.

'I ride with the Tautama Hunt. I feel privileged to be invited to ride with your father.' He touched his crop to his bowler and Sally acknowledged the gesture with a smile. He had a soft Irish brogue and mischievous blue eyes.

Sally knew her mother would consider this handsome man totally unsuitable for her to socialise with, as he looked at least ten years older than her, he was Irish and probably not considered of their class, yet Sally had no doubt he was being more than charming. He was flirting too.

An hour passed as they waited, and the horses, spread over the paddocks, shifted their weight, gnawed at their bits, flicked flies with their tails. The Irishman, who introduced himself as Sean Flanagan, and Sally talked in low whispers. He had moved from Auckland where he'd lived since he was sixteen and worked for an import company. He planned to stay in the South Island and he casually let it be known that he was single and liked dancing. Before Sally could think of how to mention the Hunt Ball later in the season, a blast from the huntsman's horn went up and they were off at a gallop. From the top of the hill a crowd of spectators, many perched on shooting sticks, watched the large field run almost full circle of the point.

Back at Ashford Lodge Sally's mother, Emily, and several young women who preferred not to ride were helping prepare the traditional Hunt breakfast. Everyone had brought a plate and they were carrying dishes through Emily's beautiful English cottage garden to the front of the house.

These girls were all part of a world that observed and revered its heritage while evolving its own customs and lifestyle. Like Sally and Yvonne, they were part of a circle of young people who came from well-to-do families, had been educated at private schools, and shared the same interests, tastes and goals. It was expected they would all marry young men from the same circle.

The speed of the Hunt increased and Sally was happily chatting with Sean. Suddenly a blind fence loomed – a wall of green she couldn't see through or over. She had no sense of any other rider being with her, and there was no chance to avoid the solid gorse hedge that rose before her. She prayed there wasn't a drop or water hazard on the other side. A conversation flashed through Sally's mind where her father had discussed setting a challenging diversion to the Hunt. She closed her eyes, leaned forward, balancing her weight as her mare lifted her forelegs, her face so close to her horse's straining neck she could feel the urgency and tension in the muscles. Then there was a moment of blissful airborne silence, before they fell, green hedge and blue sky spinning, a crash as they tumbled into the hedge, a crushing feeling as the breath was expelled from her lungs by the weight of the horse, then oblivion.

When she opened her eyes, her mother's concerned face swam into focus.

'Sal? Oh, darling. Please say something. Can you hear me?'

'Have I missed the breakfast?'

'Breakfast? Sally, dear, you mean the Hunt breakfast?' Emily asked gently.

'Sorry to drag you away, Mummy. What happened?' mumbled Sally. 'Is Rani okay?'

'She's fine, dear. That was a week ago. You've been unconscious for a week. How do you feel?' Her mother stroked her hand.

'A week? I've been out for a week. Oh, hell.' Sally closed her eyes again.

Her mother winced slightly. 'No need to swear, darling. The doctors say you will be all right. Do you remember anything?'

7

'Not much. How was the Hunt?'

'Daddy thought it all went very well . . . considering you had to be taken to hospital.'

'Oh, I spoiled it.' Sally felt her head hurt. She could imagine the chaos her accident must have caused. It would have ruined her father's organisation, the finale of the Hunt, her mother's Hunt breakfast. Her sister's joy in it all. 'Sorry, Mummy.'

'Don't be upset. The Deputy Master took over and the ambulance people were very discreet. I went in the ambulance and once Daddy made sure you were getting the best of care, even though it's the public hospital, he hosted the breakfast. By the time I got home the usual group was ensconced in the library with Daddy and the liqueurs.'

'Oh. Did the doctors know I'd be out this long?'

'Goodness me, no. We were terribly worried. But you're going to be just fine, and the horse is all right, so that's good news. You'll be home soon. Daddy thinks you'd better rest up for some of the season. But he wants you to ride in the end-of-season hunts. And there's the Hunt Ball to look forward to.'

'Was anyone else hurt?'

'Luckily, no. Now, let's concentrate on the future,' she said briskly and Sally closed her eyes, seeing for a moment the face of Sean Flanagan. She'd probably never see him again. She took a deep breath and squeezed her mother's hand. All she wanted to do was sleep.

Later, after her mother had gone, a young nurse came in with Sally's tea. 'You're a lucky girl. You had a fair-sized sleep.'

'Yeah, out for nearly a week, and I have no memory of it at all.'

'You'll be well enough to leave soon. So will your uncle be taking you home? He's been so sweet.'

'My uncle? I don't think so.' Sally couldn't imagine Uncle Richard, her father's brother, coming all the way from his home at Mearsham Park to see her. 'Did he visit me?'

'Every day. Brought you flowers. Your mother took them. He is such a lovely man. I love his Irish accent.'

The penny dropped and Sally blushed with pleasure. Uncle her foot. The dashing Sean must have taken an interest in her. Instinct told her not to mention it to her mother, who probably knew and didn't approve.

Within a few days of leaving hospital she had settled back into the family's routine. Her mother didn't talk about visitors to the hospital and no cards or flowers from the charming Mr Flanagan were mentioned. Two weeks later, on a Monday morning, Sally appeared at breakfast dressed in a neat suit, a tailored cream blouse and smart high heels with pointed toes.

'Surely you're not going to work?' exclaimed Emily.

'Why not? I feel fine. What else am I going to do?' Sally took her bowl of cereal off the sideboard and headed for her favourite armchair.

'Don't spill anything on that suit, dear,' cautioned her mother. 'You do look nice.'

'I don't see why you dress up so much when you just work for one of Daddy's friends. You could get a proper job,' muttered her sister.

'What, like yours? Counting packets of grubby bank notes? At least I'm learning about our business.'

Yvonne's job as a bank teller was regarded as an adequate pastime until she met the right man. Sally worked in the office of a stock and station agent who was also a leading auctioneer. It was an informal arrangement and there was little pressure on her, but Sally was efficient and they liked her affable manner with the clients. If she took time off for a hunt, there was no objection. Garth Mitchell and Sally's boss were old friends and drank at their club together. Her job had been mutually arranged between them and it didn't stretch her. She'd finished a secretarial course but knew she was only marking time. Until what, she wasn't sure. Unlike Yvonne she wasn't filling in time waiting to find a fiancé. No, there had to be more to life. She just had to figure out what it was and how to find it.

Garth poked his head out from behind *The Christchurch Press*. 'Girls, a job is job. Make the most of the opportunity to meet people and save a little money. Leave your mother in peace. Shall we proceed with breakfast?'

The women took the hint, and breakfast was eaten in relative silence.

The sisters made the two-hour drive to Christchurch every Monday after spending the weekend at Ashford Lodge. During the week they stayed in the family flat in town. Both had cars, a luxury for girls their age, but this morning they were driving in with their father.

He dropped Yvonne outside the bank at eight forty-five, Sally walked into the stock and station agency at five to nine, and Garth drove on to see his accountant at precisely nine o'clock. This journey could have been a sociable time between father and daughters, but they travelled in silence so as not to interrupt the NZBC morning news, rural report and finance update. Yvonne read the newspaper her father had finished over breakfast, while Sally sat in the back seat wrapped in her own thoughts. Whatever was happening in Australia or the rest of the world rarely penetrated their cosy routine.

At lunchtime Sally walked down the street to the milk bar to buy a sandwich. She paused outside *La Belle de Jour* ladies dress salon to see what new garment was on the mannequin in the window. She sighed as she studied the mink cape draped over the shoulders of the blank-eyed model.

'Now that would suit you very well,' said a friendly voice beside her.

Sally turned at the sound of the soft brogue and saw the amused blue eyes of Sean Flanagan. He whipped off his hat and ran his fingers through his unruly curls. He was smartly dressed in a suit and she almost didn't recognise him. He looked older and more sophisticated than in his hunting attire.

'I'm pleased you've made a good recovery. I was worried I might have played a part in your tumble.'

'No, not at all. These things happen.' She looked at him. 'You knew I was in the hospital?'

'I did indeed. I visited you every day. Just like Sleeping Beauty you were.'

'The flowers . . . they were from you?' She didn't say she'd never seen them, thank heavens the nurse remembered him and told her. But then, what girl wouldn't recall such a good-looking visitor?

'A small token.' Neither mentioned that Sean had called himself her uncle. 'Where are you off to? May I buy you lunch?'

'That would be lovely.' Sally's boring Monday brightened.

He held out his arm, placed his hat at a rakish angle over his eyes, tucked her arm in his and they set off to one of his 'favourite haunts'.

By the end of lunch there was a subtle acknowledgment of their mutual attraction. Sally felt light headed even though she'd only had two shandies with the meal.

They'd shared some personal details, but he'd kept the conversation around their interest in horses and hunting.

Sally glanced at her watch. 'I'd better get back. I'm half an hour late. My boss is very easy going, but I don't want him to get cross.'

'He might be worried, do you think you should call him?' Sean glanced at the flushed and sparkling Sally Mitchell, thinking he'd love to spend the whole afternoon with her. Beneath her well-brought-up manner and politeness there lurked a mischievousness that hinted she'd have little compunction at breaking the rules on occasion.

'I'll run back, it's not far.' She pushed back her chair and Sean leapt to his feet to help her. 'Thank you for a wonderful lunch. It was a lovely surprise.'

'Can we do it again? My office isn't far away.' It was in fact blocks away, he'd found out where Sally worked and had deliberately hung around hoping she'd take a lunch break.

'I would really like that. Are you joining the Saturday Rangiora Hunt?'

'I'm afraid I can't make it. Perhaps we could go for a ride sometime. Make a day of it. Perhaps one Sunday?'

'Sounds fabulous.' She doubted her father would allow her to take Rani out with a stranger. And she hadn't been back on a horse since her accident. She was being cautious, nervous at the thought of riding again. Her father wanted her back riding, but, well, she wasn't rushing into it.

'In the meantime, how about lunch on Friday. To round off the week? We could meet in Cathedral Square at twelve.'

'Wonderful. I'll be there. Don't worry about walking me back to work. Thanks again. See you Friday.'

She hoped her boss didn't mention her tardiness to her father.

Sean and Sally started seeing each other three or four times a week for lunch. When Sean finally asked her out to dinner with a small group of his friends one Saturday night Sally hesitated. She and Yvonne went home to Ashford Lodge most weekends, and her parents would never allow her to go out with him on her own. So Sean suggested she bring her sister, and Sally had agreed.

She'd told Yvonne it was a mixed group and they were going to a theatre restaurant, which sounded fun. Sally was relieved when she saw that quite a few in the group were close to her and Yvonne's age. The audience was served dinner and drinks at their tables as the performers wandered among them and a short, slightly risqué melodrama was performed on stage as the finale.

Yvonne had been a bit shocked at the show and had been watching Sally closely all night. She had guessed immediately that Sally and Sean were close friends.

As they refreshed their lipstick and powder in the ladies room Yvonne interrogated her: 'What's going on with that Sean fellow? You seem very friendly. How come you know him?'

'We met at the Hunt, he was with me when I took that tumble. He called at the hospital to see if I was all right.' Sally felt she might be skiting a bit; she'd seen how all the girls looked at Sean.

'He didn't! Does Mum know? He's far too old for you, Mum and Dad will skin you alive.'

'They're not going to find out,' said Sally, giving her sister a beady eye. She hoped her mother hadn't made the connection over the flowers at the hospital.

Yvonne shrugged. 'You be careful.' She puffed and

fluffed her hair, then a thought struck her. She lowered her voice, there was shock and concern in her tone. 'You're not, you wouldn't, you know . . . *go* with him?'

Sally's eyes widened innocently. 'Yvonne, we have to save ourselves for our wedding night. You know that.'

Her sister looked relieved. 'I don't want you to get into trouble, Sal. You stick with our own friends. They're nice boys.'

Yvonne left the powder room as Sally fiddled with the bolero of her shantung cocktail dress. Of course she was still a virgin. Damn it. She smiled at her reflection. But not for long, why save a prize for those stuffy, snooty boys in her circle. Sean might be her only chance to be wild and wicked, so she was going to make the most of it.

They went to the pictures in town at the Majestic the following Saturday night, just the two of them. She'd been at a tennis luncheon party with her friends that day and found she was starting to juggle a double life between her own social circle and the mysterious and unacceptable Irishman.

They sat at the back, paying scant attention to *Cleopatra*, the big new film starring Elizabeth Taylor. Just as Sean kissed her, Sally was aware of the usherette's torch flashing down the aisle as she seated two latecomers. In the silver glow from the screen Sally recognised the unmistakable silhouette of her parents.

'Lordy, it's Mum and Dad! I didn't know they were coming to the pictures. They'll be at the flat.'

'They're late. It must have been a last-minute idea. They didn't know you'd be here, did they?'

'Of course not. I told them I was staying the night with Pru, my best friend.'

14

'We can sneak out before the interval?'

'Let's go now.' Sally tugged at his hand.

'What do you want to do?'

She looked at his face in the flickering light, thinking he was even better looking than Richard Burton. 'Let's go to your place. Have you got some food?'

He saw the look in her eye and knew what she was thinking. 'Are you sure?'

'Dead right I am. Come on, let's get out of here.'

Holding hands they worked their way along the row and, giggling, hurried through the foyer to his car.

'This is it. Tonight's the night,' Sally told herself. She hoped it wouldn't hurt too much. Her girlfriends, none of whom knew any better, had related awful stories about this big step in a girl's life.

It turned out to be a simple and very nice event. Sean was no novice and his lovemaking was gentle and attentive. Afterwards he brought her a cloth to wipe herself and ran her a bath where he playfully joined her.

Lying back in the tub, with her legs between his knees, holding a glass of Cold Duck, Sally congratulated herself on making this decision. Boy, if only her girlfriends knew. This was no fumbling in a back seat of a car. This was classy.

She stayed the night and they made love in the morning, and with her new-found knowledge she found it exhilarating.

Sean laughed and tousled her hair. 'You're insatiable. Now all the mystery has gone, you can relax and enjoy it. But we have to be careful, Sally. I don't want you to fall pregnant.'

'So what do we do next time?'

He smiled. 'Leave it with me.'

With the worry of contraception taken care of by Sean, Sally flung herself into the love affair with the handsome older man while appearing to continue her normal social life with her family friends. The only confidante who knew about her wild romance was her friend Pru. She covered up for the nights Sally stayed at Sean's tiny flat in town. Yvonne enjoyed having the luxurious Mitchell flat to herself on these weeknights, and trusted that Sally was with Pru without giving it a second thought.

Pru suffered most through the affair, bearing the responsibility of secrecy, covering up for Sally, and trying not to say the wrong thing when they were out with their friends or visiting Ashford Lodge. Sally added to Pru's burden by wanting to share all the intimate details of her love affair. She made it sound so wonderful, so easy, so liberating, that Pru quietly decided to give in and 'go all the way' with her own boyfriend. However she never spoke of it to Sally or anyone else.

Sally and Sean rode bikes through beautiful Hagley Park, canoed along the Avon River, and found quiet spots to picnic and cuddle, screened by the weeping willows. To keep up appearances with her friends, she went along with them to the rugby then sneaked away with Sean on the occasional weekend to go skiing at Craigieburn where he belonged to a ski club and had use of its hut. It was an area the social skiers rarely went to.

Sean was more smooth and poised on skis than Sally, but he was impressed with her determination and her ready laugh when she took a tumble. Sally always wore tight black ski pants, a black parka tied around her waist and her favourite jumper, knitted by her mother in fine baby wool in stripes of blue, lemon, pink and lime. A matching knitted head band kept her curly hair off her face and her ears warm. Most girls wore goggles but Sally was very proud of her big square sunglasses, which had been imported from a smart shop in Sydney.

The beauty of the snowy peaks against the clear blue sky, the brightly dressed skiers whizzing down the slopes, the parties in the cosy bar, making love under the feather-filled eiderdown and sharing breakfast in their room, was, to Sally, the ultimate in romance and fun. She had no pangs of guilt, she was out to enjoy herself and congratulated herself on cleverly covering her tracks.

Yvonne, however, had become suspicious. While she had given up trying to remonstrate with Sally, she was beginning to fret that Sally was seeing Sean on the side and that she had taken the step that was the greatest taboo for any unmarried woman, and lost her virginity. She casually raised the matter of the Hunt Ball in two weeks' time.

'So, who are you going with?'

'What to wear is the big problem,' said Sally.

'Your dress is nearly ready. Mum has almost finished it. So who has asked you?'

'That black and white thing! Oh I hate it. She's going blind sewing on all those daisies. I'll look like a bunch of black-eyed susans on top of a lampshade.' Sally had avoided thinking about the ballerina dress with its layers of black then white chiffon over a stiffened petticoat, which was hanging in her mother's sewing room. The bodice had a ruched gathering of the two shades of chiffon around the neckline and black and white daisies sewn all over it. The narrow black velvet belt had a diamante buckle.

'I suppose you're wearing the yellow satin.'

'Of course I am. We had my white shoes dyed to match. I'm going with Lachlan. So come on, I heard Lachlan wanted to ask you to go with him.'

'You'll find out!' She danced away as Yvonne's warning voice trailed behind her.

'Sal! You'd better not do anything silly! Bring anyone . . . unsuitable . . .' But her sister had left the room. Yvonne shrugged. Sally was twenty, she'd have to look out for herself.

Her dress for the Hunt Ball was a worry to Sally. She and Sean had decided to go together and to heck with what her parents thought. But with her new status of 'fallen woman' she didn't want to go in her mother's demure daisy concoction. Emily was a fine seamstress and although the Mitchells could afford to buy a dress, there was competition between all the mothers as to who could create the best ballgown.

Two days later as Sally was hurrying to meet Sean for lunch she stopped suddenly outside Balentine's department store. In the window was a mannequin wearing the dress Sally knew she had to have for the Hunt Ball. It was made of black slinky, shimmery material that would run over her body like water. It had one shoulder, the other was bare. From below the knee it burst into a pleated fishtail with a hint of black lace at the hem. Peephole strappy sandals showed red toenails. The whole outfit was wicked. It was a stopper. It screamed, 'It's you, Sally!'

She didn't hesitate and took the lift to the third floor and asked to try it on. Looking at herself in the mirror Sally felt transformed. She and Sean would knock the eyes through the back of the heads of the stuffy Hunt crowd.

By the time she reached Beath's exclusive little restaurant Sean was waiting and he eyed the large bag she held. 'Shopping at Balentine's. Been saving up?'

'Not really. I have it on appro on Mum's account. Not that she knows.'

'What if she doesn't like it?'

'I'm not showing her and I'm not taking it back. I'm wearing it to the ball.'

He saw the firm set to her mouth. 'Can I buy it for you? I've never given you a proper present.'

Sally hesitated, tempted. But her upbringing won out. 'That's nice but no thank you. I'll pay Mum back out of my pay. After I've worn it.' She broke into a cheeky grin. 'You're going to love it.'

For Sally's and Pru's families and their friends the Hunt Ball was the event of the year. Sally arranged to stay the night at Warners Hotel where Pru's parents had taken two suites. Mr and Mrs Mitchell and Yvonne were staying at the flat. Sally had dutifully packed the black and white gown and left it in her car. Pru had brought the slinky black dress to the hotel.

Sally collected it, her new high-heeled black sandals, a red and black silk stole and a beaded black handbag, and dressed at Sean's flat. She sprayed lacquer over her hair to keep the smooth creation done by the hotel hairdresser and snapped the clasp on her grandmother's diamond bracelet, which was on loan for the occasion.

They left the flat and went to a cocktail lounge so they wouldn't be the first to arrive and she could mill in with the crowd before her parents spotted them.

Sean parked his racing green Austin Healey and they walked to the flight of stairs leading to the ballroom. Several couples were ahead of them, pausing to chat with the welcoming committee. Sally stopped and clutched Sean's arm.

'Oh, golly. Mum and Dad are the hosts greeting everyone! I didn't think they'd be right outside.'

The Master, dressed in tails, and Emily, in her long

evening gown with an orchid corsage, were standing at the foot of the carpeted stairs talking to two couples who had just arrived. Sally grabbed Sean's hand and they hurried past them, catching a lift up to the ballroom. They found their place across the room from the official table, and sat down.

With the welcoming ceremony over, the band swung into a waltz and couples headed for the dance floor. Sally could see her mother looking round the room for her. And she knew her friends, both male and female, were watching her and Sean, completely agog.

'Care to dance, my lovely?' asked Sean, and he pulled out Sally's chair.

Sally dropped her stole, revealing her bare shoulder, as Pru whispered, 'Your mother will spot you now. You'll be in for it.'

'Might as well make the most of it,' said Sally. She took Sean's arm and swept onto the dance floor. While she liked rock and roll, she was glad now of the dancing classes that had been compulsory for her at St Margaret's boarding school.

As she twirled past she caught sight of her parents' shocked faces. Each time she came within their orbit, her mother made frantic signals and inclined her head towards the ladies powder room. Sally pretended she didn't see her. But her mother walked over to the edge of the dance floor and there was no escaping her glare, which Sally knew meant, *Meet me in the ladies room in one minute, young lady*.

Her mother headed for the powder room and Sally excused herself and, head high, followed in her wake.

'Do you want me to come in and rescue you?' whispered Sean.

'It's okay, she won't make a scene in public.'

By the time Sally opened the red padded leather door,

her mother had checked out the cubicles and knew they were alone. Sally avoided her eye and opened her purse, looking for her lipstick, now feeling slightly nervous.

'Just what are you thinking?' Emily demanded. 'How dare you cheapen yourself, embarrass your father, bring shame on the Hunt. On our family.'

'I'm having fun. I'm not a school girl.'

'You're not even twenty-one, my girl, and your father and I can stop this *fun* very easily. You are not to see that detestable man again.'

'He's my boyfriend. I will keep seeing him.' Defiantly she rubbed her lips together to blot the lipstick and turned to face her mother, but she was not prepared for the swift stinging slap that struck her cheek.

'You are a brazen little hussy and I want you to go home this instant!'

Sally rubbed her stinging cheek, tears filling her eyes as her mother turned on her heel and left the room while two girls came in giggling. Hastily Sally turned back to the mirror, pulling out her compact to powder the red mark on her face.

She and Sean left immediately, but Sally made her exit as discreet as possible while the 'Pride of Erin' had most people busy on the floor, and others were at the food tables helping themselves to the venison buffet.

She cried and cried in Sean's arms. He was also rattled at Mrs Mitchell's outburst and worried he might not be invited to the Rangiora Hunt again. But neither was prepared for the Mitchells' handling of the matter of 'dealing with Sally'.

Chapter Two

SALLY KEPT HER HEAD down and stayed out of her parents' way as much as she could after the big blow up. She'd been forbidden to see Sean Flanagan again and every time she left the house she was cross examined by her mother. Yvonne stuck to her like glue, another ploy by Emily, Sally assumed. Her parents had taken an immediate dislike to Sean as a potential suitor for their daughter. He was far too old, not wealthy and, worse, hadn't been to a private school. He just didn't fit in with their social circle.

Mrs Mitchell had also been in contact with Pru's mother, Mrs Rawson, and Pru had been warned about protecting Sally as she was not to have any contact with *that* man. Pru's parents were not as well off as the Mitchells and they wanted to maintain the friendship. If Pru acted as a go-between for Sally, she would not be allowed to mix with the Mitchells again.

'Oh you poor thing! Pulling the social-climbing card,' exclaimed Sally when Pru told her everything that had passed between Mrs Mitchell, Pru and Mrs Rawson. Pru came from old money, so old most of it had already been spent. While they had the right name, they were cash poor.

'You know I don't care, we'll be friends no matter what our parents say. It's just that Mum thinks I'll meet better people, find a better prospect through you than through our family friends.'

'Well, you have! You've been going out with Gavin Summers for months now. His father is the top stockbroker in the city, no wonder she doesn't want to blow that. How are you two getting along?' Sally asked. She'd been so wrapped up in her affair with Sean that she hadn't paid much attention to her best friend's romance.

Pru blushed slightly. 'It's good. I know he really likes me, and we do have a lot of fun.'

Sally studied Pru, knowing she wasn't getting all the details. 'Have you two gone all the way?'

'Sally!'

'You would tell me, of course. So when you do, I want a full report. Now, I need you to help me. I'm meeting Sean for the weekend.'

'Oh, Sally, please! Don't get me in trouble,' wailed Pru.

'You don't have to do anything. I just want you to smuggle some clothes out for me. I'll tell Mum you're borrowing some of my things for a party.'

'What sort of clothes?'

'Some riding gear. I'm going to his place in Oxford. I've never been there before.'

'They're sure to ask where you're going.'

'There's a tennis tournament on in Oxford, it's too far away for anyone to bother with. So we can just tell them I'm going to that and a weekend house party. Yvonne and Mum are going to tea to meet that boring Lachlan's family.

I think Mum smells an engagement in the air so she wants to check it out. For once the pressure is off me.'

'Did you say you're going riding? You haven't ridden since your accident. How do you feel about it?'

'I'm nervous. Sean thinks he can get me over it. Dad just keeps telling me to get back on Rani and get on with it. But I've lost my nerve and so has she. I don't think I'll ever ride that horse again.'

'It's nice of Sean to offer to help you. He is sweet.'

'I wish my parents could see how nice he is. So what if he comes from a poor Irish family. He's done all right.'

'They think he's a scheming charmer after your money,' Pru said, giggling.

'I don't care. Come on, let's get my gear.'

Pru took the bag with Sally's casual jodhpurs and riding boots in it to her house and hid it under her bed. On Saturday morning she handed it over to Sally who waved goodbye as she set off on the drive down to Oxford.

Sean had ten acres there where he spent as much time as possible. His modest city flat was just for overnights during the week – and a convenient place to rendezvous with Sally. Mrs Mitchell need not have worried about them becoming too serious, because Sean relished his status as a single man about town. His greatest passion was his horses, which he rode in the yearly point to point. The property was lush and green, and the surrounding paddocks were bounded by old stone walls. Sean lived in the original stone cottage. This was how he thought of Ireland. But the reality had been very different for his struggling widowed mother. Sean was reinventing his childhood. Growing up he'd watched the squire trot past on his magnificent steeplechaser, seen the Hunt and field gallop across the countryside, and as a little boy hanging over a fence as they rode by, he dreamed of one day owning such a horse.

Proudly he showed Sally around. 'I've got the two hunters and they're pretty good. It's nothing like your father's spread at Ashford Lodge, but I love this place,' he said softly. 'I wish I could be here all the time, but business pays the bills.'

Sally was enchanted. The farm was small but attractive; he'd put a lot of work into it. On the nights he spent in Christchurch Sean had a neighbour feed the horses, otherwise he ran the place single handed. 'What's that horse over there?' Sally pointed to a steel-grey gelding standing close to the stables.

'Ah, you've spotted him. That's Escort. Fifteen he is, pensioned off by the Trevallyn estate when the last of them, Mrs T, died. They didn't want to sell him but preferred to find him a good home. He's special.'

'He looks in good shape. Trace clipped, hog maned, hasn't been let go to seed.'

'No, indeed not. You'll like him, come and say hello.' They ducked under the fence and walked to the horse, who calmly watched them, slowly chewing a mouthful of grass. Sean rubbed his neck, and the horse stretched a curious head to Sally who held out her hand, not moving forward.

'He's very calm, well educated obviously.'

'Escort has impeccable manners. He hunted, is a steady jumper, never pulled away, would go on the bit but mostly he's been ridden on a straight snaffle.'

'Mrs T hunted?'

'My dear, old Mrs T rode side saddle to the hounds almost to the day she died. Escort is the horse I let my city friends ride when they say they can ride when they can't.'

They both laughed.

'So my re-education is with Escort, eh?' said Sally.

'When you're ready. Let's go inside and look around the house.'

In the late afternoon, Sean took Sally – dressed in her jodhpurs and boots – down to saddle Escort. She took her time getting to know the horse, aware that Sean was leaving them alone as he busied himself with the riding tack and saddling his own horse. Sally was surprised that her fear of falling had resurfaced and she hoped Escort wasn't sensing her tension. But he stood patiently as she saddled him.

Sean walked over leading his horse. 'It's a pretty walk down the road, my land curves around to the right there. I have a couple of hedge jumps and a water jump. I also jump the stone walls. But we'll just meander today, okay?'

She nodded and turned towards Escort. 'He's very calm. How's he react to mounting?'

'He's used to being mounted from a box for the side saddle so nothing fazes him. Up you go.' Sean held out his cupped hands and she put her foot into them and he hoisted her into the saddle. Escort didn't flinch. Sally's mouth was dry and she tried to tell herself this was ridiculous, but she felt like a novice. Sean caught her mood.

'Sal, it's understandable you should feel nervous. You took a bad fall. This horse is used to everything, he's totally trustworthy. Just relax, we're not rushing anything here.'

She nodded and he mounted and led the way through the gate onto the narrow gravel road.

In the late sunlight, long shadows fell over the landscape of old trees and neat paddocks. The only sound was that of the horses' hooves and the occasional call of a settling bird. Sally felt her body relax, her enjoyment of being on horseback, the only way to appreciate the countryside, reviving again. Between herself and the mature kindly horse she felt that sense of bonding that she'd never been able to explain. It was the sense of touch, the feeling of strength and power beneath her, the instinctive swift understanding and response to commands that always made her feel a part of the horse. Sean rode beside her, glancing at her, and saw her body language soften as she fell into the rhythm of the walking horses.

'Want to trot a bit?' he asked.

Escort had a smooth gait and Sally could imagine the elderly Mrs T in her long skirt, seated side saddle, as Escort lifted his feet and head, holding her steadily aboard.

Sean began to chat about his friends to distract her so Sally didn't notice that they'd swung into the big paddock. Sean's horse Fellow broke into a light canter, but Escort waited for the instruction from Sally. She squeezed her thighs and lifted the rein, and Escort smoothly moved into a canter, which was more comfortable than a trot, and Sally rejoiced again in the sensation of feeling one with the horse. Then before she knew it a low hedge was in front of them and they sailed over it with ease, never breaking stride. Sean glanced back at Sally and she gave him a thumbs up and urged Escort to catch up and overtake Fellow.

And so she led the way, guided by Escort, taking the water jump without a splash, sailing over a hedge fence topped by a rail. It was an easy course, but it was what she needed – a steady, quiet knowledgeable horse she trusted and a gentle ride with no mishaps.

They passed another pair of riders who lifted their crops but Sally paid little attention. She didn't know anyone in the area and assumed no one knew her. By the time they returned to the stables she was flushed and exhilarated. She swung out of the saddle and hugged the grey gelding who nonchalantly accepted the spontaneous gesture. As Sean dismounted and came to her she flung her arms around him.

'Thank you, thank you.'

'Don't thank me.' He patted Escort's rump. 'A good horse is a gift. All you needed was a little connection with a horse again. You'll be right now.'

'Thanks, Sean. You're a darling. Dad's not going to believe it when I go out on the Hunt next week.'

'Better not tell him how you got your nerve back.' He grinned.

'Maybe I will, just to show him you did what he couldn't.'

'I don't think that's a wise idea. Come on, I have a good bottle of wine and the fire ready to light. Let's make the most of the short time we have. I'm going away next week for a month to Australia and Japan on business. And I'll miss you.'

Sally's elation faded slightly. Why couldn't her parents see what a nice man he was?

Looking back, Sally was always grateful for that very special weekend with Sean.

On the following Monday evening events exploded and she felt she was on a roller coaster of excitement, disappointment, frustration and trepidation.

Her mother and father had called her into the drawing room. Garth Mitchell had his arms folded; a bad sign. He spoke first.

'You have been out with that man again. Against our express wishes, Sally.'

'Oh? Who says?' Sally tried to brazen it out.

Her mother dismissed her remark. 'Goodness me, my girl. Old friends of your father down there in Oxford saw you, and told your father today. They know that man. He's considered a bit of a lady killer. Not our type.'

'I went down for a tennis tournament and met Sean and he invited me riding.'

Her father did a slight double take. 'You were riding?'

Sally seized the opportunity. 'Yes. It was Sean who let me ride his horse that got me through my nerves. Thanks to him, I'm all right.'

'I'm pleased to hear it.' Her father was noncommittal and turned his back, pouring himself a sherry.

One for Sean, thought Sally.

'That is not the point,' said her mother stiffly. 'The fact is you lied to us, you involved Prudence in the deceit, and you went against what you knew we had forbidden.'

'So, what's the big deal? C'mon, Mummy, Sean is a gentleman, he respects the same things you do –'

'Don't you dare associate me with that . . . that gypsy. We don't know his background, what sort of family he comes from. I don't know what tales he has spun you – a gullible young girl – but I imagine he comes from very poor and common stock. He is too old for you, he's in trade and he has little money. He has no prospects what-soever,' snapped her mother.

It was on the tip of Sally's tongue to retort that Sean was a great lover, a good rider and a heck of a lot of fun. That is what he had going for him. But she knew that would not be appreciated. She decided to play the gullible-young-woman card and her father, surprisingly, came to her rescue.

'I'm really very pleased to know you've regained your confidence. However, the situation has reached a point with this fellow, so your mother and I have taken matters into our hands.'

Dozens of questions flashed through her mind, she was fearful for Sean. 'What does that mean?' asked Sally, trying not to show her nervousness.

'We're sending you away. On a trip,' declared Emily.

Sally burst out laughing. 'Send me away and everyone will gossip. You know what they'll be thinking.'

Emily Mitchell blanched slightly. Girls from good homes who became pregnant were sent away to 'visit relatives' or 'have a holiday'.

'You're not going to be on your own. And most people would consider you to be extremely fortunate,' said her father. 'The SS *Oronsay* is sailing to London – we're buying you a ticket. Consider it an early twenty-first birthday present.'

Sally couldn't help the surge of excitement that ran through her. She'd always wanted to travel to Europe and explore the world away from the stifling conservatism of her home and family. 'So who's going to be the chaperone?' She prayed it wouldn't be her boring Aunt Frances or stuffy cousins.

'Seeing as you have involved Prudence in your misdemeanours, initially against our better judgement we have agreed that she go with you. We were disappointed in Pru but I believe you misled her as much as us. Therefore we are assisting with her passage on the understanding that she will be a steadying influence,' Mrs Mitchell explained. 'Her mother will make it very clear to her how she is to behave and what the consequences will be if either of you get into any trouble.'

Sally almost started laughing again. Poor Pru, no matter what she'd promised both sets of parents, Sally knew she could manipulate and bend Pru to her wishes. And Pru would probably have agreed to anything for this trip – though she'd miss her boyfriend. Of course it would make her more attractive to his family. Girls went abroad for that final polish before settling down. Sally lowered her head, pretending to mull over this news while her mind was racing, wondering if Sean could meet her over there. They could go to Ireland together – how romantic.

'So what do you have to say for yourself, young lady?' prompted her father.

'Thank you, Daddy. And Mummy. When do we leave?'

She saw the relief in her parents' eyes as they assumed the lure of this great trip had pushed thoughts of Sean to the back of her mind. 'In a few weeks. You'll fly to Sydney. Prudence's brother will come down from Brisbane to see you both. We have good friends in Sydney, with daughters your age. They have kindly agreed for you two to stay with them,' said her mother.

'They have a holiday house too, don't they?' added Garth, to make the point that these friends were quite well off.

The girls talked endlessly about the trip. Although sad at leaving their boyfriends, they were eager to see what, and who, was out there on the other side of the world.

The Mitchells' friends, the Chapmans, met them at the airport and drove them to their red brick mansion on the Hawkesbury River at Wisemans Ferry. Sons and daughters of the Chapmans and their friends swept the girls along in a social whirl of boating parties, water skiing, sailing and picnics. Pru's brother Denton, who worked for a boat designer, arrived ten days later having brought a grand Halvorsen cruiser down to Sydney Harbour to be chartered. The partying stepped up with nightclubbing at Chequers, dining at Pruniers, cruising through notorious Kings Cross, seeing the glamorous show at the Latin Quarter nightclub, shocked to discover the girls were boys. During the day they hung around Balmoral

Beach, Mosman and Neutral Bay. They were invited to the eastern suburbs to watch the first sea trials of the yacht *Gretel,* which was making the first serious challenge for the America's Cup.

They were moving in serious social circles which Sally and Pru were able to describe in letters home to their mothers, knowing they would approve. They spent as little time as possible at Wisemans Ferry, as Mrs Chapman had become tight lipped and disapproving, considering them all out of control – her own children and their friends were as party mad as Pru and Sally.

Escape came when Denton suggested they all meet up in Surfers Paradise where he had to pick up a boat and sail up north. Surfers Paradise was iconic – known as the place for honeymooners, soporific sunshine and the first bikinis. Holiday makers flaunted their suntanned bodies on golden beaches bordered by holiday units and glamorous hotels built in Hawaiian style. The air smelled of sex and suntan oil.

As a group they stayed at The Beachcomber Hotel, drinking in its beer garden where waitresses wore coloured raffia 'grass' skirts with bikini tops and plastic leis. Sally and Pru giggled endlessly at how their mothers would consider it all very low class, tasteless and cheap. There were no plans other than where to swim, where to eat, and what to wear. The girls bought sunfrocks and brilliant print silk shirts at Helen's Casuals and gold handbags and sandals from the Riviera shop. Everyone flirted and laughed, and New Zealand, parents and boyfriends Sean and Gavin seemed far away.

One morning, Sally found Pru sitting on the bed in their hotel.

'What's up?'

Pru shook her head and covered her face in her hands. Her shoulders started to shake and Sally realised she was crying. She sat down beside her and took one of her hands. 'Pru, what is it?'

'Nothing's happened.'

'What do you mean?'

'You know. No lady in red. I'm late, Sal. Real late.'

'Oh, gawd. Pregnant? Who, when? My God, you didn't tell me you were sleeping with anyone.' Sally was miffed she wasn't privy to such details. They'd promised to share everything.

Pru looked askance at her friend. 'Who do you think? I've only been with one person. What do you think I am?'

Sally quickly tried to think of ways out of this dilemma – take a hot bath and drink gin with caraway seeds? Castor oil? Vague remedies she'd heard whispered for situations like this. But she knew she couldn't suggest such a thing to her friend, who so adored her handsome rich boyfriend. 'Gavin? Well, that's all right then.'

'It was only once. Before I left and we knew we'd be apart so long. He said it'd be all right . . .' Pru dissolved again. 'It's not all right. What am I going to do? The trip and everything . . .'

Sally was practical and calming. 'Listen, you two are almost engaged. I just know he is going to propose when we get back. I thought he might have before you left, but he probably wanted you to go and have a good time. You'd better write to him today. He'll want to get married straightaway, you know, before you show, his family being so la-di-da. Then you can go overseas for your honeymoon, come back pregnant and live happily ever after.'

Pru stopped crying and looked hopeful. 'You think so? Oh, I feel so much better. But, Sal, what about you?'

'Don't you want me as your bridesmaid? I can go on the next boat.' Sally hugged her. 'Come on, you write that letter. And we'll go into town and look around the shops.'

'Hey, what do you think?' Sally in a skin-tight dress of fuchsia lace twirled in front of the mirror outside the dressing room.

Pru, sitting on a red velvet chair, cocked her head. 'I don't know, Sal. I'm confused now, you've tried on so many.'

The saleswoman tried to be helpful. 'What colour theme have you chosen for the wedding party?'

Pru looked at Sally, who giggled. 'We're still deciding. Okay, we'll go and think some more. At least we've got the wedding dress!'

'And very lovely it looks too,' said the saleswoman, beaming.

'It would want to after what it cost,' whispered Pru. They'd cashed in their tickets on the SS *Oronsay* and were busy making plans. Sally had tried to keep Pru's spirits up as she waited for an answer to her letter.

Back in Sydney they'd rented a small garden flat in Mosman and had spent two days trailing around Mark Foys, Farmers, David Jones and Anthony Hordern looking at wedding outfits, formal wear, household items, fine china and glassware, dreaming of the new life opening up for Pru.

As they went down in the lift at Anthony Hordern, the lift operator slid open the doors on a floor announcing: 'Children's wear, toys, baby furniture, infants . . .'

Pru clutched Sally's hand. 'Come on. Let's look.'

She picked her way through the aisles of baby items, stopping occasionally to smooth a satin pillow in a basinet, finger a lace net over a cot, pick up a small teddy bear. Sally followed her friend, feeling she was walking away from her in every sense. Their paths were separating, indistinctly but irrefutably. For the first time Sally felt a pang of regret that the SS *Oronsay* would sail without them. She thought of her suitcase packed with party and travelling clothes, the new diary with barely an entry, there'd been no time. They'd been too busy having fun. She thought of the adventures they would no longer share on their overseas trip. But Sally was happy for Pru, she'd got what she wanted. Sally wondered, had she planned this? But knowing the sweet naivety of her friend, she quickly pushed away such an uncharitable thought.

The telegram arrived and Sally handed it to Pru and held her breath. Then Pru ripped it open, biting her tongue, scanned the typed message and flung her arms around Sally. 'He's arriving on Friday.'

They filled the flat with vases of flowers, cleaned it well, hoping it would look less shabby, lit candles to soften its dank dimness and set up a table in the small garden. Sally bought a bottle of champagne and a little cake and gave Pru a hug, picked up her bag and blew her a kiss. She got in a taxi to go to the Chapmans and stay the night and thank them for their hospitality. For all they knew, the girls sailed in a few days.

There was no phone so Sally called out as she walked down the steps at the side of the old house at Mosman to their little flat the following afternoon. The French doors were open and she stepped into the sitting room. 'Pru? Gavin? Anyone here?'

There was a muffled noise from Pru's bedroom. Sally dropped her bag on the sofa bed in the small alcove where she slept. 'Hi. I'm back.' She didn't know what to say in case Gavin was there. The bedroom door was open and

Pru was lying curled up on the bed facing the wall. 'You sleeping? Pru?'

Pru rolled over and stared at Sally, who took an involuntary step backwards, shocked at how she looked. Her face was grey, her eyes red and swollen. She choked, barely able to speak. Sally rushed to her bedside. 'God, Pru, what is it? What happened?' For a crazy moment she thought her friend had been beaten up, she looked so . . . broken.

Pru pulled up her knees, hugging them to her side, then pointed to the bedside table. Sally reached for the white envelope and winced in pain as she saw the wad of pound notes and the address of a doctor in Bondi.

'Did he come? Did you talk to him?'

Pru nodded miserably. 'How could he, Sal? He was awful. Said he didn't want to know about it, didn't want to see me again. Ever. That it was my fault. And how did he know it was his anyway . . .' At this she burst into another fit of hoarse sobbing.

'What a sod,' exclaimed Sally.

'He did come himself but –' started Pru.

'Oh, don't give me that. He's a selfish bastard, Pru. Better you find out now.'

'What am I going to do, Sal? I can't have . . . get rid of it.' She began to wail and Sally shook her by the shoulders.

'Pru, listen to me. You don't have a choice. You go back home and have it, or have it in secret, but you won't be able to keep it, you must see that. You'll ruin your life. It's not fair to bring a baby into the world and then give it away. What will that kid think for the rest of its life? That you didn't care about it, that's what.'

'But I do, Sal. I don't want to hurt it.'

'Pru, you're going to hurt a lot more people if you don't. Go and see the doctor, get it over with. We can still go away together –'

'I can't, I've cashed in the ticket . . .' She started to cry more heavily as she thought of all the money she'd spent on the wedding dress. 'I just want to go home.' She covered her face with her hands, rolled on her back and rocked from side to side.

Sally stood up and reached for the slip of paper. 'Right, then. Let's get this over with. I'm going down to the phone box to make an appointment for you.'

When she came back Pru was making a pot of tea. They didn't talk while Sally unpacked her overnight bag.

Finally Sally spoke as Pru poured the tea. 'Monday morning. Here's a list of things you have to bring to the hospital. It's some small private place. Money too, of course. His secretary was nice, said he's a top doctor. Doesn't like to see girls ruin their lives because of a silly mistake, was how she put it.'

Pru bit her lip. 'I'll never love anyone like him. I'll never find anyone like him again. It's so unfair.'

'Rubbish. Don't feel sorry for yourself. He doesn't deserve it. He's not worth it.'

Worried about their dwindling funds, Sally and Pru caught a bus to Bondi. They found the address – it was a large double-storey house set back from the street, shielded by a high fence. Sally sat with Pru in the waiting room with several other girls who all avoided looking at each other. Two had their mothers with them, one girl had a boy holding her hand.

'I'll be all right, Sal, really. I've booked the ticket home on Wednesday.'

'Okay. When you've gone home I'll pack up the flat and go to a hotel for a couple of days,' said Sally.

'Have you decided what to do then?' asked Pru. 'What will I tell your parents?'

'Stop fretting about me. I'll let them know what I'm doing – just as soon as I know.' She gave a bright smile, trying to cover the turmoil she felt.

Pru was called in and Sally hugged her quickly, anxious to get away from the sad surroundings.

Sally was depressed and worried. She rang around some of their new friends and went out to lunch, ending up in a fashionable cafe in Rowe Street. Their group had swelled and she started chatting to a girl who had just come back from working on a station as a cook.

Sally couldn't imagine this girl, who'd done a cordon bleu course in France, slinging lamb chops and mashed spuds around for a bunch of stockmen.

'It was huge fun,' she told Sally. 'It was a fabulous place, I cooked for the family, formal dining every night. I'm going to Canberra next to work at a diplomat's residence.'

'How do you find jobs like that?'

'First one I found in *The Land* newspaper – I wanted to go outback. I registered with Dalgety's and was recommended to other people, and so it went on. If you have some qualifications and you know, breeding . . . The good families are particular.'

Sally knew what she meant. She recognised that this girl had a similar background to her own and filed this news away.

That afternoon Sally went back to the private rooms and collected a shaken, pale and upset Pru. They hailed a taxi and Pru looked out the window at the light rain and said nothing. Sally helped her into her nightie and into bed and brought her a cup of tea.

'They gave me a tablet to sleep. I'll be all right, Sal. What are you going to do?'

'I'm thinking of applying for a job in the outback. Save some money and go OS as planned. Don't say anything till I know for sure.'

Pru shook her head. 'I just want to sleep.'

'Everything is okay?' asked Sally cautiously.

'Yeah. I'll be fine. Don't worry about me.'

She held out her hand and Sally squeezed it, fighting back tears.

'Sorry, Sal.'

'Don't worry, Pru. You rest, and forget this ever happened.'

'Yeah. Sure.' Tears ran down her cheeks.

After Sally and Pru had a tearful farewell at the airport Sally packed and cleaned the flat.

She hailed a taxi. 'The Australia Hotel, please.' She'd decided to treat herself for a few days while she planned what to do.

After settling into her room she strolled up the broad space between the GPO and the buildings that flanked the Cenotaph. An elderly lady at a flower stall was singing bursts of operetta. Sally bought a small posy of lily of the valley, burying her face in its sweet smell. She felt terribly sad for herself as well as Pru. She wondered deep down if they'd ever be as close again.

At a news stand with a display of magazines and newspapers she stopped and studied the array of Australian and foreign papers. There it was, *The Land*. She bought a copy and turned into George Street heading for the cosy Repin's Inn. She ordered raisin toast and a pot of tea, then she browsed through the bible of agricultural, rural news and classified ads.

One ad jumped out at her: *Governess, quality large Gulf cattle station, three children requiring tuition prior to boarding school. Full amenities, gracious surrounds. Apply Dalgety's, Phillip Street, Sydney.*

She circled the ad and finished her tea and toast.

Chapter Three

Sydney, Australia, 1963

SALLY STUDIED HER REFLECTION in the mirror on the wardrobe door, admiring the three-quarter length leopard-skin coat. She turned the collar up around her neck and thrust her hands deep into its pockets, striking a pose. Here she is striding along the deck at night, the wind whipping the ocean as the liner ploughs through silver waves, clouds scudding over a distant moon. She is alone until she sees the figure of a tall man, standing against the rail, deep in thought. Her steps slow, he turns and later he tells her the sight of her windswept hair, her face glimpsed in the pale moonlight, her body wrapped in the luxuriously soft coat . . . was the instant he fell in love with her.

Sighing, Sally reefed off the coat. Her big extravagance would not be going to sea or with her to Cape York. She folded it and put it on top of the black and white ball gown her mother had insisted she pack. Her hotel room was smothered in clothes – piled on the bed, heaped on the chair, hanging out of the wardrobe. She then knelt in front of her suitcase and started to pack blouses, skirts, sunfrocks, shorts, sandals and cotton slacks. She held up the blue workman's jeans she'd just bought at a disposal store, wondering if she'd ever feel comfortable in the stiff denim. They looked great on Elvis, James Dean and Sal Mineo, and perhaps they'd be suitable for riding until she had her jodhpurs sent from New Zealand.

It had all happened so quickly. She had little money left, even after she and Pru had cashed in their tickets. There was no way she could tell her father she'd spent so much and she didn't want her mother to know about Pru's dilemma. She didn't know how Pru was going to explain to her family or Sally's why she wasn't going on the cruise. So Sally had rung about the ad in the paper, gone straight down to Phillip Street to Dalgety's and been interviewed for the job of governess.

She had dressed neatly in a tailored skirt, jacket nipped in at the waist, pearl choker and pearl earrings. By the time she ran through her education at one of the best private schools in New Zealand, her parents' rural background, her skills in secretarial work (she'd fudged a bit on her experience with children), her horsemanship and list of references, the man behind the desk had scribbled some notes, then reached over and shook her hand.

'The job's yours, Sally. Be ready to fly out on Thursday, okay? It's a bit of a milk run to get there. I'll ring through to Mrs Monroe and let her know you're coming.'

'She doesn't want to interview me too?' Sally asked.

'No, that's my job. The contract is for twelve months. Your pay is sent to an account you nominate, you won't need much ready cash on you up at Barra Creek. Here are the details, including the wireless phone number. Mail goes in once a week.'

'This all seems a bit rushed,' said Sally, wondering for a moment if she was doing the right thing. 'What's the nearest town?'

'Normanton. You'll fly TAA to Cloncurry, then you have to hang about for two days till the bush pilot taking the mail up to Cape York and the Gulf arrives. He'll drop you at the homestead strip; there'll be someone to meet you then.' He paused, allowing himself a small grin. 'Course you could paddle along the Norman River. Barra Creek Station fronts onto a tributary of the Norman.'

Sally wasn't taking in the travelling details. 'What about the boys' schooling, their curriculum, that sort of thing?'

'All correspondence. You have to get them, and whoever else might need schooling, on the job every day. Don't worry about the teaching side of it. Supervision is the key. Your qualifications are excellent. You'll have enough on your hands, I'd reckon.' He'd seen them come and seen them go, not many young women lasted the distance. One day he'd have to get up to Cape York and see it for himself. He looked at Sally sitting primly in the leather chair. Well, they couldn't complain he was sending them dross this time. How had Lorna Monroe described the last governess they'd sent? Common and unsavoury. Oh, and a misery guts. 'Any other questions?'

'The plane ticket? Are you sure everything is paid for?'

'The airline ticket will be delivered to your hotel tomorrow morning with some vouchers and a small amount of cash, bus fare to the airport, light meals and so on. Good luck, Sally.'

She shook his hand, thinking luck she didn't need, all she wanted was to get out of Sydney. England would always be there. The unknown outback of Queensland's Gulf country suddenly seemed an exciting prospect.

Back in her hotel room Sally opened the map she'd bought and scanned the far flung dots on Cape York. Exasperated at not finding Barra Creek she finally folded the map, stuck a safety pin through northwest Queensland and put it in an envelope, taking out the letter she'd written to her parents. She'd kept the letter vague and cheerful. She said she thought Pru had got cold feet and was homesick so instead of going to England on her own, Sally had an interesting job offer through Dalgety's Rural Agency and was going to Queensland: 'Where the pin hole is on the map,' she added at the bottom of the letter. She told them it might be a while before they heard from her as the mail plane only came in once a week.

The single-engine Cessna thrummed and occasionally bounced over the hot air thermals that rose from the bleached, seemingly empty landscape below them. Sally glanced over at Donald – 'Call me Donny' – Simpson, the bush pilot who looked relaxed and cheerful. He caught her looking at him; something he was used to as women couldn't help finding reasons to stare at his blond movie-star looks. His 'Yankee' accent helped too, even though he was Canadian.

'How're ya doing, Sally? Not sick? Too hot, too cool? We aim to please.'

'When are we going to see something? Anything. Not that anything could live down there, it's practically desert.'

'That it is, honey. You should see some of the conditions animals survive in, not to mention the white folk. I'm a snow and mountain man myself. Ever seen snow?'

'I'm a Kiwi. We ski every season in the South Island.'

The pilot was quiet then, wondering how his

passenger was going to weather the heat, the isolation, the rough conditions, the people. She was obviously used to a comfortable life. But she was a bright and spunky girl, and from their conversation throughout the day it was obvious she had no idea what she was heading into. Rushed decisions were never the right ones, in his book, despite her cheerful insistence it would be an adventure.

'Sally, I've carried a fair few people up and down the Cape, out to the Gulf, it's never what they expect.'

'You mean it's even better than they thought?' She gave him an impish smile. 'Hey, I'll be right.'

'I'm coming back down in a week, I'll stop in at Barra Creek. If you want to leave with me, let me know.'

She lifted her chin slightly and peered into the sun-streaked horizon through the plastic windscreen. 'Thanks, Donny. But I'll stick it out.'

'You don't have to, you know. Did Dalgety's tell you you're the fifth governess in the past eighteen months at Barra Creek?'

Sally shook her head. 'They must've been waiting for me to turn up then.' She looked back at the pilot she now decided looked like Tab Hunter. 'You wait and see.'

He ran his hand over his crew cut. 'Okay. I guess we'll be seeing a lot more of each other then, eh?' He gave her a wink.

Two hours later they landed at a station to deliver mail but all she could see surrounding them was red dirt, a couple of trucks and two Aboriginal men on horseback.

'Do you want to stretch your legs? No ladies room, I'm afraid,' said Donny.

Sally stood next to the plane in the shade of the wing as Donny handed over the mail bags and chatted to the stockmen. The men made no move to acknowledge her presence but Sally was aware she was being scrutinised from under low-pulled hats. Donny then lifted something off the front bumper of one of the trucks, walked back to her and handed her a dripping stiff canvas bag with a mouthpiece and wooden handles. 'Here, have a drink.'

Sally was surprised at how cool the water was. 'That's very refreshing. Thanks. I won't have too much.' This outback journey was not conducive to women travellers, she decided.

Donny threw the outgoing mail bag into the plane. 'All aboard. Next stop Barra Creek.'

'I'll believe it when I see it,' sighed Sally.

She dozed in the cockpit, her head against the side window until Donny spoke above the engine. 'Look down there. We're coming into the river country now.'

'Gosh, it's green. What's that silver bit?'

'That's the mighty Norman River, we can follow her all the way inland. Normanton is your nearest town when you're not cut off in the Wet. Barra Creek is a tributary off from near where it rises. Still a helluva big river.'

'What's down there?' Sally peered at the vegetation radiating from the snaking grey river.

'Big ugly saltwater crocodiles. Wild pigs. Birds. Stray cattle, horses, buffaloes, a few Aborigines. And barramundi, the best eating fish in the world.'

He angled the plane towards the east, circling over patchy russet earth sprinkled with trees and small hills. They were descending. She could make out dots of cattle.

'Are we getting close?'

'I'll fly you over the homestead.'

'I don't see any buildings.'

'It's four hundred square miles. So it's easy to lose a couple of buildings in it.'

She could see fences, shining pools of dams, cleared land, small clumps of trees.

'There's your new home, Sally.' He banked and she

caught the glint of tin roofs, then saw vehicles parked around buildings, sheds, the paraphernalia of a station nestled on a bend of the river. Donny did a circle leaving the homestead behind them. 'The strip is three miles down the track. It's a bit of a hike from the house but it'll never get flooded. Do they know you're coming today?'

'Of course. The agent said they'd meet me.' Sally looked down at her clothes and flicked some dust off her skirt, more a mental preparation than tidying.

Donny gave her a quick smile. 'Last chance. We can buzz straight over 'em and head south.'

'Not on your life.'

'Right.' He concentrated on levelling the little aircraft as a windsock and bulldozed length of red dirt in the flattest stretch of land near the homestead marked the landing strip.

The plane slowed to a halt and Donny muttered to himself as he got down from the pilot's seat. As Sally gathered herself to get out she heard him shouting, 'Where boss, where boys? Why you mob here?'

He came round to help Sally step down, leading her past the struts of the wing. 'Seems the welcome committee has had a bit of a problem.'

Sally walked around the rear of the plane as Donny opened the hatch and pulled out her suitcase, the mail bag and some parcels. There was no car, no adult, no friendly white face. Instead she was confronted with a knot of Aboriginal children, two boys about seven and eleven wearing sagging shorts tied around their skinny frames with rope. A little girl of about six was holding the hand of an even younger girl. Faded dresses hung from their coathanger shoulders. All had dusty hair, bare feet and running noses attracting flies. They stood by a large wooden wheelbarrow.

Donny walked over and threw the mail into the

wheelbarrow and turned back to look at Sally, who was standing dumbstruck next to the plane. They all stared at her in silence and she glanced down at her shoes: patent-leather pumps with sensible heels. In her mind she redressed herself: suspenders and nylon stockings, petticoat, pleated navy Sportscraft skirt, white blouse with a Peter Pan collar, over her arm was her Fletcher Jones plaid jacket and, of course, she wore her single strand of pearls and pearl earrings. No wonder the kids were looking at her like she was from outer space.

'What's going on?' she asked. 'Where're the Monroes?'

Donny gestured to the older boy who looked down and mumbled, 'Truck bust.'

'Means you'll have to hoof it, Sal.' Donny picked up her suitcase and hoisted it into the wheelbarrow. He avoided her eyes.

'Righto.' She made a shooing gesture at the children and the boys took a handle each and began pushing the barrow. The girls trailed behind, sneaking glances at Sally.

She held out her hand. 'Thanks, Donny. I'll be seeing you then.'

'In a week. Remember what I said.' He pulled his hat further down over his eyes. 'So long, Sally.'

She gave a wave and set off after the weaving wheelbarrow, her heels scuffing through the thick dust and gravelly stones. She concentrated on walking as straight as she could. Miss Allen, who'd taught her deportment, would have been proud of her. She heard the plane rev up and taxi but she didn't look back. Three miles to the homestead, Donny had said. A slow anger began to boil in her but she tried to calm herself and consider all the possible reasons why she hadn't been met. She heard the plane circle and Donny swooped above her.

She looked up and felt her anger melt as Donny waggled the wings.

She waited for the girls to catch up and tried to talk to them. Between their titters and sucking on fingers she got their names, but found them hard to understand. The boys were competing with each other to push their side of the wheelbarrow harder than the other. Inevitably it tipped over, spilling everything onto the ground. At first the boys were horrorstruck and quickly looked at Sally, waiting for her to shout at them. Instead she burst out laughing at the incongruity of the whole scene. In a rush of relief the children laughed too and together they repacked the wheelbarrow.

Sally lifted the younger girl, surprised at how light and frail she was, and sat her on top of her suitcase as the boys set off again.

They'd walked about a mile when they heard the sound of an engine. A truck drove towards them in a swathe of dust. Three young boys were in the cabin, the head of the one driving hardly coming above the steering wheel. He looked about twelve. A nine-year-old hung out the window and a seven-year-old was sandwiched between them. The boy leaning out the passenger side called cheekily, 'Hey lady, want a lift?'

So these were her new charges. 'Get out of that truck and get down here.' Sally spoke loudly and firmly. Surprised but with cocky grins the boys got out of the truck. 'You're late. Don't you ever keep me waiting again. Do you understand? Now unload that wheelbarrow immediately.'

The boys looked sheepish. They hadn't expected this reaction. 'Couldn't help it. The truck blew up and Dad's out with the Land Rover. We're here, aren't we?'

She watched them throw, with unnecessary force, her suitcase and the mail into the tray of the truck. 'Now come here and introduce yourselves properly. You're Ian, I suppose.' She turned to the oldest boy.

'Yeah. And that's Tommy and that's Martin.'

'Take your hat off when you speak to a lady and shake hands. You boys don't know much, do you?'

Insulted, the boys whipped off their hats and extended their hands for her to shake one by one.

'You know who I am, Sally Mitchell, your new governess.'

'Howdo, Miss Mitchell,' they mumbled, but Sally could see the resentment and hostility lurking in their eyes. They'd declared war on her even before they'd met her.

She smiled. 'I hear you fellows have quite a reputation. Four governesses in the past eighteen months, eh? Well, I'm the fifth and last. I'm not going anywhere, so get used to the idea.' She swung herself into the truck. Ian got back behind the wheel and the others climbed in the back. 'We're going to be spending a lot of time together. I hope we can be friends and get along,' Sally added.

Ian's foot barely reached the foot pedals and he let the clutch out suddenly, making the truck lurch forward. Sally took no notice. They rode in silence to the homestead, with Sally's show of bravado fading. She was hot, tired, stiff, thirsty and very aware of the challenge these boys presented. Just get through today, she told herself. One day at a time.

The homestead came into view screened by greenery, water sprinklers marking the boundary between rust dirt and emerald lawn. The mist spraying over the garden made the scene seem a quivering mirage. The house looked cool and comfortable in comparison with the harsh surrounds, but it was hardly architecturally challenging. The garden was lovely in a wildly tropical way compared to the elegant formality of her mother's gardens at Ashford Lodge.

At the gate – saplings wired together – separating the house garden from the patchy unwatered ground, leaned a tall man, nonchalantly smoking a roll-your-own and watching their progress. He came to the truck as Ian stopped and yanked on the handbrake. He opened the door and helped Sally down.

'Sorry about the delay in meeting you. These things happen.' He eyed her and smiled, showing strong white teeth in his tanned face. 'You don't seem any the worse for wear.' He pulled off his high-crowned felt hat and shook her hand. 'John Monroe.'

'Sally Mitchell. Well, I mightn't look worn on the outside, Mr Monroe, but I am on the inside,' she answered. 'It's been a long trip.'

'Come inside. Lorna has lunch ready. I'll get your bag.' He lifted out her suitcase and led the way to the house. He was tall, six foot three at least, thought Sally. Late forties, must weigh a good sixteen stone. Thick pepper-and-salt hair. He wore riding boots, long khaki army shorts and a spotless snow-white T-shirt.

Sally's first impressions of the house were that it was smothered by vines and creepers, extending even to the corrugated-iron roof, and outer walls of flyscreen enclosed a wide verandah that ran around a partitioned central living area. All along the verandah were rows of beds. The floor was concrete, covered in round seagrass mats. John led her to one end of the verandah where a small room had been partitioned off. In it was a single bed which, like all the others, was merely a canvas stretcher covered with a horsehair mattress, white sheets and cotton cover. There was also a chest of drawers and a small table. He laid the suitcase on her bed.

'Governess' quarters. You share the house with the family. Living room, dining room through there.'

Sally looked in to the living room and saw wrought-iron furniture covered in bold black and white stripes, and the same in the dining room, which had a long glass-topped table. A smaller table, obviously where the children ate, was at one side. In the open-plan living area were chairs, small tables, and a long table with the wireless and a vase of large artificial roses.

John Monroe waved his hand in the other direction. 'Bathroom across there, next to Lorna's room. Toilet's outside. Settle in and see you in the dining room.'

She heard him shout at the boys and there was the sound of boots thudding along the verandah. The bathroom was basic, with a shower and bath. She peeped around the partition to look at the screened area where there was a double bed hung with a mosquito net and a baby's cot against the wall. She noticed the sides of the cot were covered in flyscreen, making it more like a small cage. There was a wardrobe and a dressing table with a mirror. It was spartan, clean and neat.

Sally went back through the empty dining room and, hearing voices, walked into a huge kitchen filled with two tables, a long one in the centre of the room and a large one against the wall piled with ironing. The boys were settling themselves at the centre table, which could seat twelve or more, with two white men who looked like station hands. She glanced around, seeing a door, which she later learned led to a storage room that was kept locked, and a window that opened to the outside with a small counter ledge under it like a shop. This was where the station blacks came every day for rations, and to buy extra supplies or tobacco, men's shirts, cotton dresses and clothes for the children. A lubra was working at a kitchen bench adding powdered mustard to some egg mayonnaise. The men at the table half rose from their seats and nodded at Sally.

'She's the new governess,' Ian said to them.

One of the men was about to speak but began buttering a slab of bread as the back door opened and Lorna Monroe, followed by a young black woman, came in. Lorna looked completely different from what Sally had imagined. She had the immediate impression that this woman would be at home at Ashford Lodge, there was a straightness, a primness to her bearing, and she looked starched, pressed and unflustered. She wore a cotton blouse tucked into a neat skirt with white sandals. She seemed surprised to find Sally in the kitchen.

'My goodness, my apologies. Has John abandoned you?' She took Sally's hand. 'Lorna Monroe. It's lovely to have you with us. I'm sorry I wasn't here to greet you. There was a little problem with a couple of the girls in the laundry. Now, come along, you boys aren't allowed to eat out here, our lunch is ready in the dining room. Lunch is informal but dinner is a ritual with us,' she added. 'One should maintain standards no matter where you are, I believe.'

John Monroe came in and they sat at the dining table. Sally was gently probed about her life, her family, her friends, what she liked to read, and why she had applied for the job.

Her smooth answers faltered slightly. 'I wanted to travel and everyone goes to England. I wanted to see a place that was different and really experience it. Staying in one spot for a long time seemed the ideal way. And I love the wide open spaces, horses, outdoor life.'

John Monroe had a booming voice. 'There's all that here at Barra Creek, and not much else.' He gave a hearty laugh.

'It can be a challenge,' said his wife, looking at Sally.

'I'm up for a challenge,' Sally said, with more emphasis than she felt.

Monroe roared in appreciation. 'Good for you. Don't let those rascal boys get the better of you.'

'John, please,' admonished Lorna. 'What say we briefly run through the daily routine?' She motioned to the lubra hovering in the doorway. 'Take away the plates please, Betsy. And bring in the fruit.'

The kitchen girl glanced at Sally as she took her plate and Sally gave her a hesitant smile.

'Betsy works in the kitchen with several other lubras – Lizzie, Pansy, Mattie. There are four girls who rotate and do the housecleaning and laundry. Generally there are half a dozen of them at a time around the house. They're slow and need supervision. We also have a few old fellows who do the garden,' explained Lorna, watching the girl balance the plates. 'They're well looked after. They're fed from the kitchen here, get their homestead rations every day – salt beef, bread, tea, flour, sugar. Plus they have whatever bush tucker they hunt and dig up.'

'Do they eat fruit, vegetables?' asked Sally.

'They don't like them. Sometimes they eat bananas from the garden.'

'Did all the salad come from the garden?' After two days of greasy cafe food Sally had enjoyed the meal of lettuce, tomato, cucumber, tinned beetroot and pickled onions, with slices of corned beef.

'Lorna's very proud of her kitchen garden,' said John. 'And we have some fruit trees, of course. We kill and salt our own beef. There are a few sheep about for mutton. Chickens, a milker, fish, bush tucker. You ever eaten crocodile?'

'Not really. I prefer them as handbags.'

He roared again. 'I like you, Sally. A sense of humour will get you through a lot of sticky situations.'

Lorna frowned. 'John, no one eats crocodile. Don't lead her on. And let's hope we don't have to deal with any sticky situations. Now, about the boys' routine.'

Lorna talked while they ate fresh fruit salad

complemented with tinned peaches, then John excused himself, rolled a cigarette and went into the kitchen. Later Lorna took Sally around the house and garden, and showed her where everything was kept. They visited the schoolroom and Sally learned that she'd have several black children in the class as well as the Monroe boys.

'That way we get a government grant,' explained Lorna bluntly. 'Teach them about hygiene and whatever else you can manage.'

Sally considered the schoolroom barely more than basic – a slab of concrete, four corner posts supporting a corrugated-iron roof with walls of fly screen. Outside there was a pit toilet with a bit of hessian to screen it, and a tap and hose. 'The black children must wash themselves down before they can go inside, and change into clean clothes that you'll bring over from the laundry each morning. Then they change into their old clothes to go back to their camp when they leave in the afternoon,' Lorna said. She looked at Sally, still in her good skirt, blouse and heels. 'Why don't you change and freshen up? I hope you have appropriate clothes?'

'I have enough for the time being. I'll ask my mother to send my riding things over.'

'You ride?' Lorna raised an eyebrow. 'That will be nice for the boys. I don't of course. But I believe there are some quiet horses about the place.'

Sally bit her tongue. 'I'd love a shower. Is there a problem with water supply?'

They headed back towards the house. 'Not at all. We pump from the river when we have fresh water. It can be salty in the Dry, but we have rain tanks for drinking water.'

'Can we swim in the river?'

'I don't. There's a swimming spot the children use. I

would be careful, though.' She grimaced and Sally decided she'd leave the swimming for the time being.

Refreshed from her shower and wearing cotton slacks and a shirt, Sally drove with John Monroe around the immediate vicinity of the homestead to see the stockyards, past the single men's quarters, the machinery sheds, and the meat room where their meat was butchered and hung for salting. 'No freezers up here, the four big fridges in the kitchen are kerosene,' Monroe explained.

He waved towards a clump of small trees. 'That's the blacks' camp. Maybe fifty people living there all up. Some of them are good stockmen, others are lazy bastards. There are too many lubras around the place. They cause hell when the stock camps come in from mustering.'

They headed through thicker, lush vegetation to the river, which Sally found quite beautiful.

'It's very wide,' she said. 'Must be a hundred yards across.'

'It's down at the moment. In the Wet she can be double that and very fast. We have a boat moored at a landing down thataways a bit to get over when we have to. It's a long ride around. Do you like fishing? There's good barra in season.'

'Hence the name?'

'Clever. Looks like the boys have a bright teacher.'

'I consider my job more supervising than actually teaching,' said Sally carefully. She didn't have a clue about teaching.

'You teach 'em to mind their Ps and Qs. Ian's off to boarding school when he's old enough. We'll probably send Tom to board at the prep school as well.'

'Are they looking forward to it?' asked Sally.

'It doesn't matter if they are or aren't. That's how it

is.' He looked over at her. 'Unless you reckon you could teach them all they need to know?'

Sally didn't know how to take the comment or his tone of voice so she brushed it aside. 'I went to boarding school for a while. It was a very valuable experience,' she said, noncommitally.

By evening she was exhausted. Lorna made it clear that they dressed for dinner. While it wasn't formal attire, everyone had cleaned up, brushed up and changed into fresh clothes. John kept to his uniform of snowy white Chesty Bond T-shirts and shorts but switched from boots to leather sandals. Lorna had changed into a cotton dress, the boys had their hair combed and wore clean shorts and shirts. The three adults sat in the living area and John poured them all a shot of Inner Circle rum with a glass of water on the side. Neither of the Monroes diluted theirs.

'It's a good thirst quencher,' John said. 'We carry it instead of water when we're out all day.' Sally didn't believe him. Later, she learned he meant it.

When dinner was served, they went to the dining table. The boys were seated at their own table, tucking into their meal. John and Lorna discussed the plans for the following day, jobs to be done, news about men, dogs, cattle, and the mess around the blacks' camp.

Afterwards Lorna went out to the garden. It was twilight and the sprinklers were turned off and she walked around inspecting plants and making a list of chores for the men to do the next day. John sat on the verandah with a cigarette and a glass of rum, and Sally was expected to spend time entertaining the boys before they got ready for bed.

She sat on one of the spare beds near where the boys' stretcher beds were lined up and talked to Tommy and Marty about their interests, how they entertained themselves and what subjects they liked or were best at in school.

Ian wandered away and the two younger boys began regaling her with tall stories that she listened to with some amusement before saying, 'Now you don't expect me to believe *all* those stories.'

'They're true!' exclaimed Marty.

'Well then, next time you have to write a composition, I'll be expecting a really exciting story of wrestling a crocodile big enough to eat a horse,' she said.

Lorna appeared and said firmly, 'Boys, Miss Mitchell has had a long day travelling. Tonight you get yourselves to bed and no rough-housing. School at nine o'clock sharp in the morning. Now say goodnight, please.'

She turned to Sally and said gently, 'I can see you're ready to drop. Have an early night.'

'Thanks, I am very tired. I hope I wake up early.'

Lorna smiled. 'Oh you will. Goodnight.'

The governess' room was a hotbox. Sally pulled open the drawer where she'd put her night clothes and underwear. As she reached in for a nightie, geckos raced from her clothes, one jumping on her arm. She leapt back, uttering a small cry and heard a muffled giggle and the boys' bare feet padding away from her door.

'Little monsters,' she muttered.

She lay on top of the bed in her nightdress in the stifling little room, watching the sticky-footed geckos run up the wooden wall and onto the flyscreen across the window. It was certainly different from where she'd come from. She closed her eyes, too tired to think any more about the myriad impressions of the past few days.

Chapter Four

Barra Creek, Gulf Country, Queensland

IN THE COOL PRE-DAWN hours Sally managed to fall asleep after a fretful night perspiring in the hot little room, dreaming of Sean. But no sooner had she relaxed than she was jolted awake, not realising where she was or what was happening. It was sunrise, and a clanging sound was reverberating through every nerve in her body. Iron striking a large bell, then shouting. It was John Monroe.

'Get up, you lazy black bitches. Rise and shine, shake a leg.' Clang, clang clang.

Sally fell back on the pillow. Holy mackerel, was this the usual alarm clock?

Apparently so. Monroe could be heard in the kitchen, stoking the fuel stove, banging the metal hotplates and the oven door. Sally lay there wondering whether to get up and see to the boys, or wait till she was summoned. She had almost dropped back to sleep when there was a loud knock on her door and Monroe stuck his head inside. 'How do you like your tea?'

'Milky please. No sugar.'

She was sitting on the side of the bed, her hair brushed, when he appeared holding a mug of tea.

'How'd you sleep?'

'Not bad, but I'm not used to the heat at night.'

'This is nothing. Wait till the Wet. Now, fried eggs, tomatoes, toast and baked beans. Sound all right?'

'Er, yes. Fine. Thank you. I'll be out shortly.'

'When you're ready rustle up those boys and send them in to wash. Breakfast will be ready soon.'

When she emerged, showered and dressed in a simple cotton sundress, no make-up or shoes, and headed towards the kitchen, she passed Ian walking gingerly, carefully carrying a cup of tea.

'Morning, Ian. Is that for you?'

'No. It's for my mother. She likes to have tea in bed. She's not too good in the mornings, says she feels sick.'

'Oh dear. Where are Tommy and Martin?'

'In bed.'

Sally found the two boys buried beneath a sheet on their beds. It was cooler on the verandah, and the breeze came through the flyscreen carrying the scent of flowers from the dewy garden. She looked at the other empty beds and decided she'd sleep out here too. She tickled the boys, who grunted and flung protesting arms and legs at her.

'We're too big for that,' said Tommy.

She spotted some books by Tommy's bed. 'I'm glad you like reading.'

'I love it.'

'Why don't you take it in turns to make up a story and tell it to each other every night?'

Marty was enthusiastic. Sally could see the idea appealed to the younger boys. She looked at her watch. 'Off you go. Breakfast is nearly ready. And then school.'

John was at the dining table buttering a piece of toast and listening to the chatter from the wireless. 'Morning news,' he said.

'Oh, what's been going on in the world? I feel out of touch,' said Sally, reaching for the teapot in its crocheted cosy. Her hands stilled as she realised the talk on the wireless was local, between all the stations.

'Heard there's a new governess at Barra Creek. Over.'

'Yeah, wonder how long this one will last. Over.'

'I saw her at Twin Rivers. Good sort. Big tits –'

'John, turn that rubbish off, we don't want to listen to that.' Lorna appeared in the doorway in her dressing-gown, holding her cup.

Sally poured her tea as John turned to another frequency where cattle movements were being discussed. She was busting to hear the 'rubbish' but kept her eyes down. The boys giggled.

They walked over to the schoolhouse and the boys sat down at their desks, pulled out their work and showed Sally where they were up to. She had briefly studied the curriculum and saw how the lessons were organised. Each week the boys' work was sent off in the mail to correspondence-school teachers, corrected, commented on and returned. Sally was surprised at the boys' behaviour in the schoolroom. Gone was the chivvying, teasing, baiting and challenge to her authority. School work had to be done, they knew they needed to be at a certain standard before going to boarding school. There was friendly rivalry among students from other stations when they talked on the wireless about their achievements.

An hour passed and Ian looked up at her. 'You'd better get the other kids up here or Mum will be mad.'

Sally went and looked down towards the camp. 'You can't go down there,' advised Tommy.

'You boys stay here. I'll go and ask Lizzie from the kitchen to fetch them. Get on with your work.'

Lizzie and two young women were working in the outdoor dining area kneading great mounds of dough. Bread was baked every day, huge high white loaves that were sliced for the house and included, unsliced, in the camp's rations. When Sally asked her where the other children were, Lizzie just stared at her.

'You know, kids from camp. Boys, girls.' She made a gesture with her hands showing their height.

Lizzie's face cleared. 'Big fella piccaninny. Longa readin', talk 'em up proper way . . .'

'Sally. I'll deal with this.' Lorna came in from the main kitchen. 'You are not to speak pidgin. They understand plain English well enough.' To Lizzie she said, 'Send those camp kids up to school, quick smart.'

Looking sulky, Lizzie, who seemed to be in her thirties, dusted her floury hands on her apron and stomped off.

'There's a pile of clothes on a table in the laundry for the kids to change into. Make sure they wash themselves down properly,' said Lorna.

Sally collected the shorts, dresses and shirts and returned to the schoolhouse and piled them on a bench near the hose attached to the water tank. She could hear shouting and squeals as skinny children appeared from all directions, racing each other to school. She supervised the washing process, recognising the little girl who'd been at the airstrip. She was only about five years old and she attached herself to Sally's side with a proprietary smile.

By the time they were settled at desks with drawing

paper and coloured pencils it was morning-tea time. Lizzie appeared at the schoolhouse with a tray of Anzac biscuits.

'Missus say go down for johns,' she said to Sally, then began handing out biscuits to the local children. The Monroe boys ran towards the house and Sally followed.

Morning tea was set out on the dining table. There was a large pot of tea, fresh scones on silver plates, jam and tinned cream, and flowered cups and saucers. John and Lorna helped themselves as the boys took their scones to their table where orange cordial was poured into tall glasses. Fifteen minutes later, the boys carried their plates and glasses to the kitchen and escaped outside.

'What are you doing after smoko?' Lorna asked John.

'I've been telling that mob down at the camp that it's time to clean up and make a new camp. The gundies can stay but not the rest of it. They never learn. It's a bloody disgrace.'

'It always is, dear,' said Lorna, gathering the tea things. 'I hope you gave them plenty of warning.'

John stomped from the room. 'Fat lot of good that does.'

'What's a gundi, Lorna?' said Sally. The Monroes had asked her to call them by their names.

'It's what they live in. Corrugated iron on a cement slab. Two rooms with a lean-to verandah. There's a tap on the outside at one end of the verandah, and a communal lavatory and shower. Most of the old people still seem to prefer gunyahs – bough shelters or a sheet of iron propped up to keep the sun off them when they're sitting or sleeping on the ground. They live, sleep and eat around the campfire and leave the mess there. It's filthy.'

Sally excused herself and went back to the schoolhouse and settled her charges. While the Monroe boys tackled their arithmetic, she asked the older black children to show her how well they could read or write. It was a dismal response.

'They just draw pictures, Miss,' said Tommy.

Sally went through the supply cupboard and found some picture story books. 'Do you fellows mind if I read these kids a story? You keep doing those sums.'

The boys shrugged. 'They're baby stories,' said Ian.

Sally gathered the group of kids from the camp into a corner, sat down and began to softly read a story about a lost frog, holding up the book to show them the illustrations. The children were fascinated, their eyes wide as they listened. They giggled when Sally put on different voices, and jumped up to point at things in the illustrations. Sally glanced back to check on the boys and saw Marty leaning around his chair, following the story. When he caught her looking at him, he bent down, pretending to pick something up off the floor. Sally decided she'd try reading them a story that night.

It was three o'clock, and the boys were out playing while Sally helped the other children back into their camp clothes. They skipped away as she washed her hands and headed in for afternoon tea on the verandah with the Monroes. It was fruit cake this time. She came to learn that scones and biscuits were served for morning tea, and fruit cake or pikelets in the afternoon. Lunch had been substantial too. At least she wouldn't go hungry.

Lorna was taking a nap. Sally had just come out of the kitchen when she heard screams. Shrieks and howls ripped through the torpid air, followed by the sound of tin and iron being crushed, and the low growl of an engine.

'What on earth?'

She heard the boys yelling and the old truck revving

up. 'What's going on? Where are you going?' she asked as she ran outside.

Ian was behind the wheel, the other boys were standing in the tray holding onto the roof of the cabin. 'Dad's clearing out the camp.'

'What? Wait for me.' Sally pulled herself into the passenger seat, then Ian crashed the gear stick and set off over the paddock.

As the truck bounced over the mounds and ruts, they passed a line of trees and suddenly came upon a scene that shocked Sally. John Monroe was driving a big tractor with a grader blade attached in front and was roaring through the rough tin and bark shelters of the blacks' camp. Dogs and children were running in circles, there were cooking pots, cans of food, clothes, piles of rubbish, broken branches, flattened tin and unidentifiable objects crumpled and tossed aside by the rattling old tractor.

The women were wailing, flailing their arms, clutching babies and trailing possessions. Some old men stood silently to one side. They'd seen it before, as had the others. But despite the notice to relocate the camp, they never did. It was a ritual repeated every couple of months when the boss decided the stench and mess had got out of hand.

'Heck. What's going on? The poor buggers,' exclaimed Sally.

'Mum says it stinks and it's unhealthy, so Dad cleans it up. They always like their new place better.'

'I bet they go over to the trees by the river,' said Tommy. Marty didn't say anything but wasn't enjoying the spectacle the way his older brothers were.

'I don't want to watch this. Let's go back,' said Sally.

The boys protested vehemently. 'Dad lets us watch it. Sometimes we ride on the tractor.'

Sally jumped out of the truck. 'Well, I'm not staying. I'll walk back.'

She trudged through the afternoon sun, disturbed by the brutishness of the exercise. Beneath the booming joviality John Monroe had a very tough side to him, she decided. On the other hand, the camp was squalid. She'd seen and smelled it, even at a distance. It puzzled her that the women could work in the house under the fussy eye of Lorna Monroe and yet were happy to lead their own lives amidst the incredible filth that was part whiteman's trash of flour tins, rice sacks, bottles and cardboard boxes and part their own discarded half-eaten food, the chewed carcass of a wallaby the dogs hadn't finished, tools, hunting spears and digging sticks, dilly bags and dishes. She supposed it was all replaceable but the invasiveness of Monroe's actions troubled her.

Later, she saw Lorna alone, arranging a vase of silk flowers on a side table.

'The boys took me down to where John was clearing up the blacks' camp this afternoon.'

'Whatever for?'

'They weren't prepared for it. It seemed so . . . sudden. I mean the whole lot was just turned over and almost buried,' said Sally.

'That's the idea. When it gets to that point, we have to do something about it before we all get sick. By tomorrow they'll have set up a new camp. At the last minute they'll have saved their hunting gear, coolamons, bits and pieces. Or else they'll make new ones. The lubras will be up here for new dresses. And no matter how much warning we give them, it makes no difference. I sometimes think they like to make a song and dance about it all. Now, how did you find the boys today?'

Sally dropped the subject of the camp. 'They're very good in school. Really seem to want to learn.'

'They know their father will skin them alive if their marks aren't good when it's time to go away to school. He expects them to do well. And that means sports too.'

'I'm afraid I'm not much help there,' said Sally. 'I was a bit disappointed that the big kids from the camp can't read or write at all.'

'Don't worry too much. They just need to show up and keep out of mischief. They'll figure out how to sign their name eventually, I suppose.'

Changing for dinner Sally found a dead snake amongst her shoes. She bit her tongue, determined not to squeal. She could tell the instant she clapped eyes on the way it was draped through her gold sandals that it was dead. She'd never seen a snake before and was thankful this one was quite small. She had no idea what type it was, so she steeled herself, swept it into a dustpan and carried it out onto the verandah and left it on Ian's pillow. Being the oldest she figured he was the ringleader in their anti-governess campaign. While there she turned down the pristine white covers on the adjoining bed and left her book and dressing-gown on it.

None of the boys mentioned the snake, but Marty couldn't resist giving her a sly grin as she sent them off to get ready for dinner.

Sally and Lorna had pre-dinner drinks on their own. John was nowhere to be seen and Lorna looked slightly distracted. When the boys came into the dining room, Sally asked her, 'Shall we wait for dinner? Or should I eat with the boys?'

'Yes, yes. Good idea. John is still down at the machinery shed. I'll wait for him.'

Sally carried her plate to the boys' table and pulled out a chair. They looked at her in surprise but went on eating.

She noticed they had starched linen napkins on their laps and held their knives and forks in the prescribed manner. Lorna was a stickler for doing things the right way. As if to challenge Sally, Tommy leaned one elbow on the table, and Martin picked up a piece of meat in his fingers. Ian sent his peas and carrots spilling off his plate. Then Tommy knocked over his drink, splashing Milo over the white tablecloth. Martin giggled.

Sally slammed her knife and fork down with a bang. 'Right. Enough. Leave the table. Take your dishes into the kitchen and put the food in the chook bucket.'

'We haven't finished,' wailed Tommy.

'Too bad,' said Sally unsympathetically. 'And there was a nice dessert too.'

'What?' cried Martin. 'I'm hungry.'

'Then don't play with your food and try to stir me up,' she said. 'Think how much you're going to enjoy breakfast.'

'You're mean,' hissed Ian as he marched past her.

Sally finished her meal alone, wondering what had happened to John. Lorna seemed to make such a big deal about having dinner together.

Young Betsy hovered at the door. 'You finished? Me clean up?' she asked Sally.

The women were always anxious to clear away the dishes and clean up the kitchen so they could leave the house. Lorna made them wait until the meal was over and the two kitchen girls on duty would hang around in the garden, smoking or chewing tobacco. If there were visitors, or if John Monroe was in an ebullient mood, it could be a long wait.

'What about the missus? The boss?' asked Sally.

'The missus got dinner in her room. The boss . . .' she looked around and mimicked a drinking gesture to Sally.

Sally thought she'd better not probe in case Lorna

67

could hear. 'Then go ahead and clean up the kitchen, please, Betsy.'

She could hear the boys playing in the dark garden. The door to Lorna's room was shut. Sally helped herself to another glass of rum and sat in a chair in the living room. For a moment she felt lonely, then decided to relish these moments alone.

The clock on the sideboard struck eight. Sally had dozed off. She jerked awake and saw a light had been turned on and the dining table was set for breakfast. The kitchen was neat, the dishes washed and put away, every surface wiped clean. She went outside and called the boys.

There was no answer. 'If you don't come now, there'll be no treats and extra homework tomorrow,' she threatened in a loud voice.

Martin came out of the gloom. 'We're just playing hide and seek.'

She smiled at him. 'You blokes have an answer for everything. Come on, Martin, bedtime.'

He followed her along the verandah. 'Can you please call me Marty? And you know what you said about a story . . .'

'Course I do. What's your favourite?'

'*Wind in the Willows.*'

'That's one of my favourites too. Do you have a copy? We could read some if you like.'

He rushed into the room that served as John's study and Lorna's sewing room and came back with the book.

'Get ready for bed. Do you want to tell me where the others are hiding?'

'Don't say I told.'

She put her finger to her lips and he whispered, 'In the tree near the chooks.'

Sally picked up a torch and strolled through the garden to the chook pen.

'Nighty, night, chickens. Watch out for that big snake. I have a gun so I'll fire up this tree here and scare him away. Might catch a bat or two as well.' She lifted the black torch. 'Looks like a couple of big ones up there in the branches.'

'Hey! Watch out,' cried Tommy. 'It's us.' The leaves rustled.

'One . . . two . . . ready . . . aim . . .' Sally pretended to squint along the barrel of the torch. 'Did you know I was the best pistol shot in the South Island of New Zealand?'

Tommy swung down from the tree. 'What are you doing?' he demanded.

'If I don't see two boys in their pyjamas quick smart, you might be surprised what I'll do.'

Tommy sprinted for the house and Ian climbed down and stood in front of her, his hands on his hips. 'You think you're so clever.'

'Do I?'

They glared at each other, then suddenly heard John's voice. 'Where is everyone? Sally? What's going on?' His voice sounded tired, thick and not himself. Ian turned and bolted round the side of the house. Sally took the cue and hurried after him, sensing maybe it wasn't a good time to run into John.

Marty was in bed with the book. Sally sat beside him and began to read. He sat up so he could see the illustrations.

'Can you do voices? Like for Rat and Mole and Toad?' he asked.

'Let's do it together. You be Mole and Rat and I'll be Toad and the others.'

The older boys took no notice and pulled up their

sheets, pretending not to listen. But both were quiet. At the end of the first chapter, Sally closed the book.

'It's late. More tomorrow. G'night, Marty.'

He waved at the other bed. 'You sleeping out here too?'

'Yes. That room is too hot. Goodnight, boys.'

There was a grunt from Ian. Tommy was asleep.

'G'night, Miss,' said Marty quietly.

Sally went into the bathroom to brush her teeth and wash her face. She stopped as she heard voices coming from Lorna's room.

'C'mon, Lorn . . .' there was the thud of a boot, the unmistakable squeak of wire bed coils under the big inner-spring mattress. The only one in the house.

'Go away, John. You're drunk. Too drunk.'

'Ya reckon? Move over, love. Just a little cuddle.'

'Get out of my bed.' Her words were low but ferocious, hissed between clenched teeth.

Sally tiptoed into her room to change as she heard gasps and grunts that sounded like a physical wrestle. She shut the door and lay in the dark as John Monroe forced himself on his unwilling wife, pounding and grunting until he groaned, gave a gasp, and started muttering to himself.

'Don't you dare go to sleep. Get out. Go to your own bed.' Lorna's tone was icy and she must have pushed him as there was a stumble before Sally heard him bang into the partition wall and stagger out to the far corner of the verandah where, Sally now realised, he slept.

She waited in a lather of perspiration as she heard Lorna go to the bathroom and wash herself. When the house was quiet save for John's snoring, Sally crept to the back part of the verandah. She discovered the boys, well, Ian, she assumed, had pushed her bed away from theirs, leaving a big gap between the governess and her charges.

Grateful for the cool starched sheets and balmy breeze from the garden she settled on the bed, disturbed but sexually aroused, and thought of Sean. Had he thought of her? Suddenly she wished he was with her and she vowed to write to him tomorrow. The young woman who'd set off to conquer England without a backward glance now felt very, very lonely.

The following morning after showering and dressing, Sally went into the dining room where the boys had already started breakfast. John bellowed at Lizzie in the kitchen and strode in and took his place with a cheerful good morning. If he was embarrassed about the previous night, he didn't show it. Lorna was still in bed. Her custom was to sleep in and let John organise the women to prepare breakfast. One of the boys would bring her a cup of tea, then she'd wait till the others had finished breakfast and emerge, neatly dressed with powder, lipstick and smoothed hair, and eat a small bowl of rolled oats followed by a piece of toast and fresh tea. It was Lorna's time to herself, which was respected and never intruded upon unless it was important.

The static sound of the wireless, a modern version of the old pedal wireless, was coming from the living room, the boys were talking about something they were doing with their father that afternoon, and Sally sat at the table, eating cornflakes and tinned peaches.

'What's going on after school?' she asked.

'Boy stuff,' said John Monroe, pouring himself a mug of tea. 'Ridin', shootin', cowboy stuff.'

'Sounds exciting. Can I come too?'

'We're going riding,' said Ian.

'I can ride,' said Sally.

'We're going to get a killer,' added Tommy.

Sally looked at John, who roared with laughter. 'Not some outlaw on the run. A killer is a steer we knock on the head for house beef.'

The boys laughed. 'Didn't you know that?' cried Marty.

John's head swivelled over the laughter, alert to a call on the wireless. 'That's us being called in. Let's see what's up.'

He went into the living room and picked up the receiver. 'Barra Creek here. Receiving on channel six. Over.'

Sally and the boys took no notice as they argued over what horse Sally could ride.

Monroe walked back in holding a piece of paper. 'That was about you, Sally.' He spoke quietly and looked slightly concerned.

'More gossip?' she sighed.

'No. It was a telegram. From your parents in New Zealand.'

'What! Is everything all right?' Sally's hand shook as she put her cup down.

'They're a bit worried. Wondering where you are. They tracked you down through Dalgety's.' He gave her a steady look.

'Ooh, er. Did you run away?' asked Tommy. All three boys were looking at her with wide eyes.

'Of course not,' said Sally briskly. 'They haven't got my letter yet, that's all.' John Monroe dropped a hand on her shoulder, sensing her discomfort. 'Don't worry, Sal. I'll send a wire back. Tell 'em you're with us, and we're delighted to have you here too. Not to worry. Letter following, eh?'

Sally looked at him gratefully. 'That would be nice. Thanks very much.'

Monroe glanced at the boys. 'Stop your carry on and finish your breakfast. You don't want to be late for school. Any trouble and you don't come out with Fitzi and me this arvo.'

The boys put their napkins by their bread and butter plates as taught and left the table, pushing in their chairs. Tommy spoke up. 'We'll be having spare ribs tonight won't we, Dad?'

'Of course we bloody will! Killer night is spare ribs on the barbecue.' He grinned at Sally. 'One of the few times we eat fresh meat. Starting with the ribs tonight, steaks tomorrow and a roast the day after.'

'Sounds good to me,' she said. The boys had left the room when she turned back to John Monroe. 'Thanks for sending the message to my parents. They tend to fuss a bit.'

'Most parents would if their pretty young daughter was heading to England and ended up in Queensland's Gulf country. You got any problems, you tell me, okay?'

Sally nodded, suddenly choked up at the unusually soft tone of his voice.

'Lorna and me are real glad you're here. I hope you'll hang around, Sally. I know the boys can be a pain in the backside.'

'Oh, no. They're lovely. I really enjoy them,' she said quickly. 'They're just trying it on. Testing me out. That's natural.'

'I'm glad you see it that way. Lorna keeps telling me it's my fault they get out of hand. Learn it from me, she says. Ah, struth, you can't teach an old dog new tricks, I reckon. Most times, it's just the grog or the boredom that gets to you up here. Keep busy, that's the ticket.' He went back into the living room to send the telegram and as he dictated it over the wireless, Sally realised everyone in the district would have heard the exchange and she'd be the cause for more gossip.

The boys were well behaved in school, nervous that if they played up they might not be allowed to go out riding.

Over afternoon tea Lorna handed round the plate of sliced fruit cake. 'Sally, are you sure you want to go out with them? You don't have to, you know.'

'I want to! I'd love to go for a ride, and see a bit more of the station.'

'We're only going to the main home paddock,' said Ian.

Sally had been told that the paddocks closest to the house were twenty and fifty acres. Barra Creek was over 240,000 acres, far bigger than anything in New Zealand.

'Good, I won't get lost then.'

'If, by chance, you do get bushed remember there's always a dead patch on the western side of quinine and ironwood trees. If it's overcast and cloudy you can tell west because of the bare patch,' said John casually.

The boys were anxious to get going and raced to change from their school shorts into their moleskins.

'What do you have to wear to ride in?' asked Lorna.

'I bought some boy's dungarees. But I don't have any boots. I'm writing to my mother tonight to ask her to send some of my things over.'

'There's a pile of boots out by the laundry. There'll be a pair to fit you,' Lorna said in a tone that implied *if you must*.

Sally found the boys at the stables, saddling their horses. Ian helped Marty, but once he was in the saddle he looked perfectly at home on the pony.

'So which is my horse?' She had seen some good-looking horses around the station but when Ian pointed over his shoulder at the fifteen-hand black mare standing tethered to a tree, Sally wondered if she should back out.

'That one. Dad saddled her.' Sally stared at the strange bulky, high-backed stock saddle in some dismay. She was used to small, light hunting saddles. She adjusted the stirrups and attempted to make friends with the horse, but to no avail. This was a horse who had been ridden hard, treated rough and now in her golden years had been relegated to hack work. The mare was bored, tired, disinterested.

Once the boys were ready to ride out, Sally mounted, embarrassed at how clumsy she felt in the cumbersome saddle. The boys rode leaning back, legs straight and sticking forward in a manner that went against all the riding rules of British-equestrian-trained Sally.

Once clear of the yards, they broke into a canter and Sally followed, but she was slipping and sliding in the saddle. She couldn't feel the horse with her legs, and her frustration and mounting fury were communicated to the animal, which pulled on the bit and strained against her commands. The boys glanced back at her struggling and, giggling, they galloped away.

They darted between trees and raced across the open ground before reaching an area covered in feather-tipped spear grass, young bloodwoods and to Sally's amazement, huge red termite mounds. The boys kept changing direction, cutting around the ant hills and she realised they were trying to lose her. It was country like nothing she'd ever seen or imagined. She cursed as she kept losing her balance, furious at the stubborn horse and mad at the boys. She couldn't see where they had gone so she kicked the horse with her heels and let the animal have her head.

It was wild country and Sally knew how easy it would be to become disoriented and lost. To her eyes, there were few landmarks. But the horse either knew the country or where the other horses had gone for soon Sally saw puffs of dust kicked up by the three horses cantering behind John Monroe's truck.

She kicked the mare into a canter, trying to keep her balance on the slippery saddle, hanging onto the horse's mane. As she got closer she saw the truck was nudging along half a dozen cattle with the boys spread out on the wings nosing them towards a stand of trees. A black stockman was standing in the tray of the truck, directing the boys, and near a large tree she spotted a ringer who had swung into the low branches. The truck stopped a little distance away and the boys jumped down and sat on the ground watching the cattle mill around under the trees. It was very quiet and still. Monroe got out of the truck, leaving the door open, and studied the cattle. Sally dismounted, watching the scene. The stockman in the back of the truck sat down and rolled himself a cigarette. Sally sat on the grass beside her horse like the boys.

They were there for about four or five minutes watching the cattle, which were standing quietly in the dappled light of the trees. Monroe, who'd been leaning against the truck, slowly lifted his arm, pointing, giving a signal. She heard the crack and saw a steer fall to its knees, the others running in a panic into the bauhinias. With the calm suddenly shattered John Monroe and the stockman ran forward, tying a rope around the dead beast as the marksman climbed out of the tree, a rifle slung across his back.

'Get in and stick him,' Monroe called and the stockman swiftly cut an incision at the jugular, then stabbed the knife down into the bullock's heart.

The men began opening the hide and cleaning as they went. 'Got to bleed him properly. Makes better meat,' Monroe explained to her.

Leading her horse, Sally followed as the beast was tied to the rear of the truck and John Monroe got back behind the wheel and dragged the animal to a solid tree with low branches. They threw a rope over a branch and adjusted it so that when John moved the truck slowly forward it winched the beast on the other end of the rope off the ground by its haunches.

The stockman, whom she recognised now as Fitzi who also worked around the yards and garden, took a long-bladed knife and removed the hide. He then slit the belly, letting the guts spill out. John Monroe called to the boys to help and they pulled an old tarpaulin from the truck and threw it onto the ground.

Sally crinkled her nose as the grisly process of cutting away at the carcass continued with precision, and great sections of it were thrown onto the tarp.

Monroe glanced up and saw her. 'How do you like your steak?' he shouted.

'Not moving on my plate, thanks. Why did you wait so long before shooting one?' she asked.

'You want the adrenalin to get out of their system. The calmer they are the more tender the meat. I don't believe in killing 'em on the run. Wait till you taste this meat.'

'I'll wait till it's cooked, thanks. I'll see you back at the house.'

'Can you find your way back?' he shouted.

'Yes.' She was going to make a sarcastic comment about the boys but bit her tongue. Struggling to mount and stay as steady as possible in the saddle, knowing they were all watching her, Sally wheeled the horse about and trotted away, hoping she looked more confident than she felt.

On her own, she began to relax and enjoy the scenery. The thicket of trees and undergrowth lining the river was away to her left so she turned the horse in that direction, wondering if there was a track along the edge of the river.

She saw tyre marks in the grass that had made something of a track to follow and discovered it came out at a clearing where there was a wooden landing, big enough to hold two people, jutting into the river. A small wooden clinker-built boat with no cabin, but a seat, a tiller at the stern and an inboard diesel engine covered with a piece of canvas, was tied to the pylon near the landing.

The river looked cool and inviting. Sally dismounted, tethered the horse to a sapling and, breaking off a small twig, walked onto the landing and threw the twig into the water. It glided along in the current at a speed that surprised her. On the other side of the river she could see another landing. This must be the crossing Monroe had told her about. One day she'd like to explore over that side of the river. It looked less penetrable, though. A glossy green vine had climbed across the tree tops and the undergrowth around the landing was thick, smothered by the now uncontrollable Madagascar rubber vine that was killing the natural vegetation. She wondered whether this might be a good place to fish. Perhaps this would be something she could do with the boys. Although, she'd only ever fished for trout with her father in a stream on their farm.

She turned around and froze mid step, her mind trying to come to terms with what she saw. There, stretched across the landing at the edge of the bank, was a crocodile. Motionless, it had scaly plates, a greyish brown, was about five feet long, with a horny snout and hooded ridges over mean, deep-set eyes.

Her head started to spin. There was no going forwards as it blocked her path, stepping backwards meant falling into the river, where, she had no doubt, more crocs lurked. A mere two yards separated them.

She remained frozen to the spot, aware its green eyes were watching her. The monster was simply waiting. Sally had only ever seen crocodiles in pictures and she had no knowledge of how they behaved. But she figured it would not be easily intimidated if she rushed at it. She felt like she was about to pass out then realised she'd been holding her breath. She gasped, drew a deep breath and yelled with all her might.

Her scream for help shocked the mare, who'd been dozing. Her head shot up as she pulled backwards, her back legs losing balance, scrabbling in the loose earth. The sudden action behind it startled the crocodile, which flicked its tail and was in the water in a movement so fast Sally scarcely registered it. She waited a few seconds then leapt along the landing in three strides, grabbed the horse's dangling bridle, flung herself awkwardly into the saddle and kicked the horse, who was now thoroughly startled and so confused that she bolted for the homestead. Sally clung to the animal's neck, her trembling arms communicating her fear to the horse.

The mare went straight to the stables and stopped at the gate. Almost crying with relief, Sally slid to the ground and patted the old nag she now regarded as her saviour.

She was hanging up the saddle after grooming the horse, keeping busy to calm her nerves, when she heard the truck heading back. She walked towards the house and saw it stop outside the flyscreened meat room. A cloud of black flies swarmed above the bright red chunks of beef. She turned away as the men carried it in to butcher it on the wooden bench.

The boys were excited about dinner, dancing up and down chanting, 'Spare ribs, spare ribs.'

Sally didn't think she could eat the meat after seeing it slaughtered and her stomach felt wobbly after her fright at the river. She hadn't said anything, but after two glasses of rum, the smell of the meat sizzling over the open fire was tempting. On this occasion, manners were relaxed, and even Lorna picked up the fat ribs in her fingers to gnaw at the meat.

Sally chose her moment, fortified with rum, and announced casually, 'I saw a croc at the river this afternoon. It came and sat beside me on the landing, where the boat is.'

'Oh yeah, how big?' asked Ian sceptically.

'About as big as you,' said Sally. 'No, bigger.'

Lorna raised an eyebrow. 'What were you doing at the river? Be careful walking down there please, Sally.'

'Oh, I was riding and decided to take a look at the river.'

'What did you do?' asked Marty.

Sally shrugged. 'Ah, I sent it packing into the river. Spooked that old mare though. I had to catch her. But no problem.' She bit into her spare rib, which was delicious, enjoying the impressed looks from the two younger boys.

John thumped the outdoor table. 'A 'gater, eh? Good for you, Sal. I thought you were having a bit of trouble with that old nag.'

'It's the saddle. I've never used a stock saddle before, it's awful.'

'Not if you're sitting in it ten hours a day,' he retorted.

'I've written home and asked my mother to send my saddle over,' said Sally.

'Goodness me, there're plenty of saddles about the place,' said Lorna.

'I'd like to do a lot more riding. With my saddle and a *decent* horse you fellows won't catch me.' Sally smiled and winked at the boys.

John Monroe studied her, but didn't say anything. Instead he reached for another spare rib.

Sally sat on the edge of Marty's bed when the three boys were in bed.

'Tell us again, what happened when the croc sneaked up behind you on the landing,' said Marty.

'Well, I didn't hear anything. But I just knew something was behind me, the hairs on the back of my neck stood up,' Sally began. 'And when I saw it I knew I'd have to jump in the river, in the boat, or charge it . . .'

Ian sniffed and rolled on his side with his back to her, but Sally knew he was listening as she embellished the tale until she saw Marty's eyelids flicker and his breathing slow then steady as he went to sleep. She stood up and smoothed the sheet.

'Night, Tommy. Night, Ian.'

Ian didn't answer and she wasn't sure if he was awake. But Tommy mumbled quietly, 'That black mare is a stupid horse. Don't ride her again, Sally.'

'Okay. You tell me what's a good horse,' she said softly, ignoring his use of her first name.

Sally was very tired. She got into bed, noticing that it was still pushed down the verandah, leaving a long gap between her and the boys, and fell asleep almost immediately.

Chapter Five

SALLY HAD SEEN DONNY'S mail plane flying over the station and wondered whether he was thinking about her. She had no way of leaving the property, even if she had a vehicle or a horse she wouldn't get far. She didn't know how to use the wireless, and no one had visited the station since she'd been there – nearly a month now. John Monroe was omnipresent, shouting at the young station hands and browbeating the old black men who plodded through their work, indifferent to his shouts and curses. The house girls went about their tasks under Lorna's direction, and life was orderly and routine. The boys assured Sally, however, that this was the quiet time with both stock camps out mustering. It would be much more exciting when Rob and Snowy brought their cattle in, they told her.

She mentioned this to Lorna who raised her eyebrows. 'The boys are right. These times are the eye of the storm.' She had taken the opportunity to set up in her sewing room, surrounded by yards of damask and polished white cotton, making new pillow cases, table-cloths and napkins.

It never ceased to amaze Sally how Lorna kept such an immaculate house despite the circumstances. She assumed it was her nursing background. Lorna had told her that she came from a good middle-class Melbourne family, and the fact she lived in the outback was no reason to lower her standards. Sally realised Lorna had recognised her own privileged upbringing in New Zealand and understood that her family knew how to conduct themselves. The subtle questions, the times she'd watched Sally, listened to her conversation, had been enough for Lorna to give Sally a tick of approval. Lorna had even forgiven her for not knowing how to wash up properly, iron or fold sheets, or do other domestic chores when she'd asked Sally to take over or show one of the house girls how to do something *properly*.

Sally had thrown up her hands and confessed, 'We always had a housekeeper, I never had to do this stuff.'

Lorna had nodded but then said seriously, 'Sally, you must know how to do these things. Even just to show the help what to do. You must have your standards.' And so she taught Sally how to do hospital tucks on the bed sheets, how towels were folded long and flat and kept fluffy. How linen was pressed and folded and smoothed. How to clean glass and mirrors. Never to go to bed while food or dirty plates remained in the kitchen. How clothes should be tightly pegged on the clothesline, avoiding creases. Sally had absorbed the social graces from her mother but hadn't wanted to know how to run a household.

Out here, of all places, it all seemed overdone, but perhaps it was a gesture by Lorna to maintain links with society, to feel they were living a life as controlled and ordered as anyone in a metropolis. Her intentions were kind and helpful, and Sally wasn't made to feel like a servant but like a supervisor, to instruct the house girls and learn for her own benefit. Lorna told her that no matter how well she married, or if she didn't have any help at all, Sally would know how to do these things – *properly*.

At morning-tea time, as Lorna took a break from her sewing and John and the boys were busy elsewhere, she suggested Sally take one of the vehicles and do the mail run. Sally grabbed the opportunity.

The plane was a faraway dot when she left the house in the unregistered Land Rover used to run around the station. As she parked by the landing strip and got out of the vehicle she thought back, such a short time ago, to her arrival and how kind Donny had been.

The plane landed and he leapt out and came over to her with a big grin.

'Are you staying or leaving? I've been worried about you. You're the talk of the Gulf country, you know.'

'I am not.' Then she remembered the talk on the morning wireless session. 'Golly, I hope I'm not. What are they saying?'

'That you're a good sort. You've run away from a secret past in Kiwiland, you've been kidnapped, you're looking for a rich husband. Lots of speculation.'

'All rubbish,' she said briskly.

They walked to the rear of the plane. 'So how are you getting on? Coping all right? Or do you want out? You won't lose face if you leave now. You've given it a fair old bash.'

'I'm not about to quit. It's pretty good. There are still a few things to sort out, but I'm liking it.'

'Really?'

'Truly, ruly.' She grinned.

'Give me the mail and I'll shout you morning tea.'

'I've had morning tea, but okay.'

They exchanged the mail bags and as he tucked the sack from Barra Creek into the plane Sally gave it a pat. 'Couple of mine in there.'

'Letters home? To the boyfriend?'

'What makes you think I have a boyfriend?'

'Course you have. I bet you've broken a few hearts in your time.'

She laughed lightly, but as well as writing to her parents, she had sent Sean a short letter. She watched as Donny pulled a small icebox from behind his seat.

'Come on, hop into the Land Rover and head for those trees down near the river,' he told her.

'Are you serious?' She hesitated, glancing at the line of trees about a mile away.

'Yeah, I know this area. I went fishing around here with buddies. Rob showed me a few good spots.'

They got in and Sally started the engine. 'Rob? Who's he?'

'Ah, you haven't met him yet. Or Snowy?'

'Who are they?'

'Hell, no wonder you've stuck around. It must be bloody quiet without the stock camps at the station. Those boys are the stock camp kings. Snowy runs the Barra Creek stock camp with the local boys from the blacks' camp on the station. Rob is the contract musterer, has his own fellows. Very particular. The two of 'em are chalk and cheese, I'd say.'

'The Monroe boys told me things would hot up when the stock camps came in.'

'Yeah. You be careful. Snowy is a rough ol' redneck, Rob is off the land in the Territory. He had a falling out with his dad over something, I gather, and he took off on his own. Came from a big station, good family. He went to the King's School down in Sydney.' He gave a chuckle.

'So did John Monroe, I think it irks him that his contract musterer had the same schooling he did.'

'That's where he's sending his sons, I suppose.'

'Eventually. I think Lorna and John were married in the King's chapel.'

'So do they all get on together?' asked Sally, sensing she needed to sort out the undercurrents of the situation before these two mysterious men arrived back at the homestead.

'From what I've heard I don't think they have a lot in common other than cattle and work. I don't imagine there'll be smart dinner parties at the homestead.' He laughed. 'Go left, see over there, that big tree, pull up near that. We can walk through to the clearing.'

'We're not going near the river bank, are we? I had a run in with a croc when I was on my own the other day.'

'Is that so? Honey, you're really acclimatising.'

They pulled up, and with Donny leading and carrying the icebox they walked among the stand of trees. Sally was surprised to see a clearing with a distant view of the river through bushes and smaller trees.

'Great little spot, huh? There's a bit of a path that goes to a muddy sand spit where you can fish.'

He brushed twigs and stones aside for them to sit down and took two bottles of cool orange juice and a plastic container of small finger buns covered in pink icing from the ice-chest.

'Courtesy of Mrs Rydge at Mallee Station.'

'Oh, is this the custom? Feed the mailman? I'll have to whip up something next time.'

'Do you cook? How's the food at Barra Creek?'

'No, I'm not a cook or very up on domestic things like ironing and folding. Lorna is teaching me the finer points. She supervises the food – except breakfast – but

I'm getting tired of salads, and vegetables and corned beef. Hot, cold or curried.'

'Sally, you do realise how lucky you are, don't you? Not many, in fact hardly any, of the governesses stay in the house with the family. Of course, a lot of the governesses are rough as bags. Some of them have been nice-enough girls, but stuck out in quarters on their own or with the house staff, too close to the single men's quarters, well, that's asking for trouble. Or else they just want to go home. I can't blame them.'

'I wouldn't have stayed if they treated me like a servant,' snapped Sally. But Donny's information surprised her. She had landed on her feet.

'John can seem a bit rough and tough, but he has a good business head, I gather. Lorna runs a tight ship,' said Donny. 'She was a sharp little nurse who came up here from the big smoke. For a long time after the war a lot of smart city women came to the bush as teachers and nurses looking for husbands.'

'How come you know so much about everyone? Do you read their mail?' teased Sally.

'I ferry agents, accountants, bankers, solicitors and locals from station to station. I hear things.'

'You'd better not gossip about me.'

'You haven't shared anything worth telling. Now come on, how's life really treating you?' And as she gave him a quizzical look, he added, 'I promise not to breathe a word.' He bit into a bun. 'It's nice to have a pal to talk to. I don't s'pose there's anyone you can do that with at Barra, huh?'

Sally was thoughtful. 'No, there's not. Lorna is kind, but sometimes withdrawn. John has a good heart, I think, underneath the bluster. I feel there's a bit of tension between them though. Privately.'

'And the boys, how do you get on with them? They

managed to rip through the other governesses. Not that the kids were the sole reason they left. None of them could measure up to Lorna's exacting standards, a couple got into trouble with some stockmen, then there was the isolation, the boredom and no social life.'

'Individually the boys are okay. Though Ian, the oldest, is testing me a bit. But nothing I can't handle,' she added.

'You're a self-reliant, stubborn young lady, aren't you?'

'I can be. I had a strict upbringing, but my parents were fair. I've been a bit of a rebel, though, so I can't say I blame them for packing me off to England.'

'But you didn't go. Was there a guy in the picture?'

'If there was I wouldn't tell you.'

Donny leaned back and reached in his pocket for a packet of filter-tip cigarettes. He offered her one and Sally took it, mainly to be sociable. She'd only ever smoked for effect, to appear sophisticated and worldly. 'Any time you want to talk about things, I'm happy to take time out, Sally. It's a lonely place out here for women.'

Sally narrowed her eyes as she expelled smoke. 'I bet you have a lot of lady friends on your route, eh?'

'I like to think of them as friends. Often I'm their only visitor for weeks at a stretch.' Donny was thinking that, despite her touch of world weary airs and tough banter, Sally was really an innocent in this part of the world. She'd obviously come from a protective family. But she was in for a few shocks down the track. 'Just remember that you have a friend who you can dump your woes on, have a bit of a break with on occasion if you'd like – no strings – I enjoy the company. You intrigue me, I kinda feel responsible for you.'

'Why's that?'

He shrugged. 'I fly a lot of people around. I was real concerned leaving you out here the day you arrived, all dressed up, looking so damned well bred. And there you were stranded with a bunch of grubby kids and a wheelbarrow.'

Sally looked away for a moment, a pang hitting her, then she laughed. 'Those kids must have thought I'd dropped in from another planet. That little girl, Alice, she's like my shadow now.' They both laughed at the memory. 'I just don't understand the blacks, though.'

'It's easier not to try. Different worlds, honey. Come on, let's go for a bit of a walk, I'll show you the fishing spot. No crocs, although there's one that lives further up river. They're territorial and tend to hang about in the same place. Unless they're hungry and start stalking prey further afield.' He picked up the icebox and led the way.

When they got back to the plane and Donny had swung into the pilot's seat, Sally was sad to see him leave. They'd talked about all manner of things on their walk and she'd learned a lot more about his life and family in Canada.

'See you next week if I can,' she called. 'Morning tea's on me.'

'Sounds good. Don't worry if you can't make it. We'll catch up. Look after yourself, Sal.'

'See you, Donny.'

She waved and waited till the little plane skimmed into the air, then turned back to the Land Rover with a light heart. Driving to the homestead, she tried to analyse her feelings. She wasn't attracted to Donny, despite his handsome looks, but he was a nice man in a big brotherly way. She'd enjoyed his company and suddenly she missed Sean and especially Pru. Remembering their shared confidences, their adventures, their closeness, she was overwhelmed with a sense of guilt. God, what had happened to Pru? Well, she assumed she'd hear when her mother wrote back. Sally started to think of the list of things she'd asked her mother to send and prayed her parents would agree to send everything she wanted. Or would she get a summons to come home? She'd signed an agreement and her father had taught her that her word was her bond. There was no going back. But from what Donny had said, she should be grateful she'd landed in the middle of a decent family who respected her upbringing.

She gazed out at the great red land surrounding her, there was still a lot of country to explore. She'd love to go riding with the boys a couple of afternoons a week. In the distance she saw a straggling group of lubras from the camp walking slowly, gathering food to supplement station rations, she assumed.

She pulled up to the homestead and saw John Monroe in the front yard, rolling a cigarette. Lorna was telling Fitzi how to prune a shrub, and the boys were sitting on the verandah steps absorbed in braiding strips of leather. It was a pleasant domestic scene that etched itself in Sally's mind.

The next morning John was banging around in the kitchen when Sally ventured in for a cup of tea. 'Bloody Lizzie and Betsy aren't here. What do you want to eat?'

'I'll fix it. Cereal is fine. Are they sick?'

'Pretending to be. A mob of the lubras have walked out.'

'Left? Gone walkabout you mean?'

He didn't answer for a moment as he stuck a thick slice of white bread on a long fork and faced it into the wood fire at the bottom of the stove. 'Thought they seemed a bit toey last night. Anxious to get away.'

'Now that you mention it they did kind of whip the plates away and clean up the kitchen quickly. Where've they gone?'

'With the rest. Some of the girls left the camp yesterday. Those black bitches are walking out to meet the boys. A stock camp is coming in. Probably that lazy bugger Snowy.'

'How do you know?' asked Sally. 'How do they know?'

'You ever hear of the bush telegraph? They know stuff somehow way before we hear about things. Damned if I know. Those women can smell a man coming, that's for sure.'

Sally couldn't understand his anger. 'Does that mean there's no one to work in the house?

'Ah, maybe. You and Lorna might have to help out. They generally send some of the young girls up to work for 'em. They need training up and watching. Don't give an order unless you're able to stand there and watch them do it.'

'Might as well do it myself then,' said Sally lightly. If John was so put out, Lorna was going to be livid. 'Does this happen every time?'

'Every couple of months. Now get those boys in here. Don't mention about Snowy coming in or you won't get any sense out of 'em in school, they'll be wanting to get down to the yards.' He turned his piece of toast and looked sullen.

Sally took her bowl of Weet-Bix into the dining room and joined the boys who were whispering excitedly.

'What are you fellows talking about?'

'Nothing,' said Ian.

Tommy's eyes were shining and he couldn't stop grinning.

'Go on, tell her,' said Marty.

'You mean about the stock camp coming in? Is it Snowy?' said Sally calmly, trying to keep a straight face at the deflated expressions.

'Who told you?' demanded Ian.

'Who told you?' countered Sally.

'Fitzi. He said he heard them coming,' said Marty. 'He's clever.'

'Heard them? How close are they?' she asked and it was the boys' turn to look smug.

'He puts his ear to the ground. Reckons he can hear the vibrations from miles and miles away,' said Tommy. 'He's teaching me.'

Ian glared at him to be quiet. Sally knew Lorna's orders were that they weren't to mix with the blacks. Sally had seen the boys playing with the older kids from the camp and had turned a blind eye.

'So when will they get here? And what happens?'

The boys all talked at once until Sally held up her hands. 'Whoa, it can't be all that thrilling.'

'Mum doesn't think so and Dad always yells, but it's fun!' said Tommy.

'You come up to the yards and see,' added Marty.

'All right, I will. But not if it's school time.'

Their faces fell and the two younger boys looked at Ian.

'They won't get here before dark. Maybe tomorrow,' he said.

'Good, then we can get through our work. Perhaps do a bit extra and then we could take a little time off, eh?' suggested Sally.

The boys brightened. 'Yeah. Let's go.' Tommy gulped down his breakfast. 'Can I be excused please, Miss?'

'Me too,' said Marty.

'There's no rush,' said Ian, wiping a piece of bread into the last of his eggs and tomato sauce their father had cooked.

'Well, I'm looking forward to seeing all the cattle come in.' Sally stood up and carried her plate into the kitchen, leaving Ian alone at the table.

It was late afternoon, Sally was sitting with Lorna on the verandah having a cup of tea, when the boys raced across the lawn.

'They're here. We're going to the yards!' And they dashed to the stables where they had their horses already saddled.

Sally jumped up and peered towards the home paddock. She could see a drifting cloud of red dust and hear a low rumble like distant thunder and the occasional ringing, snapping crack. 'It sounds like a thunderstorm coming this way.'

'Snowy always makes a racket. He tries to make it all look and sound more important than it is,' sighed Lorna. 'I hope he's brought in a decent-sized mob or John will be cranky. And, Sally, under no account go anywhere near the blacks' camp or the single men's quarters. Snowy camps in there and I think he's got a couple of white men with him, bore runners. That means trouble, especially when the boys will be back with their wives and lubras. It'll be on for young and old tonight. It's disgusting.'

'What are bore runners?' asked Sally.

'Fellows that run round all the stations checking and repairing the bores, troughs, windmills. They also do a bit of maintenance work on the machinery or odd jobs.'

'Shall I go and keep an eye on the boys?' She was dying to get up to the yards.

'Take the Land Rover. John said you aren't to ride that black mare. It's probably better you're there watching them and make sure they're back and cleaned up in time for tea.'

Sally was cross about Lorna's remark that she wasn't to ride the mare, but she got into the Land Rover and drove as fast as she could to the yards in the home paddock.

It looked like utter mayhem. She stopped the vehicle as

she saw the seven hundred head of cattle charging towards the stockyards, men on horseback galloping on either side and to the rear, cracking whips, yelling and urging the leaders towards the open gate. The poor beasts, all wild cattle – cleanskins – that had been plodding round the open country undisturbed, were frantic at this mad rush.

As the cattle poured into the yards, the men dismounted and ran to slam down the rails. Sally saw the boys sitting on top of a yard railing so she got out and went to join them.

The dust was choking, the noise deafening and she wondered why everything had to be done at such a frenetic pace. She climbed up and sat beside Marty, the boys barely acknowledging her. Then she spotted the man who must be Snowy. He was directing everyone by shouting, waving his whip, kicking his horse this way and that. He was stocky, with a ruddy face flushed with sun and exertion. And when he took his hat off to wipe his brow Sally saw he had ginger hair.

She leaned over to Tommy. 'Why isn't he called Bluey instead of Snowy?'

Tommy shook his head, looking puzzled. Sally leaned over to Ian. 'I thought in Australia red-headed blokes were always called Blue.'

'Snowy came up here after working on the Snowy River scheme.'

'I see.' The boys weren't interested. This was a place where men could be known only by a nickname and where they could bury their pasts.

Several lubras and children were also watching the activity. Frankie and Ginger from the school joined them on the railing and they discussed the cattle and horses. Some order replaced the chaos as the cattle were marshalled. John Monroe appeared and pulled Snowy aside and there was an intense discussion. Monroe then strode away, studied the cattle, turned on his heel, got in his car and drove back towards the homestead.

Sally looked at her watch. 'Boys, we'd better get back and clean up for dinner.'

Reluctantly they got down from the rails. Sally looked at Frankie and Ginger. 'See you tomorrow.'

They hung their heads. 'Nah. Big come home jump up. Big pella come back. Mebbe school. Mebbe not.'

Sally caught a warning look from Tommy so she let it go. 'See you later then. Come on, boys, get back to the house and clean up.'

John Monroe was agitated at dinner. He'd had more than his usual two pre-dinner rums.

'So what is Snowy's mob like?' asked Lorna. 'Can they be sold on or do they need a bit of fattening?'

'Of course they need fattening up. He's run them into the bloody ground to get here. Lazy bastard never stays out long enough. Barely six weeks this time. There're a lot more cleanskins roaming round out there. He and those boys are always in a rush to get back to the mob at the camp.'

Lorna narrowed her eyes, reminding him the boys were in the room.

'Where have the cattle come from?' asked Sally, trying to change the focus of the conversation but also because she was curious.

'Most are off our land. But there are no fences out back of beyond. Cattle and horses run free, breed and are there for the taking. First in best dressed, in a way. Sure there are other cattle breeders, but, hell, look at the distances. It's hard to say whose cattle have strayed where. The outback runs on cleanskins. And poddy dodging.'

'What do you do with them?' asked Sally.

'Put your brand on 'em quick smart,' said Monroe.

'Branding is exciting. Almost as good as breaking,' said Tommy, glancing at the adults' table.

'I'd like to see that. You boys can explain to me how it all works,' said Sally.

'Got to draft them first. Later we cut 'em. You reckon you know a bit about horses, eh Sally?'

Lorna cut in. 'John, that's all disgusting work, not the sort of thing Sally should be bothered with.'

'Oh, we had horses at home. Thoroughbreds for hunting –'

John Monroe gave a bawdy laugh. 'Hunting! You mean the la-di-da business in red jackets chasing some poor bloody rabbit? I'd like to see them run down a rogue bull or catch a steer. That's bloody riding.'

'Now, John, don't be insulting. I doubt Sally has any interest in buck jumping or bull catching,' said Lorna.

'I do like horses,' began Sally, trying to get across the idea that maybe she'd didn't ride like a stockman but she loved riding and would like to do more. Lorna obviously thought riding was not a ladylike activity. And judging from what Sally had seen around the yards with the wild men bringing in the cattle, she could see her point.

'Bet you'd like the stallions but,' began Tommy.

'Don't end sentences, in "but", Tommy,' said Lorna. 'Finish your meal please, lads.'

Later as she sat on Marty's bed when the three boys settled down for the night, Sally asked about the stallions.

'They bring up good breeding stock from down south, or any brumbies that look good are sent out to mix with the wild horses,' Ian explained. 'So in a season or two we get better horses to use or sell.'

Sally listened attentively, it was the most Ian had spoken to her since she'd arrived.

'I see. Is there a horse I could ride? Your father won't let me ride that black mare.'

'You really like riding?'

'I do. If I had a horse we could go out riding together, couldn't we?' she said. 'I'd love to go exploring over the station more, especially when my saddle comes.'

The boys exchanged looks. The two young ones looked at Ian accusingly as if it had been his idea to put Sally on the mad mare. Then they seemed to make up their minds.

Ian settled himself under the covers, saying nonchalantly, 'I'll talk to Dad.'

'Mum doesn't like horses,' Marty whispered to Sally.

That night Sally was restless. The noise from the cattle was disturbing. The penned beasts were frightened and annoyed. They moaned and roared, the metal gates clanged as they banged against them, and Sally wondered what would happen if they broke free and thundered towards the house. She turned over, opened her eyes and sat up.

The usual bulky silhouette of the sleeping boys wasn't there. Their beds were empty, the sheets thrown back. She got up and looked around, cocking her head to listen in case they were whispering nearby. Wondering whether to alert Lorna or John, she padded along the verandah and saw that John's bed hadn't been slept in.

She hurried back to her bed, pulled on her boots and stepped into the garden.

It was bright moonlight and the noise from the cattle seemed closer. She wasn't sure what she was going to do, but she walked around the garden to the front of the house. A distant flash of a torchlight near the stables caught her eye and she heard a horse whinny. Surely the boys weren't over there.

Seeing the Land Rover parked by the fence surrounding the homestead garden, she ran over to it. As usual the keys were in the ignition. Worried that Lorna might hear her, she released the handbrake, put it in neutral and felt it start to roll. Then she turned on the ignition and drove slowly down the driveway. The headlights didn't work but it was bright enough to follow the ruts to the stables. She stopped a little distance away.

She could see a light in the stables, so she got out and walked towards them. Now she could hear voices. But not from the stables, they were coming from the single men's quarters. Lights were on and there was a sudden burst of laughter. Must be Snowy and the runners who'd driven in with the cattle, she thought. Maybe that's where John was as well. As she came closer to the stables, she could hear horses moving. Then she heard Ian's voice low and urgent, directing Tommy.

She stopped, her eyes adjusting to the darkness. Soon she could make out a small figure atop a fence railing. Someone was moving in the yard with the horses. The animals were distressed, snorting and whinnying. Sally inched closer. Tommy was holding onto a rope slung around a horse's neck. Ian was standing in the small yard with a stockwhip, keeping several other horses at bay. Marty watched from the railing.

The horse must have been broken in as it was calmer than the others, although it still appeared a little nervous. Sally paused, afraid to go closer in case she spooked the horses and they trampled Ian.

Tommy was shortening the length of rope, slowly winding it in, moving cautiously closer to the horse, murmuring soothing words all the while. Ian held the other horses back until Tommy was standing beside the horse, who was breathing heavily and looked poised to rear on its hind legs. Slowly he reached out and placed his hand on its neck and although it recoiled it didn't jerk away. Sally inched closer, holding her breath.

Now Tommy was walking with the horse, leading it quietly to where Marty was holding open a gate that led into a smaller stall. Once the horse was inside, Tommy slipped the rope through the half hitch so it slipped off its neck. Walking backwards, he climbed out of the stall. Ian swung onto the railing and jumped outside. The horse lunged forward into the yard, looking for a way out. The boys climbed onto the railing and studied the animal, unaware Sally was now behind them.

'What's going on?'

The boys started in surprise.

'How'd you get down here?' asked Ian.

Sally suddenly realised she was standing in her pale blue nightdress, the borrowed work boots on her feet. 'So? What are you up to? Looks pretty risky.'

'We wanted to get this filly out from the others. Before they send them away in the morning,' said Tommy.

'Where are they going?' From what Sally could see in the moonlight these horses were fine boned, with a good build and nice heads.

'Snowy is going to let them go with the brumbies. We wanted this one,' said Marty.

'Does your father know what you're doing?'

'Course not,' said Ian.

'Then you get back to bed before I yell for him.'

'Don't do that, Miss,' pleaded Tommy.

Marty leapt down and grabbed her arm. 'We're not doing anything wrong . . . it's a surprise.'

'Shut up, Marty,' said Ian.

'Get in the Land Rover, we're going back to bed,' said Sally firmly.

As they all squeezed into the vehicle they heard shouts, laughter and what sounded like women squealing, coming from the men's quarters.

Sally glanced in the direction of the converted sheds. 'What's going on? Sounds like a party.'

Ian answered and Sally was surprised at the vehemence in his voice.

'Don't go near there.'

She bit her tongue and drove slowly to the gateway and switched off the engine.

'We'd better stop here so we don't wake anyone.'

As they walked quietly to the back verandah Tommy tugged at Sally's arm. 'You won't say anything to Dad, Miss?'

'Isn't he going to ask about the horse?'

'We're going to tell him it was pulled out by a couple of the stockmen. Fitzi's idea. It's a good horse. Too good to go out with the brumbies.'

'I see. We'll talk about it in the morning.'

The boys hurried ahead and by the time Sally had pulled off her boots and climbed into bed, they were under their sheets, backs turned away from her. She lay there listening to her heart, which was beating quickly.

After a few minutes Marty murmured, 'G'night, Miss.'

'Goodnight, Marty. Go to sleep. Night, Tommy, night, Ian.' She paused. 'Next time you want to go messing around in the middle of the night, take me with you.'

There was a muffled giggle, then Ian said gruffly, 'Thanks for not dobbing us in. Night.'

He shrugged into the bed and Sally smiled to herself. It was the first time he'd ever said goodnight to her.

Sally was sound asleep but woke with a start; she'd heard a high-pitched scream. Or had it been the cattle? All was silent now. As she drifted to sleep she heard the thump of John Monroe's boots, a crash as he bumped into something. He fell onto his bed. The house slept.

Chapter Six

John Monroe was up early despite his late night. He hung onto the bell, whacking it with extra might. No one had surfaced from the men's quarters but as the bell shattered the morning silence, Sally heard faint shouts from the lubras: 'Shut up, bloody old man.' That was how all the blacks referred to John Monroe.

He thumped around the kitchen, where Lizzie was setting out breakfast for the white men and the woman from the stock camp who'd arrived with the two white bore runners. He rang the cow bell one more time. 'If you lazy bastards aren't up here in five minutes,' he yelled, 'the grub's off.'

He stomped into the dining room and sat down muttering, 'You have to hunt down that Snowy, he's always late. Lazy bugger.'

'You starting to draft the cattle today, Dad?' Ian asked.

'If that bloody Snowy and his men get off their backs. Have to cut and brand 'em before Rob brings his mob in.

I hope to hell he stays out longer than Snowy. Seven hundred head isn't much to show for six weeks' work.'

'When's Rob coming back?' asked Tommy eagerly.

'Not for a while, I reckon.'

'Can we come and watch the cattle drafting?' asked Marty.

John gave Sally a slight wink. 'Depends on the ol' governess here. How's their work coming along?'

'Ahead of schedule. They've been going flat out. I think they've earned a bit of time off.'

The boys looked pleased. Ian spoke up. 'Dad, we want to show you something. Can we see you outside when you're finished?'

'S'pose so.' The flyscreen door banged as Snowy and his mates came in for breakfast. 'I'll just sort those sleepyheads out first.'

'I'll take Mum her tea then,' said Ian, and he brought his plate into the kitchen, followed by the other boys.

'What's going on?' asked John Monroe.

'I've no idea,' said Sally. She'd promised that she wouldn't mention anything about the previous night, and she wasn't going to break her word.

Sally was alone at the table, relishing a few quiet moments as she sipped her tea, trying to block out the rumblings from John Monroe in the kitchen and the raucous laughter from one of the men and a woman. Lorna came in, dressed in a pretty flowered housecoat, satin slippers, her long hair coiled on her head, her face shining with face cream. 'Any tea left?'

'It's a bit cold, I'll top it up.' Sally jumped up. 'Anything else?'

'No thanks. I'll eat something later when I'm dressed.'

Sally returned with the refreshed teapot and poured Lorna and herself a refill. 'Who's that lady with the runners?' she asked.

'She's no lady! She travels with those two men, cooks for them when they're out fencing, checking bores and so on. She camps with them even in the desert. Her name's Gloria – rough as bags,' sniffed Lorna.

'Are they related? It's odd there're three of them.'

'Oh, they're quite up front about it. She sleeps with both of them. I don't think even the most desperate stock boys would go near her.'

Sally was shocked at this and also at Lorna's matter-of-fact tone. 'Oh. How long will they be here?'

'Two or three weeks, I suppose. They'll get stuck into the jobs John has lined up for them.'

'Hard way to make a living,' said Sally.

'They wouldn't be hired for anything else. They're not bright men, Sally. Keep away from them, and that Gloria. And especially don't let our boys hang around them.'

The boys were fidgety in class and raced away once Sally dismissed them. They didn't appear at morning tea and nor did their father. Lizzie took smoko up to the yards, leaving Lorna and Sally alone on the verandah with the tea and scones. Sally was itching to find out what was going on, so as soon as she could she excused herself and headed for the yards.

Gloria pulled up beside her in the runners' beat-up utility truck. 'Yer wanna lift down t'the yards?'

Her accent and voice set Sally's teeth on edge, but she grabbed the door handle and got in. 'Yes, please. I have to find those three boys and I figure they're where all the action is.'

'That'd be right.' Gloria had a cigarette stuck to her lip and, as she wrestled with the shaky steering and gears, Sally took a good look at 'the runners' bird'.

She was plump in a doughy way, years of starchy bread, sugar and rum rolled around her frame, and the sun had baked her skin to a crispy, shrivelled brown. Her once-permed hair was dusty dry, her breasts swung, and her calloused hands and elbows showed she'd worked as hard as a man with straining wires and fence posts. She hadn't touched her face with anything resembling a cosmetic or cream in many years, but her eyes were startling blue in her weathered face, and her teeth looked strong despite the nicotine stains. She smelled appalling and Sally couldn't imagine how the men could find her attractive. But then she'd heard the old joke about lonely men and sheep. If one was desperate enough . . . she turned away. Gloria was only in her forties she guessed. Is this what happened to women up here? No wonder Lorna kept indoors and was such a slave to her grooming.

Gloria was equally curious. She looked at Sally. 'So, how're you finding it here? The old man give you a hard time?'

'Mr Monroe? He's been really nice. And Lorna is lovely. The boys can be a bit of a tease, but we get along okay,' said Sally, knowing she sounded prim.

Gloria chortled and gagged on her cigarette. 'Struth, you are the new bloody chum. You been here, what, a couple of months? You haven't seen anything yet.'

'I'm managing all right.' Sally was terse. 'I'll see my contract out.'

'You won't mind if I don't put money on you, love? Christ, this ain't no finishing school. You might live in the house and think you're as good as them, but believe me, no one has lasted the distance.'

Sally was relieved when they arrived at the busy

cattle yards. 'I'm here because I want to be, and if I want to go, I will. And frankly, I don't think it's any of your business.' She banged the passenger door of the truck and strode off.

In the yards, the cattle were pressed so close together the working dogs were running over their backs, nipping their ears, barking and helping push them into the race where they were quickly assessed by Snowy and a stock-man and divided up into the various yards. John Monroe was down in one, gesticulating and yelling at which beasts he wanted in the main yard, moving recalcitrant ones along with a short gidgee stick.

Sally spotted the boys sitting on a railing along with Frankie and Ginger, pointing and talking. Some of the younger kids from the camp were running around outside the yards, calling out in pidgin to the Monroe boys. Sally was starting to realise that there was a strong bond between the three boys and the black children, although Lorna had forbidden it. The kids needed playmates and it seemed they shared common interests in what went on around the station.

When she asked them what was happening, Tommy shouted above the din, 'They're drafting out the best ones, the ones to go back for fattening, getting them ready for branding.'

'Why do they have to be so rough?' Sally was upset at the men's handling of the cattle, the way the animals were crammed in, stamping on each other, their eyes roll-ing and their fear starkly obvious.

'They're only cattle,' said Ian.

Ian said something in pidgin to Frankie, who nodded. Marty translated to Sally, 'Ian says he could do Dad's job better than that.'

'Well, you're not about to start. Come on, back to school, you can come back after lunch.' She'd spotted the

Land Rover Ian had driven and started to walk towards it.

'You coming, Frankie, Ginger?' Tommy nudged Ginger and reluctantly the two black boys climbed into the back while the Monroes sat in the front next to Sally. She let Ian drive, marvelling at the young boy's easy skill behind the wheel.

'Are you going to come and watch the branding tomorrow, Miss?' asked Marty.

'Depends. I want to learn everything I can about life around the station. We'll see.'

Sally was thinking about their afternoon activities, wondering what she could give them to do as she knew Lorna was going to ask her to keep the boys away from the cattle for part of the day at least. Her ears were still burning from the string of expletives that had bounced around the yards. Language the boys would certainly pick up.

They went back to the schoolhouse and finished their project and the boys raced to lunch. Sally supervised Frankie and Ginger's change of clothes and Frankie gave her a mischievous smile.

'Me 'n Ginger goin' to pish 'im river. Mebbe catch one barra. Missy bring horse, go pish?'

Sally thought quickly. Fishing would keep the boys away from the yards. 'Sounds good, Frankie. Plenty barramundi about?'

'Mebbe.'

'I don't have a horse to ride. Can we drive there? Or walk?'

He gave her an odd look. 'No good drivin'. Horse.'

'You come back to the schoolhouse after lunch, see me. Okay?'

He nodded and walked off, his stick-like legs looking even thinner in the pair of loose men's shorts bunched at his waist.

She was putting away the school books in the cupboard when Marty stuck his head in the door.

'What are you doing?' she asked. 'Lunch is ready.'

He joined her as she headed for the house, but in the garden he grabbed her hand. 'Come round the back. I gotta show you something.' He could barely conceal his excitement.

'I hope you boys aren't up to any mischief . . .'

They walked around the back near the kitchen garden to find Ian, Tommy and their father standing by the water tank with a horse. It was the small filly the boys had cut from the mob last night. How much did John know, she wondered, but from their big grins it was obvious the boys weren't in trouble.

'That's a lovely little horse. Looks a bit shy.' She quickly assessed her to be around fourteen or so hands. Good head and legs, a dark bay with white flashes. She was lightly saddled but looked uneasy. 'How come she's broken in?'

'Rob broke her last season and then we put her out to spell her.'

'She's real smart,' said Marty.

'So what's happening with her?' she asked, moving slowly forward, stretching out her hand to the nervous young horse.

'She's yours, Sally,' said Monroe. 'We can't have you taking the boys out on the old black nag.'

'She's still shy but if you can ride, she'll listen to you,' said Ian with a faint hint of a challenge even though his eyes were smiling.

'Mine! What do you mean?'

'You said you wanted to ride and the boys spotted this filly. It would be good if you could spend time with the boys, take 'em out, see they don't get into trouble.'

'Oh, my.' Sally's eyes filled with tears. 'I don't know

what to say.' She laid her hand gently on the horse's throat and felt her skin twitch, but she stayed still.

John Monroe looked pleased as punch. 'I don't want to have to come and rescue the lot of you now –'

'No fear. I just have to get used to your flaming Australian saddles,' said Sally, who was going to ride this little beauty no matter what.

John left them to it and Ian and Marty disappeared into the house. Tommy quietly walked the horse around the back garden, then made her trot and briefly canter. Sally was amazed at the authoritative but gentle control and rapport Tommy had with the animal.

He was a gifted rider and a joy to watch. Sally was entranced. He was no longer a little kid in her care but a boy who instinctively knew how to handle a horse and with the added advantage of the local skills he had learned, she could tell he could handle even a difficult animal.

'How did you learn all this, Tommy? You're a natural with horses,' she said.

He didn't answer for a moment as if deciding what to say, then he muttered, 'Rob and Fitzi, they show me stuff. They're the best. They know how to do everything.'

He dismounted and helped her into the saddle, the horse standing quietly while Tommy was close by. Then he stepped to one side as Sally settled and found her balance in the unwieldy saddle and headed onto the track from the house towards the river.

It was quiet away from the cattle, so Sally took the horse on, slowly rising to a trot. The horse realised the difference in riders and when Sally slipped in the saddle, threw her leg a little, counterbalancing her weight. Sally was elated that this was a horse who wanted to learn, she was intelligent and smart. Tommy had spotted it in a minute and he'd been the one to suggest they cull the filly for her. But as Sally rode smoothly towards the trees she was more surprised at this gift from John Monroe. Maybe because he didn't want to spend time on horseback with the boys himself. She knew the boys could work with the stockhorses and cattle if needed, or when they begged to be included. It was Lorna who hated to see them out with the men and in the stock camps. But it was part of station life and she was overruled by her husband.

By the time Sally cantered back to the house she'd come to a basic understanding with the little horse she'd named Dancer. Her feet were so dainty, her steps so precise that she was a bit of a Ginger Rogers, Sally decided.

Tommy was sitting on the fence with Frankie beside him and they gave her a thumbs up. Sally slid down and handed Tommy the reins.

'Never been riding in a skirt before,' she said. 'Tommy, she's a princess, a fabulous horse. Now we can all go out. In fact Frankie suggested we go fishing this afternoon.' Suddenly Sally realised that Frankie must have known about the horse. 'Is she up to it?'

'If we take it slow and easy, get her used to the other horses. No races,' said Tommy solemnly.

'Let's go find the others.' Sally loosely tied the horse to the railing.

After lunch she changed into the moleskins borrowed from the stores, preferring them to the stiff denims she'd bought in Sydney, riding boots, a shirt tucked in and one of the battered Akubra hats off the peg on the back wall near the kitchen. She passed Lorna carrying a basket on her way to pick flowers and vegetables from the garden. She looked at Sally's flushed face. 'Where are you off to? I hope not near the yards and the men up there.'

'No. The boys and I are going for a bit of a fish. Might bring home supper,' she said gaily.

'How are you getting down to the river? Don't go anywhere but the usual spots.'

'We're riding. Oh, Lorna, I'm so thrilled about the horse. She's just fabulous.' Sally hurried outside and didn't see Lorna's expression of surprise, anger and tightened lips.

'Be careful!' she called and Sally gave a salute on the run to show she'd heard, but she didn't look back.

It was the best time Sally had enjoyed since arriving at Barra Creek. Away from their parents or other eyes around the station, the five boys and Sally laughed, teased and thoroughly enjoyed the fishing expedition.

The Monroe boys and Sally walked the horses while Frankie and Ginger trotted ahead. They rode parallel to the river, which was hidden by a tangle of undergrowth and trees, till they came to a clearing and the horses were hobbled in the shade of some bloodwood trees. They walked along a track to the river bank where there was a landing bigger than the one Sally had discovered on her walk. There was a dinghy and two old canoes beside a traditional log canoe, all turned upside down and tied to a tree. The boys pulled out fishing gear from the dinghy.

'We're not going in that!' said Sally, pointing at the shallow hollow log canoe.

'That's Fitzi's. We tried it and kept tipping over,' said Marty.

'I wouldn't like to fall in the river,' Sally said nervously.

'No croc round 'ere. Close up bend, longa way, big 'un stay,' said Frankie.

Unconcerned, the boys tipped up the dinghy, pulled the oars from beneath the seats and dragged it into the river. 'C'mon, Miss, you get in the front. Marty, you go next,' instructed Ian as he and Tommy prepared to push the small boat out into the river. Frankie and Ginger took a canoe each, stowed their fishing gear and pushed off. The three little craft moved slowly along the river. It was hot, Sally turned down the brim of her Akubra, but around a bend Ian rowed closer to the bank where there was dappled shade, then let the dinghy drift.

The boys shocked her for a moment when they pulled out a blue Capstan cigarette packet but it was filled with silver paper from other packets and chocolates. Expertly they showed her how to wrap the silver paper over tin lures dangling above the triple hooks at the end of her line.

'I'm not used to a rod like this. I've done a bit of fly casting for trout at home,' she said.

Tommy cast his line out and slowly began to wind it back in. 'Barra go after live bait, they're not bottom feeders, so you have to make it look like a little fish swimming along,' he explained.

'It's easier when you have a motor and can just trawl slowly,' said Ian.

'I reckon the engine puts 'em off,' said Tommy.

'Oh well, it gives you something to do rather than just sit holding a line. How will I know if I get a bite?' Sally asked.

The boys laughed. 'It'll almost pull you out of the boat, then run like billyo,' said Tommy.

They drifted, casting and reeling in, chatting casually as the two boys in the canoes kept pace with them.

'I hope they don't get a big one,' said Sally. 'Those canoes look very flimsy.'

Before the boys could answer, Tommy's rod jerked and bent low to the water as the line went taut. He clicked the reel and began winding in as fast as he could. The other boys wound up their lines to help him.

He strained against the bending rod. Ian picked up a large steel hook from under a seat and crouched close to the water, ready to gaff the fish and bring it into the boat.

Marty kept his distance to give them room. Sally just sat and watched, stunned at the strength of the fish on the end of the line, oblivious to her own line.

'A strike,' yelled Marty.

The surface of the water cleaved and there was a flash of silver as the fish appeared to shake its head, trying to get rid of the hook.

'A beauty,' shouted Ian. 'C'mon, Tommy.'

All eyes were on the stretch of water in front of Tommy, waiting to see what came to the surface. At that instant Sally felt her arm almost yanked from its socket, and the instinctive reaction was to pull her rod backwards to save losing it. She began reeling in.

'Cripes, it's a big 'un,' shouted Marty to Tommy. 'Fifteen pounds, I bet.'

Ian leaned over to sink the hook into the fish as they had no net in the boat, when with a surge the fish spun, there was a ping as Tommy's rod straightened and the line went slack.

'Oh bugger. He's gone!'

'I missed him.'

'How'd he get off? He was so close,' cried Marty.

'Must've ripped his mouth off,' said Ian, sounding disappointed.

There was a grunt from Sally as she panted and wound in her line with difficulty. The boys now spun around to her. 'You got one, Sally?'

'Yeah, hooray,' cried Marty.

'Get it in the boat first, bring it round the side here,' Ian told her. 'Can you see it?'

Sally shook her head and then her heart leapt as she saw its yellow-white belly. 'Oh my gosh, what'll I do?'

'Throw it in the boat, just bring your rod here.' Ian reached for her line and together they lifted the gleaming barramundi into the boat.

Sally was shrieking in delight as Tommy and Ian grabbed the fish, releasing the lure.

'Cast back in, same spot,' said Ian and Tommy threw his line back in.

'I have no idea where it was. Maybe back there a bit opposite that leaning tree,' said Sally, determined to catch another.

Ian jammed his rod into a wedge on the side of the boat and grabbed the oars. 'I'll row back there. Keep the lines out.'

Tensing his muscles he pulled strongly on the oars, picking up a bit of speed as he hit a slight current. The two boys and Sally cast again and began slowly winding through the water as they moved.

Marty got a strike, Tommy handed his rod to Sally to hold and Ian shipped the oars to help him, but Marty brushed them away. 'No, no I want to do it.'

They let him struggle. It seemed to take forever, as it had for Sally when she was pulling in her fish. Finally a six-pound barramundi was landed.

'Only half the size of yours,' said Marty. He brightened. 'But it's your first one.'

'I hope I get many more. This is fun!'

The boys in the canoes caught some small fish including a couple of catfish.

Ian glanced up at the sun. 'We'd better get going.'

'Oh, what time is it?' Sally had been enjoying herself, and dinner time had gone out of her head.

Tommy squinted at the sun and held up his fingers. 'After five.'

The three boys and Sally went ahead, leaving Frankie and Ginger to tie up the boats and make their own way home carrying the cleaned fish. Cantering through the late sunlight, Sally was elated. The afternoon had been a real breakthrough with the boys and she hoped there'd be more times like it. As the homestead came into view, the horses broke into an impromptu race, but Sally pulled Dancer back, feeling uneasy as she slid in the saddle. The horse wanted her head, but obeyed her rider's restraining touch. Sally could tell this horse had a lot of power in her small frame.

John Monroe was several drinks ahead of Lorna and Sally as they gathered in the living room, and he roared in delight as she related the tale of their fishing expedition. Lorna sat quietly sipping her drink.

'So where are these monster fish?' he asked. 'You haven't seen barra until you get out in the Gulf. We'll do that one day, go into Karumba and get out in the Gulf. Unless we find some mate with a boat big enough to take us down the river and out to sea. Then you and the boys will know what fishing's all about.'

'And how was the horse?' asked Lorna.

Sally bubbled over with enthusiasm. 'She's magic. Just great. She's so well behaved for hardly being ridden in so long.'

'Rob does a bloody good job breaking a horse,' said John Monroe, downing his drink as Lizzie brought in the food and the boys filed to their table. Sally was disappointed dinner had been prepared as she was looking forward to eating their catch.

'You're honoured to have a horse like that,' said Lorna to Sally. 'A lot of the men, even the boys, had their eye on her.'

There was something in her voice that caught Sally's attention but she couldn't put her finger on it.

Monroe brushed it aside with a magnanimous gesture. 'Too small. She's a good little lady's horse. Too bad you don't ride, Lorna.'

There was a short sharp glance between them, John Monroe was still smiling, but there was no warmth in his expression. Lorna was saved from answering by the runners and Gloria banging into the kitchen. Similar expressions of distaste flashed across Lorna and John's faces.

'I hate them bringing that woman into the house,' said Lorna in a low voice.

'Well, there's not much we can do. Can't send her down to the blacks' camp. Mind you, she probably goes there anyway. She's not fussy.'

'John!' admonished Lorna. 'The boys.'

He turned to where the boys were discussing the fishing trip. 'So you caught a few, eh? Enough for a feed?'

'You bet, Dad. They're in the fridge. Sally caught a good size. Maybe twelve pounds.'

'Is there no end to the governess' talents?' demanded John Monroe with a proud smile at Sally. 'And Ian? Nothing huh?'

Lorna made no comment and passed the plate of vegetables.

'Marty got a decent fish too. Ian helped us land them,' said Sally. Monroe's attention was making her feel uncomfortable.

There was now so much noise coming from the kitchen, mainly Gloria's raucous laughter, that John got up from the table and walked out, and they heard him bellow, 'Keep it down, won't you? We're eating tea too. We can't hear ourselves shout.'

The boys talked quietly and John, Lorna and Sally finished their meal in silence as the voices in the kitchen soon rose again.

'Can't help themselves, can they?' said John.

'They've been drinking. She drinks more than the lot of them,' said Lorna.

Sally suggested the boys do a bit of homework after

dinner and they settled in the living room with their exercise books. John Monroe turned the wireless on to hear any local gossip and Lorna retreated to the verandah to watch the last of the day fade behind the peppercorn and palm trees.

Sally sat with the boys checking some school work and occasionally picking up one of Lorna's many *Home* magazines to flick through. The flyscreen doors banged and Gloria – with the bore runners, Dougie and Harry – left the house. Lizzie and Betsy flew inside to clean up the kitchen.

Later, when the boys had gone to sleep, Sally noticed with pleasure that her bed had been moved closer to the boys'. She was being subtly welcomed to their inner circle.

She changed into her nightie and cotton housecoat and decided to take a short walk around the garden. It was cool and refreshing as night settled but she was surprised to see Lorna still on the verandah where'd she been since dinner. Sally went and sat down beside her.

'It's lovely in the garden at night, isn't it? You should wear covered shoes though, Sally. You could tread on something nasty.'

Sally glanced down at her feet in her pastel scuffs. 'These are more for the bright lights of Surfers Paradise, I suppose.'

'Are you missing the bright lights?'

'No. I'm not, really. I like it here. Today was especially nice, with the boys.'

'They like you. I'm pleased. John is too.'

'Yes, well, I mean the horse and all. That was such a nice thing to do. It will give me more to do with the boys.'

'He tried to get me interested in riding. I'm just not comfortable. I'm a city girl.'

'Do *you* miss the bright lights?' asked Sally, suddenly.

'Indeed I do. More than I care to admit.' Lorna sighed and Sally wished she hadn't asked. 'I knew it would be lonely out here and I thought I knew what it would be like. But things don't always turn out to be quite what you expect.'

'How did you meet John?' asked Sally, hoping she wasn't venturing into sensitive territory. But Lorna seemed relieved to talk.

'Don't ever think you can run away from problems, they come with you. I was having a fling with a married man, it took me some time to realise he wasn't going to leave his wife. So I decided to go as far from Melbourne as I could and got a job at the Cloncurry hospital as a nurse. I met John up there, he was doing some droving and mustering and got banged up so he was in the hospital. I couldn't help liking him, he can turn on the charm, you know.' Sally nodded, she could believe that. 'Anyway he kept coming into Cloncurry and we saw a lot of each other. Too much.'

'Oops,' said Sally. 'You mean?'

'I was so mad at myself for getting pregnant. I decided to go back to Melbourne. I knew doctors who could help me . . .'

'You didn't tell him?'

'No. But you know what, and to this day I don't know if it was accidental, but guess who had the seat next to me in the plane? John.

'After a few days in Melbourne I told him and he insisted we get married. The full works – King's chapel, his old school. A quick honeymoon in Fiji. Then I had Ian in Cloncurry. We bought into this place with a mate of John's. We bought him out later. So here we are.'

She fell silent and Sally wondered whether to pursue the topic.

'You like music, don't you?' said Sally. There was a pile of LPs by the gramophone, which was powered by the generator, and during the day in the schoolhouse Sally could hear classical music playing loudly.

'I do. I'm afraid my taste doesn't fit in with John's. He's more a country music fan.' She gave a wry smile. 'I miss symphony concerts. I used to go all the time. And to the ballet and theatre.'

'Do you get the chance to go when you're away on holidays?'

'With the boys and John? It's the beach, big hotels, noisy restaurants.' She was silent a moment. 'I think Tommy would like to see a show or a concert. He's a bit of a performer. He loves to sing and dance.'

'Oh.' Sally filed this away. Maybe she could persuade the boys to put on a show; do a short play perhaps. 'Do you play the piano? I noticed one in the study the other day.'

'Why do you think it's tucked away? I can play, though not well. But well enough to teach the boys.'

'I haven't heard them play. Do they practise?'

'They've never had a lesson. John thinks it's sissy, no use to them. Tommy taught himself the harmonica and that's all right. Ian has no interest in anything much outside the station. Marty is too young.'

'Maybe when they go away to school their horizons will broaden,' said Sally.

'Then they'll be mixing with other boys off the land most of the time. Ian already has his own views about this place. He clashes with his father when he's allowed to speak up. John always knows best, of course. I wonder how the three boys are going to sort things out between them. John doesn't want to see this place broken up.'

'Can't the boys run it together, eventually?' asked Sally. 'Anyway, it's a long way off, surely.'

Lorna rose. 'I suppose so. I'd better go to bed. I have a feeling there's going to be a bit of partying going on in the single men's quarters tonight. I hope the noise doesn't bother you.'

'After all that riding and fishing, I'm going to sleep like a log. Goodnight, Lorna.'

'Night, Sally.'

Sally stayed on the verandah waiting for Lorna to finish in the bathroom. How sad and defeated she'd sounded. Sally wondered if Lorna would still be here if it weren't for the boys. She rarely talked about her family in Melbourne. Sally felt sorry for her and now had a deeper understanding of why Lorna was like she was – a perfectionist, house proud, coming from a more cultured background that she couldn't indulge at Barra Creek. And not sharing a bed with her husband except when he demanded. No wonder she was lonely.

Sally did sleep soundly at first, but there was no way she was going to sleep through the mayhem that was unleashed outside. She sat up and swung her legs over the side of the bed as she tried to work out what was going on. There was shouting, screaming, banging coming from a distance. The workers' party. Except it sounded violent.

Tommy, who was the only one awake, whispered to her, 'Don't go outside. Mum will sort it out.'

Sally didn't think there was any way Lorna would be involved in the fracas. 'Stay in bed. I'll just peep out from the kitchen.' She certainly wasn't going to set foot anywhere near the men's quarters. Sally passed Lorna on the verandah. She had her housecoat wrapped around her and her boots on.

'Go back to bed, Sally. Do not leave the boys and don't go out.'

'You're not going down there?'

'I've handled this before,' she said grimly.

Sally wondered where John was. He was probably either out cold in a drunken sleep, or in the middle of it.

Lorna tightened the belt of her housecoat and hurried across the darkened grass thinking, I knew that wretched woman was trouble. As she reached the men's quarters – a long basic shed, raised on stumps above the ground with single, two-, four- and six-bunk rooms, with a wash block at one end – two men stumbled out of a doorway, throwing punches, grappling and pulling at each other. They fell into the dust at the bottom step, rolling and punching wildly. Snowy appeared in the lighted doorway, swaying and shaking his fist.

'You silly bastards. Have a go then, go on.'

Lorna walked over to the men on the ground, lifted her foot and with all her might kicked it into one man's ribs and the shoulder blade of the other. 'Stop that brawling, this instant!'

'Christ, is that you, Missus?' Snowy, drunk as he was, tried to focus. He staggered and went out to drag Harry and Dougie to their feet. Lorna stepped onto the narrow verandah, nudged him aside and walked into the lighted room. Bedding hung from the bunks, bottles, tin cans and cigarette butts littered the floor. A card table and four chairs were overturned. Gloria, dishevelled and wearing a grubby ripped petticoat, was sitting on the edge of a bunk dragging on a cigarette. She didn't lift her head as Lorna marched in.

'What's going on? You causing trouble, Gloria?'

'They're drunk as skunks. Nothin' to do with me,' she mumbled.

'You're all drunk. What set those two off? I want answers or the lot of you are out of here tomorrow. I mean it.'

Although she was a slight build and still looked every

inch a lady, Lorna Monroe's tone of voice brooked no arguing.

Snowy appeared in the doorway again. 'It's her fuckin' fault. Slut.'

'You didn't mind a piece of it,' shouted Gloria suddenly.

Lorna wheeled on Snowy. 'Talk. Straight and quick.'

He began to crumble. He didn't want to face John Monroe, let alone Lorna, and he wanted to keep his job. It didn't matter so much to the others, they were drifters. 'Dougie and Harry got pissed, slagged off at Gloria. They had a blue. Anyway one thing and 'nother, she hopped in the sack with me. The buggers came in and it was on. That's it.'

Lorna stepped in front of the slatternly lump as Gloria hitched her petticoat strap back on her shoulder, hoisting the sag of her pendulous breasts. 'You're a whore. And a filthy one at that. I don't want you in my beds or under any roof of mine. Get your gear and get out. Go to the blacks' camp or throw your swag outside.'

Lorna turned on her heel and pointed at Snowy. 'Get her out of here and tell those men if they want work, see John tomorrow morning. And keep her out of sight. She is not welcome here.'

'You think you're so high and mighty,' shouted Gloria to Lorna's back. 'I could tell you a thing or two about your old man, you frigid bitch . . .'

Snowy reached her in two strides and whacked her hard across the mouth. 'Shut up, bitch.'

Lorna didn't look back, but as she walked, slowly this time, to the main house, she threw a glance towards the blacks' camp and back at the single men's quarters, where further along, a door opened and a man stepped outside buckling his belt. Lorna knew who it was.

Hearing Lorna return, Sally went into the kitchen

where she was making a cup of tea. 'Is everything all right?'

'I suppose so. That woman would sleep with anything breathing, man or beast.'

'Oh dear, a ménage à trois or something?' Sally really had no idea what had happened, this was all so far removed from the delicate indiscretions she'd heard about in New Zealand.

'They are just a bunch of drunken low-lifes. They live like animals and they act that way. Do you want a cup of tea?'

They were sitting with their tea in the living room, talking quietly, when John Monroe came in. He seemed a bit surprised to see them.

'Was there a blue down there? I've been at the yards, Fitzi said there was a problem with some of the cattle.'

'Everything is taken care of, John. You'd better talk to Snowy in the morning. I've sent that woman packing. You decide if you need those runners around the place.' Lorna was frosty and put her cup down with a clink in its saucer.

John gave a yawn. 'I hate the bastards. Waste of fucking space. Trouble is we need a few hands around the joint to do some new yards and repairs. I'll sort 'em out tomorrow.'

Sally looked at him, thinking Lorna had done a pretty good job of sorting things out herself. She was still amazed at the strength radiating from Lorna. She wouldn't like to be at the receiving end of her displeasure. It was the first time Sally had seen the steel in Lorna and suddenly she saw that while John was all bluster and noise, his wife wielded a sharp and withering power.

She was staring at John, wondering if he was drunk or sober. He gave her a half smile. 'Sorry the buggers woke you, Sally.'

Lorna gathered up the tea cups and stood up. 'Let's not lose any more sleep. Go to bed, Sally.'

Sally fled back to bed, the tension between Lorna and John was palpable.

Tommy sat up and asked quietly, 'Is everything all right?'

'It's fine, go to sleep.'

'G'night.'

'Goodnight, Tommy.'

As he settled down, he whispered, 'It was a good afternoon, wasn't it? We'll do it again, eh?'

Sally felt the tension of the past hour begin to melt.

'Yep, we certainly will.'

Chapter Seven

JOHN MONROE FINISHED BREAKFAST, virtually ignoring Sally and the boys. The kitchen was quiet, Lizzie was waiting to dish up breakfast for Dougie and Harry.

Monroe stuck his head around the door. 'No sign of 'em eh, Lizzie? Dish it up and leave it on the table.'

'Steak 'n eggs get cold, boss.'

'Too bad.' He slammed his hat on his head, picked up his .303 rifle from its rack above the assorted bush hats and headed outside. Lizzie went into the dining room and stood there shuffling her feet for a moment.

'What's up, Lizzie?' asked Sally.

'The old man got 'is rifle, goin' shoot dem bore pellas. Mebbe Snowy.'

The boys looked up. 'Nah, he won't,' said Ian.

'He just wants to scare them,' Tommy added.

'Should I get your mother?' asked Sally.

'She won't do anything,' said Ian. 'Dad's on the warpath.'

They continued eating and Sally shrugged at Lizzie.

John Monroe roared away in the truck to the single men's quarters. Holding the rifle, he stepped onto the narrow verandah, went to the middle room, flung open the door and lifted the rifle. The stale odour of booze, vomit and close living hit him in the face. He didn't look to see who was still in bed but aimed at the back corrugated-iron wall and fired through it. The shot reverberated in the quarters as if in a hollow drum.

Two bodies rose from the bunks, rubbing their eyes and shaking their ringing heads.

'What the fuck?'

'Get up and out there, you lazy sodden bastards. You've missed breakfast. I want you down at the yards, working, in ten minutes.' He turned on his heel and drove back to the homestead. It was 8 am; the day had begun.

Sally was as anxious as the boys to get up to the yards to watch the branding, so she struck a deal with them to catch up on their school work after hours. Then they headed to the noisy big home paddock where Snowy and three stockmen were working as a team, lassoing the cleanskins and big weaners, throwing them to the ground, two holding them down, castrating the males while two other men did the branding – heating the irons and searing them onto the hide of the animal, which leapt away with the stinging BC brand on its rump.

The boys were all over the place trying to get as close to the action as they were allowed, looking like smaller versions of the men in their Cuban-heeled boots and battered Akubras. Sally stayed by the fence, intrigued by the activity but wincing as the hot iron seared into each hairy hide.

John Monroe swung up beside her. 'You really interested in all this? Or just keeping an eye on the boys?' He sounded cheerful and more relaxed than earlier in the morning.

'Both. It's a bit rugged on the poor animals but I suppose it has to be done.'

'Bloody oath. This isn't such a good haul, a few decent weaners. Rob'll come in with a better mob, I reckon.'

'Who is this Rob I keep hearing about? When's he coming back?'

John gave her a hard stare. 'Now listen, Sally, you keep your distance. These blokes are bushies, not for the likes of you. Even the well-educated ones.'

'What's that mean?'

'You know what I mean. You had the makings for being a good bush wife, but it's too late now. You've been spoilt.'

'I wouldn't say that!' Sally's chin lifted. 'If you get away on a decent holiday every year – this is a good life.'

John slid down from the railing with a rueful grin. 'Glad you think so. The trouble with holidays is that sometimes someone doesn't want to come back home.' He strode away and Sally realised he was talking about Lorna.

Before their talk the previous night it had struck Sally how different John and Lorna were, how little they had in common outside the family. Imperious, immaculate Lorna. John, the ruddy, muscular, rough diamond. At least now she knew why they were together but it seemed a one-sided arrangement.

Sally only occasionally saw any overt and spontaneous displays of affection between Lorna and her family – mostly the youngest, Marty. Between Lorna and her husband, never.

When she returned to the house, leaving the boys at the yards, Sally found Lorna supervising the cleaning.

The tableau would burn in her memory for years whenever she thought of Lorna, or indeed if domestic matters came to her attention. Lorna was standing outside the bathroom, her arms folded, back straight, expression stern. Not a hair was out of place, her dress was pressed perfectly, she wore her pearl earrings and watch. In front of her Mattie, the youngest house girl, was on her hands and knees, wiping the bathroom floor tiles. Again.

'Do it again. You're missing the corners. Wash every inch. Thoroughly.' The girl swished the wet cloth.

'Wring out the water in the bucket, girl. Don't just wipe dirty water over the floor.'

Sally made herself a glass of cordial from the bottle in the fridge. Lorna came into the kitchen. 'Do you want a glass, Lorna?'

'No, thank you. Have one of the girls make a pitcher of lemonade. There are masses of lemons on the tree. It's much better for you than that sweet stuff.'

'I know. I was never allowed cordial or soft drinks at home.'

'Then you shouldn't drink them here. There's water in the pitcher on the sideboard.'

The silver water jugs were filled several times a day from the rainwater tank. Lorna followed Sally into the living room carrying a plate of biscuits, which she slipped onto a serving dish on the sideboard.

Sally took one and watched Mattie carry out the bucket from the bathroom to throw on the rose bushes.

Lorna went in and inspected the bathroom floor. Returning she remarked, 'Well it's taken her four tries.' Seeing Mattie shuffle back into the room to await her next instruction, Lorna pointed at the rubbish basket next to the table where the wireless sat.

'Empty the basket, Mattie.'

Sally choked on her drink as she saw the girl pick up

the basket filled with papers, up-end it on the floor and put the basket down.

The pitch of Lorna's voice deepened but the velocity rose. 'Put the rubbish back into the basket.' Confused for a moment, the girl then quickly stuffed the papers back in. 'Now take the rubbish basket, *with* the rubbish *inside* it, and put it with the burn rubbish. Outside. *Now*.'

The girl scurried away and Lorna shrugged at Sally.

'I hadn't realised how much effort is involved in keeping a tidy house. I never noticed it at home,' said Sally.

'I'm sure you would have noticed if things were not exactly so, though,' Lorna said with a slight smile. 'When you've been brought up a certain way it shows and you aren't comfortable with anything less.'

Sally wasn't sure if Lorna was referring to her. 'I hadn't planned on doing a lot of domestic chores when I married.'

'Nonetheless you must know how things *should* be done, isn't that so?'

Sally munched on her biscuit. 'I thought I had absorbed it all subconsciously.'

Sally had accepted how Lorna ran things, but it seemed a lot of effort when the dust descended so quickly and visitors were rare. Every morning and afternoon tea was served on the best china and the boys were expected to observe and appreciate the niceties of life.

The cement floors of the house were swept twice a day, the seagrass mats shaken and replaced, then each week everything was carried out of the house and the floors hosed down. The silver was polished once a week, and doing the laundry took two days. Lorna had two beater washing machines with a wringer on top that ran from a petrol-driven motor. Everything was rinsed in Reckitt's Blue wash then dipped in liquid boiled starch. Table linen, sheets, pillow cases, most clothes including

John's shorts, Lorna's housecoats, the boys' clothes were crisp and smooth – very little escaped starching. Sheets had to be folded in a particular way and were laid neatly in the linen cupboard.

'I'll be glad when those lubras settle down and get back to working properly. They're too busy lying on their backs now their men are home,' said Lorna in a matter-of-fact tone. 'At least the squabbles have stopped.'

When the mail plane was due, Sally suggested she go and collect the bag. She was looking forward to seeing Donny and had planned on taking a small picnic as promised. But Lorna refused. In a firm voice, she told Sally that she must keep the boys occupied.

Sally skulked to the schoolhouse, surprised at how disappointed she felt at not seeing Donny. She wanted to share some of her experiences, talk about the incident with Snowy, the runners and Gloria. She thought Donny could give her the lowdown on Gloria, who, to quote Snowy, had been 'Up and down the Cape like a bride's nightie.'

'There's the mail plane,' she said.

Marty looked up from his work. 'We haven't been to see Donny for ages.'

'He lets us sit in the pilot's seat,' said Tommy.

Sally seized the chance. 'Well, next week, let's go and see him!'

Ian shook his head. 'Mum says we can't.'

'She wants him all to herself,' said Marty.

Tommy hastily explained. 'They sit and talk, talk, talk. It's boring.'

'Maybe your mum wants to talk to someone . . . outside, catch up on the news,' said Sally, thinking that no one had long conversations with Lorna that weren't to do with Barra Creek. Maybe she should make an effort to spend more time with her, just the two of them.

'You get the news on the wireless,' said Tommy. 'Everyone gossips.'

'The problem is everyone else listens too,' laughed Sally. 'Back to work, now.'

Sally noticed a slight change in Lorna when they all sat down to afternoon tea. She seemed more relaxed and cheerful and when John asked what was in the mail, she made a small joke.

'Your pile is on the table, all the bills. Mine is all the magazines and catalogues.'

John grinned at Sally. 'She spends, I pay. You girls have it worked out pretty well.'

'You don't scrimp when you want something,' said Lorna. 'Those Elders people can sell you anything. Sally, come and let's go through the David Jones' catalogue.'

'Can we order something, Mum?' asked Marty.

'I don't think there's anything you'd like. Look in the Anthony Hordern's one.' She smiled at him. 'I hope you've saved your pocket money.'

She laughed and Sally realised she hadn't even seen any cash since she'd arrived at Barra Creek, not that she had anything to spend it on. Her monthly pay cheque was deposited into the bank account she'd set up in Sydney.

Lorna took her cup of tea and the shiny mail-order catalogue out onto the verandah. 'Let's have a look, Sally.'

They settled themselves on the two-seater lounge and Lorna opened the book on her lap. 'Now, if there's anything you want, just say so. We'll sort it out later.'

Together they spent an hour going through pages of household and kitchen luxuries, linens, clothes, shoes and cosmetics. Lorna turned over page corners, marking things they liked, then sent Sally to fetch a notepad and pencil and they made a list of sandals, tablecloths and serviettes, a vase to replace one Betsy had broken, nice soap, some blouses and new underwear. It was an enjoyable female spree that became a regular event for them, evoking remarks and anecdotes.

'My grandmother had a dinner service like that!' from Sally.

Or, from Lorna, 'Maybe I should re-cover all the cushions. I rather like this material, what do you think, Sally?'

And eventually the order would arrive, lugged in boxes from the plane by Donny, and it was like Christmas with something for everyone. Sally was never shown an account and she soon realised she was not expected to pay. It became the two women's 'day for going shopping'.

As they wrote out their order John would sometimes pass by and ask, 'Did you two get something nice for yourselves from me? Some nice perfume perhaps?'

Lorna would nod and say graciously, 'Yes, thank you, dear. I've ordered you and the boys new T-shirts and socks, too, and some books.'

Sally knew Lorna ordered beautiful, expensive lingerie, cosmetics and trinkets, many of which lay unused, wrapped in tissue in the chest of drawers in her room.

To John the mail-order catalogues were for women, kids and house stuff. He was a serious buyer of equipment, machinery, horse gear and restored vehicles. Often they were quickly thrashed beyond repair and added to the pile of rusting metal, empty oil drums, broken pipes and bits and pieces that was known as the spare-parts department. This 'snake harbour' was kept well away from Lorna's garden, because she was as particular about the grounds as she was about the inside of the homestead. Nothing unattractive was to come into her line of vision from any vantage point in the house.

Periodically she would insist that John get the men to paint or oil the garden fences. He in turn tried to persuade her to trim back the dense foliage of bougainvillea and grape vines that swarmed over the outside of the house.

'I don't want that greenery cut back,' she said firmly. 'It softens the outline of the house and keeps it cool.' Privately to Sally she confided, 'Men don't seem to notice the dust and barrenness. I like to think of the house as an oasis.'

Sally thought it was a strange and beautiful jungle, but scary. She could lie in bed and watch small green snakes slither through the vines.

For Lorna the house was her island, marooned in a sea of cleared red earth and a broad dark river bordered with almost impenetrable undergrowth harbouring danger.

The three boys had thawed to such a degree with Sally that instead of reading a story to Marty alone at bedtime, she would now lie between the three of them and tell them stories about New Zealand – a country foreign to them except for the All Blacks rugby team. She talked about her parents' farm, their horses, about hunting, about skiing, and the childhood stories she'd been told.

Some evenings after dinner, John would tell Sally about wild bush characters he'd known, of business deals and entrepreneurs gone bust, the rise and fall of cattle stations, or mad experiments like growing rice and cotton. At these times Lorna would excuse herself to sit on the verandah with her rum as John topped up his own and Sally's. She assumed Lorna had patiently and politely listened to these stories many times. Ian would sometimes hover, but generally he'd heard the stories before, as had the other boys who made one last escape to play in the garden before being summoned to get ready for bed.

'How's that horse going?' John asked Sally one evening.

'She's smart as a whip. The boys and I go riding every afternoon.'

'You should take them out to meet the stock camp later in the week. The lubras, with their bush knowledge, tell me Rob's on his way in.'

'Could we?' Sally's eyes lit up. She was surprised after his warning to stay away from the stockmen, then realised it would be more for the boys. 'That'd be terrific. How far out?'

He gave a belly laugh. 'Good on you, I figured you'd be up for it. The boys are always on to me to let them go out. But I've got too much else to do without keeping an eye on them. Clear it with Lorna first, though.'

Lorna wasn't enthusiastic at the idea, merely saying, 'Let me think about it.'

After Sally told the boys, there was no peace as they badgered her to get their mother to agree to let them ride out for half a day to meet Rob's plant of horses. Finally Marty was coerced into buttering up Lorna as 'he was her favourite'.

'That's not true,' admonished Sally in fairness to Lorna. 'Mothers don't have favourites. They sometimes feel a bit more protective towards their littlest one, that's all.' But Sally had also decided that Lorna held a very tender spot in her heart for her last born.

Finally Lorna agreed, laying down firm rules that Sally and the boys listened to, nodding their heads like a row of soldiers being given orders by their general. 'And I hold you all personally responsible for the safety of each other.'

John looked at the boys. 'So no playing silly buggers, all right?'

'That means everyone,' said Lorna evenly, and Sally went to laugh but saw that John was looking slightly abashed.

'They'll be fine with Rob and Fitzi along. It'll be an experience for the governess here.'

Lorna looked at Sally. 'You are there to look after the boys. I'm only agreeing because I know how much it means to them.'

'I'll stick to them like glue. We're the four musketeers these days,' promised Sally.

Two days later Fitzi appeared at the back door and spoke to John Monroe. 'Reckon he's gettin' close, boss. Mebbe tomorra night. Good mob, too.'

They packed all the gear they needed, including their swags as they planned to camp out. The boys were in a lather of excitement, as was Sally, although she tried to look restrained and sensible about the exercise. School work was abandoned for the day and they set out after a big breakfast. Many of the women from the camp had set off the night before on foot. Fitzi was on a solid stock-horse, Sally on Dancer and the boys on their own horses. Marty rode beside Sally on his pony and, remembering Lorna's quiet aside to her to 'keep an eye on Marty, he's so young', she glanced back at the homestead and saw the upright figure of Lorna standing by the garden fence gate watching them ride away.

'Doesn't your mum ride at all?' she asked Marty.

'I dunno. Don't think so.'

Tommy had wheeled around and heard them. 'She does so. She came to the river with us a couple of times.'

'The horses walked!' scoffed Marty. 'That's not riding.'

Sally decided not to ask why their father wasn't joining them, she was glad of the respite from his over-powering personality. Frankie, Ginger, Alice and a string of kids from the camp ran ahead, then followed them for a short distance before calling out and waving goodbye.

They rode east for two hours then stopped at a bore.

Two of the women who had left the night before were sitting on the ground at its edge.

They had a quick word with Fitzi who had made a billy of tea, then the riders set off again. Fitzi rode in front, anxious to reach the camp. He knew where they were going although there were no features, landmarks or tracks to follow other than the thin paths made by the cattle that led from the bore. Sally remembered the stampede of frightened cattle that Snowy and his men had whipped towards the stockyards and she was nervous of what lay ahead.

Fitzi stared into the distance then spoke to Ian. 'I tink dem cattle be heading for Meeka Well. We camp dere night, I reckon. Rob never hurry 'em up.'

'That'd be right.' Ian glanced back at Sally and his brothers. 'Looks like we'll be camping out tonight.'

The other boys let out whoops of delight.

'Let's hope the plant is set up before we get there,' said Ian.

Fitzi nodded. 'I reckon. Rob send dem stock camp boys ahead.'

The reality of what they were doing began to sink in for Sally and she started to feel even more nervous. 'Will the cattle be there too, where we're camping?'

'That's the whole idea. Rob won't push them the last leg to the home paddock. He pokes them along nice and quiet. Well, as quiet as a big mob can be,' Ian said.

'And why is he going slowly? Is he paid by the day?'

'Nah, he's on contract. He says if the cattle run they get upset and lose weight,' explained Ian.

'Is Meeka Well on Barra Creek?' she asked.

'Yeah. It's a bore that was put down on a spot where the old drovers camped. There's an underground spring the blacks showed them. It's about four hours' ride.'

It was a hard and long ride, and Sally was feeling

hot, tired and very uncomfortable trying to stay balanced as they followed Fitzi across the trackless country. The landscape changed now they were so far from the river. The ant hills and scrubby coolibah trees were interspersed with expanses of hot, flat country and a distant ridge or low line of hills floated above the horizon line in a haze. She kept peering ahead looking for a telltale cloud of rising dust. Everyone seemed to be expecting Rob to bring in more cattle than Snowy.

'There's Meeka,' shouted Ian, pointing in the distance. Sally squinted and for a moment couldn't see anything. Then she saw a thin wisp of smoke and a small black dot that gradually grew into a couple of horses and the stick figures of two men. They had set up camp by an old pipe projecting from the ground beside a boggy patch of ground.

It was four o'clock when they trotted into the camp, and the sight of a camp oven hanging from an iron tripod over a low-burning fire was most welcome. Two lean black stockmen met them, helping the boys from their horses and casting curious sideways glances at Sally. They had come ahead of the mustered mob due in at sunset so they could get settled before dark, one of the men explained. An older white man bent down and fussed with the fire. Sally looked around, wondering where she could find some privacy and Tommy was quick to realise her discomfort.

'Over there. Couple of sticks in the ground with a bit of canvas wrapped around them. Take the small hand-shovel with you.'

Sally nodded gratefully and pulled the roll of toilet paper from her pack. 'I'd better take the home comforts.'

'It's not so bad,' he said. 'There's water at the bore. It's warm too.'

'Good. But I don't plan on taking a bath out here,' she said. The temperature would drop at night and the hot water would be a luxury, but she was very aware of being the only woman in the group.

'There they are!' called Tommy as Sally walked back to the camp, and immediately the boys were back on their horses. Tired as she was, Sally remounted to follow them.

A long brown cloud of dust spread across the featureless horizon. Sally began to recall scenes from dreadful old Westerns where the cavalry faced the thousands of mounted Indians streaming over the hills.

But as the gap closed between them she saw that this was no galloping frenzy of terrified beasts being shunted by men cracking whips and shouting. Instead the animals were walking at a leisurely pace, kept in control by men on horseback and well-trained dogs. There must have been a thousand or more head of cattle and even the boys hung back as the river of animals was herded towards them.

'How are they going to keep them here, there aren't any yards?' she called.

'Horses, dogs, watch patrol,' replied Ian. 'Rob does this all the time.' And sure enough the men began herding the animals into a close circle and slowed them down as they headed towards the bore.

'Boys, keep back, stay back here,' warned Sally, worried that if these plodding animals suddenly started to panic they'd run right over them. 'Let's move on the outside and get behind them.'

But the boys were keen to get close to the action and their horses danced and weaved, and finally broke to run forward to the outer western flank of the mob. Sally went to follow but Dancer was being difficult, sidestepping rather than obeying the forward command, snorting and flattening her ears. Sally got mad and kicked her and she reacted in anger that almost threw Sally from her back.

Even though the cattle were walking slowly, their grunting and lowing and their steady surge of movement was unnerving.

The boys had gone ahead and she could see Marty with Fitzi. Ian had gone to the head and Tommy was near a stockman. Somewhere, guiding all this organised chaos must be Rob.

Some of the stockmen moved up and down the edges of the mob, their horses turning and swerving, keeping the animals together, chasing the occasional beast who decided to make a break for it. But on the whole the group streamed slowly forward as though they'd been strictly drilled. The leaders lifted their heads, smelling the water at the bore.

Dancer was still flighty and anxious. She hadn't been around a big mob of cattle before, and decided the best course of action was to take off. Before Sally knew it, she'd reared slightly, then split in the opposite direction, cutting across the path of the cattle. For one moment she saw the lead beasts look up and wonder about taking flight before shouts and a crack of a stockwhip reminded them of what they were supposed to be doing, and they ignored the sudden bolt of the little filly with the slim figure on her back, sliding in the bulky saddle.

After what seemed an eternity, Sally finally pulled her horse up and then tried to turn her in the direction of the camp. Dancer saw that was where the cattle were also headed and refused to move, baulking at Sally's heels digging into her ribs.

'Hold up. Leave her,' called a voice. Sally looked behind her to see a man on a grey horse cantering towards her.

'Your horse been around cattle before, has it?'

'No. I don't think so. She's been with brumbies.'

'What's wrong with your saddle?' He was now riding beside her and Dancer seemed to relax in the company of another horse.

'It's me, I'm afraid. I'm not used to an Australian stock saddle.'

The man grinned. 'I can see that.'

Sally looked at him and was shocked at the dishevelled ruffian who had appeared from nowhere. He was filthy and unshaven, obviously one of Rob's stockmen. His clothes were dust covered and around his throat was a grubby, bloodstained bandage, which crossed under his shirt and over his chest and shoulder.

'Pull up and dismount.' He reined in his horse, swung out of the saddle and reached for Dancer's bridle as Sally hesitated then did as he asked.

'What are you doing?' she said as he began adjusting Dancer's buckle on her girth.

'Take my horse, try my saddle, you can't go past a western saddle. It might suit you better. It can be dangerous when your horse hasn't been around a mob. I don't want to have to scrape you off the ground.' He spoke well, with gentle authority. He was in his early thirties but acted like someone much older; someone who knew what he was doing. Sally was about to protest, but glancing at the horse and its saddle she could see this was no rough stockhorse and the western saddle would be easier.

The man held Dancer and watched Sally swing onto his horse. He swiftly shortened the stirrups for her. 'How's that feel?'

'Fantastic. It's like sitting in an armchair.'

He gave her a quick look. 'You can take him as close as you want to the mob, either on the flank, follow along behind or circle around and bring up the tail, just in case we have a lagging stray. Just move slowly. Okay?'

139

'Will do,' said Sally, feeling so much more confident on this man's horse. He might look like something the cat dragged in but he had a fine horse and a great saddle.

'See you at supper.' He settled onto Dancer then turned towards the lead cattle.

'Right.' Sally lifted her hand. 'I'm Sally Mitchell, by the way.'

'Are you visiting?'

'No, I'm the governess.'

'Ah. I'm Rob Donaldson.'

'I've heard about you.' Sally grinned.

'All good, I hope. I'm at a disadvantage, I haven't heard about you. Maybe later.' His attention was back with the cattle and he cantered off without a backward glance. Sally was irritated to see Dancer had no qualms about heading close to the cattle she'd been so nervous about when she was riding her.

She caught up to the boys and was fascinated to watch the cattle settle as they made camp. Two stockmen on horseback and a couple of dogs quietly circled the stationary mob as the other stockmen looked after the horses, threw down their swags and sat around the fire. Nearby, three black women and an adolescent girl sat around their own small campfire. The stockmen took no notice of them.

The white man at the fire turned out to be the cook, a short, lean man who looked like a strip of tanned leather. Sally watched him expertly handle the camp oven over the fire and dig out the coals surrounding the damper. When he slid the iron lid off, the bread smelt delicious.

'That looks as light as a sponge cake,' she complimented him.

'Be orright. Been doin' it long enough,' he grunted.

'Just cooking?' She noticed he walked with a limp

and wondered if he'd taken up the job of camp cook after an accident.

'Done a bit of everything. Horse breaking, bull dogging, buffalo hunting, even had me own camels.' He tossed a handful of tea leaves into the boiling billy. 'Got thrown and trod on, buggered me hip and leg. So I started cooking. One way to stay out in the scrub.'

'You don't like towns?'

'Nah. Not fer me. Me missus is half Abo, we stick to our camp.'

Fitzi materialised with the boys carrying their swags. 'We set 'im swags down dis way, Missy?'

'Right, Fitzi, whatever you think is best.'

'We want to be near the fire. It gets cold,' said Tommy.

The boys dropped their swags in a semicircle around Sally's and sat on them, reaching their hands out towards the glowing coals.

'What's for tea, Wally?' asked Marty.

'What yer given,' said the old cook.

When the simmering stew was dished up in tin plates with chunks of the crusty warm damper, Sally declared it one of the best meals she'd seen.

'That's because it's served under the stars round a campfire,' said Rob. 'Hard to beat that.'

He sat away from Sally and the boys, and Fitzi sat behind them. Wally crouched by the fire ready to hand around seconds, and across the other side of the fire sat the stockmen, their dark, creased faces gilded in the firelight. There seemed to be a hierarchy around the fire in who sat where and in what order they were served. Wally deferred a bit to Rob and it became obvious that they had been working together for some years.

After eating, the men lit up cigarettes and a second billy of tea was passed around. It was the time for yarning and the boys pestered Rob to tell them one of his stories.

He gazed at the glittering sky and thought for a moment. Then he grinned at them. 'Did I tell you about the wildest rodeo bull no man could ever ride?'

'Wow, how wild was it?'

'What happened?'

'Ah, now that's a very strange story,' said Rob, leaning back and everyone moved around to get comfortable and listen to one of Rob's tall tales.

At its conclusion a great debate was sparked when Wally declared, 'That's nothing! I once saw a bull try and climb up the rails. He was one smart bugger.'

The stockmen chuckled and then Rob got to his feet. 'I'll do the first nightwatch.' He nodded at Sally and winked at the boys. 'Night, one and all.'

Fitzi began to help Marty settle his swag and Tommy cleared away sticks and stones, scooped a bit of a hollow and unrolled his swag. He glanced up at Sally. 'Do you want me to walk over to the toilet with you?'

'Yes, that would be good. I have a torch.'

They glanced back at the camp where dark figures were silhouetted against the fire that had been boosted with fresh wood.

'Let's turn the torch off for a minute,' said Tommy.

Their eyes soon adjusted to the darkness, and Tommy tilted his head back. 'Look at the stars – trillions and trillions.'

'That's the Milky Way.'

'And there's the saucepan.'

'Do you know the constellations? Maybe we could study them at school.'

'Rob showed us all of them one night. I can't remember them but, I mean, though,' he corrected himself.

It was obvious the boys liked Rob, and Sally could

understand why they warmed to a man who could handle cattle and horses and knew his way around rodeos and the outback.

The boys settled down for the night and fell asleep immediately, but Sally tried to stay awake to savour the sense of freedom and adventure that was almost overwhelming. Two horses were saddled and hobbled nearby to stop them straying, but ready to be ridden if the cattle broke and rushed during the night. And she heard the gentle singing and humming of Rob and one of the stockmen on the first watch. Rob sang almost to himself but his song told the animals and the sleeping group in the perimeter of the fire that all was calm and safe.

Chapter Eight

WHEN SALLY WOKE UP, the sun was rising. The air was crisp and she'd slept like a log. She rolled over, stretched, then sat up. Wally was sitting by the fire smoking, the stockmen had gone, their campfire extinguished.

'Gosh, how did I sleep through? Where is everyone?'

'Gone to move the cattle, start the day, love. You slept well. Want a cuppa?'

'Yes, please. I'm surprised I didn't hear anything. Where are the boys?'

'With Rob, checking on the mob. I slept in too.'

Sally got out of her swag. 'It's barely sunrise. I can't believe I slept on the ground without waking up. It must be the fresh air.'

Wally grinned. 'That'd be it. I always reckon a mob of happy cattle is a great lullaby. Now, how's toasted damper and cocky's joy sound?'

'Good. I'm getting a taste for golden syrup.'

Sally returned from the primitive toilet facility and took the tin of warm water Wally had ready and splashed her face. She watched him spoon the thick syrup from the green and gold tin and slather it over the toasted damper.

'So we head back to the homestead this morning?' she asked.

'Yep. I'll go ahead with the packhorses – you and the boys can come along with me. Rob moves the plant nice and slow. Won't get there till dusk, probably.'

'Oh, I think the boys will want to stay with Rob and the cattle. Me too.'

Wally's face creased with a smile. 'You seem pretty at home out here.' He poured the tea into a mug and handed it to her. 'There's more damper if you want it and cold beef. The blokes will be back for some grub soon enough and then we'll be on the move.'

She took the hint. 'I'll be ready.' She rolled the canvas swag and blanket into a tight bundle, fastening the leather straps around it.

As the sun began to light the tops of the trees, Rob, several of the stockmen and the boys rode back to the camp.

Breakfast was eaten hastily and Rob threw the last of his mug of tea into the fire and nodded at Sally. 'You coming with us or going with Wally?'

The boys were gulping down their breakfast and cast her an anxious look.

'I'll stay with the boys.'

'We're okay with Rob,' said Ian quickly.

'He's got a lot of cattle and men to watch. I'd better keep an eye on you three,' said Sally. She knew the boys wanted to stay where the action was. Travelling with the cook wouldn't be very exciting, and she had to admit she also liked being in the thick of it. Though she was still a bit nervous about Dancer, and the spread of huge beasts overwhelmed her. Wally had told her some horror stories of cattle getting spooked and rushing, running straight over a camp, flattening everything, including sleeping men. But if Rob took them slowly, and with the stock-men and dogs around, it seemed unlikely they'd break or rush.

Rob jammed his hat on his unruly sun-bleached hair. 'Just keep out of the way and follow my instructions, especially when we get close to the home paddock and they smell water and other animals. They can get a bit excited. Under no circumstance do you and the boys yell at the cattle.'

'Right,' said Sally, giving the boys a pointed look. She certainly didn't want to ruffle Rob, whom she thought looked a bit thuggish with his stubbly growth of a beard, matted hair and the filthy bloodstained bandage wrapped around his neck. He was very businesslike and didn't seem the type who'd have much patience with kids and their governess tagging along.

When Sally and the boys got to their horses, she was surprised to find Dancer was already saddled with Rob's comfortable western saddle.

'Who did this?'

'Rob. He's got your saddle,' said Tommy.

'He rides in rodeos,' added Ian.

'Oh.' Sally was a bit embarrassed but grateful. 'That was nice of him. My riding must have made a bad impression, huh?'

The boys giggled and Marty spoke up for her. 'Your horse isn't used to a lot of cattle.'

'Nor me,' laughed Sally.

Later, as they walked behind the plodding cattle with the ringers, she felt her nervousness subside. The whole manoeuvre was a revelation to her and she had to admire Rob's quiet firm control over the men and the cattle. The stockmen were wonderful to watch, able to make their horses respond in an instant to their commands, smoothly changing direction when they had to nudge a stray beast back into line. Under Rob's instruction they avoided using whips and never raised their voices, allowing the horses to work the cattle. The men's respect for Rob was obvious and they behaved very differently from the stockmen Snowy had working for him. Wally had told Sally that Rob handpicked his men.

Rob seemed to be everywhere, materialising from the cloud of ochre dust as he skirted the perimeter of the slowly moving beasts. He caught up with them mid morning and rode between Sally and Marty.

'We'll stop for a break at the next water. Then it's the last long haul home. We've made good progress.'

'What happens when we get to Barra Creek?' asked Sally.

'We spell them in the big home paddock and the next day start branding and culling in the smaller paddock. They'll be sent off in small mobs for sale. John will probably keep some a bit longer. Depends on prices, demand, availability of transport, that sort of thing.'

'And what do you do after this?'

'Same again. I'll hang around for a bit then go out when I get a lead on more cleanskins. I might go after a pack of brumbies I heard about.'

'Can we go fishing down at the river, Rob?' asked Tommy.

'You bet. Well, if it's okay with your governess here.' He flashed Sally a smile and she wasn't sure if he was being polite or facetious.

'Only if I can come along too,' she countered lightly.

'Course you can. I hope you can paddle a canoe and bait your own hook.'

The boys laughed and Sally ignored the remark as Rob swung his horse and headed up the outside flank. She wished the boys had told him that she'd already caught a barramundi. He probably thought her a real outback novice.

When they got to the bore, they found Wally had left two young boys to tend the campfire and the lunch of damper and cold pickled meat and billies of strong black tea. Four packhorses were hobbled nearby. Wally had continued ahead with his plant.

Sally was glad to stretch her legs and the sweet strong tea was welcome. The Monroe boys squatted round the fire as the stockmen filed in to get their food and retreated to sit in small groups. Rob and a few others stayed with the cattle.

She smiled at her three young charges sitting back on their high Cuban-heeled boots, sipping black tea, and it flashed into her mind, what was their future? Would they be here, as adults, doing the same as the other men in years to come? She thought of Lorna with her music and books and love of city life and John, a determined man of the land but one who rarely sat on a horse or got his hands dirty. Whose influence would be stronger? Station life gave them a lot, but she could understand Lorna's frustration at not being able to enrich her son's minds and tastes.

She studied each of the boys in turn: Ian – gangly, serious, defensive, already butting heads with his father's decisions; Tommy – happy-go-lucky, curious, interested in the world away from the station. And Marty, sensitive and shy, still a little kid. She wondered why, after such a short time, she cared so much about these boys. It was a job, twelve months if she stuck it out. At this moment she felt quite confident she'd last the distance. She couldn't imagine spending all day in an office now. The drab little stock and station agency she'd worked in back home would be so boring and claustrophobic after being out here.

The shadows lengthened and Sally was sorry the trip was coming to an end. From the talk around the campfire the night before she had learned a little about the appeal of droving. These men could not stand to be hemmed in by crowds and cities. Wally explained that the attraction for the whitefellas was the sense of freedom, being under the canopy of sky with no walls or fences. The black stockmen were treated as equals on the track, respected for their horsemanship and bush skills. They shared the same conditions, the same tucker. They would stay with Rob for most of the year, only going home to their camps and towns when the Wet came and it was too difficult to muster the wild cattle. That was when Rob worked at Barra Creek or returned to his family station in the Territory.

There was an hour or so of daylight left when they arrived at Barra Creek. The great swarm of cattle filled the home paddock. John Monroe roared up in his Land Rover, pausing to stick his head out the window. 'How'd you find it? Saddle sore, I suppose.'

'Not really.' Sally patted Rob's saddle. 'It was fabulous.'

'Rob got over a thousand head, Dad,' called Ian.

'You bloody beauty. That's more like it. See you at dinner. Your mother wants to see you.' He gunned the car and took off. The boys kicked their horses and raced each other to the homestead.

Lorna was all smiles as they rushed onto the verandah to greet her once they'd stabled their horses. 'I've missed you all. I hope it was worth it. You all look like gypsies.' She hugged them and then touched Sally's hair. 'Your hair is like straw, Sal. You should look after yourself out here. Your skin too. Don't let yourself go,' she admonished.

In the bathroom Sally looked at herself and had to

admit Lorna was right. She was sunburned, her auburn hair looked like burned chaff, fingernails were broken, her heels were cracked and her legs hadn't seen a razor in weeks. Sighing, she promised herself she'd make a bit of an effort.

Once the boys were scrubbed clean and dressed for dinner, Sally had them sit quietly on their beds and do some reading so they could catch up with their school work. She wrote a long letter to Sean describing everything. She thought the droving and horsemanship would appeal to him.

John Monroe was pouring the drinks in the living room when Sally and the boys walked in.

'Well timed. Here you are, Sally.' He handed her a glass.

'Are you pleased with all the cattle Rob brought in?' she asked.

'He'd better be!' came a cheerful voice and Rob strode into the room.

Lorna came in from the kitchen, and everyone seemed to be talking at once as the boys jostled to sit on the lounge next to Rob. Sally was glad of the distraction for she was stunned at the change in him. Rob had showered and was dressed in freshly pressed pants and a new blue shirt she recognised as one from the storeroom. He had a neat dressing on his neck and his hair had been cut. He caught her look of surprise and grinned at her. 'Lorna cleaned me up a bit.'

'Scrubs up quite well, don't you think?' said Lorna, with warmth in her voice.

'You run into a pair of bull horns?' commented John, glancing at the dressing on Rob's neck as he handed him a drink.

'Something like that.' He turned and gave the boys a pat on the shoulder. 'What do you blokes reckon about it, then?'

'It was great.'

'Wally told us stories and Rob played the mouth organ round the fire,' said Marty.

'They're in good nick, aren't they, Dad?' said Ian.

Listening to them, Sally realised that the boys were anxious that their father approve and praise the contract musterer. She was surprised at Lorna's obvious fondness for him too; she couldn't imagine her cutting the hair of any of the other workers. Sally now saw what an attractive man he was beneath the weeks of dust, sweat and lack of water. She'd noticed Rob's well-spoken manner in contrast to Wally and the stockmen, and he seemed perfectly at home in the Monroes' living room. Lorna had gone to some trouble with a flower arrangement and setting the table, and it appeared everyone was vying for Rob's attention.

When they were seated and Lizzie carried in the silver serving dishes, Rob finally turned to Sally. 'How did you enjoy our little adventure?'

'A lot better after you loaned me your saddle. Thanks very much for that,' she said.

'She hasn't got the hang of an Aussie saddle yet,' chuffed John Monroe. 'She's one of those poncy tally-ho types. Rides to the hounds and so on.'

'John, don't make fun,' chided Lorna. 'They take hunting very seriously in New Zealand.'

'Ah, ha. I see. That's why you ride well then,' said Rob and Sally tried not to look as flattered as she felt.

'She's got a damn fine little horse, that helps,' said John Monroe. 'How'd Dancer do with the cattle? She's not used to being around a big mob even though you broke her in well.'

'She was a bit skittish at first, but settled down. Or I

151

did,' Sally answered and Rob gave her a quick smile.

John sawed through his giant steak. 'You should take some of the colts out next time, Rob, get them used to being ridden and working.'

'I'd rather not, unless I break them in. Flighty, hard-mouthed animals waste time and money.'

The men talked horses, beef prices and cattle sales, until Rob glanced at Lorna and Sally and attempted to swing the conversation back to them.

'Any news from down south while I've been away? What's happening in the world?'

Before Lorna could answer John cut in. 'Those bloody bra burners are marching in the streets, would you believe? What a bunch of no hopers, they all need a man to keep 'em in line. Demanding this and demanding that. Women aren't equal, never will be.'

'Next thing you know women will be chaining themselves to the gates of Parliament House,' said Lorna quietly.

'What do you think of these new bra burners?' Rob asked Sally.

'I don't know much about them, the women's movement hasn't registered in New Zealand yet. But perhaps if I was in Sydney I'd be marching.' She grinned. 'But then, I've always been regarded as a bit of a rebel.'

'Better not try it on here,' grumbled John. 'Just as well we don't have daughters, eh?'

He shot a glance at Lorna who raised an eyebrow and said calmly, 'What's the difference? I think part of this new attitude is trying to get our sons to appreciate a woman's point of view. I hope my sons will be better husbands because of this feminine revolution.'

'Oh? Better than what?' John Monroe's voice rose with a three-rum edge. 'There's no place for wimps on Barra Creek.'

'Oh, we know that,' said Lorna smoothly. 'Rob, are you ready for dessert?'

The boys had kept their heads down during this last exchange. Tommy saw an opening to pour a little oil on the troubled water.

'What's for dessert, Mum?'

'Watermelon and mint salad, or tinned peaches and custard.'

'A choice? Rob must be back in camp,' said John, leaning back in his chair.

Rob let the barb slide by. He looked over at the boys. 'Got a story planned for tonight?'

'Sally reads to us,' said Tommy. 'Or tells us stories.'

'Terrific. That's good news. I used to tell these fellows a bit of a yarn each night.'

'Well, go ahead, I wouldn't mind a night off and they seem keen as mustard,' said Sally. She was starting to see the subtle dynamics of the family group where Rob was a pawn sought by each of them.

Lorna rose. 'Would you gentlemen excuse us, please? Sally, bring your drink.' Before either man could say anything she blew a kiss to her sons. 'Goodnight, boys. Back to school in the morning.'

Sally followed Lorna out onto the verandah, breathing in the scent of the night flowers and enjoying the cool air. Sometimes they lit a candle or small kerosene lamp, but tonight Lorna chose to sit in the darkness. She struck a match that flared, illuminating her face in an unflattering light. She only smoked on occasions and Sally had never figured out what mood justified a cigarette.

'So, the expedition was worth it? I know the boys enjoyed it. And you did too?'

'I did. The landscape, the whole exercise, the open air, the thrill of it all . . .' She broke off, wondering if Lorna could really appreciate this. She didn't ride and never seemed to venture from the homestead. 'The boys loved it,' she finished lamely.

'Yes. I know. That worries me.'

Sally watched her drag on the cigarette. 'Why? It's boys' own adventure stuff. How many kids wouldn't want to be part of what the boys experienced the last couple of days?'

'It's not a life, Sally. It's not how I see their future.'

'You mean, even if they come back to run this place?'

Lorna sighed. 'It's difficult. Traditionally properties are shared between sons, but if some aren't cut out for it, or are no good at running a station . . . I can't stand them being sent in a direction they might not want to go.'

'So what do you want for your sons, Lorna? Maybe when they go to school they'll make other decisions.'

'Not on your life. By then it will be too late. They're handed over to boarding school masters who are just like their fathers and grandfathers, to make men of them. Then they are sent back to the land. John wanted to send them to school last term. Finding you has given them, well me, a reprieve.'

'They seem so young. I hated boarding school, even though I went home at weekends.'

'Tommy will start at Tudor House at King's then go into the big school. Ian is ready for school, then he'll come back. But he'll want to do things his way. He and his father clash already. I want the boys at least to have the chance to explore other options.' Her face crumpled slightly and in the shadowy light Sally saw a fearful mother.

'Have you talked about this with John?' she asked, knowing full well he was not a man open to discussions.

'As much as one can with John. We talked while you were away. It got a little tense. In fact I'm taking a break and going down to Sydney. I have every confidence in you caring for the boys while I'm away.'

'Of course. Sounds like a good idea.' Sally couldn't help wondering about being left with John Monroe and was glad Rob would be around for a while. It would give her an opportunity to see Donny too. Lorna had been meeting the mail plane for weeks.

'I'll tell the boys in the morning. I'll go with Donny into Cloncurry on Wednesday and I'm booked on a TAA flight down to Sydney. I'll pop into David Jones so think of anything you want.'

'Thanks. What I need is a trip to a beauty salon,' laughed Sally. 'You did a good job on Rob, maybe you can give me a trim.'

'When I come back I'll see if my friend Toby wants to come up for a holiday. He's a hairdresser in Sydney and loves it up here. He comes for a week or more and does my hair while he's here, so he can style yours at the same time. John can't stand him, calls him Fruity. But he's great fun, always up with the latest theatre and film news.'

'He sounds terrific.' Sally couldn't imagine such a person fitting in to Barra Creek so she wouldn't hold her breath. Lorna would undoubtedly be through the Elizabeth Arden Red Door at Farmers the minute she hit Sydney.

She heard the low murmur of Rob's voice as she went to prepare for bed and when she came back from the bathroom she found him sitting on the edge of Marty's bed.

'Right, that's it, chaps. The boss is here. It's been a big few days. Sleep tight,' he said softly.

Sally stood awkwardly by her bed waiting to grab her nightgown. 'Thanks again for the saddle. I'm hoping mine will arrive soon. My mother is sending a care package.'

'No trouble. Borrow it any time. Once you get the hang of the stock saddle it's okay. You did well, Sally.' He added, 'Sorry I couldn't spend any time with you and the boys on the muster. But one of the men was keeping an eye on you all the time.'

'Oh. Thanks.' Sally hadn't been aware of that and was touched by his obvious concern for the boys. And her, it seemed.

'Well, I'm ready to hit the sack. I'm not getting into a drinking session with big John tonight.'

'Where are you staying?'

'I have a room in the single men's quarters but for the next couple of nights I'll doss down with my boys at their camp. Keep the lubras at bay for as long as I can. They're probably fed up with Snowy's boys and looking for fresh blood. My fellows are good blokes but temptation can win out. See you round, eh.'

He left and by the time she'd changed and slipped into her bed, the boys were sleeping soundly.

The boys shot out after breakfast to see Rob start to cull the cleanskins, calves and bulls. They'd promised to be in school by 9 am. Lorna wasn't up, so Sally decided to go for a ride. She took Dancer in the opposite direction to the calls from the cattle yards and headed towards the river. She trotted beneath the paperbark trees, keeping away from the thick undergrowth that fringed the river bank. She still had a dread of crocodiles. The morning air was fresh and she was glad of the solitude. She was always surrounded by people, and she decided she needed this time to herself. She'd been thinking about home, her family, Sean, and realised she was a little homesick. She turned away from the river into a stretch of long grass and broke into a canter. As the grass thickened she reined Dancer in and

156

at that instant something rose from the clumps of Mitchell grass, startling the horse who pranced sideways.

Some creature leapt at them, half man, half beast.

Then Sally realised it was a tall emaciated black man daubed in mud and some kind of grease. He was dressed only in a loin cloth. A putrid smell hit her as he gave her a leering grin showing a few yellow teeth. His hair, plaited in a long braid almost to his feet, was also smothered in dried clay or mud. He looked evil and, feeling frightened, Sally kicked Dancer and bolted for the homestead. Her heart was pounding and she rushed into the house and found the boys in the kitchen with Lizzie.

'What's the matter?' asked Tommy.

She started to describe the weird man she saw, but before she'd finished they had all started laughing.

'Mr Stinky!' they cried.

'Who? What is he?'

Even Lizzie was chuckling. She rolled her eyes. 'He old pella teach 'em up girlies.'

'Ask Mum,' mumbled Ian. 'We're going to the schoolhouse.'

'What are they talking about, Lizzie?'

The woman thrust her hips back and forth suggestively and laughed some more as Sally looked embarrassed and hurried from the room.

At the morning break Lorna took her aside and explained about Mr Stinky.

'I know how you felt. He still makes my skin crawl. He knows he's not welcome here, but he often turns up at the camp.' She paused then went on. 'I don't approve, but it's their way and John says we mustn't interfere.'

'So what does he do?'

'The young girls approaching puberty are sent to him to learn the sexual arts,' said Lorna primly. 'And the boys are sometimes sent off with the old women.'

Sally couldn't get past the idea of young girls being sent to have sex with the strange old man. 'That's shocking. He seems such a creep. Yuk!'

Lorna shrugged. 'There's never been any trouble. The girls come back and are married off. They all seem quite happy with the arrangement. He obviously doesn't . . . hurt them.'

Sally shook her head. 'It's immoral, shouldn't be allowed.'

'By whose law? They live by their laws. We've learned that if we try to make them live totally by our ways, things fall apart and there are more fights. We try to find the balance between our world and theirs with as little disruption as possible.' She sighed. 'But there's always some damn drama happening.'

This was the nearest Sally had heard Lorna come to swearing. 'Well, I hope I don't run into him again.'

Lorna rose, sounding tired. 'He's harmless, I suppose. He's not allowed near the camp, they walk out to meet him. They must have some arrangement.'

Sally went back to the schoolhouse wondering how much the boys knew about the details and why John tolerated Mr Stinky. Anyone Monroe regarded as a troublemaker was given short shrift at Barra Creek.

Lorna left the station with a minimum of fuss. She hugged the boys, who stayed behind to finish a project in the schoolhouse while Sally drove her out to the mail plane. She hadn't been privy to Lorna's farewell to her husband, who was down at the cattle yards. But they slowed as they passed the crowded stockyards and John, sitting on top of a railing, gave them a wave and turned back to the action.

Donny brought the little plane to a halt, jumped

down and opened the rear door, pulling out the mail bag, then sauntered over to them.

'All ready, Lorna?'

'Absolutely.' She looked happy, the tension Sally had observed in her all morning was slipping away.

'G'day, Sally, long time no see. Got all your instructions?'

'I hope so. Everything will be fine, Lorna. Don't worry.'

'I'm not going to. I'm glad you're here, Sally.' She reached over and kissed her cheek. 'Look after my boys.'

'All four of 'em, eh?' grinned Donny, taking Lorna's bag. 'See you next week, Sal.'

'See you, Donny.'

'Have a good trip, Lorna. Enjoy David Jones!'

She watched Donny settle Lorna into her seat as if she were a piece of fragile china.

The plane was out of sight before she got back to the homestead where Monroe was sitting on the verandah, rolling a cigarette.

'Let me know if the kids give you any strife, Sally.'

'They'll be good, John. I'd better see if they've finished their sheets.' Sally walked to the schoolhouse feeling the weight of responsibility settle on her shoulders.

Chapter Nine

DESPITE HER RARE APPEARANCES outside the home-stead gardens, Lorna's absence was subtly felt about Barra Creek. Within days there was a general slackness among the women, and John bawled at the men louder, more aggressively and more often. He was also drinking heavily. In the schoolhouse the children played up more frequently than usual, especially little Alice. One morning she refused to sit at a desk and draw, and instead she crawled around the floor and sat by Sally's feet. The smoko bell rang out and when Sally went to slip on her shoes, which she always kicked off under her desk, Alice had disappeared with them.

'Ginger, you go find that Alice. Bring back my shoes.'

Giggling, he ran off and Sally waited while the boys went to the house for morning tea.

She was planning the afternoon's worksheets when she heard a step and Rob appeared in the doorway.

'I passed a couple of scallywags playing catchings

with these. Don't walk around bare foot, there are scorpions and hookworms.'

'I know. That's why I'm sitting here and not tucking into scones. But thanks.' She took the gold sandals that she'd bought in Surfers Paradise.

He gave a small smile. 'A bit fancy for out here. Do you have good boots?'

'I've been borrowing some riding boots. I've ordered some sandshoes from the catalogue and my boots are on the way from home. I hadn't planned on wearing them in London.'

'You got a bit sidetracked, I hear.'

'Yes. My girlfriend had to go back home to New Zealand instead of going overseas with me. This seemed like a good idea. I can always go to England,' she said, putting on her shoes.

They walked towards the house. 'So, how are you finding it way out here?' he asked.

'I like it. I can't believe how I've settled in so quickly. The boys tested me at first but we get on really well now.'

'They're good kids. John comes down a bit hard on Ian sometimes. But that's the cross you bear being the oldest son.' There was something in his tone, a slight edge that made Sally glance at him and notice the set of his mouth.

'Are you the oldest son?'

'Yeah. My dad and I don't see eye to eye about a lot of things. I took off to work for myself. They think I'm wasting their expensive education. I'm a King's boy too,' he added. 'But I do all right. And I like the lifestyle, especially being my own boss.'

'Will you go back home eventually?'

'I'm saving for my own place. My brothers are running our station in the Territory. I don't really know where I'll end up.'

They stepped onto the verandah and saw John Monroe banging around in the kitchen as Snowy, Harry, Dougie and Gloria came through the screen door.

'Don't be looking for bloody scones. The lubras have walked off the job,' he snapped. 'It's tea and a biscuit.'

'Lazy bitches. Do youse want me to whip up some scones?' Gloria asked.

'No fear.' John knew Lorna wouldn't want the runners' woman mucking about in her kitchen. 'Lizzie can make a cake for this arvo.'

'Things are falling apart a bit,' said Sally as she and Rob walked into the dining room. 'I'd better keep an eye on the lubras. The trouble is they don't take a lot of notice of me because I don't speak pidgin.' She poured them each a cup of tea.

'John will haul them over the coals. You'd better chase them about doing the housework and the washing. The boys can translate for you.'

'Lorna doesn't like them speaking pidgin.'

'If you ask them to do it, that's different. They know not to let on to their mother.'

There was a burst of raucous laughter from Gloria and Rob rolled his eyes.

'She's one tough bird. They're due to move back out to the boundary in a day or so.' He hesitated as if debating whether to say anything or not. 'Gloria might get a bit out of control, especially when Lorna's away.'

'We've already had one blue with her,' said Sally. 'In fact, I'm surprised John lets her come into the house.'

'They can all drink, that's for sure.' He drained his cup. 'I'll see you at dinner.'

Rob picked up his hat and went outside. John was talking with the two bore runners in the kitchen, they seemed to be making plans. There had been a lot of noise and laughter coming from the single men's quarters at night and Sally thought she'd heard John's voice. He was always up first but was looking very seedy and hadn't bothered to shave for a few days. He still dressed in his spotless white T-shirts and ironed shorts, though. Sally went into the garden to look for the boys.

'Ian, can you find the kids from the camp and tell them to send Lizzie and Betsy up to the house? They haven't done their work today.'

'Mum won't let us go down to the blacks' camp.'

'You can get the big kids to run a message. Lizzie and the girls had better get up here before your dad does his block.'

'Dad can handle it,' said Ian.

Sally decided not to press the point. Ian had his stubborn look and tight expression that invariably led to an argument. 'Fine then. You boys go back to the schoolhouse. I'm going for the mail.'

'Can we come?' pleaded Tommy.

'Not this week, you're behind because of the time out at the stock camp. Next week when you've caught up you can give Donny your school work to post.' She tried to sound firm. Again, without Lorna to back her up she was being challenged by the boys.

Donny gave her a thumbs up as he jumped down from the plane.

'Here you go. What you've been waiting for, parcels from home. Two big cartons.'

Sally saw her father's writing and winced at the row of stamps. 'Dad must have had a fit at how much these cost to send.'

'You've got your saddle and all your gear now.'

'Looks like it.' She felt suddenly homesick.

'How are things back at the ol' ranch?'

'Slacking off. Since Lorna's been away I've had a bit of a hard time keeping the house girls in line. John drinks a lot and disappears after dinner. I reckon he goes and drinks with the bore runners and that Gloria.'

'She's trouble, always has been. She banged around the Kimberley and the Territory before landing in a bit of hot water and ended up in the 'Curry. Then she picked up those runner blokes –'

'Dougie and Harry.'

'And she left Cloncurry with them. Odd arrangement, a threesome. Guess none of them are choosy.'

'What sort of trouble did she get into?'

'She was known for being light fingered and she bashed a young bloke. Near killed him.'

'What for, did he make a pass at her?'

Donny laughed. 'That'd be the day she'd carry on about that! Nah, he called her an old slut and a few other choice words, said she'd stolen his wallet. She took offence and slammed him with a broken beer bottle. Flying Doc said he was cut up pretty bad.'

'No wonder Lorna doesn't like her in the house.'

'And how are you getting on with Rob?' he asked as he carried the mail bag to the Land Rover.

'He's been great. He's really nice. The boys love him.'

Donny cast her a sideways glance and said casually, 'And you? He's a decent fellow, hard working, knows his job, well brought up, smart, bit of a loner. Seems like he could be a good mate – or more.'

Sally tried not to smile. 'You think so? I thought he looked a bit of a hooligan when I first met him at the stock camp. Lorna tidied him up. They seem very friendly.'

'She's got a lot of time for him. He treats her as a lady, and she's a very lonely woman.' Donny pulled out his cigarettes. 'Did you bring morning tea as you promised?'

'You bet. I have a Thermos of tea and some fruit cake,' said Sally. 'No scones, Lizzie didn't turn up this morning.'

'They'll take advantage where they can. Try to crack the whip, Sally. Lorna has a lot of confidence you can manage things.'

'My job has expanded a bit,' said Sally. 'But I don't mind helping where I can.'

'It's a way of life out here, Sal. People have to rely on each other. Lorna is very happy you're here. She thinks you do a good job with the boys and she enjoys your company.'

'She tells you a lot,' said Sally.

'Ah, most of the ladies I drop in on need a chance to bend a friendly ear.'

'You're not a mail man, you're a flying father confessor!'

He laughed. 'I s'pose I am a bit. Tell you what, why don't you take a couple of hours off next week? We'll go for a proper picnic. I know a great place down the track.'

She looked a bit dubious. 'I suppose I could. The boys could stay with Rob, he's offered to show them roping calves or something.'

'It's a date then. You bring the food and your swimmers. There's a billabong where we can swim.'

'It sounds lovely. You're on.'

He stubbed out his cigarette and handed her the mug. 'I'm proud of you, Sally. Looks like you'll make it to the end of your contract.'

'I'm not a quitter.'

'And then what, eh?' He gave her a shrewd look.

'Crikey, that's a long way off. Do you know what you'll be doing in say, eighteen months' time?'

'I'd like to have my own plane. Be in love. Might even leave the bush and try for my commercial licence.'

'Really?'

'We all have dreams, Sal. See you next week. I'll bring some drinks, fresh fruit. Don't forget – food, towel, swimmers . . . or you can forget them if you like.'

'Fat chance. See you, Donny.'

'Take care, kiddo.'

The boys ran out of the schoolhouse to see what mail had arrived and Marty demanded Sally open her packages. She'd wanted to go through everything by herself but the boys' curiosity was infectious. They brought the parcels into the living room and Sally pulled them open. She put the letters from her mother and sister to one side, then pulled out the jar of Paul Duval face cream with a note from Emily Mitchell: *Look after your skin in that dreadful Australian sun.* Next came her riding boots and hard hat, which made the boys giggle. There were the clothes she'd asked for and a few new ones – blouses, skirts and a nightdress chosen by her mother as being appropriate. Sally just sighed. In the second box was her saddle and when she pulled it out and unwrapped the soft blanket protecting the light hunting saddle, the boys screamed with laughter. John Monroe walked in and stopped to see what all the fuss was about.

'That wouldn't fit on a bloody jack rabbit!' he said, looking at the saddle.

'It's too small even for Marty!'

'How'd you be on that all day!'

'I'm glad you think it's so funny,' snapped Sally.

'Does it make the horse go faster?' said Tommy, laughing.

'I know! We'll enter her in the races at the 'Curry!' Monroe slapped his knee then looked around. 'Say, that's not a silly idea, y'know.'

'They have ladies' races, don't they, Dad?' asked Ian.

Sally stood up and gathered an armful of her belongings. 'I might just show the lot of you one day. Any time you want to race, let me know. See how well I can do!'

'How about tomorrow?' shouted John Monroe.

'All right, you're on.' She stomped along the verandah and sat on her bed to read the letters. As well as the mail from home she'd received a letter from Sean. It was a sweet letter, he missed her and asked when she'd get a holiday as maybe he could meet her somewhere. The idea sounded very appealing, but she knew her holidays were a long way off. Perhaps Sean could come out here. No, bad idea. She re-read the letter, savouring the sexy and romantic bits, then read the letters from her mother and sister.

By lunchtime the word was out that Sally on Dancer with her stupid little saddle was going to race young Ian on his father's big bay gelding, Shooter. Sally hadn't taken the suggestion of the race very seriously but as she walked into lunch Rob said to her quietly, 'Are you sure about this race idea?'

'Oh. I guess so. I mean it's no big deal. Bit of a run down to the river and back or something.'

'Ian on his dad's horse. It's creating quite a diversion, bets are being taken.'

'Oh hell. Well, that's all right. Dancer is a great little horse but I'm not going to be responsible if anything happens to Ian. I know he's a good rider but Shooter is a big horse. Do you think I should call it off?'

'Up to you. If you want to prove a point, this is your chance.'

'Fine by me.' Sally lifted her chin and marched into the dining room.

The news of 'The Governess Cup' flashed around the

station and the stockmen ambled in and hung around the yards. The runners and Gloria started jibing Snowy to 'have a go'.

The red-faced, heavy-set musterer started boasting about past triumphs and ended by saying, 'Ah, there isn't a horse strong enough to race with me on board.'

Dougie spoke up. ''Course there is. That big bastard of a stallion that John keeps in the old yards. He's been penned for a bit, so he'll go like the clappers.'

'Struth, it's only a kids' race,' interjected Gloria.

'That governess is no kid. Not with those knockers,' said Harry.

'Why doesn't Rob go in it?' asked Gloria.

Snowy nodded. 'That's a good idea. But it's gotta be worth our while. What's the prize?'

And so it went from a short sprint between Sally and Ian to an event that promised to be the highlight of the week. John Monroe put up a case of rum and planned the course.

Chilla, one of Snowy's stockmen, decided to enter when he heard Snowy was racing. 'I want ta beat that big mouth. Him full of bulldust,' he said to one of his mates.

The black stockmen watched the activity the next morning with slight amusement and finally Rob threw up his hands in disgust, knowing no work was being done. He went to the schoolhouse and called Sally outside.

'This damn thing has got bigger than Ben Hur's chariot race. Snowy is pissed – he started on the rum after breakfast – and he's insisting on riding that black stallion. Chilla's gone in it to see Snowy come a cropper and now that John has put up a case of rum Dan is running too. Do you want me to ride in your place?'

'What for? I'll do my own riding, thanks.'

'These blokes take risks and don't play by the rules. There's no hunt master out here.'

'Dancer is smart. I'm more worried about Ian. I think you should talk him out of it.'

Rob ran his hands through his curly hair. 'He wouldn't like that. Geez, how did this all happen? Let's hope no one gets hurt. Lorna's not here to patch them up.'

'I don't think we'd be doing this if Lorna was here,' said Sally.

'That's true. Send Ian out and I'll have a word with him.'

Ian refused to withdraw from the race and Rob saw this was one of those stepping stones towards manhood for Ian. He would lose face with his little brothers if he withdrew, and it was an opportunity to prove himself to his father.

'Righto. Seeing as how everyone else seems to want to have a bit of a run, do you mind if I ride along?'

'Go for your life,' said Ian.

It was a 3 pm start over one mile. John had driven over the track and Fitzi had hammered in marker posts at the half and three-quarter points. The track wound across open country, around the western well, looped behind the small dam, back over the bottom creek, up the rise in the home paddock and down past the closest boundary fence, ending at the stables.

The horses and riders lined up for the start behind a rope held by two stockmen. There was much hilarity at Sally's small saddle. Her legs were bent high, causing comments about lady jockeys.

Snowy flailed in his saddle, sticking his legs forward and flinging his reins about and yodelling. Dan sat dourly, straight-backed, ignoring Snowy's mocking remarks. Chilla sat easily in the saddle, grinning from ear to ear. Rob was beside Ian, giving him a few last-minute instructions about safety and keeping out of trouble. Sally had drawn the outside and tried to relax, softly murmuring to Dancer.

John Monroe was the starter and he stood to one side, waiting until they all looked as ready as they'd ever be, facing the same direction in a vague shifting line. He motioned to the men to drop the rope, lifted his rifle, pointed it away from the riders, and fired.

The horses leapt forward from fright or instinct before the riders had registered what was happening. Immediately Sally felt the thrill of the chase that always came during a hunt. Ian broke free, wildly kicking his horse and Rob took off after him, swearing under his breath. Dan hung behind Sally, and Snowy, bringing up the rear, started to shout and curse, whipping his horse as he went after Chilla.

The watching mob scrambled to catch sight of the race as the horses galloped off.

Dan overtook Snowy, then Chilla and Sally, and then went after Ian and Rob, who glanced back over his shoulder to check on Sally. Snowy caught up to her, and in a frenzy of shouting and thrashing, bolted past her, Ian and Rob, his big horse showed the whites of its eyes, ears flattened.

They swung around the small dam in a tight pack and Sally saw Snowy shove between Ian and Rob, cutting in front of Rob and almost causing his horse to fall. She gritted her teeth, muttering, 'Stupid bastard', and looked for the right moment to move up with Snowy and Dan, who were in the lead.

Dancer, though smaller than the other horses, was fast and sure footed, and with the light saddle and confident rider began to enjoy herself. Sally could tell she hadn't reached her limit, there was still a reserve of energy in the horse, so she gave her a nudge to open up a bit more. Dancer responded and flew past Rob, then Ian, to tuck in behind Snowy and Dan.

The ground was open but those in the lead were following the faint track left by cattle and horses. Sally had been over this land a few times and suddenly recalled how she'd tried to take a shortcut back to the homestead but had been foiled by a fence that marked the boundary of the home paddock creek. The creek was dry, although she'd been told it became a small river in the Wet. Their instructions had been to head for the home stables after the dam. She grinned as she wheeled Dancer to the right.

Dan's horse was tiring and dropped back behind Ian. Snowy was now in the lead and still yelling, cheering himself on, cursing the horse as he belted its hide. Rob glanced back and saw Sally take off across country. 'No, not that way,' he shouted, knowing she couldn't hear him. He looked at Ian, who was gaining on Snowy, his young face showing grim determination.

They were now in sight of the yards and the onlookers were standing on top of vehicles, a shed, in a tree and perched on the rails. John Monroe watched through binoculars. Snowy was just ahead of Ian but when he glanced over his shoulder and saw the boy he yanked his horse directly in front of him to cut him off. The crowd hollered at the dirty trick but despite his horse swerving, losing momentum and some ground, Ian stuck in the saddle. Rob caught up with him and could have overtaken but paced him, calling out, 'Move away from him, widen the gap.'

Ian understood and wheeled Shooter slightly, making a wide turn which momentarily confused Snowy and his horse. As they started to follow, Ian spurred his horse forward, cutting across Snowy and racing ahead. The mob cheered. Snowy's horse was labouring but he let it have all, whipping it with the long greenhide reins, kicking in his spurs and flogging the tiring animal to continue. Meanwhile the crowd had spotted Sally cutting across to the home paddock.

'Silly bitch is going to hit the deep creek bed.'

'Outsmarted herself this time.'

'Christ, she'd better pull up, she must see the damn thing,' muttered John Monroe.

At that instant Snowy's horse had had enough, and by will or physical exhaustion it staggered, baulked and stopped, sending Snowy flying over its head to hit the ground with a heavy thud. He rolled and lay there. Dan shot past and Snowy's horse cantered away. Chilla rode straight past the weaving Snowy, his big grin still in place. Eventually Snowy sat up and rubbed his head. Seeing the smug expression on his stockman's face he shook his fist, shouting, 'You'll be sorry, you yella fella!'

Sally saw the creek bed, which was several feet deep with logs at its edge. She leaned forward. 'Come on, Dancer, we can do this, lift your bloody feet up.' Without breaking stride Dancer understood and as they reached the creek there was a faint tremble in the horse's body but Sally had her head down close to her neck, her hips raised out of the saddle and urged Dancer up. And across. The animal kicked her back legs high, stretched out, and they cleared the creek. No one knew that Sally had been training Dancer to jump over logs and obstacles around the home paddock.

There was a moment of silence from everyone watching, then a burst of cheering and disbelieving laughter as Sally raced up to the yards ahead of Ian and Rob, then Dan and Chilla.

John Monroe reached her first and gave her a slap on the back as she dismounted. 'You bloody beauty. Fooled us all, more style than the jumping at the Royal Easter Show.'

'Ian rode brilliantly. I thought Snowy was going to dislodge him. Very underhand,' said Sally as Ian rode up.

'Ah, Snowy is pissed. A few rums too many before he started. I'm amazed he didn't fall off sooner.' Monroe turned away, 'Hey, send someone to pick up Snowy and get his horse.'

Sally waited for John to congratulate Ian. When he didn't say anything she called out, 'Fantastic ride, Ian. You were great, very good reactions when Snowy cut in on you.'

The boy looked sour. 'I didn't win but.'

'No, a bloody sheila beat you. We'd better send you to one of those posh riding schools,' called his father.

Rob overheard the comment and went to Ian and shook his hand. 'You had me eating your dust, kid. Good on you. That was a hard race.'

Ian looked mollified and Sally smiled gratefully at Rob.

'Dancer is a damned good horse. Told you so,' said John Monroe.

'She is. Depends who rides her, of course,' said Sally, smiling.

'Yeah, well you could have come a bad cropper,' said Monroe. 'And if Dancer had been hurt you wouldn't be laughing.'

'No. I wouldn't,' she said. 'Any time you want to borrow my saddle, let me know.'

She went to Ian and dropped her arm around his taut shoulders. 'You were winning, Ian. I'm sorry. I just decided to tackle the creek on the spur of the moment. I shouldn't have.'

'S'all right,' he muttered and shrugged away from her.

'Don't be mad at me, friends, okay?'

'I'm not mad at you.' Ian glanced at his father who was talking to Dan, and leading his sweating horse, walked away.

For the next few days everything was out of kilter. Everyone found it hard to settle down after the impromptu race. Lorna would be back soon and John Monroe was making a last drinking stand. Harry, Dougie and Gloria were drinking in the single men's quarters. Rob and his men were working at the yards, separating calves and cows, watched by the Monroe boys.

Sally took the opportunity to have a leisurely shower, shampoo her hair and rub the face cream her mother had sent her over her skin. She wondered what Lorna was doing, quite aware that the race wouldn't have happened if she'd been home. For a few moments she felt isolated, realising how much she relied on Lorna's company. They were the only women there who could relate to each other.

When she emerged in a fresh sundress and sandals there was no sign of Lizzie or any of the women preparing dinner. Sally went outside and found Fitzi carrying a pail of milk to the house.

'Goat milk. Good one make 'um cheese an 'tings.'

'Yogurt. Where're Lizzie and Betsy? They haven't started tea.'

He looked down. 'Dey be cookin' at de campfire. Boss doin' plenny big cook up.'

'You mean down by the men's quarters? Sounds like a party.'

'Dat Snowy and dem bore pellas drink longa time.'

'Get one of those girls up here please, Fitzi. The boys have to eat properly.' She didn't ask whether Rob was with the mob at the campfire shindig.

She took the goat's milk, poured it into a bowl and set it by the warm Aga stove that was always alight. Lorna had shown her how the girls set the milk on the back of the stove with a spoonful of yogurt culture in it. Idly she opened the fridge, wondering what was there for the boys' tea.

'I hope you're not thinking of cooking,' came Rob's voice.

'Someone has to, we're a bit short staffed,' said Sally with more heat than she meant. She didn't seem to have Lorna's firm control over the women. 'John is rather out of it, drinking down at the single men's quarters.'

'I'll go rustle up those lubras. They go to pieces with their men in camp.'

'Thanks. Er, are you eating with us?'

'Of course. But I doubt John will make it back up. Your rum is flowing pretty freely down there.'

'My rum? Oh, the prize. Rescue a bottle for me, would you?'

'I'll do better than that. You don't want to drink that rough cane juice. I'll bring us something decent for dinner.'

Sally was glad Rob was around as he brought the reluctant boys back to the homestead to clean up for tea and chased Betsy back into the kitchen. To her surprise she discovered Rob throwing steaks on the open fire outside the kitchen and in the living room was Betsy's salad, mashed potato and bread on the table set for five. A bottle of red wine was open and two good wine glasses stood beside it. Sally picked a spray of wisteria from the vine around the verandah and laid it in the centre of the table.

'Hey, this is a neat turnaround. I like a man who can cook. And where'd the wine come from?' she asked as Rob walked in with a plate of steaks.

'Lorna keeps a secret stash for me. She doesn't mind a good glass of claret occasionally. John thinks it's a wog drink.'

'He would. Though he's a bit of a contradiction in some ways. He spends so much money on his own toys, only the best will do. He's damned fastidious about his laundry and Italian leather sandals. But he won't spend money on other things like the house or the kids.'

Rob handed her a glass of wine. 'Lorna makes up for that. The "Catalogue Queen", Donny calls her. Come on, the steaks are getting cold.' He gave a shrill whistle and the three boys raced in and shyly sat at the 'big' table, eyeing the candles, flowers and bottle of wine. Their cold Milo was poured into matching crystal wine glasses.

'How well do you know Donny?' asked Sally. For some reason it hadn't occurred to her that the two men might share information about the household. She'd better be careful what she told each of them. She'd thought of Donny as someone with whom she could share her frustrations and feelings about life at Barra Creek, remembering their last conversation when she'd teased him about being a flying father confessor.

'So what's the big deal?' asked Ian, as Rob served up the steaks.

'Sally won the race!' exclaimed Marty, and Ian cast his youngest brother a dirty look. Sally overlooked the use of her name. Lorna insisted on Miss, or Miss Mitchell.

Rob stepped in quickly. 'It's a celebration for all of us!'

'You would have won, Ian, fair and square,' said Sally, raising her glass to him. 'I took a short cut and it was stupid of me.'

'Is that cheating?' asked Marty.

They all looked at Rob.

'Well . . . it is if you meant to. The rules weren't very clear, it was just a spontaneous move by Sally.'

'What's spontaneous mean?' asked Marty.

'Unplanned,' said Sally. 'Come on, let's finish dinner then we can all have a game of Monopoly.' She smiled at Rob, including him, but he narrowed his eyes.

'I might have to check on things down at the camp. Make sure my men don't get into any trouble.'

The boys looked disappointed. They were loving having Sally and Rob to themselves, being treated as grown-ups, almost.

Betsy hovered at the dining room door and Sally waved her in to clear the table. 'Tell you what then, how about a quick game? A couple of rounds of snap.'

They sat at the table where the boys normally ate and Sally dealt the cards as Rob poured the last of the red wine. Lizzie was talking to Betsy in the kitchen and there seemed to be some spat ensuing.

'I'll go and see what's going on out there,' said Rob.

Sally could hear their voices but couldn't grasp what they were talking about as Rob was also speaking pidgin. The boys glanced at one another.

'Tonight? They going out tonight?' Tommy looked at Ian.

'Sounds like it.'

'Can we go?'

'Go where?' asked Sally. 'What's going on? Hey, Rob, what's happening?'

He came into the dining room looking tight lipped. There was a short explosion in the kitchen as John Monroe lumbered in, shouting to the women to shake a bloody leg. He burst into the dining room and headed for the drinks.

'Off to bed, you fellas. And stay there.'

'You going out with them, Dad?' asked Tommy.

'Out where? It's nearly nine o'clock,' said Sally. 'What the heck is happening?'

John lifted his glass of rum. 'Here's to the little lady jockey.' He took a mouthful. 'Fortification. Need it on the river.'

'The river. Are you blokes going fishing?'

'You might say that,' he chortled. 'With a bloody rope and a gun.'

'They're going croc shooting,' explained Ian, his eyes bright. 'Dad, can't we come down and sit in the Land Rover?'

'Not without me, and I'm not going,' snapped Sally.

'Now boys, you know the rules,' said Rob. 'Not tonight. I want your word on that. Okay?' He looked at each of them in turn and they nodded slowly.

'That's the way. You are still little blokes. This is men's business.'

'Gloria's going,' said Ian. 'Lizzie just said so.'

'She's a bloke,' roared John Monroe, adding with a leer towards Rob, 'Not that them runners give a shit.'

Sally stood up. 'Right. Clear the cards and let's go to bed. You can read for half an hour. And we're up and out of here early. A ride before breakfast, okay?' The boys loved to do this so she threw it in to ease their disappointment.

'Can I borrow your saddle?' asked Tommy quickly.

'You think it's going to make you go faster,' said Marty and Ian glared at him.

'Goodnight, fellas. We'll have that game tomorrow night, okay?' added Rob.

'If you catch a big one can we see it later?' asked Marty.

'We'll wake you up, for sure,' said his father. 'Might tie it up to the end of your bed. Be careful where you step in the night if you have to take a piss.' Roaring at his joke he headed down the verandah.

The boys went to get into their pyjamas, and Sally turned to Rob.

'Are they really going out this late and half shick-ered?' she asked. 'Who's going with them? It sounds dangerous to me.'

'Could be. Dougie, Harry and Gloria will go in one boat, John and someone to look out for him in another.'

'Who's going to be silly enough to go out in a din-ghy with John cockeyed on rum among a bunch of giant crocodiles? Snowy, I suppose.'

'Me, I'm afraid.' He gave a rueful grin. 'Snowy's passed out.'

'You! What for? You don't have to do that.'

'I know, but Lorna would want me to go. Besides, under good conditions, it's exciting.'

'What are good conditions?' asked Sally.

'Full moon, no wind, sober shooters. And big crocs.'

'You're mad.'

'I know. Say, you want to come?'

'You must be joking!'

'Yeah, I am. Another time maybe. It can be quite romantic on the river at night.'

'Without the crocodiles, thanks.'

'Well, that's their territory. We humans are the invad-ers; you can't blame them for protecting their turf.'

'That's one way of looking at it. What's the point of this exercise anyway?'

'Bit of fun for the boys. When the croc hunters come in it's serious business. The skins are valuable. Ever had a crocodile steak?'

'No. I'll stick to beef and lamb. I'll pass on the snake too.'

'You don't know what you're missing, Sal. See you in the morning. Make sure those boys don't sneak out of bed.'

'They gave their word.'

'Remind them of that. And, Sally,' he looked at her

179

and was serious again. 'If you hear any ructions or revelry in the night, ignore it.'

'Righto. Happy hunting. Be careful.'

'That's why I'm going. See you at breakfast.'

Rob walked away from the house hoping Sally would heed his advice. She was impetuous – spontaneous, he grinned to himself and it occurred to him that she might decide to come down to the river to see what was going on. He had been on a few croc hunts and had listened to the croc shooters' stories around many a campfire. And even separating the exaggerated myth from the truth, danger seemed to be the common thread. The blacks talked of old rogue saltwater crocs living in the quiet upper reaches of the Norman River that were so big they would grab a calf, a dog or a piccaninny.

Croc shooters along with doggers were tough men who made a living from skins and dingo scalps. When they called into Barra Creek to shoot crocs, it was a serious business. The few pounds they got for a good hide seemed little compensation for the risks to life and limb. It was a rough life. If they lost a leg, arm, hand or life, that was part of the business.

At first Rob thought they must be mad men. Yet, more often than not, he found them to be reticent, monosyllabic, careful individuals while they were working. Around a campfire, away from the river, with the rum being passed, they told tales of near escapes, of the hunter being hunted. Some white men savoured well-cooked croc meat, but the smell that seeped from the skin of blacks who feasted on it turned Rob's stomach. And after his first croc-shooting expedition, he was more convinced than ever that crocodiles were evil. He'd joined several of the croc shooters he trusted who came to the property and he'd watched and learned. He had little choice now but to go and keep a sober eye on the inebriated John

Monroe, who considered himself bullet proof no matter what the circumstances.

It was a merry group that unloaded gear and untied the dinghies at the landing on the river. They left the headlights of the Land Rover shining onto the bank as they threw ropes, a harpoon, rifles, wire and heavy spotlight torches into each boat. Gloria insisted on sitting in the rear of a dinghy which sank low to the water beneath her weight.

'You could get a bite on the bum,' shouted Monroe.

'Not from you,' she retorted.

He muttered under his breath to Rob, 'That's for bloody sure.'

'Since when have you been so picky?' said Rob, and they both laughed.

Dougie arranged the gear in one boat, John Monroe sipped from a hip flask and watched as Rob loaded their boat. Then they pushed off, talking quietly to each other. Rob and John went ahead, while there was some disagreement between Harry and Dougie, with Gloria arguing from the stern.

The river was sluggish, lit by a pale moon and overshadowed by trees. Some clear stretches of the river bank looked safe enough to pull in a boat. However they all knew better. They paddled slowly past, Dougie in the bow of his boat and Rob rowing the other boat with John standing in the stern peering at the banks. He held his torch ready but for now they were guided by the watery moonlight.

It was Gloria who hissed first. 'Shit! Over there.'

Harry swung around and saw the two glowing red points.

'Over there, Dougie. Whaddya reckon?'

'Not so big. Let's keep going. He'll stay around.'

'Well, how big is big, for Chrissakes?' hissed Gloria. 'I want a hide that'll fetch me boots, bag and bra.'

'Hard tits and a horny pouch . . . that'd be right,' muttered Dougie.

'Who's gonna skin and tan the bastard? A good skin can fetch a decent price,' said Harry.

'Let's see what we get. Whatever we land, bloody Monroe will want half of it.'

'So let's get a fuckin' big bastard,' exclaimed Gloria, turning her attention back to the muddy river bank.

Rob and Monroe changed places. John Monroe stroked strongly through the thick water. Rob felt sober and alert watching the dark banks on either side of them. He spotted tiny pinpoints of red but none of the others noticed them so he made no comment.

Slowly, rising to the surface a few yards from the boat, appeared two bright red eyes, gleaming in the torchlight.

Monroe spoke first. 'Fuck, that's big.'

'Yippee, let's go!' hollered Gloria.

The second boat was slightly behind Rob and John Monroe and now Harry stroked beside them. 'So, what do you want t'do?'

'Hold that light up, shine it straight at him,' instructed Rob, stepping into the bow, feeling for the harpoon as Monroe drew on the oars.

'Tell me when, Rob. I'll shoot him –'

'If you shoot him now he'll sink and we'll never bring him up. We have to get the rope into him.' He picked up the harpoon with a thick rope attached to the spearhead, which a croc shooter had given John Monroe some time ago.

'You gotta get it in the right spot. Want me t'do it?' asked Monroe.

Rob didn't want to undermine him, but knew he was still swaying from an evening of drinking. 'I'll shoot the rope into him when we get him close to the boat again, then put a bullet between the eyes.'

'What are you blokes doing?' Gloria's voice was agitated. 'That's a big bastard, longer than the bloody boat. Got t'be a fifteen footer.'

They swung their boat closer.

'Keep the damned light on him,' shouted Rob to Dougie. 'If he thinks he's outnumbered he'll take off.'

'They're cowards, y'know,' said John Monroe.

'Well, I'm not taking any chances.' Rob took aim as Harry's torch shone along the broad horny back that was now visible above the inky surface. The massive tail disappeared out of sight. 'Watch his tail, don't get too close or he'll flip you blokes,' warned Rob.

Dougie took several quick strokes backward, swinging the dinghy side on so the massive croc was between the two boats.

Rob took aim and plunged the harpoon into the croc and instantly the thick rope spun out of the boat as the water churned around the thrashing crocodile. It dragged Rob and John's boat behind it as Rob feverishly tried to haul in the rope to get it alongside. Monroe had the .303 rifle cocked.

'It's going to hit the other boat!'

'Pull the bugger in!' screamed Gloria, who was sitting on the gunwale watching the heaving animal with jaws that were over two and a half feet long.

'Shoot the bloody thing,' panted Rob.

'Wait, if I don't get it in the head it'll be madder than a cut snake.' Monroe took aim.

At that instant, there was a snap and the rope broke, sending Rob and Monroe to the bottom of the boat and the bullet shooting into a tree on the bank. The crocodile, now unrestrained, lunged at the nearest object in retaliation, a move so swift it was a second or more before the horrible realisation struck them.

Gloria's scream rang along the river above the

slashing tail. Harry saw her look of disbelief as he and Dougie reached forward, knowing the animal would take its prey straight below the surface. He clutched a handful of her hair in a desperate tug of war. The crocodile had her by the buttock and thigh in a precarious grip it seemed, for it opened its jaws to take in the entire width of her body. In the moment it loosened its grip both men pulled Gloria up the side of the boat as another shot rang out.

'Oh sweet Jesus. Did you get it?' screamed Harry, as he and Dougie struggled to pull Gloria into the boat. She'd stopped screaming and was a dead weight.

'Get a light. Shit, how bad is she?' Rob asked, pulling their boat up alongside.

'Oh fuck. She's a goner, has to be, her whole leg's been ripped off,' said Monroe.

'Stop the bleeding, quick, tie something around her,' snapped Rob. 'Throw me the tow rope.'

John Monroe pulled hard and fast for the bank, towing the boat while the two men kneeled with the flashlight on a seat. Gloria's blood flowed over the floorboards as they tied their shirts around the severed leg and missing buttock where the croc had rolled and wrenched, sawing through the soft fat.

She was still unconscious as they lifted her into the Land Rover and John Monroe drove like a mad man towards the homestead, Dougie and Harry taking turns to twist and tighten the blood-soaked shirts.

Rob sprinted from the vehicle to call the emergency channel on the wireless for the Flying Doctor.

Sally was woken by the sound of the speeding truck and, hearing Rob's urgent tone, came into the dining room.

'What's happened? Where's John?'

'Gloria. A croc got her. Bad. Real bad.'

Sally's hand flew to her mouth. 'What can I do?'

'Not much unless you're a surgeon.' He started to give details to the Flying Doctor base.

Or a nurse, thought Sally, knowing Lorna would be better in this emergency. 'Where are they?'

'Outside. Grab a sheet.'

She ran along the verandah, ripping the sheet from the nearest bed, and stepped into the garden. The men had Gloria on the ground in the headlights of the truck. John was giving her mouth to mouth. Dougie was pushing a cloth into the bloodied flesh where her hip and buttock used to be. Sally felt her stomach heave and she thrust the sheet at Harry.

In seconds it too was blood covered. Dougie leaned over and put his ear to her chest. Harry picked up her limp wrist then dropped it. They looked at each other.

Dougie was first to shake his head. Sally fled into the house.

'It's too late, Rob. She's dead.'

Rob relayed the message over the radio.

Sally turned around to find the three boys staring at her with ashen faces. Their father came into the room and they gasped at the sight of his blood-stained clothing and shocked white face.

'What'd they say?' he asked Rob.

'Be here about 6 am. Bloody unbelievable.' He could feel his knees start to shake with delayed shock and a sense of guilt that they hadn't checked the rope on the harpoon. It was old and had been rotting in the sun for months.

'Sally, get the rum,' snapped John Monroe. He went to his room and ripped off his clothes.

Rob took the decanter from Sally, sloshed it into two glasses and went outside to where Dougie and Harry were sitting on the ground beside the wet, bloodied body of Gloria, her face a ghostly white.

Sally poured herself a drink. 'Boys, go back to bed please.'

'Will you tell us what happened?' whispered Tommy.

'Yes, later. I don't know much myself.' She gulped a mouthful of the rum then her head shot up. 'What the heck is that noise?' It was a howling moan that rose to a high wail.

'The blacks. They know someone's all finished,' said Ian.

'They'll go on all night,' added Tommy.

'Well, go back to bed. I'm going to make a pot of tea.'

'Can I have a Milo?' asked Marty. He looked worried.

'Sure you can. I'll bring you one in bed. Off you all go. Your father has enough to deal with.'

The boys took the hint. It wasn't a time to get in his way.

When Sally went back to the verandah she found Marty curled up in her bed. She handed him the mug.

'Can I sleep with you? I'm scared,' he whispered.

'Okay. But don't be scared. It was an accident. A terrible one.'

'He's going to have nightmares,' said Tommy.

'Go to sleep. Or at least just stay there. I'll tell you what's happening.' She pulled on her cotton dressing-gown and went back inside.

John Monroe and Rob were slumped in the lounge chairs with the bottle of rum in easy reach.

'Can I do anything for the two men?' she asked.

'Leave them be. They'll be looked after down at their quarters. Snowy has come to, he'll handle it.'

Sally didn't ask where Gloria's body was. She hoped she wouldn't see it on the lawn in the morning.

Rob looked at Sally distractedly tightening the belt of her dressing-gown. 'Go to bed, Sally. The plane will be here at daybreak.'

She nodded and turned away.

The boys had put out the light. She slipped into bed and was grateful for the warmth of Marty curled on his side next to her.

How was Lorna going to take the news, she wondered. Sally tried to sleep but was overcome with feelings of inadequacy. It seemed there'd been nothing but dramas and now tragedy since Lorna had left.

Chapter Ten

BREAKFAST WAS A SUBDUED pot of tea and piece of toast at daybreak before the Flying Doctor was due. They heard the plane land and the boys rushed out onto the verandah in their pyjamas, then came running back inside, agog.

'There's blood all over the grass!'

'Yuk, worse than when we kill a calf!'

'That's enough!' roared John Monroe.

Rob joined them and asked Monroe, 'Are you going to talk to the Doc? The coroner will have some questions, I imagine.'

'Yeah. As if I didn't have enough to deal with,' John said morosely. 'Lorna is due back today anyway. She's in Cloncurry waiting to hook up with Donny.'

'Do you think she'll know about the accident yet?'

'Everybody heard the call last night. It'll be all over the Cape by now.'

'We'd better make sure everything around the house is in order,' said Sally. 'Are you meeting Lorna's plane?'

'I might be tied up. Got to get the men back to work

and settle them down. Besides, I don't want to be the first up for a towelling from Lorna. You go, Sally. Calm her down.'

She glanced at Rob, who raised his eyebrows behind John's back. What a coward John is, thought Sally. 'Okay, boys, let's get cracking. No riding this morning. Clothes, house, kitchen and garden inspection. I don't want your mother to think we've been living like blackfellas while she's been away. And no kicking clothes under your beds.' She turned to John Monroe. 'What about the house girls? I'll need them up here and working, no moping and wailing about the place.'

'I'll get a rocket up their bums when I get down there.' John rose and left the room.

Rob picked up his plate and cup as there was no one around to clear the table. 'They're very superstitious but they'll also use this accident as an excuse to get out of work. Lorna will give them a dressing down for sure. She knows what it's like when she's away. John on the booze, the lubras slacking off.'

As the boys carried their plates into the kitchen Sally said to him softly, 'I feel guilty I haven't kept everyone in line. How is Lorna going to take this? I feel so badly the accident happened while she was away.'

'It was not your fault, Sally. Accidents happen. But she's bound to have a few choice words to say. She'll blame the boozing. I'm the one who feels like shit. I was sober. I went along to keep an eye on everyone. Didn't do much of a job.'

'Rob, please, don't feel badly. What could you have done differently? It sounded like it was all so fast.'

'Bit late for if onlys . . .'

'I'd better make sure everything is in order, Lorna's such a neat freak.' Sally tried to sound brisk and efficient, then she hesitated. 'Where is she? Gloria.'

'They took her to the men's quarters, but the Flying Doctor is taking her now.' He grabbed his hat and went outside.

The two black women finally shuffled back to the house to clean up, bake bread and do the laundry, rolling their eyes and shaking their heads. Fitzi spoke firmly to them in pidgin then disappeared. Sally left the boys working in the school room, spruced up in clean shirts, polished boots and combed hair. None of the children from the camp had appeared.

Sally drove to the plane feeling nervous. She hadn't seen John Monroe since he'd left to see the Flying Doctor at breakfast. The plane had stayed for over an hour, and John had taken the police officer down to the river.

She watched Donny taxi the Cessna and wait till the props stopped spinning before he jumped down to open the passenger door. Sally was really looking forward to their picnic when he flew in next week and hoped Lorna would agree to let her have a couple of hours off. The pressure of the last twenty-four hours was telling on her and a break would be good.

Lorna stepped down looking smart as always. Sally went to greet her and take her hatbox as Donny opened the hold.

The older woman gave her a brief hug then her mouth set in a tight line. 'Dreadful business. It was a stroke of luck I was on my way home anyway. Donny, bless him, agreed to bring me back early. How are the boys?'

'Absolutely fine. They've been kept well away from the whole thing as much as possible. We were asleep when it . . . happened,' her voice faltered and Lorna touched her arm.

'Thanks for staying with the boys. I can imagine the scenario. Was John down at the single men's quarters?'

'Well, yes. A few drinks after dinner . . .' Her voice

trailed off and Sally glanced at Donny, who was keeping his distance, putting Lorna's luggage into the Land Rover.

Lorna sighed. 'It's all right, Sally. I'll deal with it.'

'How was the trip?'

For a moment Lorna's face softened then tightened again. 'Lovely. I brought you back a present. And I have some news, but it can wait.'

'Anything else I can do, Lorna?' Donny leaned on the vehicle.

'You've been so kind, as always.' She smiled at him.

'I thought I'd take Sally for a bit of a picnic next week. Can she have an hour or so off?' He spoke easily so refusal would seem unsporting.

Lorna pursed her lips again then shrugged. 'I imagine you're due for a break after the past week or so. I'm sure it will be okay.'

'I'll just have to tell everyone so my regulars aren't waiting out at the strip.'

Sally felt uncomfortable. 'It doesn't matter, Lorna, unless the boys want to come along too?'

Lorna got into the passenger seat, lifting her skirt away from the door, a faintly amused look on her face. 'Oh, I don't think Donny planned on that. See you again, Donny. Thanks for everything.'

They drove in silence towards the homestead and as the stables came into view Lorna touched Sally's hand on the steering wheel. 'Stop here, Sally. In case we don't have a quiet moment together for a bit.'

Sally turned off the engine. 'What is it?'

Lorna looked distracted and turned to stare across the home paddock. She spoke almost to herself. 'I wish I wasn't here.'

'Why? What's wrong? Did something happen in Sydney?' Sally was concerned. She'd never seen Lorna quite like this.

Lorna slowly looked around to face Sally, folding her hands on top of the leather handbag on her lap. 'I'm pregnant. Again. I thought I might be when you first arrived.'

'Oh!' Sally was shocked and didn't know how to react. 'That's great! I mean, that's good, isn't it? Maybe a little girl. The boys would like that.' She was babbling. She bit her lip.

'I suppose so. It means John will stop trying to jump on me, at least. But it also means I'm tied here even more.'

'Can't you go to Brisbane or Sydney and have the baby? Is there a problem?' Sally thought Lorna was too old for this. She must be nearly forty at least.

'My age is a concern. John won't care one way or the other, whether it's a girl I mean. The boys might be worried if it's another son. That would mean splitting up the property even more.'

'Oh.' Sally thought of her sister Yvonne and herself and wondered what her father planned to do in his will. She'd never had such thoughts before.

'I'll help you all I can. In the house, I mean. Are you supposed to rest?'

'The usual. I don't want you to feel obligated in any way about staying on here.'

'I like it here and I'm still on contract. For as long as you like, Lorna.'

'Thank you. But any time you get fed up – remember you haven't been here for the Wet – you tell me and you go home.'

'Ah, New Zealand seems a bit small these days,' laughed Sally, starting the engine again.

'We'll give you a nice holiday soon enough. We'd better think about that before the Wet and while I'm still fairly mobile.'

'Sounds good.' Sally drove on feeling confused, wondering how the boys would take their mother's news.

'Sally, don't say anything. I haven't told John yet.'

Sally didn't see the reunion between husband and wife, but John Monroe appeared at lunchtime immaculately dressed and wearing his best sandals. Rob wore a clean shirt and the silver buckle on his plaited belt had been given a polish. Both were subdued, though it seemed to Sally that John was being solicitous to Lorna. Whether it was because she'd told him about the baby or to avoid getting an ear bashing over the drinking and accident, Sally wasn't sure.

Rob took her to one side before they sat down and whispered, 'Don't talk about the race with Ian, Lorna's not impressed.'

The boys were back at their small table and the adults listened to Lorna quietly talk of changes in Sydney. All avoided the subject of Gloria's death.

'Don't tell me you didn't shop,' said John.

'I did stock up on a few things. And I bought a few presents.'

John rolled his eyes. 'I knew it. You going to stack them away or do we get 'em early?'

'I don't think it's very appropriate at the moment, given how Snowy and the men must feel,' she answered stiffly. Then seeing the disappointment on the boys' faces she added, 'Maybe before bedtime tonight. Just a small thing each.'

'I hope you brought something back for the governess here,' said John, looking at Sally. 'She's had her work cut out for her trying to keep those lubras in line.'

'I think I need pidgin lessons,' said Sally.

'No you don't,' Lorna shot back. 'They understand

perfectly well, there's no need to lower yourself to their level. Get Fitzi to speak to them in the house, or Snowy in the yards if there's no one else around.'

'Yes, Lorna,' said Sally meekly.

'We can manage, don't you concern yourself with yard work and such, Lorna,' said John and when Rob gave him a strange look, Lorna smiled.

'I've told John and the boys, and Sally, that I'm expecting.'

Sally glanced at the boys knowing they were busting to talk to her about it and Rob looked shocked but quickly recovered. 'Congratulations, great news. Lovely surprise.'

John pushed back his chair looking smug.

Sally glanced at Rob, who avoided looking at her. Lorna's expression was stern, and Sally had the feeling there was an undercurrent at the table she didn't understand.

'I'll go and unpack. See you before dinner, okay boys?' said Lorna. 'I might have a surprise or three.'

'How about we go for a short ride, then back to the schoolhouse and finish the arithmetic?' suggested Sally.

Lorna turned in the doorway. 'I trust this will be a sedate ride. No dangerous racing. I do not want any more accidents around here, if you please.' She left and the boys and Sally grimaced, knowing they were in trouble.

'What's happening about Gloria? Where's her family?' Sally asked Rob.

'No one seems to know. Snowy said Dougie and Harry thought she had a sister down south.'

'How are they taking it?'

'They're still shaken. I gather Snowy and the two of them are going back to the river tonight.'

'To get the croc? Do you think they will?'

'They're going to try bloody hard. The creepy thing

194

is that Snowy reckons it's a bull; he said Gloria was menstruating. It's not the first time a bull croc has gone after a woman when she's bleeding.'

As they walked the horses from the stables, Sally spoke to Ian. 'I should never have agreed to that silly race. Your mother is right, you could have had an accident. Or I could have. If anything had happened to you I'd never forgive myself.'

Ian looked mollified but tried to shrug it off. 'Doesn't matter. It wasn't anything that special anyway. Mum treats me like a baby, so does Dad.'

Sally let that slide and changed the subject. 'So what do you fellows think of the idea of a new baby round here?'

'Nice, I guess,' said Marty. 'I won't be the youngest any more.'

'Isn't Mum too old? She's so tired all the time. Will you look after the baby, Sally?' asked Tommy.

'Hey! I'm the governess remember, not a baby nurse. Your mum will get help, I'm sure.'

'Hope it's not a boy,' muttered Ian.

'Why? Do you like the idea of a little sister?'

'Nah, but Dad might change his mind and leave Barra Creek to the new kid.'

'Rubbish. Why would he do that?' said Sally, thinking as she often did about how threatened and antagonistic Ian felt towards his father.

'He always says that when he's mad at Ian,' said Tommy.

'Ah, don't take any notice. That's just to shake you up. C'mon, let's go over to the home paddock and see the calves.' Sally wanted to distract them. These boys were worrying far beyond their years. It wasn't fair.

For dinner that night John and Rob had brought in fresh meat from a killer and cooked it over the open fire outside. They gathered for drinks before dinner and Lorna handed out the presents – new boots for the boys, a new hat and Bonds white T-shirts for John, good shampoo, French soap and deodorant for Sally. She also gave her a set of wire hair curlers and a bottle of Napro hair crème.

'Take care of your hair, Sally, it looks very dry. Toby, my hairdresser friend, thought this might brighten up your auburn highlights.' She added a floppy cotton hat to shade Sally's face and a pile of glossy overseas fashion magazines. For the house she'd bought new bunches of silk flowers and black and white embroidered cushion covers. She handed Rob a big box of Darrell Lea chocolates to share with the boys. If it hadn't been for the shadow of Gloria's death hanging over them, the meal could almost have been festive. They were all aware that down on the dark river Snowy and the two bore runners were looking to trap Gloria's killer by setting a snare.

In a pause during the meal Lorna raised the issue of holidays and John exploded. 'Christ, Lorna! You haven't been back twenty-four hours and you want to take off again!'

'I was thinking of the boys and Sally. There's a school break soon, and it makes sense to travel before I get too cumbersome.'

'We always go away at Christmas. If we can get out in the Wet.'

'That's still a long way off.'

'You lot go then. I'm too busy.'

'We don't have to go away, Mum,' Ian spoke up. 'It's more fun here if we don't have school.'

'I don't need a big holiday,' said Sally. 'A couple of hours off next week for the picnic with Donny sounds good to me.'

'Where's he taking you?' asked Rob.

Monroe leered at Sally. 'Sneaking off for a skinny dip in a billabong somewhere, eh?'

'We're not sneaking off, every station on the mail route knows,' said Sally.

'Donny is very thoughtful,' said Lorna.

'Yeah, isn't he just,' mimicked John Monroe.

'Can we go too?' asked Marty.

'No,' said Lorna.

Rob leaned back in his chair. 'I was thinking I'd go bush again, trap some brumbies.'

'When did you decide this?' Monroe asked. 'If there's a mob been spotted I want to know about it.'

'How long you going for?' asked Ian.

'Depends where they are. Two weeks maybe.'

Lorna put her knife and fork together in the centre of her plate and dabbed her mouth with her napkin. 'I'm going to book that holiday, somewhere on the coast. Sally can have a few days on her own in Darwin then join us.'

'Why'd I want to go there on my own?' asked Sally in surprise. She was thinking about Sean. Darwin sounded a long way from Christchurch, she doubted he'd travel that far for a few days.

'You need a holiday away from all of us as much as getting away from Barra Creek,' said Lorna.

'So I'm driving, am I?' John Monroe looked resigned. 'Where're we going?'

'I haven't decided yet. You shouldn't care, you spend your time in pubs and restaurants anyway,' said Lorna. 'And it won't be for a few weeks at least.'

There was silence at the table as Lizzie came in to take the plates away.

'Can we have a chocolate now, please?' asked Marty.

Lorna excused herself. 'Yes, you may. I'm going to sit outside for a little while. Sally, do you want to join me?'

Sally walked over to the boys' table. 'Don't pester Rob for chocolates. I want to come back in soon and find you cleaned up, ready for bed. Then a story.'

'I'll do the story tonight, if you like,' offered Rob, and immediately the boys jumped to their feet, clamouring for his attention.

John Monroe topped up his rum and sank into a chair, turning up the wireless to catch the relay broadcast of the ABC news.

'I know it's been hard on you, Sally, with me being away. Especially with the accident. No matter what happens round here, remember my sons always come first. That's your main responsibility.'

'Of course.'

'I want you to take a holiday. The Wet is a hard season, and the run up to it when it's humid, muggy, oppressive is not easy either. Tempers get short.'

'Whatever you say, Lorna. So when should I go?'

'Next month.'

'I don't know anyone in Darwin. What's it like?'

'All the governesses go there. It can be a bit of a wild town, but there're lots of young people. I'm sure you'll be sensible about things. We'll put you up at the Darwin Hotel, it's very nice. Reminiscent of Raffles Hotel in Singapore.'

As the Monroes were paying for the trip Sally didn't argue. There'd be enough time to see if Sean could meet her there. She started to look forward to the idea. 'So how did the boys react to the news about the baby?'

'They haven't said much. It's all too far away. It won't register with them till it's here.'

'A girl?'

Lorna allowed herself a soft smile. 'I hope so.' Then

she sighed. 'Of course I'm not the only one expecting around here.'

'Really? You mean one of the lubras?'

Lorna didn't look pleased. 'Yes. Young Betsy.' She was about to say something more when John Monroe stuck his head out of the living room.

'Guess what? Camel Head Races have been moved up. I reckon we should go. It's next week, what do you say?'

'The boys would like it,' said Lorna. 'Maybe we should do that instead of going to the coast. It certainly is fun.'

'Sally, you'll love it. You'll never see riding anywhere like this, there's a rodeo too. It's not the Melbourne Cup but it runs a close second,' said John, pleased with his idea. 'Eating, drinking, dancing, betting, competitions, goes on for days. You're up to it aren't you, Lorn?' he asked, remembering her condition.

Later as Lorna sat on the edge of her bed in her nightgown, brushing her hair, John appeared around the partition.

'You all right?'

'For the moment. Ask me again in a few months.'

'This baby is a bit of a surprise, eh? A nice one though.' He gave a brief smile.

'I'm glad you think so.'

'Anything you want, Lorna, just ask. The races is a good idea, eh?'

'I still think Sally should get away to Darwin and be with people her own age. She's the best we've ever had. I don't want to lose her.'

'That's for sure.'

'John, keep Rob away from her. He's a nice boy, but not for the likes of Sally.'

'What d'you mean? There's nothing going on, is

there?' He sounded surprised at the idea and a little annoyed. 'He can get too big for his boots, if you ask me. I think you made a mistake inviting him into the house. He's just a bloody contract musterer. He works for me.'

'He comes from a very good home, he's as educated as you are and runs his own business. Don't talk down to him,' snapped Lorna. 'Until Rob came along, I didn't have much company.'

John opened his mouth to say something but closed it and kept the thought to himself. If she wanted to talk about feelings and books and music with Donny and Rob, good luck to her. He'd talk horses with Sally any day. He'd keep an eye on Rob and Sally. John knew that word had spread about the Monroes' attractive governess who could ride better than a lot of the men. 'You tell her to watch out for the blokes then.'

'If she was my daughter so far from home, I'd hope the family she was working for would be protective of her. Sally comes from a very good family. You can tell,' said Lorna. 'Breeding shows.'

John looked down at the floor. 'I s'pose you want a daughter.'

'It would be nice. You have the boys. They'll keep Barra Creek going.'

He was silent a minute then lifted his gaze. 'That's going to be a problem. We'll see how they develop. Dividing the property isn't on the agenda. They'll have to learn to work together.'

'What are you saying? That the three boys will have to run this place when we're not here? Together? Even if they're married with their own families? That might work for some but not our boys. They're too different.' She closed her eyes as if in pain, then began brushing her hair again. 'It's a long way off. Forget I mentioned it.'

He turned away. 'Goodnight, Lorn.'

'Goodnight.' She put down the hairbrush and swung her legs onto the bed, laying her arm over her eyes. Dear Lord, she prayed, please let my boys find their path in life, be fairly treated and be happy. Would it be possible for them to run the farm together, she wondered. It worked for some families. The man she'd married was a complex, contradictory person. She ached for her sons.

In the morning Lorna seemed refreshed. Rather than stay in bed and wait for her cup of tea, she was up not long after Sally and the boys.

John gave Sally a wink at breakfast. 'Look out, Lorna's on the warpath.'

Life settled back into its routine with the lure of the race meeting as the only excitement on the horizon. Rob left a few days before Sally and the Monroes, driving his ute with his dogs, swag and supplies in the back. He was planning to stop at a station along the way to discuss a mustering contract they had offered him for the following year before meeting them at the races. Dougie and Harry also left to start work on a job for the station adjoining Barra Creek. In the back of their ute was the rolled and salted giant bull croc skin.

Once while she was out riding near the river, Sally wondered who had mourned Gloria, if she had a family somewhere. It was only a passing thought, though the river still gave her the shivers.

It was arranged that Donny would charter a bigger plane and fly the family to the Camel Head Races near the Gilbert River. He'd been hankering to go to the races for the past few years, so he was happy to take leave from his mail run to go along.

Sally hadn't minded that they'd postponed their picnic. The races sounded like a fun diversion.

Up in the air John Monroe, sitting next to Sally, shouted in her ear, 'Who knows how many wild cattle are down there! I tell you though, Sal, I reckon the writing is on the wall for those big holdings, the old ways are going. No one can compete with government meddling and so-called development.'

They flew over the temporary township that had grown up for the races. There were clustered encampments of canvas, bough shelters, temporary wood shelters, the fenced racecourse, judges' box, and a rough and ready grandstand. Big tents served as the dance hall, mess hall and bar. A dam, windmill and cattle yards were part of this spread that was fourteen miles away from the main homestead. Light aircraft and vehicles were parked next to grazing horses.

As Donny circled, Sally counted nearly thirty campsites. 'How many people are here?'

'Several hundred, plus the blacks and all their mobs.'

'How are they all being fed?'

'We'll eat our way through several bullocks and wash it down with tanks of rum,' said John.

They landed and were soon settled in to one of the big tents. The three boys quickly met friends their own age from other stations who they had talked to on the wireless. People were still coming in from all directions. They'd come long distances and made it a special occasion. From the backs of vehicles came tables and chairs, cooler boxes, even a playpen or two for the babies. One family arrived on packhorses, a child and baby tucked into the saddle bags on one horse.

The jackeroos and ringers were dressed to the nines in new RM Williams gear with big buckles, polished boots and new Akubras. Sally had been dubious about the clothes Lorna said she should bring but many of the women had gone to town with frilly frocks, heels and hats, though most seemed to favour shirtmaker dresses and white shoes that were soon covered in dust. A lot of younger women stuck to their casual clothes but Sally enjoyed wearing a good sundress, her pearls, her gold sandals, smart sunglasses and make-up. She'd eschewed a hat, knotting a silk scarf over her hair. Lorna, as always, was impeccably dressed, in a loose linen skirt, silk blouse with a matching linen bolero jacket – understated but smart.

The predominantly black jockeys, garishly dressed in brilliant silks, were skilled riders, but it seemed that almost anyone with a horse was prepared to have a go. And everyone wagered accordingly. Odds were short, betting frenzied. The two bookies looked frayed around the edges and both had raucous gravelly voices. They set up business beneath faded beach umbrellas, stuffing money and tickets into their worn leather bags.

The bartenders in the long bar next to the racecourse were run off their feet serving keg beer, rum and warm fizzy soft drinks. In the mess tent, food was served non-stop. You could eat steak and eggs with fried onions for breakfast and morning and afternoon tea as well as dinner. Fried potatoes were optional. Bread was tipped out of camp ovens and slabs of it were served with meals or with golden syrup any time. The hours merged. People drank through the night to sit down to rum with breakfast. There was a grubby, rickety merry-go-round and a fairy floss stand heavily patronised by the black kids.

Rob found the Monroes and threw his swag down on the ground next to the tent Sally would be sharing with the boys.

'I've never seen anything like this,' she laughed.

'Wait till you see Rob ride in the rodeo,' said Tommy.

'Are you going to go in the gibber races?' Marty asked Sally.

'There are foot races after the rodeo,' explained Rob. 'Anything from rock and spoon, sack races, three legged and the ladies' barefoot run. The women dash across a track, maybe a hundred yards or so, in their best gear but they take off their shoes and stockings first.'

'It's over gibber stones,' said Ian.

Sally knew how sharp the hard little stones could be. 'I'm not going in that.'

'There a big dance tonight, you mustn't miss it.' Rob grinned at her.

'Can we come?' asked Tommy.

'You bet,' said Rob.

The five-piece band thumped into the wee hours as the dust rose from the swinging high-heeled boots of the men and shoes of the women. Men wore their denim trousers and coloured shirts, sleeves tightly rolled up over muscles. Skirts swirled as the girls were spun, and everyone laughed and squealed above the music. Sally danced with the boys, with Rob, Donny, John and a string of young men.

The men made frequent forays to the bar and no one seemed to mind that they were eating steaks at four in the morning. A cheerful young waitress slapped food onto the tables announcing she hadn't slept in two days, hadn't laughed so much in a year and wanted a couple of matchsticks to keep her eyes open. Fortified with rum, Sally, Rob and Donny sang their way back to their camp.

Lorna spent time with some women from other stations, chatting and laughing. The boys finally fell into their swags as Sally and Rob followed them back to the tents. John settled down at a campfire with old friends from all over the Gulf, Cape and Territory swapping yarns and drinking themselves into oblivion.

The following day was the rodeo and Sally watched the cattle and horses being brought into the pens and wondered at the wisdom of the hung-over stockmen preparing to ride these rough beasts. There was a big crowd, and the MC stood on the back of a truck with a microphone, screaming descriptions and encouragement at the mayhem in the main ring. All the blacks gathered on the far side of the ring to laugh and applaud. While they were there to help out when needed, their skill as jockeys acknowledged, they didn't mix with the whites. Whites and blacks, station owners and managers, stockmen, jackeroos and ringers, all had their own areas.

As the rodeo got under way hell-bent riders raced after maddened steers. The buckjumping was violent and wild, the pick-up men in the ring swift to pluck a rider to safety and wave away a beast determined to trample the men who dared to straddle their backs. Rob pulled on his spurs and carefully lowered himself onto a mean-eyed steer with a set of dangerous horns. Released from the chute into the ring the animal twisted and leapt, then tried to scrape Rob from his back against the rails. Deflected by the pick-up men the steer bucked around the ring in a crazed dance until a metal clang announced that Rob had gone the distance. He scrambled over the rails and Sally and the boys rushed to slap him on the back.

Egged on by John Monroe and the three boys, Sally entered the rock and spoon race, and won the sack race to uphold the honour of Barra Creek.

The days and nights were a blur and finally even John Monroe had had enough rum and fun. They took off into a clear sky, a wedge-tailed eagle angling away from the

aircraft as it rose above the township, which was folding its tents and packing up for another year. The plains
stretched to the horizon, broken only by the lines of cattle tracks radiating from waterholes. Sally had enjoyed
herself enormously and had to smile as she thought back
on the smart races she'd attended in Christchurch and the
regimented formality of the hunts.

Lorna's laughter and relaxed manner disappeared once
they returned to Barra Creek. She stalked through the
house and gardens, quietly but firmly issuing instructions, directing tasks. The night before Sally's picnic with
Donny, as she and Lorna discussed what food to take,
Rob came into the kitchen.

'Lorna, I need to get stores. I'm heading out to trap
brumbies and I'm taking six of my fellas. We'll probably
leave at the end of the week.'

'I suppose John is going.'

Rob gave a small shrug, a little embarrassed that
Monroe hadn't told his wife but he wasn't surprised.
Lorna, no doubt, was used to it.

'We'll miss you round the place,' said Sally with a
smile.

'Ah, plenty of company round here. Foxy the bore
mechanic is coming in for a day or so,' he said. 'He needs
spare parts and tucker.'

'I don't imagine Sally will be interested in passing
the time of day with that dreadful man,' Lorna said
tartly.

'He's handy. Keeps those bores flowing. You can't
expect everyone to have charm, patience and time on his
hands, like Donny.' He gave a wink and picked up the
box of bread for his camp. 'See you later.'

'Well, if they're going to be away for a week or so,

we'll have some peace and quiet.' Sally didn't comment and Lorna continued to slice the fruit cake. 'Once the boys know about the brumby trapping they'll probably want to go, especially Ian.'

'Could they go along? The two big boys?'

'I'll have to think about it. Let's see if they raise the idea. Marty would hate to be left behind. Now he's no longer going to be the baby of the family, he's trying to keep up with his brothers.'

Sally had her swimsuit on under her sunfrock and was wearing her fancy catseye sunglasses and gold sandals but despite Lorna giving her a cotton sunhat, she'd chosen one of Ian's old Akubras to shade her face and protect her hair.

Donny looked different as he grinned at her and took the box of food. Then she realised he wasn't wearing his usual uniform of navy shorts and white shirt and his pilot's cap, but casual shorts and T-shirt and sandals instead of his leather shoes and long white socks.

'All ready?' He helped her into the passenger seat.

'I certainly am.' She buckled her seat belt as he got in and slammed the pilot's door closed.

It was almost impossible to talk over the noise of the engine. Sally enjoyed the scenery but the gap where her door met the body of the plane made her nervous as daylight and a cold draught came through.

The nose of the plane dipped slightly. Raising his voice Donny said, 'Look down there, that's where we're going.'

'Looks like jungle to me! Where will we land?'

'There's a deserted strip that was part of a mining enterprise that failed. Gold, tin or something. There's a shack, a strip and a truck we all keep in working order.'

'We?'

'Those of us who know about it. Serious fun seekers – fishermen, shooters, buffalo and boar hunters. Don't blab, you're one of us now,' he shouted.

'God, I've no idea where we are. Is that a track down there?' She peered at the thin red line weaving between trees, an open plain and lush wetland around a watercourse of some kind.

'Yes. Flying in is much easier.' He banked and aimed the plane at what Sally could now see was a roughly cleared stretch of land. 'It's a bit bumpy but don't worry.'

'How do you keep it cleared?' She clutched her seat as they hit the ground, which was studded with small rocks.

'Drag a log behind the truck. Here we are.'

Sally stepped down and saw a rusty galvanised lean-to, an ancient Bedford truck, some oil and petrol drums, rusting equipment and an upturned dinghy. She thought she was used to silence after spending months at Barra Creek, but here it was oppressively quiet. There were no sounds of men, the blacks' camp, horses or cattle. A bird screeched and she jumped.

'Crikey, this is the middle of nowhere.'

'Perfect place for a murder, isn't it? No one would ever find a body out here.'

Sally went cold for a moment. Were all her instincts wrong? Then she thought of Lorna and John, encouraging her to take a few hours off and go flying with Donny.

'I always think about it when I come here,' said Donny, unloading gear from the hold. 'I wonder about some of the blokes who camp out here, get on the piss, have an argument . . .'

'Could we talk about something else. Like where's this famous swimming hole?'

'Okay, throw the food and that swag into the tray

of the truck. I'll bring the drinks. There're towels and a blanket to sit on in the swag.'

It took a bit to start the truck as it hadn't been driven for a while, but eventually he got it going. They drove through the bush, Donny's unerring sense of direction taking them in fifteen minutes to a clearing. They got out and she followed him, ducking beneath giant pandanus and paperbark trees, through knee-high grass to the edge of a huge billabong. It was beautiful. The water was clear green, dotted with blue waterlilies. There was a red sandy bank partly shaded, which was a perfect spot to picnic.

'This is gorgeous.'

Sally spread out the swag with the blanket and towels while Donny tied the box of food into the fork of a tree branch away from ants.

'Right, let's swim. This water is like a bath.'

'You're sure it's safe?'

He swung his arms around in an arc encompassing the remote landscape. 'No river, or crocodiles, for miles. Wait till the Wet though, all the waterholes link up, it's amazing. That's when a croc might get up this far.'

Sally gingerly followed him into the water, stroking quickly into the centre away from the reeds fringing the edge that could be hiding goodness knows what creatures. Gradually the sheer pleasure of the caressing water, the tranquil setting and Donny's easy company relaxed her and she felt the tension of the last weeks flow from her body.

Lying on the blanket, drying in the sun as Donny set out the picnic, her hat over her face, Sally sighed contentedly. 'This is so great. It's hard to really relax when I always have to be watching the boys.'

'So enjoy this little break, until you take your holiday. Ever been to Darwin?'

She lifted her hat and glanced at him. Did Lorna discuss everything with Donny before making a decision, she wondered. She hadn't mentioned her trip to him while they were at the races.

'I suppose when you have your sights set on the bright lights of London, Darwin doesn't cross your radar,' he said.

'I don't want to go there at all. I don't feel the need to get away. I'm still discovering this area, like today.'

'I s'pose Lorna thinks it will do you good. After Gloria's accident and all that.'

'She tells you a lot, doesn't she?'

'Yes, we chat,' he said easily. 'She didn't have anyone much to talk to about things, until you came along.'

'So what else did she say? How am I doing?' Sally sat up and although she was smiling her voice was challenging.

'As a governess? Top marks.'

'But? It sounds like a but is hanging in there.'

He looked at her, his face more serious. 'She's worried about Rob.'

'Rob? What's he got to do with me?'

'She's worried you two might have a fling.'

'If we do, it's nothing to do with her!'

'Yes it is. She feels some responsibility towards you, besides it could be very disruptive. And more importantly he's not good enough for you!'

'She said that?' Sally was both irritated and flattered. 'She doesn't mind him eating with the family or playing with the boys.'

'Lorna is a snob. I like her enormously, but she has her standards as I'm sure you know. Rob doesn't have his own place. That's important to Lorna. It's the difference between managing a property and owning one.'

'I gather he had a blue with his father and he went out on his own. That's admirable, isn't it? Anyway, I'm not here for romance. I don't want it to bugger up a nice friendship, with anyone,' she added pointedly.

'So how's the lover left at home? Still pining?'

'I doubt it. But he does send me sexy letters, and he says he misses me.'

'Is he going to Darwin?'

Sally laughed. 'You're one step ahead of me. I was thinking I'd ask him. There's not much time, though. And I don't want the whole of Cape York to know about it if I ring him up or send him a telegram.'

'I could send it for you. Write it out and I'll send it from Cloncurry with my return address.'

'Why would you do that for me?'

'Why not? Pals help each other, right?'

'Okay, be cupid. Thanks. Darwin sounds a bit dull on my own.'

'The place has a lot of drawbacks but dull isn't one of them. You and whatsisname will have a ball.'

'His name is Sean.'

They were silent for a while and Sally thought back to her romance with Sean. How distant and unreal it seemed. Or was it that this place and her life in it seemed so unreal. Her parents – and Sean probably – couldn't imagine what it was like. She smiled, remembering how she'd jumped on the mail plane for the last long leg of her trip up here with no idea of where she was going or what it would be like.

'What are you smiling about? Fond memories of Sean, eh?'

'No. Actually I was thinking about first coming up here with you. How unprepared and naive I was.'

'Yeah. How do you feel now?'

'Still a bit of a greenhorn but I've struck a few blows. I won that damned horse race. It was stupid to do it because of Ian, but now the lot of 'em want to borrow my saddle. They think it makes the horses go faster. Everyone wants to be a jockey.'

'Be careful though, Sal, you walk a fine line between being an employee and part of the family. Lorna is a fierce lioness as far as her cubs are concerned.'

'You know her news?'

'Yes. It's lovely, but it might take a bit of a toll. I don't think Lorna's health is one hundred per cent. She's more suited to a grand drawing room in town than a cattle station.'

'She does seem to miss the culture, concerts and so on.'

'Yes, she loves music,' said Donny.

'I like dancing, I enjoyed myself at the races.'

'Then you've got something to look forward to – dancing under the moon in Darwin with Sean.'

She started to feel a quiver of excitement at the thought of handsome Sean dashing up to Darwin to meet her for a romantic interlude. She closed her eyes and fantasised in the sun.

When they landed the boys were there to meet her, Ian driving the Land Rover. After giving them time to climb over the plane, sit in the pilot's seat and chat to Donny, Sally thanked him and they watched him take off. Then the three boys jumped around her.

'Dad says we can go brumby trapping!'

'Rob says there's a big mob out by the gorge.'

'Dad says we're leaving on Friday.'

'But you have to come too. Otherwise we can't go.'

'What?' Sally looked at the three excited faces. 'What's your mum say?'

'She says okay. She wants a rest.'

Sally gave Marty, sitting on her lap, a quick hug.

'Well, brumby trapping it is then. I'll have to ask Rob to tell me how it all works,' she said and felt Marty stiffen. He looked at Tommy, but Ian answered.

'He's a bit crook about us going. Says we shouldn't go, it's too dangerous.'

'We really want to go, Sally.'

'Then we're going,' she said, and meant it.

Chapter Eleven

LORNA STOOD IN THE cool shadows of the verandah watching her three boys and Sally sort through what they were taking on their ride the following day. Rob was supervising the swags, rations, clothes and gear spread over the front lawn.

'You're each responsible for your own stuff. What you leave behind, stays behind. Yella-fella Bluey will be keeping an eye on you, and you obey anything he says. Wally is camp cook and in charge of the trap. Your dad will come along in the truck to herd the animals down to the water.'

'I don't understand how it works,' said Sally.

'There's plenty of time to explain. When you're on horseback you are in charge of your horse – its safety, saddling, hobbling, watering and feed. Clear enough?'

The boys nodded and Sally cheekily saluted. 'Aye, aye captain.'

'Don't be flippant, Sally, this is dangerous work. You're there to watch out for these three.'

'Of course. I understand that,' she said, somewhat chastened.

Sally's banter was a veneer over the fear she felt. She knew enough about horses to imagine how wild stallions, some never having seen humans, protective of their harems, could react in a stressful situation. She'd have to keep her wits about her, knowing what little cowboys the three youngsters could be when they were on horseback.

A scuffle broke out between Ian and Marty who were both tugging at Marty's blanket.

'No, stop it. Leave it!' shouted Marty.

'I saw it. Don't be a baby,' teased Ian. 'Baby, baby, baby.'

Sally stepped in and separated them, realising what Marty was hiding. She crouched down in front of him. 'Did Pooh want to come too?'

Marty nodded, looking at his boots.

'There's nothing wrong with keeping something very special close to you,' said Sally gently. 'See, I have a little kiwi a good friend gave me.' She pulled out a silver chain from inside her shirt with a good luck charm on it that Sean had given her. 'And Rob has his special silver belt buckle.'

'That's different. A teddy bear is baby stuff,' sneered Ian.

'Pooh Bear isn't just a teddy bear,' said Marty crossly. The little bear was a special talisman for him.

Sally knew that at eight years old he was possibly too old to cling to his Pooh Bear. 'Tell you what, Marty. Sounds like it's going to be pretty rough where we're going. Might be a bit dangerous for Pooh. Why don't you leave him here with your mum? She can look after him and Pooh will keep her company while we're all away.'

He looked doubtful for a moment then gave a short nod and went over to his mother. He held out his worn

Pooh Bear with a stiff arm. 'Will you look after him, please, Mum?'

'Of course I will.' Lorna crouched down and reached for them both. 'I'll be very pleased to have him with me while you're gone. He'll keep me company.'

'I want him back though.' He hesitated. ''Course if the new baby wants my Pooh . . .'

'No, Marty. He's yours, always has been and always will be.' Marty had begged for the Pooh Bear after hearing the story and it was one of the few toys that hadn't been handed down to him. Lorna watched him run across the lawn with a twist in her heart. She had no doubt Pooh would eventually travel to boarding school in the bottom of Marty's luggage. At least when the boys left home she'd have a new child to fill the hole in her heart. Instinctively her hand went to the swell in her belly. 'Please, Lord, keep my children safe.' She tried not to think of the problems of what she'd been told could be a difficult childbirth and being so far from help.

The younger boys plunged into the bath that night with gusto, their shyness in front of Sally long forgotten. Tommy was out first. Dripping and naked he led them in a merry 'Aborigine dance' along the verandah, with Ian and Marty giggling and mimicking his emu antics. Sally chased after them, grabbing the slight figure of Marty and wrapping him in the towel in her arms.

He hugged her tightly, his damp hair against her cheek. 'This is going to be an adventure, isn't it, Sal?'

'I suppose so. You sure you want to go? No one will think you're chicken if you don't go. I'm worried about your mum being alone.'

'I really want to go, please. I don't want Dad and Ian to keep calling me a baby.'

'Oh, Marty, they don't think of you as a baby. You know how they are. They just don't want you to grow up.'

'Why?'

'It makes your dad feel older when his youngest child starts to think and act for himself. And Ian feels threatened too. It's natural. You just be yourself.'

He looked doubtful. 'But I don't want to grow up. I like being me.'

She rubbed the towel on his back. 'Marty, you always just be yourself and you'll be okay in this world.'

The dinner bell rang. Not the clanging cow bell John Monroe bashed for breakfast, but a discreet tinkle from the dining room. Lorna was getting impatient. She wanted them all to gather before dinner, this being their last meal together for a little while. Sally slicked the boys' hair, checked that their shirts were neatly tucked in and sent them ahead as she quickly looked at herself. The new shampoo and hair crème had made her hair shine with bright red-gold streaks, her complexion looked better and she was paying attention to her nails. She smoothed her dress, slipped on her sandals and walked into the living room where the family was gathered. Rob, in an ironed clean blue shirt and hair smoothed with Brylcreem, looked relaxed. Again Sally was struck by how much a part of this family he seemed. And it hit her that she too was finally fitting in, comfortable with life at Barra Creek. When she woke each morning now her thoughts turned to the day ahead rather than days back at home. She couldn't recall the last time she'd felt homesick.

Rob smiled at her and raised his glass. 'Cheers. I'll hold the memory of how you look now for the next couple of nights.'

'I might surprise you,' said Sally with a grin.

John Monroe handed her a rum. 'Sally is always full of surprises.'

She smiled at Lorna who gave her a look in that unspoken language women shared. It was a swift understanding of the difference between men and women, of women's sense of superiority, that men were simple creatures and that women understood each other's motives. Especially how easy it was to manipulate men.

This evening the boys were included in the pre-dinner drinks. Sitting in the living room, sipping their cordial, they endured the questioning of their father and the testing of manners from their mother. Shooting quick glances at Sally for approval, noting the faint shakes of her head if they weren't doing something right, they were on their best behaviour. This was the price they paid for being allowed to 'go wild' over the next few days.

Lorna insisted on playing a new LP record she'd brought from Sydney, by Nat King Cole, and as the boys sat with bored faces, Rob came to their rescue. He put down his glass and went to Sally, giving her a short bow.

'May I have the pleasure of the next dance?'

She smiled and rose. Rob swept her up and swung into a full dance, no half-hearted shuffling. The boys applauded as he spun her along the verandah.

'Go on, Dad,' sang out Marty.

John Monroe, looking as attractive as Lorna always remembered him, took up the challenge. 'You're as beautiful as the day I first saw you, Lorn. Shall we?' She stepped into his outstretched arms with a slight smile.

King's School had taught him well and he swung into a waltz. They spun and dipped to the claps of the boys.

'What did I ever do to deserve the likes of you?' John asked softly.

'You were just yourself, I guess.'

'With all my flaws and troubles?'

'I like to think I know what's in your heart, John. You're a good man.'

'Remind me more often, love.' He spun her around, the moment now lost.

'Careful,' she gasped. 'I don't want to fall.'

Rob and Sally danced back to the room after their circuit of the verandah and fell into their chairs as the boys laughed and cheered. Lizzie, looking somewhat taken aback, stood stiffly in the doorway.

'You wantum grub?'

'Yes, yes, put it on the table please, Lizzie,' laughed Lorna.

As the last track on the record played, Marty stepped shyly forward. 'Can I try, Mum?'

John poured drinks for Sally and Rob. Ian and Tommy went to their table as Lizzie carried in the food. And in the shadows on the verandah, Marty formally slipped his arm around his mother's waist, took her outstretched hand and, concentrating hard, counting to himself, solemnly danced with his mother.

This was the end of the dry season and the brumbies, desperate for water, were coming down from the surrounding hills to the waterhole on the boundary of Barra Creek's far western paddock, half a day's drive from the homestead. Two fences ran from the base of the small hill ten miles into the big waterhole that abutted the fence of this paddock. They made a direct funnel to the waterhole where the men had built a permanent trap. The fences corralling the water were partially pulled down when not in use. Rob and Wally had gone ahead a few days earlier to erect the trap yard and the bough hides where they would wait during the night until the brumbies came to water.

When they'd finished the trap they returned to the homestead to let the brumbies get used to coming down to the waterhole past the fences. They were suspicious creatures, and smart, but after several trips they became familiar with the look and smell of the fences, humans and the yard.

Rob, Sally and the boys set out to ride to the camp established by Bluey and Chilla. There was a campfire with the packhorses hobbled nearby, the men and their horses were settled under trees a short distance away. Everyone was prepared to move downwind at a moment's notice. John Monroe would drive out in the Land Rover two days later.

They arrived mid afternoon and Rob showed Sally and the boys the waterhole with the yards and the trap railing gates ready to be slammed in place once the brumbies went in.

'Tomorrow night we'll sit in the hide to see what mob turns up. If it's a decent group, we'll try to trap them the next night.'

'There's no water up there?' asked Ian.

'Nope, and the small waterholes close to the hills have dried up. This is the main watering place, always has been.'

'How many horses are out there?' asked Sally, looking at the silent, still landscape.

'Thousands. Some escaped from stations, most have bred in the wild, but John and some other station owners have released decent bloodstock over the years to build up the quality of the herds. This is payback time, we hope.'

'Sometimes they're mangy and scrappy, with no good horses in the mob,' explained Ian.

'Can we watch them being broken?' asked Tommy.

'It's a rough business, we geld the young colts straight-away. The breaking is pretty exciting.'

'Rodeo time, huh? Is that how you won your silver buckle?' Sally teased.

Rob didn't answer and swung his horse, leading them away from the marshy water.

That night, grouped around the campfire after their meal of salt beef and damper, the men started telling stories. The boys sat entranced as the stockmen told of ghosts, of mysterious murders, strange events, Aboriginal beliefs, great rides, bronco and buffalo busting, and accidents. Sally and Rob sat behind the ring around the fire, watching the light flicker over the faces of those who talked and those who listened. Sally was fascinated but Rob leaned near her and whispered, 'Don't believe a half of what you hear. Bushies' tall tales!'

'Don't disillusion me. I was intrigued by the mummified family.'

Bluey had told of working years back in the sandhill country. A sand storm had blown away half a sandhill showing something buried in it, so they dug and dug and found an old shack. Inside was a family sitting around a kitchen table. A sand storm had buried them alive and in the dry airless heat the bodies had mummified.

Rob shrugged. 'Could be true. Though these fellows tell some strange stories at times.'

Sally turned to say something and caught Rob looking at her. They were sitting close, the firelight catching a gleam in their hair, their faces in shadow, but their eyes bright. It hit her forcibly as if she'd been burned, how attractive, desirable, strong and dependable Rob looked. She closed her eyes for a second, almost winded.

'Are you all right?' He touched her arm and she felt again a searing tingle.

She nodded and scrambled to her feet. 'I have to go pee.' She could have kicked herself for saying something so common – as her mother would say. But it was all that came to her mind. She wanted to put a little distance between them, catch her breath. The sensation she felt shocked her.

'Take the torch and look where you walk.'

She headed into the darkness taking deep breaths. Why had such a feeling just hit her? She'd always liked Rob and, despite her first impressions, he was a handsome man. And a nice man. She respected him and enjoyed his company. She and Rob and the three boys were a solid unit in the face of John Monroe's bluster, Lorna's bouts of withdrawal and the unpredictable life at Barra Creek. While she hadn't thought of him exactly as a brotherly figure, she had always felt comfortable and secure around him. This wild spark of sexual electricity was unexpected and confusing. She turned the torch off and stood quietly. Glancing back she saw figures moving around the campfire as swags were unrolled. Glad of the diversion of settling the boys, she headed back.

The three boys, as usual, encircled her swag and she saw old Fitzi nod to them as he joined the group of stockmen who were settling down. Sally stood by the glowing embers, warming her hands.

Rob crouched down and stuck a length of wood rolled inside thick grass into the fire where it flared then glowed and smoked. 'I'm going down to the hide. See what kind of a mob turns up and if it's worth the trouble.'

'When do the horses come and drink?'

'Not long after moonrise, when it's bright. They feel safer. I want to get settled before then.'

'Can I come?' The words came naturally but Sally thought that her voice sounded strange.

Rob didn't seem to notice. 'Settle the boys and rug up, it'll be cold.'

He tested the wind direction and quietly told her the rules. 'No talking, no smoking, no strong odours.'

'John told me before I left not to wear any perfume, deodorant or use any fancy soap.'

'Right. I'll show you some hand signals. We'll be there for about two hours. If they haven't turned up by then, Wally will take the next shift.'

He was businesslike and, after checking the boys, Sally pulled on her fleece-lined jacket and gave a brief wave to the boys, rolled in their swags, their heads just visible. The campfire had been put out.

'Tell us how many brumbies there are, and pick out a good one for me,' whispered Ian.

Holding a smoke torch, which she waved in front to light her way and keep insects at bay, Sally followed Rob down to the waterhole. It took fifteen minutes through the open country following the fence line. Rob stopped as the dark water came into view and signalled for Sally to go to one side where, twenty yards away from the waterhole, she could see a little shelter made of brush and boughs.

Inside there was just enough room for the two of them to sit, leaning against a rock, and peer through gaps between the branches. They were on a slight rise, which gave them a good view of the hill and the waterhole in front of them. The boundary fences led from the base of the rocky, tree-studded hill straight to the yard around the waterhole. As Sally's eyes grew accustomed to the dim light she could make out the gates that would bar any exit when they were swung shut across the corridor.

They sat quietly, barely moving. She heard the rush of a bird's wings, the crackle of insects in the grass, the croak of a frog.

The proximity of Rob, hunched in his jacket, staring across the water, was becoming claustrophobic. Sally wished she hadn't come and hoped either the brumbies or Wally would come to relieve the building tension she felt in her body. She put her head on her knees, willing the suffocating sensation to pass, and Rob gently stroked her hair. She didn't move, didn't dare lift her head to look at him, but gradually she felt her neck and shoulders relax and the knot in her stomach loosen. Then he slid his hand onto her shoulder and pressed it firmly. Sally looked up. The moon was now shining across the still water, lighting the reeds and waterlilies around its bank. Rob tilted his head, listening, then she heard it too. A loose rock rolled, a gentle snort, a cracking twig. She imagined she could smell the horses. Shadowy movement on the hillside caught her attention. The pale glimmer of one shadow followed by others. The leader emerged alone into the clearing at the start of the run down to the water.

It was a bay stallion, about fifteen hands, broad chest, long neck and a huge proud head. He stood cautiously alert, testing the air with his ears and nostrils. Slowly he walked ahead, ears flattened, stopped and turned, pacing back and forth. Listening, sniffing the air that held smells his instinct told him were dangerous. Behind him Sally could now see his herd. The horses seemed to stand nonchalantly, waiting and trusting that their dominant male would signal when it was safe. Despite their thirst they would not step away before the stallion made the first move. Sally's heart was pounding, she was hardly breathing.

Slowly the stallion stepped closer to the water and stopped, lifting his head once more. His tail twitched. He knew something was not right. He walked slowly and deliberately down to the waterhole, lowered his head and sucked up huge draughts of water.

His mares and a couple of colts walked quietly forward. There was no noisy rush, but with a calm and steady tread they splashed into the marshy shallows to drink.

Rob and Sally counted, using the system Rob had shown her, Rob tapping her arm for every five horses he counted. The stallion had a herd of fifteen mares and two young colts. Some looked in poor condition but there was no doubt that several horses were big and strong. The colts would eventually challenge their leader and each other to be the dominant one. But for now the stallion was older, wiser and in charge.

As the mares held their muzzles in the water, the stallion lifted his head, took one last deep drink, turned and broke into a gallop, splashing through the water and causing a great silver spray as he raced from the waterhole and headed back to the safety of the hill. The herd and young horses galloped behind him in the moonlight, long tangled manes and tails waving as they pounded away, their unshod hooves smashing the grass and undergrowth.

Sally had never seen anything so magnificent and moving. As the brumbies thundered off she turned to Rob, too choked up to speak. He saw her expression, sensed her exhilaration and spontaneously leaned forward and kissed her smiling mouth. It was meant to be a quick kiss but to both their surprise the powerful effect of the light touching of their lips turned into a burning, hard, gasping, lingering passion. Eventually they drew apart, breathless and shocked.

'Sally . . .' Words failed him and he leant to her again.

The kissing was unrestrained.

Finally he whispered, 'We'd better get back. I'll tell Wally he can stay in his swag.' He was struggling to get back to normalcy.

They walked through the bush, which to Sally now seemed friendly and embracing. With the tall figure of Rob beside her, what harm could come to her? They held hands.

'It was exciting, wasn't it?' he said softly.

'Kissing?'

'Well, yes, that too. I meant the brumbies.'

The vision of the wild horses led by the stallion flashed again into her mind. 'Yes, it was. I'm looking forward to tomorrow night.' She gave him a look and they both laughed.

Rob suddenly sounded serious. 'It can be dangerous as well as exciting, Sal.'

'Don't worry, we'll be careful.' They knew the conversation could be interpreted two ways. They were stepping into uncharted territory. Rob dropped her hand as they came to the camp with the circle of sleeping figures.

'Everyone's asleep,' she whispered.

'Fitzi's not.'

She tried to see where the stockman had put his swag. 'How do you know?'

'I reckon John has told him to keep an eye on you, and me. And report back.'

'The bugger. I suppose it was Lorna's idea.'

Rob gave a small chuckle. 'Go to sleep, Sal.' Despite her self assurance, Sally was naive in many ways. It hadn't occurred to her that Monroe might find the young governess very appealing.

Rob crouched by Wally's swag and murmured, 'A good mob, eighteen. They're gone.'

'They'll be back tomorra,' he grunted sleepily and huddled further down in his swag.

They worked throughout the morning. John Monroe drove into the camp with tomatoes, fresh bread and a fruit cake, and Wally cooked up a big lunch. It would be a long night.

Mid afternoon, Monroe and Wally checked the fence

around the waterhole. The horses always drank at the same spot, not knowing they were surrounded in a triangle with the apex a narrow entry along the fence corridor. There was a giant tree stump in the middle of the track that the horses went past each time, unaware that the massive wooden gates could be swung from either side and latched onto the centre tree stump post, shutting them in. The men in charge of closing the gates and getting the sliprail in place had to move swiftly at the right moment.

Sally watched Rob go about his work and occasionally they exchanged secret smiles. The boys were everywhere, racing on horseback between the waterhole trap and the yards being readied for the brumbies.

'Where can we watch?' Tommy asked Rob.

'What about the top of the Land Rover? Then we could drive it down to the yards,' said Ian.

'Can we all squeeze in?' said Marty, worried he might be left behind.

'The country is too rough for you to drive, Ian,' said Sally.

Rob glanced away and Sally saw his expression tighten and knew their presence was worrying him. 'I'll stay with the boys. Do what you have to do,' she said quickly.

He gave her a relieved smile. 'Good. As soon as the horses are all locked up, come down. Don't get near the railings or climb up on them under any circumstances, understand? I've seen stallions throw themselves at the rails like they were climbing out. They're bloody dangerous. They're wild creatures, got it?'

The boys nodded.

'I'll see you when I see you, do as you're told, okay?'

'Pick me out a nice horse, Rob,' called Tommy, who

desperately wanted a special horse of his own and not just one of the stockhorse ponies. It was another sign of maturity when you had a horse that you looked after and rode exclusively.

As the light melted away the campfire was extinguished and the men drained their mugs of tea. Everyone took up their positions and made themselves comfortable to wait for the horses to come down. There was no talking, no smoking, everyone was to be still and patient. The boys, Sally and Wally were left close to the camp. John Monroe and Rob crouched in the rough brush hides on either side of the gates. Chilla and Bluey were out of sight at the waterhole, ready to throw up the sliprail as the horses headed back up the corridor to the safety of their hill. Rob sat hugging his knees, remembering Sally's kiss. Was it just the moment or was this the start of something? It would be tricky to indulge in a romance with the governess under the Monroes' roof.

John, sitting on the ground, reached for his silver hip flask and took a sip of rum. Further up the hill between the track taken by the horses and their rough campsite, where their own horses were hobbled, Fitzi waited. The men had spread out on either side of the corridor, out of sight, ready to spring to the yards once the horses were in.

It grew dark. Eyes turned anxiously to the sky, fearful the moonrise might be dulled by cloud. A change could mean the stallion might not bring his herd down. The slightest thing could spook them.

John Monroe had told Fitzi to wait and if the horses didn't appear after a reasonable time to check if they were around. He didn't want to spend unnecessary hours in the uncomfortable hide if the horses had left the hill.

The night sky cleared, the stars came out, the moon rose slowly, majestically.

A shadow in the immense silver landscape was barely noticeable. It drifted, reed like, one moment motionless, the next appearing in a different spot. No sudden movements, the figure of Fitzi blended in with the terrain, keeping upwind, making no sound, as light as the breath of night air, as alert as the wild night creatures. Fitzi saw the freshly trampled grass, could smell the horses, intuitively he sensed what their next move might be. He was at home in this country.

He faded into the stillness of the night knowing that soon the stallion would come down the hill.

Led by the stallion the horses moved slowly, cautiously but with definite intent. They'd been watering at this spot, on and off, for many seasons. But wild stallions are quick to protect their harem from any threat and they are constantly alert. The mares and young colts flowed single file behind the leader as they walked through the wide end of the funnel-shaped yard. Sally tried to pick out the brush and bough shelter where Rob and John were probably holding their breath as the horses passed.

The stallion reached the edge of the water and looked around, arching his neck, shaking his head, threatening and asserting his superiority, then lowered it to drink. The other horses trotted forward and immediately began drinking. All was peaceful.

With a scraping, dragging sound, then a thud Rob and John Monroe pulled the gates shut across the yards.

The stallion reared as if hit, arching his neck, rolling his eyes, ears laid back, nostrils flaring, he spun and, whinnying in alarm, splashed from the water, thundering back the way he had come, the harem following in a panic.

Chilla and Bluey rushed from their hide at the edge

of the waterhole, dragging the long wooden sliprails and banging them in place across the narrow entrance to the fenced waterhole.

Fitzi came and stood beside Sally, who could hear the noise below. 'We go down.'

The boys charged ahead as she shouted, 'Keep back, wait for us.'

Racing behind the boys, dodging round the ant hills, it seemed to her that total chaos had broken out below. It was the noise that hit her first – neighing and snorting, the banging of hooves on the fences, the frightened squeals of the other horses.

If there was one thing wild horses feared above all else it was confinement. The stallion's anger, frustration, helplessness, drove it into a frenzy. He reached the massive gates – railings of solid wood, seven feet high, secured in a steel grip to the central tree trunk. The rest of the panicked horses were close behind him, there was no room to turn. And then the stallion's head lifted and he screamed. He felt in every twitch and fibre of his body that he and his herd were hemmed into this space between the heavy wooden railings. Sally had never heard a sound like it. The horses flung themselves against the wooden rails and the men surged forward, shouting and cracking whips. The boys hung back as the men moved in close to the trapped brumbies.

Fitzi was shaking his head as they watched. 'You stay back away dem yards. Bad blood. Bad debils.'

Bluey, John and Chilla moved closer. Rob went down to the waterhole and looked at the sliprails, making sure they were secure.

'Reckon we could have a go? Some of them are going to kill each other if we don't start getting them separated,' said Wally.

'No bloody way, we'll wait till morning. That stallion

is mad as hell. They'll settle down by daylight. Can't keep this adrenaline up,' said John.

'That stallion'll be singing a different song tomorra,' said Bluey.

'Yeah, you get to do the honours, mate. Come on, let's go back to the camp. Leave a couple of blokes to watch them.' Monroe turned on his heel and headed over to where the Land Rover was parked out of sight. The boys ran after him and climbed into it. Fitzi waited with Sally until Rob came over, then set off on foot back to their campsite up the hill. Rob and Sally began walking after him.

'I feel sorry for them. They're so distressed,' she said.

'Tomorrow we'll cut and brand the ones we want. When they're broken and working they'll forget this life.'

'I wonder,' mused Sally. 'Running free must be better than a working life on a station.'

'Good feed and water, learning to work the cattle, being cared for is a lot better than always looking for tucker and water, and other stallions wanting to usurp your dominance.'

'Yes, I did see a lot of bites and scars on that stallion.'

'He's a tough bastard. Too bad John wants Bluey to take the fight out of him tomorrow,' said Rob.

'I don't think I'll be able to sleep with that dreadful noise,' said Sally.

'We'll hear it up the hill for sure. Have a couple of rums.' Rob dropped his arm around her shoulder and gave her a brief squeeze. ''Course I could keep you warm.'

'Not with Fitzi, John and the boys around. I feel like Mata Hari,' said Sally, grinning.

'Wait till we get back home. We'll find a way.'

Sally slipped her arm around his waist and didn't press him for details.

The boys went to sleep, it was late for them. The campfire was built up and the rum was passed between Rob, Sally, John and Wally. Sally was first to give in and crawl into her swag. Despite the alcohol it was hard to sleep hearing the squeals, whinnies and frustrated banging of hooves on wood and metal coming from the yards below.

Breakfast was hasty, the men were tense, the horses subdued but wary. The boys, however, were excited and although they were kept at a distance with Sally, they were quickly assessing the horses.

Sally watched the men move in on one young colt and with a startled leap after a stinging whip on his haunches, he stepped into the narrow chute. A rope was slung around his neck and he was pushed to the exit, the race opened and he was let loose in a small yard. Two men with lassoes faced him and as he reared to kick them away, his head was cruelly yanked as the rope tightened and another was thrown around his back legs and he was unceremoniously thrown to the ground. A stockman then raced in and sat on his head. Bluey stepped forward with a cruel grin.

Tommy stood close to her and Ian darted over to his father, who was helping get the other colt into the race. Marty started to cry and ran forward. Bluey took no notice and one of the stockmen handed him the red hot branding iron and the smell of burned hair and flesh hit the cool morning air.

Marty started shouting hysterically, 'Don't hurt him, Bluey!'

John Monroe yelled at him, 'Grow up, for God's sake!'

Sally took Tommy's hand and, seeing Fitzi, moved

away from the yards towards him. 'Come away, Marty,' she called, but the young boy, stung by his father's words, didn't move.

Ian, against Rob's instructions, was up on the fence rails beside his father, intent on all the action in the yard. Marty, now alone by the gates that held back the terrified mob of mares, stood with trembling lips as the men let the other young colt from the race into the yard where the stockmen quickly had him on the ground.

Fighting back tears, Marty sprang forward in the corridor to clamber on the gates secured to the cut tree.

Rob took in the scene in a flash and shouted, 'Marty, no!'

Sally stopped and spun around, gripping Tommy's hand.

The men dealing with the colt in the small yard took no notice of the frightened squeals of the mares. Marty stood in front of the gate, too afraid to climb the rails where angry hooves battered and shoved. With nostrils flaring, ears flattened, teeth barred, the horses made one last attempt at freedom, the front mares kicking at the gate pushed by the others behind. The sea of straining angry horses looked to Marty like devils. He hovered and as his courage failed him, he turned his back on the gate.

John Monroe, straddling the race, shouted at Marty. But his shout of exasperation at his youngest son was never heard.

There was a splintering, a crunching and a surge of energy as the gates gave way from the pressure as the horses penned behind it rushed. Despite all the men's precautions the fury of the horses couldn't be held back.

The lead mares had jumped through the gap before the gates had fully parted. The rest of the horses, fast on their heels, pushed through the gates, trampling several mares in the front of the mob. They rushed on either side of the tree stump where the iron band holding the latch dangled uselessly from wrenched nails. Smelling escape the horses pounded in a mass into the corridor, back the way they had walked so calmly the previous night, taking no notice of the small figure they trampled underfoot.

It happened so swiftly. The horses were gone, heading for their hills. The stallion, still penned, shrieked, urging them on, knowing he would never run with them again. The crumpled remains of Marty, face down, his back a mat of hoof marks, lay in the dust of the well-worn track.

Sally heard a distant scream then realised it was from her own throat and chest. A deep wail of anguish.

Everyone was running, except Tommy, who flung himself into her chest, trying to blot out what he saw and pretend it hadn't happened.

Later Sally had only blurred memories – of Ian flinging himself at his father, pummelling him and shouting. Rob kneeling down and stroking the matted back of Marty's head, not prepared to turn over the crumpled shape. Fitzi drawing her and Tommy firmly away. And in the distance, the sound of galloping hooves.

That night at the homestead, Sally pulled the three stretcher beds close together so she could reach out and touch Tommy and Ian on either side of her. The Flying Doctor had given them all tablets to help them sleep but Tommy slept fitfully, a sob escaping as the dreadful scenes reeled through his subconscious. Ian was a coiled spring of anger directed at his father. Sally felt sick in her stomach and wished she could blot away forever the scene of Lorna – dignified, immaculate Lorna – crouched on the lawn nursing the bloodstained horse blanket that held the shattered remains of her youngest son.

Chapter Twelve

SALLY SAT ON THE garden seat almost hidden by the long branches of the peppercorn tree next to the rain tanks that supplied water for the kitchen. The lawn was velvet green scattered with fallen frangipani flowers. Rob walked up and sat quietly beside her.

'I wondered where you'd got to. Everyone is gathering inside. They've come from Melbourne, Sydney, across from the coast. People they haven't seen in years.'

Sally didn't answer for a minute but continued to stare across the garden to the schoolhouse and further away, to the home stables. 'Odd, isn't it, how a place can look so different? Nothing has changed out there physically, yet everything has changed.' A tear rolled down her cheek. 'All because a little boy has gone. I used to think this was such a pretty outlook. Now it's just . . . sad.'

He put his arm around her shoulders and pulled her close to him as he looked across to the school where Ian was solemnly leading a group of kids towards the house. He felt he saw Marty racing after them, eager and smiling as always. 'I know, I know,' he whispered supportively.

Sally lowered her head, eyes closed, a look of pain on her face. 'I can't help blaming myself. I should have held onto him, all the time. You told us not to go near the rails –'

'Sally, stop. Stop it. You cannot hold a child's hand every minute of the day. If there's any blame . . .' he bit his lip. 'You have to help Tommy and Ian through this. And Lorna.'

Sally nodded, wiping her eyes with the back of her hand. 'God, I hope this doesn't upset the baby. If she loses it, I can't imagine . . .'

Rob spoke firmly. 'She's doing fine. You told me the doctor said she was in good shape. It's going to be later, when all this is over, when she's alone, that she'll fall apart. In private.'

'Oh, do you think so? Maybe I shouldn't go away then.'

'Go? Go where?'

'Lorna is insisting I take that holiday in Darwin.'

'That's a good idea. You need to get away from here. At least I get away on the stock camps. I'm heading out again. I think it's best to leave the family on their own for a bit.'

Sally was doubtful but said nothing. She certainly needed a change of scenery. And she was still hoping Sean would fly over and meet her.

'We'd better go inside. The minister is all ready for the service.' He took her hand, pulled her to her feet and led her onto the verandah.

They had all brought something, the kitchen was piled with boxes of food and bottles of beer and liquor. Women thrived at these times of upheaval. Like a swarm of worker bees they knew what to do, moving from the kitchen to the verandah in a choreographed buzz of making sandwiches, dishing out plates of food, making urns of tea, peeling back greaseproof paper from plates of cakes, slices and biscuits. Those off stations directed the house lubras in authoritative tones, the city women avoided them.

Light, lacy cloths were thrown over the food, the bustle slowed, the mood subdued as they gathered on the front lawn.

Reverend Hector, who'd come in from the mission down the river, waited in his cassock, prayer book clasped to his chest. Then, at a nod from John Monroe, he turned and led the assembled family and friends through the garden, past the schoolhouse, along the track that wound past the stables to the rise above the homestead where Lorna had planted a magnolia among the fruit trees beside a lone white gum flecking shadows on the grassy knoll. At certain times of the year a little red wildflower crept up between the stones and grass, and from here one caught the first breeze, the first raindrops. You could see across the river and hear the sounds of cattle and horses, men singing and, sometimes at night, the songs of a corroboree. Lorna had planned to landscape this as an extended garden. She and John had chosen it to be a resting place should either of them die on the property. Never had they anticipated one of their children dying before them.

The coffin was made from trees that grew by the river. When the men were building it at the back of the workshop they had looked up to see Lorna standing in the twilight watching them. Awkwardly they stopped work and Bluey came forward. 'What is it, Missus?'

Silently Lorna thrust out the soft yellow bear in its red jacket with its cheerful honey-licking smirk. 'Put this in with him. It's my son's favourite toy.'

'Yes, Miz Monroe. We do dat. For sure.'

Lorna, in a straight dark dress, her face set as if in constant pain, walked stiffly beside John, who was dressed in dark pants, white shirt and a tie. Sally wore her arrival clothes of pleated navy skirt, white blouse and pearls and walked beside Rob. Most of the men, including Rob, wore long-sleeved blue or checked shirts, buttoned up, and a tie if they owned one. It was too warm for jackets and Lorna, for once, had not bothered to insist on correct attire. She did not care or notice.

Everyone from the blacks' camp squatted or stood on the fringe. The school children hung back behind the old women, their eyes wide and frightened that the little white boss fella had been spirited away to his ancestors. Fitzi and Bluey stood with Snowy and his men. Fitzi wore a black waistcoat and whitefella tie, his silvering hair not covered by his usual battered ten-gallon hat. The house girls had on their best frocks of bright colours. Some wore old shoes, one carried her prized possession of a voluminous peeling patent-leather handbag. They had wailed around their campfire for two nights, and now curiously watched the whiteman's ceremony.

It was simple, short and formal, too painful an occasion for long speeches and prayers. The minister spoke of the short life of a sweet child, chosen to be with God. The coffin was sealed and a bouquet of flowers from Lorna's garden, sprays of bougainvillea and frangipani, lay on top.

They sang the twenty-third psalm, '*The Lord is my shepherd, I'll not want . . .*' accompanied by Rob on his harmonica, which sounded so unbearably sad to Sally. To her surprise, Donny led them in the hymn, his sweet rich voice ringing above the stumbling voices of the small congregation.

As the coffin was lowered and the red soil of Barra Creek rattled on top, covering the raw wood, the family stepped forward to pay their respects, dropping flowers into the grave as the minister intoned, 'We have entrusted Marty to God's merciful keeping and we now commit his body to be buried in the ground in sure and certain hope of the resurrection to eternal life through our Lord Jesus Christ who died, was buried, and rose again. To God be glory for ever and ever. Amen.'

Ian and Tommy stood close to their mother, their faces pale, Tommy silently crying. As John led Lorna forward to the graveside, Tommy looked wildly round and Sally quietly stepped between the boys and took their trembling hands.

Reverend Hector continued, 'Earth to earth, ashes to ashes, dust to dust.'

Lorna knelt, her shoulders shaking, and John opened his palm and let the fistful of earth crumble into the grave.

Tommy tugged at Sally. 'I don't want to go and look,' he whispered.

He looked distraught and Sally led him back to stand with Rob and Fitzi. Donny finished the hymn, dropped a flower onto the coffin and then joined them, taking Tommy's other hand.

Ian, standing on his own, looked grim and defiant, determined not to cry. John took Lorna's arm and with head bowed, she turned her back on the grave and walked towards the homestead.

Ian glanced at the minister who held out his hand to the young boy. Ian stepped forward, leaned down and scooped up a handful of the soft dirt, and stood looking at it. Instead of dropping it into the grave, he spun, threw the dirt at the sky and ran as fast as he could down towards the river.

Sally jerked but Rob put a restraining hand on her arm. 'Let him go. Fitzi will bring him back.'

Donny led Tommy away and a straggling procession headed for the house.

Lorna was the gracious hostess for a short while, catching up on news from the visitors, but her attention would quickly waver and she'd excuse herself to move on. Then she quietly disappeared.

The gathering broke into groups, men and women. The Aborigines had returned to their camp, including Rob's men who forsook their separate camp to join the Barra Creek mob. The white men sat on the verandah knocking back the rum and beer, the women settled in the living room with the leftover food, fresh pots of tea and an occasional glass of rum. The late morning tea ran through to lunch. Some people stretched out on the beds along the verandah for a kip, a few of the men repaired to the single men's quarters and continued drinking.

As sunset approached, preparations began for dinner. Ribs, steaks and chunks of meat from a freshly killed steer sizzled over the open fire on a sheet of hot iron and pots of boiled potatoes bubbled on the side. In the kitchen the women prepared vegetables and salads.

Sally and Donny stayed with the boys, busying themselves with six nanny goats and one billy that a couple had brought with them from their property. They thought the little herd might help distract Ian and Tommy, as it did with the Aboriginal children who giggled hysterically at the goats' antics.

'Make the blacks understand these are *not* for eating. Milk and cheese only,' Donny told Ian.

The lubras hovered, waiting to clean up. They looked anxious. There was a big gathering at the blacks' camp. All the men were in and there was competition amongst the women, the old men and the children for attention. At the men's quarters there was heavy drinking among the white workers not included in the homestead activities. The noise level rose as the booze flowed.

Donny took Sally aside and, as they walked to a quiet corner of the garden, he handed her a piece of paper. 'Loverboy can't make it.'

'Sean? Oh.' She skimmed through the brief message on the telegram. 'I guess there wasn't enough time.'

'He says he'll keep waiting though.'

'Well, that's easy to say when I'm tucked up here and he's over in New Zealand getting on with his social life.'

'Do you want to marry him?'

'No, not yet. There's still too much to do.'

'The trip to England?' Donny took her arm and tucked it in his. 'Don't delay too long Sal, sweet. This part of the country can suck the juices out of you. Before you know it you're a dried-up bush bird with a string of kids, a tired husband constantly battling the weather and all the other hassles of outback life.'

'Thanks, but you might like to dust your crystal ball. My mother would be over here like a shot and haul me back on the next plane if your prediction was a possibility.'

'He'd have to own his own station at the very least, eh?'

'Mother couldn't imagine life on a station. Owning a million miles of land might sound impressive but I think she sees my sister and me in elegant houses in town and a nice little farm for weekends.'

'Married to an accountant or a bank manager, or a solicitor?'

'You got the picture.'

'All the more reason for having a fling with someone unsuitable, eh?' He grinned.

'Sean?'

'Or someone around here, like Rob.'

'You're taken?'

'I'm your best friend – that's better.' He squeezed her arm. 'By the way, don't be surprised if Lorna or John suggest you take off for Darwin earlier than planned.'

'Your crystal ball is getting a workout.'

'Seriously, Sally. I think it would be a good idea for you to get away soon. Let the family grieve in their own way. Now that you don't have a definite rendezvous with loverboy . . .'

'I'll wait till I'm asked.'

The wake turned into a serious drinking session and occasional bursts of raucous laughter echoed from the men's quarters. Along the verandah conversation drifted in the darkness. Sally sat with Tommy and Ian on her bed telling them a story about New Zealand. She was trying to remember the Maori folktales she'd heard from a cook who'd once worked for her mother. The boys liked the new setting of these stories, which differed from the Aboriginal legends they'd been told. Sally was surprised to see Lorna appear on the verandah.

'I wanted to say goodnight to the boys. And, Sally, could we have a word in a few minutes?'

Sally nodded, knowing what was coming. She slid off the bed. 'I'll go brush my teeth, see you soon.' She left them alone. It wasn't often that Lorna came out to where they slept. The boys looked slightly uncomfortable, hoping their mother wasn't going to cry or talk about Marty. So far no one had uttered his name.

Lorna was brief, almost formal, as she suggested that it might be best for Sally to take her break in Darwin now. John had made a reservation at the Darwin Hotel, she could fly out the next day with friends, the Hardys, who'd flown in for the funeral in their own plane. 'The wet season is coming so you'd better go before then. Leave some school work for the boys to do.'

Sally wanted to ask, *Why Darwin?* but knew Lorna would tell her once again that it was where all the governesses went. Instead she said, 'Whatever you think best.'

'I'm not thinking too well, Sally, but thank you for being so accommodating.' Then she looked away and added, 'I need time with my family.'

Sally couldn't pinpoint the tone of the remark. Was it part sadness, remorse, or a hope they could come closer together in this time of tragedy? A feeling of despair swept over her and she wanted to embrace Lorna. But Sally's own pangs of guilt over Marty's death stopped her. Lorna held herself stiffly, as if frightened of crumbling. A moat surrounded her and she was not letting down the drawbridge.

As Sally turned away, Lorna said, 'Oh, and Sally . . . with everything . . . there's some mail for Rob on the bureau. I think you should take it down to him. I'm afraid I haven't been very organised.'

Sally dismissed it. 'I'm sure it's not important.'

Lorna swung around, her eyes bright. 'Oh, but it is. It's not right of me to neglect these things . . . I want you to take his mail down to him. Now, please.'

She spoke carefully, enunciating every word. Sally shrugged. Lorna was not functioning properly and who could blame her? Perhaps by observing these little niceties she was clinging to the normalcy of life.

'Of course. I'll do it right away.'

The men's quarters were forbidden territory. Lights blazed and there was the unmistakable noise of the raised voices and drunken laughter of those escaping the reality of the moment. Sally knew Rob usually camped with his own men away from the influence of the rough likes of Snowy, the white stockmen, ringers and workers passing through. But on occasion he stayed in a room in the bunk-house. She stood outside in the darkness, clutching the small parcel of mail, then chose the loudest room where all the activity seemed to be happening. She stepped onto the narrow verandah and, realising no one would hear her knocking, pushed the door open.

It took a moment for the scene to register in her brain. Yet it was an image that stuck in her head for years.

Like some rough Australian version of a bacchanalian orgy, bodies were sprawled over bunks and the floor, and the pervading smell and sense was one of slovenly lust, overindulgence, loose morals. There were men with their shirts off sitting around drunk, and girls with laughing black eyes, hitched skirts and exposed breasts commanding their attention as they straddled laps and bodies. They glanced at her with some bemusement, even arrogance.

'I was looking for . . .' she stuttered. Then she saw Rob on a bunk bed, obviously passed out, too drunk to move. She looked wildly round the room, Snowy leering, Chilla and Bluey with women, young Betsy huddled in a corner. Sally dropped the letters, turned and fled. She never mentioned her visit and never knew, or cared, if Rob got his mail.

The boys were upset at her sudden departure for Darwin and their feelings were mirrored by the black children who were confused at the coming and goings of so many people. Now Sally was flying away and they lined up by the edge of the runway watching Tommy hug her.

'You promise you'll come back,' he said.

'Of course. It's just a little holiday. You fellows have to look after your mum and dad. Cheer them up.'

Ian gave her a defeated look. 'Mum's sad and Dad's mad. How are we going to make any difference?'

'Be patient, be good, stay close with them. Try to do things together.'

Ian rolled his eyes in exasperation but Tommy nodded. 'Okay. And when you come back will we start school again?'

'Of course we will,' said Ian. 'We've got to pass and get good marks for King's.'

'You have some essays to write and homework to do. It's all with your mother. There's something you can do together.'

'The black kids too?' asked Tommy.

'Ask your mother.' She turned to the rest of the group and wagged a finger. 'You be good piccaninnies. All right?'

They nodded and shuffled their feet then suddenly little Alice rushed at Sally, holding onto her legs and howling as the realisation that Sally was getting on the plane hit her.

Frankie pulled her away and held her. 'We draw pictures. Make good one for you,' he said.

Mr Hardy was beckoning and Sally grabbed her handbag. 'Bye. Drive back carefully, Ian.' She knew Ian drove the old Land Rover better than she did but now she was terrified of accidents.

As the Cessna rose and banked, she saw a scatter of horses in the home paddock and recognised Rob on horseback, waving his hat. In seconds he was out of sight but she was touched by his gesture.

The Hardys only stopped overnight in Darwin on their way back to their property.

Sally took a taxi to the Darwin Hotel. The town looked a rough and ready sort of place; some shops still had chicken wire and reinforced mesh in the windows replacing the bombed-out glass.

'Is that from the war?' she asked the Greek taxi driver.

'Yair. No one hurries up here.'

'Twenty years is a pretty slow reaction,' said Sally. 'So where's a good place to eat?'

'Milk bar. Caff. The pub. You with a bank, government or something?'

'No. I work on a property.'

'Then you can't eat at the mess.' He glanced at her over his shoulder, looking at the way she was dressed in a sunfrock with short bolero, expensive sunglasses and a nice bag.

'Go to the Darwin Hotel's dining room. My son plays in the band.'

The houses looked temporary and with many there was nothing but dirt in their front yards. The ugliness of the streets, though, was relieved by flowering poincianas, frangipanis and some sprawling hibiscus and bougainvillea. The port was bustling but the damp humidity seemed to slow every other activity. They passed the Don Hotel and men who looked like station hands or workmen stood in its doorways and on the steps holding large glasses of beer. She caught a glimpse of a group of blacks squatting in the dirt under a tree out the back, hopeful that someone would sell them some illicit grog. It was a pretty basic township but to see people and shops, after months at Barra Creek, was a novelty. She was relieved when they pulled up outside the Darwin Hotel and she saw the pleasant building with its wide verandah and green gardens.

On the ground floor large rooms opened onto each other, filled with cane furniture and slow-turning ceiling fans. The receptionist had been contacted by the Monroes so she put Sally in a verandah room.

Sally carried her bag upstairs to a plain, spacious room

of polished dark wood smelling heavily of Johnson's floor polish. Narrow double doors with lace curtains opened onto the verandah that overlooked the Esplanade. In the beer garden below, tables and chairs were set among tropical plants. It wasn't stylish but it was comfortable and obviously the best place in town to stay. She was tired and went down the hall to the bathroom to wash. But she didn't step into the shower until she'd swatted all the cockroaches.

She lay on her bed listening to voices, laughter, cars and wondered how she'd sleep after the quiet nights at Barra Creek. In the early evening when a breeze brought the strong salty tang of ocean smells, Sally walked through the town. She found little to interest her and feeling nervous at the rough men and drunks that hung around the Don she went to Smith Street, glanced at the Victoria Hotel and saw some young women sitting on a car bonnet sipping pink drinks. One called out to her, 'You on your own? New in town?'

Sally slowed. The girls were nicely dressed and seemed pleasant. 'Yes. I've just arrived. Do you live here?'

'For the time being. We're nurses up at the hospital. Where are you from?'

'New Zealand originally. I'm working out on a station.'

'Ah, governess eh? What's your name?'

'Sally Mitchell. What is there to do for entertainment here?'

'Depends.' A girl with bottle-blonde hair gave her a big grin. 'I'm Joyce. We're with some Army fellows.' Two casually dressed men joined them carrying refills for the girls.

'This is Sally. A governess, just arrived,' said Joyce.

'G'day, Sally. Want a Shirley Temple?'

'No thanks.' Sally was used to drinking with the men.

The ban on women in the public bar of hotels irritated her.

'We'll probably go for a drink at the Darwin soon. Maybe we'll see you there in the lounge then.'

'Probably. Nice meeting you.' She continued walking and returned to her hotel.

It was Friday night and the lounge bar was filling up. Sally sat at a corner table, watching the various groups – men at the bar, women at the tables and lounges. The waiter had told her that mostly people from the bank or government offices came here; the RAAF, Navy and Army boys had their own messes for meals and drinking. The Victoria was 'just a pub', and the Don was the drinking home of the waterside workers, builders' labourers and the 'rough' bushies. She saw Joyce and her gang come in and they quickly spotted her and made their way over to join her, pulling in chairs for the girls as the men headed for the bar after taking their orders.

'We've been with a gang from Vestey. Boy, can they drink when they come to town.'

'It can be isolated working on a big station,' said Sally, and she wondered what Rob did when he left Barra Creek.

The men talked to each other, only asking the girls what they wanted to drink. Or they kidded around with a remark or two before turning their attention back to the topic of driving a vehicle, on a road with really bad corrugations that wrecked the radiator, and other driving troubles from cooked engines to bad injectors, getting spares, breakdowns and bush mechanic improvisations.

The girls laughed a lot and talked about people who were new in town or moving on; escapades at the hospital smuggling fellows into their quarters; the gruesome injuries of croc shooters; and a local man who'd come in with an embarrassing predicament to do with his penis and a soft drink bottle.

Sally was bored. She glanced around the crowded room wondering what on earth she was going to do here for a week. There was a man looking at her. She did a double take as he was so different from everyone else in the bar. He was slim with a high brow and fine nose, a sculptured mouth that was smiling in her direction, thick dark hair and almond-shaped eyes. He must be Oriental, she thought, but not how she'd ever imagined an Asian to look, never having met anyone from the East.

He was smiling and began to walk across the room towards her. Sally glanced around in mild panic and saw that Babs beside her was also smiling and beckoning him over. Sally shrank back feeling silly. Babs, like Joyce, was boisterous, blonde and jokey.

Babs nudged Joyce, 'Front and centre, look who's here.'

'Ooh. Doctor Dreamboat.'

The man gave the girls a big smile and nodded at the group, but addressed Babs. 'Evening, Barbara. Enjoying yourself?'

'That's the idea. We've just started.'

He laughed and glanced at Sally. 'Are you with us? I haven't seen you around.'

'This is Sally, she's a governess out bush, not one of us. This is Doctor Lee,' said Joyce.

Sally leaned forward and shook his hand. 'You wouldn't want me on your medical team, I'm afraid.'

'Surely you have to cope with the occasional medical emergency on a station. Where are you working?'

'Barra Creek. Yes, we've had our share of . . . accidents.' She looked down, suddenly overcome. For a little while she'd almost forgotten about Marty.

She was relieved when one of the boys said cheerfully, 'Who's shouting?'

Babs and Joyce finished their drinks quickly. 'Listen, we have to go on for dinner. There's a hillbilly singer on at the Victoria and we want to get good seats. You coming, Sally?'

She shook her head. 'I'm supposed to meet Mr and Mrs Tsouris here, they're friends of the owners of Barra Creek. Thanks anyway.'

'Oh, they own the big Greek restaurant. See ya round.' Joyce and Babs rose, followed by the other girls and trailed by the men after they downed their schooners.

'Would you care for another drink, Sally? I know the Tsourises well. They'll look after you.'

'I suppose so. I think I'd like a gin and tonic please, Dr Lee.'

'Please, call me Hal. It's Harold, which I detest.'

Sally had seen how deferential the nurses had been towards him, even though they were about the same age.

'Thanks, Hal.'

They exchanged small talk, and Sally was intrigued by him as he told her about the time he'd spent in Singapore.

'Is that your home?'

'No. Believe it or not I'm a genuine Darwinian. My great grandfather came here to seek his fortune. He thought this country was a paradise where a man prepared to work could prosper without being under threat from the powerful tongs.'

'Is that like a kind of Chinese mafia?'

'Yes, in a way. Imperial China was not a place to advance from the coolie classes. Like so many others from around the world, he saw Australia as a land of opportunity.'

'And your family did well and have been here ever since?' asked Sally, quite fascinated.

'Yes, that's right. And what about you? Where are you from? From your accent I detect a touch of New Zealand vowels.'

'You're right. My family's story is rather mundane compared to yours.'

He glanced at his watch. 'Dinner is being served in the main dining room, would you care to join me for a meal?'

Sally was finding the handsome and exotic doctor interesting company. 'I'd love to, though I'm supposed to meet Mr and Mrs Tsouris for a drink and maybe dinner, the invitation was a bit casual.'

'Casual is the operative word up here,' said Hal, rising to his feet and holding out his hand to Sally. 'We can send word to them that we're in the dining room.'

She walked beside him into the dining room, aware that eyes were following them with interest. Joyce and Babs had told her they'd met some of the governesses and they weren't like Sally. They tended to be rough or good-time girls lusting after bull catchers, jackeroos, or any bloke ready to play up in town. They rarely lived in the house or dined with the boss and his wife. Quality governesses were hard to find or moved on from the tough life of the outback. Joyce and Babs had figured Sally as having rich parents who'd lined her up for a cushy job for a couple of months' experience.

They were halfway through dinner when George and Despina Tsouris came to the table, greeting Hal and shaking Sally's hand in welcome.

'I hope you're comfortable,' said Despina. She was very round, dressed in a bright silk floral dress and lots of expensive jewellery. Her dark short hair had a dramatic silver swathe in the front.

'Very comfortable, thank you. I'm sure I'm going to enjoy staying here.'

'I hope so, dear girl.' She sat in the chair Hal was holding out for her.

'How is Lorna?' George asked.

'It's hard to say. Lorna is such a private person.' Sally didn't imagine the Tsourises were intimate friends but more social acquaintances of the Monroes, so she wasn't about to gossip.

George had flicked a nod to the waiter and a bottle of wine and a plate of olives appeared. 'And you, Hal, how come you have found the prettiest guest in the hotel? Do you know Lorna and John too?'

'No. I rarely get a chance to go bush. It sounds fascinating from Sally's description, though. One of the girls from the hospital introduced us. I hope you don't mind my intruding on your dinner?'

'Of course not, we're sorry we're so late. We had to organise the chef. You can help entertain Sally, you know Darwin better than we do,' said Despina, patting his arm.

George poured the red wine from a bottle that Sally had never seen before. She'd never tried fresh olives before either.

Despite being much older than Sally and Hal, the Tsourises were entertaining and generous company. They insisted that the meal was on them and hoped Hal would be able to show Sally a few of the sights as they were snowed under with their restaurant at the moment.

Sally thanked them and turned to Hal. 'I don't want to impose, I imagine you're busy at the hospital too.'

'Not too busy, thankfully. It's no imposition at all. I'd enjoy it. I'm due for a few days off my roster anyway. How about we start tomorrow lunchtime?'

Despite her initial trepidation at being alone, Sally made sure her room was locked, turned on the fan, draped the soft mosquito net around the bed, turned out the light and, relishing the privacy and big soft bed, slept like a log.

Hal greeted her the next day as they'd arranged and opened the door of his red MG convertible. He was casually dressed and looked like a thirty-year-old out for a day's fun rather than the more serious doctor in coat and tie of the night before.

'There's a scarf in the glove compartment for your hair if you like.'

Sally wondered where it had come from, but said casually, 'That's okay, a friend of mine at home has an Austin Healey. I like the wind in my face.' She wasn't about to appear impressed by his snazzy sports car.

'It's a bit of an indulgence and impractical for up here as you can't take it into the bush, but I love it. I suppose you drive a Land Rover at Barra Creek.'

'No, I ride everywhere. The oldest boy drives the Land Rover. You know how country kids learn to drive the minute they can see over the steering wheel? Although Ian wouldn't have a clue about parking or traffic,' she added as they eased into the Esplanade.

He drove her around Darwin and the outskirts, past Fannie Bay and produced a picnic lunch, which they ate on Mindil Beach. Afterwards he showed her where his great grandfather had started a market garden and later built a store that had grown into an emporium. 'He came here to dig for gold but actually made his fortune digging a market garden and selling food. I'm the first not to stay in the family business of trade and be a merchant.' He laughed. 'Sorry for the humble origins tour but I do feel immensely proud of my family. My grandfather was one of the few non-whites to hold public office in Darwin.'

'Does living in Darwin satisfy you? Don't you want to go to a big city hospital or overseas?'

'Eventually. The hours are long, it's demanding and challenging. But I get to do a lot of different things here; I plan on specialising in the future.'

'So you'll leave?'

'Yes. Darwin is a place where time gets away. Months become years before you know it. I have a lot of family history here that draws me back, but I'll have to strike out eventually.'

'Do you still have family here?'

'Only a couple of old aunties. My mother's relatives are in the UK. I have family in Singapore as well.'

Later he took her past his family home, a large house facing the port. 'Auntie May and Aunt Winifred live there. I have a small place close to the hospital.'

'What was the attraction of medicine?'

His face clouded. 'My mother died when I was young. It was cancer, and I wished so hard that I could make her better. So I gravitated towards healing people.'

'Do you remember her well?'

'I was ten at the time and I have some very special memories. She was English, my parents met in Singapore. My father was working with his uncle in his import business, my mother's father was there with the British Army. They married at the British Residency and lived in Singapore for a while. Then my father decided to come back to Darwin to take over the family business. Fortunately my family didn't lose much in the bombings during the war. The shops in town were damaged but we owned a lot of land so he rebuilt.'

Sally was getting the picture that the Lees were a well-established family in Darwin. 'Where did you study?'

'Sydney Uni. I did my residency there but I couldn't

resist the chance to take up a position in my home town. I'll move on pretty soon.'

'To do what?'

'I'm interested in treating children. But come on, what about you? You told me last night you were sidetracked on the way to London. What are your plans?'

They were parked by the port and Sally was suddenly taken back to the excitement of sailing to England. 'At the time it was the thing to do. I never imagined myself on a cattle station. But I love horses and the life out there, and I've become very attached to the family.'

'How are the family coping after the tragedy? I read about it in the paper here of course.'

Sally felt a pain at the unexpected opening of the wound of Marty's death. It had been so intensely personal that it hadn't occurred to her that strangers in other parts of the country would know about it. Tears began to roll down her cheeks. Furiously she turned her head and brushed them away.

Hal quickly dropped his arm around her shoulders and, in a quiet caring voice, comforted her. 'That was thoughtless of me. You must have been so close to him. It's all right, Sally, go ahead, let it out.'

His words, the tone of his voice, his bedside manner – as Sally had already come to think of his gentle, caring attitude – unleashed a flood of feelings. She found tears rolling from her eyes, her voice cracking and a desperate desire to talk about Marty's death. She poured out the story of what had happened, how guilty and responsible she felt, how Ian and probably some of the men, including Rob, blamed John Monroe for baiting the boy and pushing him into a dangerous situation. She wondered if Lorna blamed her.

He listened, and when she finally ran out of words she was crying uncontrollably.

Hal drew her close and stroked her hair. 'There will always be questions and doubts in such a situation. But you must put it to one side, as indeed must the brothers, Ian especially. There is no going back.'

It was the first time she'd truly cried for Marty. Hal was right, she'd never given in to her feelings. She'd had to be strong in front of Tommy and Ian and everyone else. Hal's gentle manner had caught her unawares. He stroked her hair until her shoulders stopped shaking and the tears eased.

'I'm sorry, I shouldn't let this get to me . . .'

'Sally, you have every right to feel rotten. It seems there're a lot of people leaning on you and you don't have anyone to support you. It must have been hard for you. I often see how the death of a child can splinter and even destroy a family, or make them stronger. You have a big responsibility to help them get through this.' Hal wiped her tears and, impulsively, softly kissed her.

Sally returned his tender kiss. There weren't the fireworks of the first kiss she'd exchanged with Rob but the care in the depths of Hal's dark-lashed eyes, the strength of his smooth face and hands, made her feel secure.

'Don't feel embarrassed. Shall we walk a little bit?' He helped her from the car and it seemed the most natural thing for him to take her hand as they walked along the foreshore.

Over the following week Hal made himself available to escort Sally around Darwin, taking her to the Saturday night pictures and to dances at the Victoria Hotel and the RAAF officers' mess. They dined at the Darwin Hotel each evening, once with two other doctors and their wives. He took her for tea with his aunties at their large home, which was filled with Asian antiques. It was a very

English tea with fine bone china. Her mother would have approved. The two sisters had inherited different features. Auntie May was small and delicate and looked very Chinese; Aunt Winifred was tall and thin and looked very British, because of her English ancestors.

Sally and Hal became something of a well-known couple about town in a few days. She was aware women watched her with some envy as she and Hal walked into the bar for drinks before dinner. The Tsourises were delighted at their friendship and commented on what a striking couple they made. Sally had asked Hal about his love life and he laughed easily.

'I see a couple of girls here and there, in Singapore and London. Professionally it's best I don't socialise with any of the hospital staff,' he said diplomatically.

Sally held her tongue. The likes of Babs and Joyce were not in his class, that was for sure. Then she caught herself and laughed inwardly, thinking she was being just like her mother.

'What about you? What's the social life like at Barra Creek?'

'Wild, crazy, hectic!' They both laughed. 'My parents tried to pack me off to England because I was seeing someone unsuitable at home. They have no idea I'm surrounded by – what they'd consider – unsuitable men in the outback.'

'All those bull catchers, jackeroos and stockmen, eh?'

'Not my type, I'm afraid.'

'What are your plans when your contract finishes? I can't see you staying a governess.'

'Funny, I don't think of myself like that. I really feel part of the family. I can imagine Lorna and John and the kids being at my wedding when that day comes.' Sally paused, her future was a question she hadn't liked to think about. Now with the new baby on the way and the trauma over Marty, she knew Lorna would be relying on her even more.

While the social life in Darwin didn't measure up to the mad whirl of Sydney or the formal scene of Christchurch, she'd really enjoyed being taken around the town and its surroundings, and the dinners at the Darwin Hotel with stimulating and sophisticated conversations with Hal and the Tsourises. The thought of returning to the property and listening to John Monroe being the know-it-all and sounding off, Rob talking about horses, the two boys and their interests, Lorna's depression, and the sad cloud of Marty's death hanging over them all was not pulling her back.

Hal was well-travelled – he skiied in Europe every year. He was a cultured man, who was used to having money. It was no hardship for him to be a dedicated doctor in Darwin when he could fly off to the glamorous playgrounds of Europe in his holidays. A sudden comparison with Rob flashed into her mind and Sally wondered if Rob knew how to ski. She could imagine him fearlessly tackling the big slopes. But she couldn't visualise Hal on a horse amongst cattle. They each had a different calling, yet there was some streak in them both that was similar. Hal was a very caring doctor, his love of children showed in his compassion. Equally she had watched Rob around horses, his calm, intuitive manner and gentle handling of the horses he loved was far different and more effective than the rough treatment handed out by many of the other stockmen.

'Can you afford to go to England as you planned?' Hal asked her.

'I suppose so, I never touch my pay. But it's not a lot of fun on your own. Once my friend Pru dropped out I lost interest in going on alone.'

Hal squeezed her hand. 'I go to London every so often. Maybe when I go over to do my specialist training I could meet you there.'

'Who knows?' said Sally lightly, but the seed had been sown.

Hal took her to the airport and surprised her with a beautiful spray of purple orchids in a cellophane container. 'I had them sent down from Singapore. They're in water so they should last for some time. Perhaps you could share them with Mrs Monroe.'

'Oh Hal, they're gorgeous. Lorna keeps the house full of silk flowers, she'll love the real thing. Thank you.'

He kissed her goodbye and there was a firmness and a promise in his lingering kiss.

'Crikey, are they real?' asked Donny when he saw the orchids as he loaded her bag onto the plane in Cloncurry.

'They certainly are. I'm giving them to Lorna. But, darling heart, wait till I tell you how I got them,' said Sally, grinning.

'Oh, a tall, dark, handsome stranger?' Donny clasped his hands together in mock excitement. 'Darwin did you good. I can tell.'

She laughed and shook her head in a coquettish move. 'Actually, yes. I'll tell you all, but don't gossip.'

Donny put a finger to his lips. 'Promise. So what was he like?'

Chapter Thirteen

THE ORCHIDS STAYED IN the centre of the dining table for two weeks. Small, delicate and exotic, the flowers were a rare specimen in the surroundings of Barra Creek. Lorna did her work around the house as usual, though she took a long nap each afternoon. Sally spent a lot more time with the children in the schoolhouse 'catching up' for, despite Lorna's good intentions, the work schedules Sally had left for the boys were only half done.

Now the Monroe boys and the black children, including little Alice, busily applied themselves to school work as a welcome distraction from thinking about Marty. Sally was taken with the drawings done by Frankie and Ginger, but most of all she was impressed with a composition Tommy had written. He always wrote good 'stories' but he was quick and sloppy. Sally wanted him to pay attention to what he'd been told to write about and to mind his handwriting, spelling and grammar. This little story had been dashed off but it captured the scene and mood of fishing down at the river quite wonderfully.

'Tommy, this is such a good composition. I feel I want to rush down to the river and throw a line in.'

'Why don't we?' He grinned and the black kids jumped up and cheered in agreement.

'Why's he writing about that? We had to write about an event that changed history or our lives,' sniffed Ian.

'Here, read how he has cleverly brought that in. Ignore the spelling and punctuation,' said Sally. She decided to encourage Tommy with his writing. He had real flair. 'You both need to read more. I'm going to arrange to get some good books sent from the library.'

'We have enough to read for school,' moaned Ian.

But Tommy was all for it. 'Dad has a library of books but we're not allowed to touch them.'

Sally had seen the books in John's office area but never paid much attention to them. 'What sort of books?'

'Old-fashioned, smelly books for old people,' scoffed Ian.

'I'll check them out tonight,' said Sally.

'When we feed 'em up goaties?' asked Frankie, causing an immediate eruption in the class. The little herd of goats had become household pets, and loved attention and being hand fed. They were locked up at night in a pen with a small shelter next to the home stables. Fitzi was helping make a billy cart with a harness for the goats so the children could ride in it. He'd also spent time putting chicken wire around the garden fences to keep the goats away from Lorna's flowers and vegetables.

John Monroe had scoffed at Sally when she said she was trying to teach one of the black kids to read and write. 'He only needs to sign his name to a bit of paper occasionally. Don't waste your time.'

Ginger, with his dark skin and shock of yellow hair, was bright and keen and the same age as Marty, as near as they could estimate, and had always wanted to do what Marty did. He seemed to be putting in a special effort now so Sally encouraged him and with great concentration he gripped the pencil, his tongue poking from the corner of his mouth, as he laboriously scratched out the letters that spelled his name.

After lunch Sally and the boys followed Fitzi and the camp kids down to the yards where Rob was breaking in the big stallion. The horse had been left alone since the brumby rush that had killed Marty. It looked wild eyed, its apprehension covered up with aggressive head movements and pawing at the ground. Being confined had not calmed him, if anything it had made him more determined to break free.

Ian was besotted with the beautiful horse, but John Monroe refused to have anything to do with it. 'Sell it, get rid of it,' he told Rob.

'It has the makings of a good stockhorse,' said Rob.

'Bullshit. It's a mad horse, a jinxed horse.' He strode away from the yards leaving no doubt that he blamed the horse for the stampede that felled Marty.

Snowy hovered. 'Give him to me, I'll get him working.'

Ian ran at him. 'No! Leave him!' He'd seen Snowy beat a horse until it cowered.

Rob stepped in quickly. 'Calm down, Ian. No one's going near that stallion but me.'

'He's *my* horse. I want him.' Ian seemed close to tears. Rob threw Sally a look and she put her arm around Ian's shoulders.

'It's okay. Let Rob break him in. He'll do a good job. Then the horse will treat you well when you're strong enough to ride him.' Sally knew the slim boy would not be capable of controlling such a big horse for a while.

Ian nodded. 'Yeah. Rob's the best. Sally, will you tell Dad? Please?'

'Tell him what?'

'That he's my horse. He didn't hurt Marty. He was just . . . doing what a wild stallion does. He wanted his mares to be free. Isn't that right?'

Sally was struck by the pleading in Ian's eyes and voice. She saw how much this horse meant to him. For this young boy it was a link with his brother; unlike his father he didn't blame the horse.

'Yes. Yes, you're right. I'll talk to him.'

Rob and Sally exchanged a glance over Ian's head. Each knew what the other was thinking: this could turn into yet another cause for friction between Monroe and his eldest son. Sally decided to ask Rob for his advice on how to handle the situation. There was no question Rob should tame the big stallion. It suddenly struck her how quickly her rapport with Rob was re-established and her time with the charming Doctor Lee seemed remote and unreal.

They decided to start breaking in the horse the following morning when Monroe was out checking on the bore runners and would be gone overnight. Sally would give the class a break to watch Rob work with the stallion and they'd make up the school time later.

They trailed down to the yards, even the black children's exuberance was subdued. It crossed Sally's mind that it felt as if they were going to church, or maybe to the theatre to see a serious opera. Rob had assembled his gear and was laying out his mouthing bits, ropes and a secret mixture he kept in an old jar. He would rub it on cotton cloth wound around a mouthing bit to cool the gums. He squatted on his haunches and rolled a cigarette while studying the stallion.

Sally crouched beside him. 'He's a beautiful animal, Rob.'

'I was thinking how different it is with humans. You can pick a good horse by his looks and movement, but it's hard to see a person's pedigree.'

'I suppose it's something inside humans that's not immediately obvious.'

'Where're your spurs and whip?' asked Ian.

'I'm not here to be cruel, break his spirit. Like Sally teaches you things at school, I'm going to educate this fella, make him a smart horse.' Rob's eyes didn't move from the horse. He was absorbing the way his legs and feet moved, which side he seemed to favour, the language spoken in the movement of his ears, the flare of nostrils, mouth action and head movements.

Sally had seen horses roughly and cruelly broken-in that would always carry bad habits and a resentful attitude, but Rob's technique was different. He could see the potential of this horse. Ian sensed it too and wanted the stallion very badly.

'How long is it going to take?' Ian asked.

'As long as it takes.' Then after a few minutes Rob added, 'I'm tuning in to his wavelength, getting to know what he's thinking.'

'Ah, how can you do that?' Sally asked. She wasn't sure if he was leading Ian on or really meant it.

After a few moments, Rob asked Ian, 'So what do you reckon he's thinking? See how he paces up and down, keeps looking back at the hills, nods his head and tosses his mane.'

'He looks like he wants to get out of there.'

'That's for sure. He's frustrated, he's worried about his herd. His whole world has been reduced to the small space in the yard, with strange creatures around him. He's scared of us but he won't show it.'

'Will he fight though?' asked Sally.

'Wouldn't you after what's happened?'

'Yes. I would.'

Rob finished his cigarette but seemed to drift off into a world of his own so Sally and Ian moved away.

'I reckon we make ourselves comfortable and sit it out, eh?'

They watched in silence as Rob picked up his plaited cotton lasso, deftly dropped it over the horse's neck, flipped it over his head and, moving the horse anti-clockwise, gave a light pull so the loop was under his throat. He then stepped in front of the stallion turning him clockwise, threw a half-hitch over his nose and pulled it taut, which pulled up the horse. He made eye contact with the wary animal and immediately had the horse's full attention. There was fear and defiance but neither came to the fore as the man and horse locked eyes.

Rob spoke softly. 'See, I've got you, old boy. So I'm going to lead you, gently, but you get the message, right?'

He then relaxed the pressure on the horse's nose and took several steps backwards and sideways, never breaking eye contact, letting the animal inspect him. He passed the rope to his left hand and slowly but surely approached the horse, who suddenly swung to the side. Rob increased the pressure on the rope slightly, bringing him back to face him. The horse reared, but Rob seemed to be expecting it and merely released all pressure on the rope so the animal didn't roll and fall.

Facing each other again, the stallion glared balefully at Rob, and Sally realised that he knew that by staring into Rob's eyes he may be able to puzzle out what this man was thinking. Rob advanced slowly, stopped, and held out the back of his hand for the horse to smell, his eyes still not wavering from those of the horse.

The horse sniffed and Rob ran his little finger up the side of the stallion's head then slipped his palm over one eye and closed it, retaining firm pressure on the rope in his left hand. He closed the horse's eye a few times then stepped back and let the stallion absorb what had transpired.

Moments passed as they studied each other and Rob repeated the process twice more. On the third time he rubbed behind an ear. Gently he worked the rope loose from under the throat, widening the noose, and then stepped back, until he was standing several paces away but in front of the horse, maintaining eye contact. He lifted the noose and, instinctively as it went over the eyes, the stallion ducked and the rope dropped off. Rob broke eye contact and the stallion stepped away as Rob slowly wound up the rope and left the yard.

'Is that it?' asked Sally.

'For today. He won't be so fearful tomorrow. He knows I'm boss, but I won't hurt him. He'll be less worried when I take him around the yard tomorrow and we'll do a little more mouthing, put on a bridle.'

Ian left to find Tommy, and Sally helped Rob release the stallion back into the main yard. Walking back to the stables Rob gave a wry grin. 'So, how was Darwin? You look decidedly happier.'

'It was good for me, just what the doctor ordered.' She laughed inwardly. 'The Tsourises looked after me really well. I met a few people, socialised, went to the pictures, a couple of dances. But it's not the most glamorous place for a holiday.'

'I like the ocean myself, Surfers or up the Cape.'

'Me too. I adored Surfers. I'm nervous swimming too far north, though. Too many nasties.'

'Maybe we could do that sometime. Go to the coast. I'd like to see you in one of those two-piece jobs.'

Sally laughed. 'The new thing is a bikini . . . though my mother would shoot me if I wore one.'

'Let's go for a swim tomorrow, it's so hot.'

'I'm too scared. What if there are more big crocs around?'

'We'll be okay at the old swimming hole. We'll take the piccaninnies with us and chuck them in first, see if it's safe.'

'Rob! You're joking!'

'I am. But the old people told me that if you have to swim in a croc-infested river, splash in first and put an old woman behind you, by the time the croc is alerted to the noise, he'll grab the old one at the rear and you'll get over.'

'Even if it isn't true, that's a terrible story. Crocodiles are the biggest problem about living by the river, beautiful as it is.'

They reached the stables, which were deserted in the hot afternoon. Suddenly Rob spun around and swept Sally into his arms behind the lean-to shelter, kissing her long and hard.

She responded instantly to his scorching mouth and felt her legs go weak as she pressed against him.

'I missed you,' he murmured as they drew apart. 'I thought you might find some bloke over in the big smoke and not come back.'

'In a week?' teased Sally. 'And Darwin's scarcely the big smoke.'

'It must be lonely for you here. Lorna's a bit out of it these days.'

Sally felt a rush of emotion – guilt over her attraction to Hal, the fact she'd secretly tried to meet Sean in Darwin, disloyalty to Rob. Yet there had never been anything between them but friendship and now this powerful physical attraction. 'I would be, if it wasn't for you. You're my best friend up here.'

He held her tightly to him. 'Can we be more than friends? Seems like we've jumped a barrier or two.'

She didn't answer but lifted her face to be kissed as his hands ran along her back, over her firm buttocks and drew her hips into his. Then they grinned at each other.

'So what are we going to do about this?' asked Sally.

'Leave it to me. We'll have to be careful that John or Lorna don't notice anything different.'

'Do you feel different?'

He laughed. 'Yes, I do.' Then he grew serious. 'I promise not to hurt you, Sally. Hurt your feelings or do the wrong thing. I don't want you to think I'm taking advantage or anything. I was knocked over by you the first time I saw you. I tried hard not to show it.'

Sally recalled the dishevelled man she'd first seen. 'I thought I was getting in the way and you hated having me around.'

'Sally, I'm glad we're friends.'

'Me too.' She kissed him quickly. 'I'd better get back to the boys. If you see the rest of the kids send them up to the school, please.'

All was quiet in the schoolhouse save for the scratching of a pen, the scrape of Frankie's coloured chalk as he drew on the board and the heavy breathing of a cattle dog under a desk. Sally was checking their homework before it went off in that week's bag of work to the correspondence school. She glanced at her watch, it was almost time to finish for the day. Then there was an eruption of noise, laughter, shouting, a car horn blowing.

'What the dickens?' Sally ran to the door.

The women were running from the house, Fitzi and two stockmen were in the yard on horseback having ridden up from the front gate. They were followed by John Monroe, who swerved the Land Rover up to the house and jumped out, calling Lorna.

'What's going on?' called Sally.

Fitzi was closest to her and he shouted, 'Mizta Charlie Chan come. Got him van, plenny good tings!'

The black children raced off before she could dismiss them. 'Who on earth is Charlie Chan?'

'He's the hawker man. He comes round all the stations twice a year selling things,' said Ian. 'Can we go now? I want to see what he's got.'

'What sort of things does he sell?' Sally's curiosity was piqued and the idea of a travelling salesman was appealing.

'All kinds of things. Ask Mum.' Tommy and Ian were racing towards the house to raid their piggy banks.

Lorna was getting into the Land Rover. 'Come on, Sally, let's go shopping.'

'I don't have any cash on me.'

'Don't worry about that, just pick out what you want,' called John Monroe so Sally jumped in the back with the boys who were clutching their pocket money.

The old hawker had parked his big truck, covered with a canvas awning and piled with bags and boxes on the side and top, near the home stables but close enough to the blacks' camp for them to see he was there.

'My God, look at those old girls run,' said John. 'Never stir themselves any other time.'

Sally laughed at the sight of the women, the plump, the skinny, those with a piccaninny on their back, kids and dogs chasing at their heels, all hurrying as fast as they could to the van where a short man was rolling up the canvas sides of the truck. The boys rushed over to him as Lorna, John and Sally greeted him.

'G'day, Charlie. Thought you wouldn't get here before the Wet,' said John.

'No fear, Mister Monroe, I wouldn't miss you out. How do, Miz Monroe.'

'Hello, Charlie. This is our governess, Miss Mitchell.'

Sally nodded and gave him a big smile, unsure whether to shake hands as neither of the Monroes had. Charlie was a mixture of Aboriginal, Chinese, European and Afghan. He had wrinkled olive skin, narrow bright black eyes, a high forehead and a long dark pigtail.

Lorna said to Sally, 'Charlie is carrying on an old family tradition. His father and grandfather were Afghan camel traders. They travelled all around the Territory and north selling to the stations, prospectors, outstations, missions, everywhere. It used to be the only way we could get things sometimes.'

'Me more modern but,' laughed Charlie. 'I hated them camels when I was a kid.'

'So what do you have to show us, Charlie?' Lorna was businesslike; she was ready to stock up on her store supplies. The black men hovered, but the women were pulling things from the truck as the kids squealed and jumped around them. Soon some of the stockmen came over to join them. The word of Charlie's arrival had been spreading for some time as he'd driven along the track to Barra Creek.

It was a small riot of a bargain bazaar as items were spread on the ground. The men wanted to see whips, belts, holsters, boots, hats, smelly hair cream, scarves, buckles and fancy satin Western shirts. Lorna put aside work shirts, pants, some baby nappies and cleaning utensils along with dresses and blouses for the women. The boys were pulling out toys and books, paints and crayons, slingshots and a badminton set. John Monroe stocked up on bullets, rope, snake oil and nails. Sally found a bright red nail polish, a couple of books and a fancy plaited leather belt.

Charlie nodded approval at the belt. 'That a good belt that one. Made by old fella Jack at Brindley Station. His eyes are goin' and hands are shaky. He won't be makin' many more like that one.'

A voice behind her whispered, 'How about a silver buckle to go with it?' Rob held out the buckle engraved with a prancing horse. 'A present for you.'

'Hey, thank you, Rob.' Sally wanted to hug him but was aware Lorna was watching them.

''Scuse me, I gotta fix up them girls or they'll have every bit of cloth unrolled,' said Charlie, heading into the melee at the back of the truck. The women had grabbed bolts of bright red and yellow cloth and Charlie was kept busy cutting off lengths for them. Others were buying colourful patterned dresses.

Lorna and Sally shook their heads. 'They like the colours of the dresses,' said Lorna, 'never mind that big fat Daisy has bought an XSW.'

'But she can't wear it!' exclaimed Sally.

'Oh, she'll find a way. They can sew a very basic running stitch, big over and under. You've seen some of their frocks – a hole for the head and stitched up the sides. Sometimes they'll go to the trouble of adding a big gusset in the sides. So long as they like the colour they're happy.'

Lizzie was elated and held up her red material. 'Make 'em plenny corroboree dress. Got 'em lachtik, fix 'em up good.'

'What's lachtik?' asked Sally.

'They buy wide elastic, put it round their waist and tuck the fabric into it. Hey presto, a skirt. They'll tear a strip off one side and tie it round their hair.'

That evening there was much laughter from the blacks' camp as everyone shared their booty. In the homestead Sally took out her silver buckle and turned it over in her hands, touched by Rob's gesture. She decided next time she went away she'd have something engraved on it to remind her of Barra Creek. Then it struck her, where would she wear a stockman's leather belt with a big silver buckle? It was so unlike the conservative gear and subdued accessories she was allowed to wear for Hunt events. She'd ask Rob to attach the buckle to her belt tomorrow.

The following afternoon, after school had been out for an hour or so, Sally went looking for the boys to go for a ride. She wandered down to the stables and asked Rob if he'd seen them.

'They've gone hunting with Frankie and Ginger and the lubras. They're having a corroboree tonight.'

'What for?'

'Ask Fitzi. It's a bit of a party.'

'I hear them singing some nights,' said Sally. 'It's kind of mournful.'

'I'll take you down, if you like. After the boys are in bed.'

'Should I tell Lorna?'

'Why not? But she's never been interested. It's not a special ceremony or anything.'

'Right. See you later then.'

Lorna sipped a soft drink as they gathered before dinner. Rob and John were deep in conversation about station matters. The boys were in the kitchen talking to Lizzie. The nanny goat had been milked and there had been a discussion about how to make goat's cheese.

'Rob says the camp blacks are doing a corroboree tonight. He's going to take me down to watch,' Sally told Lorna.

'Sally, I wish you wouldn't. Has Rob checked it out with Fitzi? Sometimes it's not appropriate for women to watch. Why on earth do you want to go down there anyway?'

Sally hesitated. 'Rob thought I might be interested.'

Lorna gave her a sharp look. 'You make your own decisions, Sally.' Pointedly she changed the subject. 'Have you heard from your nice doctor in Darwin?'

'Heavens no. Now come on, Lorna,' she cajoled. 'You don't want me to move to Darwin, do you?' Sally kept her voice low so Rob, across the room, didn't hear.

Lorna's lips twitched in a near smile. 'I doubt that will happen. You're meant for better things. Though we don't want to lose you just yet.'

'I'm not going anywhere, Lorna. I love it here with you, the boys . . .'

'And?' Lorna glanced towards Rob.

'C'mon, Lorna, we're mates. Good friends. There isn't a lot of company my own age around here. Unless you count some of the stockmen or the runners . . .'

Lorna held up her hand. 'Very well, I take your point. Sally, when you're out here, and lonely, you don't want to build more into something than is there.'

Sally leaned over and touched Lorna's arm. 'I understand what you're saying. Really I do.'

Lorna looked relieved. 'That's good then because I have to go to Cairns. They're a bit worried about my condition. The doctor wants me on hand to monitor me.'

'Oh, I see. Well, that's sensible, much safer,' said Sally, wondering how she'd manage on her own for so long. John had got out of hand when Lorna was down in Sydney. 'When will John go over?'

'Heavens, I don't expect him to leave. I'll be all right.' But her face looked tight and sad.

'The baby is the most important thing,' said Sally softly. 'Don't worry, everything here will be fine.'

'I hope so. I know what happens when I leave. I trust you, Sally. You know what I mean.' She rose and rang the bell for Lizzie to serve.

Sally knew what she meant. Her responsibility was Ian and Tommy. Lorna couldn't bring herself to mention how one boy had been lost. Not that she blamed

Sally. She didn't have to, Sally still blamed herself in some ways for Marty's death. She glanced across the room and caught Rob's eye. He'd heard Lorna's last remark. Thank God he was there. Life at Barra Creek would be much more difficult without his company.

By bedtime the boys had heard that Rob was taking Sally down to the corroboree and wanted to go as well.

'You know your mother has forbidden you to go near the blacks' camp. It's a no-go area.'

'She doesn't like you going there either,' countered Ian.

'Yes, but Rob is watching out for me. I'll just stay in the background.'

'He can look after us too,' said Tommy.

'Come on, you chaps. I've never seen real Aborigine dancing. I've seen Frankie and Ginger showing you at the back of the schoolhouse, but that's all.'

'All right then,' laughed Tommy. 'We'll put on our own corroboree!'

Trailing towels, the two boys rushed along the verandah and dragged from under a bed a didgeridoo and clap sticks. Ian perched cross legged on the floor and started playing the long, hollow pipe Fitzi had made from a straight tree branch. Tommy played the clap sticks, banging the small cigar-shaped sticks together, swaying to their rhythm. Then he began to dance. Sally had seen him do this in wild spurts before, but tonight the boys performed with great seriousness, conscious that the third member of their group was missing. Marty had always kept to the beat by clapping and slapping his thighs.

Sally marvelled at the nimble movements of Tommy's slim body, lithe one minute, jerky the next as he imitated the bush creatures, the warrior and the hunter. He was depicting a story that came to a conclusion as the hunter closed in on his prey. The didge music got louder and as the hunter raised his spear Lorna stepped out onto the verandah.

'Just stop that rubbish, this instant!'

Shocked into silence, Ian tried to hide the didgeridoo, Tommy stopped dancing and Sally stepped forward and took the clap sticks from him.

'Okay, that's enough, finish getting ready for bed.' She pushed the sticks into her pocket.

'Sally, don't let them do that. I will not have them behaving like wild native bush boys. Ian, give me that thing.'

'Aw, Mum, it's special.' He tried to hide the didgeridoo that was almost as tall as Tommy. 'It's not mine anyway.'

'Then all the more reason why you shouldn't have it.'

'It's Fitzi's favourite,' cried Tommy.

'No it's not. It's Rob's,' said Ian, hoping that might make it more valuable.

Lorna took the musical instrument. 'It's firewood now. Off you go to the bathroom.' She turned to Sally. 'I'm putting this in the fire. It's hard enough trying to stop them growing up like little heathens, allowing this sort of behaviour doesn't help. You are to oversee their manners as much as their school work.'

'Yes, Lorna. I'm sorry. They wanted to go down to the corroboree. Of course I told them it was out of the question.'

'Why can't they listen to proper music or learn the piano?' sighed Lorna. 'They'll be at such a disadvantage when they go to school next year.'

From what Lorna had told Sally, most of the boys from the country were just like Tommy and Ian; she doubted they'd be misfits.

'I won't go down to the corroboree then.'

Lorna's anger had dissipated slightly. 'Go, as long as Rob stays with you. These things go on all night, I'll expect you back at a reasonable time. Then you won't need to go near that camp again. When I'm away I want to know I can trust you.'

'Of course.'

'I'm still going to burn this thing,' said Lorna.

The boys flung Sally a desperate look, but her expression silenced their moans at losing the didgeridoo. Sally hoped Fitzi would make another one that was just as good.

Once the boys were settled in bed Rob and Sally drove in his ute towards the camp. As they came close they saw the glow of the campfires and a smoky cloud of dust in the yellow light. There was a lot of movement from swaying dancers and an occasional leaping figure.

Rob walked ahead and Fitzi materialised beside them, though for a moment Sally didn't recognise him. He and the other men wore loincloths that looked to Sally like nappies; the men called them cockrags. Some wore old shorts, their bare chests daubed with thick white markings. Their hair was caked with grey ash and mud, and some wore elaborate headdresses. The women wore their new skirts sewn up as Lorna had described along with strips of material around their heads. Their bare breasts and faces were also painted with ochre. They sat on the ground, singing and playing the clap sticks.

Fitzi showed them where to sit and crouched beside them.

'What story this one?' asked Rob.

'Dis longa time, good chory, how camel men come 'ere.'

'The Afghans?'

'Dem good people. Camel go everywhere, carry every ting.'

'Like the hawkers?' said Sally.

'Dat be one. Dem come round in motor car now. No more camel chop.' He nodded at the dancers. 'Dere be camel in dat dance.'

Sally immediately recognised the two dancers pretending to be a camel. 'I wish I could follow the whole story. They're wonderful mimics.'

Fitzi returned to the group and she and Rob became absorbed in the saga being played out on the dirt stage. It was difficult to recognise the same slow lubras and stockmen, the blacks who sat down around the station, as these energetic, exuberant performers. It was mesmerising, the singing and rhythmic clapping hypnotic. Sally had no idea how much time had passed when Rob nudged her.

'We should make a move soon. It's been nearly two hours.'

'Righto.' Sally stood and as she turned she froze. Across the edge of the fire she saw the weird and creepy figure of the strange old man the boys called Mr Stinky. His wrinkled skin, cut with initiation and ceremonial scars, looked saggy, his yellow hair through the fire haze looked to be ablaze and his eyes glowed like red embers. He was staring directly at Sally, a slight smile on his face. Beside him stood two young girls of about twelve. Rob caught her involuntary shudder.

'What's up?'

'That old man, Mr Stinky. Those girls with him. Surely he's not going to . . . take them away with him.'

'Looks like it. It's the custom, Sal. He teaches them.'

'It's disgusting, they must hate it.'

'He must be pretty good, apparently the girls don't want to leave him when he brings them back to camp.'

'I don't understand it.'

Rob was about to say something, but changed his

mind and turned away. 'We'd better get back, Lorna is probably sitting on the verandah waiting for us.'

'She wouldn't!'

Rob grinned. 'Let's not rock the boat. Besides she'll be gone for a couple of weeks.' He leaned down and kissed Sally. 'And then who's going to keep tabs on us?'

Sally laughed and relaxed, the glimpse of the old man forgotten. 'The boys, John, Fitzi. We'll have eyes on us the whole time if you ask me!'

When they drove up to the homestead all was in darkness; everything was peaceful. The moon was blurry bright and Rob glanced up at the night sky. 'Looks like the Wet will start early. Didn't have much of a wet season last year. It would be good if we got a decent one this year.'

'Ugh, I hate rain.'

'This isn't rain, it's an upended river.' He drew her to him and they stood in the garden, arms entwined around each other.

'Thanks for taking me down tonight. It was really interesting. Listen, you can still hear them.'

'Don't expect the women to turn up on the dot tomorrow morning. G'night, Sal.' He kissed her softly on the lips. But the gentle kiss quickly became a rush of passion.

When they drew apart, Rob shook his head. 'My God, Sally, you run me over like a steam train. I can't believe what you do to me. You're a dangerous woman.'

Sally felt the same, amazed at how her body surged at his touch. 'We seem to have some sort of electrical current between us.'

They leaned closer, their lips touching again. 'So what are we going to do about it?' whispered Rob. 'Up to you . . .'

In answer, Sally tightened her arms and kissed him harder, giving him all the answer he needed.

He took her hand. 'Come and say goodnight to Jasper,' and began to lead her away from the house.

'Who's Jasper?' she whispered.

'The stallion. He's the colour of jasper. That's what I call him anyway.'

'But he's still pretty wild, won't he get upset?'

'I don't intrude. He knows me now. I just stand and let him know I'm there, speak softly to him. I go every night.'

They stood in the pale moonlight watching the horse standing almost motionless in the yard. His head was inclined to the side, ears twitching, his tail flicking. He watched Rob approach the fence.

Rob hung over the rails and called softly. 'Just checking on you, mate. Hope the corroboree didn't scare you. I brought a friend. She thinks you're a pretty handsome fellow. I told her you're going to be one heck of a smart horse when we've finished training you. Isn't that right?'

Sally smiled at Rob's crooning, soothing voice, like a father talking a child to sleep. The stallion took a few tentative steps forward then stopped, nostrils flaring, head erect.

'He smells you, something different. He's wary.'

Sally picked up Rob's calm, gentle tone. 'I just wanted to see you were okay too. I suppose you miss your herd. But they might join you some time.'

The horse listened but would come no closer. They watched him for a few more minutes then Rob took Sally's hand. He led her into the shed next to the stable and flicked on his lighter.

'Careful, this place is full of hay,' said Sally.

'It's okay.' He lit a small kerosene lantern that hung on a wire from a door. In the small circle of yellow light Sally watched as he pulled down a couple of clean horse blankets and lay them over a pile of loose straw. 'It's not wildly comfortable and not very romantic but . . .' He held out his arms with a shy half smile. Sally willingly surrendered to his embrace and, giggling quietly, they settled onto the makeshift bed.

It was hard to leave. Sally wanted to sleep in Rob's arms, despite the occasional prick of hay, but they knew they'd better go. He kissed her quickly and silently under the willow tree and waited till she was tiptoeing along the verandah before turning and heading to the room he sometimes used at the end of the single men's quarters. No one stirred.

Sally lay on top of her bed feeling flushed with sensations of love and being loved. The physical pleasure they'd shared had been exhilarating, but she'd seen another side to Rob in their whispers and knew how he had been creeping under her skin for many weeks leading to this moment. For the rest of her life, the smell of straw always brought back memories of this sensuous warm night with him.

Chapter Fourteen

SALLY AND LORNA SIPPED their afternoon tea on the verandah. As usual at this time of day the banks of clouds rolled across the sky, seeming to suck the air up into them and leaving everyone on the ground panting, tired and ill tempered. The weather had made it an exhausting couple of weeks, but Sally didn't like to complain. She could only imagine how uncomfortable Lorna must feel so far into her pregnancy. Just when Sally felt as if she was going to expire with the oppressive weather, a great storm would roll in. A dry storm. Dust would rise from the ground and fall from above, covering everything in a heavy red layer.

It blew straight through the flyscreens into the house, falling onto the beds, seeping into chairs and lounges, covering every surface. Sally had the taste of dust in her mouth from the moment she woke up in the morning, even her hair was coated. She hated it.

Then after three weeks of this, lightning started flashing along the horizon. At night Rob had pointed out the glow of fires – spinifex and dry grass hit by lightning and bursting into flame. They had word on the wireless of a fire on a property boundary to the east running on a sixty-mile front, driven by the strong winds.

'The Wet will come, and then you'll be sick of it,' sighed Lorna.

Rob sat on the rough fence rail and watched Sally slowly and calmly approach Jasper, keeping eye contact. The stallion had adjusted to his new life, if not to the loss of his herd. But he no longer had to fight for dominance, and he had water and feed and shelter. He had come to trust the tall quiet man with the gentle voice.

The horse watched Sally, smelled her, and felt no fear. She was trying to remember all Rob had told her, his 'unteaching' of her traditional British dressage and hunt riding techniques.

Once mounted with the leathers shortened a little so she had the power to swing straight into the saddle, she pushed her feet right into the heel of each boot. Sit well forward, lean slightly back, keep straight without any weight in the stirrups unless she needed to pull on the horse's head. No squeezing with the knees. Shoulders back to find the point of balance where she felt secure and in control. She rode Jasper around the yard for a few minutes before Rob agreed to open the gate.

'Ride him loose, Sal. You have to be able to change reins from left to right quickly or bring them back to two for shortening and steering. Shift your weight from side to side to change direction. Put the weight in the iron on the side you want him to turn. Use your hands, feet and your voice.'

Sally had been intrigued watching Rob break in the wild stallion in a series of short lessons with pauses in between, so Jasper could 'think about it'. After all the handling and frequent blindfolding, Jasper had become so accustomed to Rob that he offered no resistance when Rob first rode him. Now Jasper had become a smart, well-mannered horse and Rob intended to keep him that way and not let him learn any bad habits.

Sally trotted Jasper down to the smallest home paddock, executed a figure eight, stopped, walked him backwards, then moved forward again. Only on the last leg back to the yards did she allow the horse to canter, an easy powerful gait, when her position in the saddle felt exactly right. She'd become used to Rob's American-style saddle and rarely used her own from New Zealand. She knew her father would be appalled to see her riding like this, like a cowboy, he'd say.

Rob gave her a big thumbs up as she brought the horse into the yard and dismounted.

'He's a magnificent horse, Rob. Too good to be chasing cattle.'

'He'll make a good stockhorse, he's so strong. I'm going to ask Monroe if I can buy Jasper. This horse and I will work well together.'

'Where will you take him?'

He didn't answer for a minute. 'Well, eventually I want to have my own place. Maybe Dad will split up the station between my brothers and me. Whatever happens, I want to start a horse breeding program. Good stockhorses, like good working dogs, are worth a lot of money.' He squeezed Sally's arm. 'I'm glad you like horses. They're better than sheep. Sheep are silly animals.'

'Well, I grew up on a sheep farm so I'm not about to argue with that,' she said, laughing.

'Yeah, I hear New Zealand has six million sheep and two million people. You'd better not tell Ian you've ridden Jasper. He's after me to let him have a go, but I want to hold him back a bit.'

'The boys are talking a lot about leaving for school next year. It will be the first time they've been separated,' said Sally as they turned back towards the homestead. They walked closely, their arms touching as they carried the gear.

'What do you reckon will happen to them? To Barra Creek?'

Sally stared at him. 'It will go on, Ian will see to that. And Tommy, I s'pose. Monroe is not one to retire to a unit on the Gold Coast. Though I bet Lorna would like to go to the city more often.'

'Yeah, she'll be able to enjoy time away from here before the baby comes.' He glanced at the sky. 'She'd better leave soon though. The clouds are building, I think it's going to be a pretty decent wet season.'

In a lull between dust storms, Lorna, despite the weight of the baby and her swollen ankles, embarked on a frenzy of cleaning. Lizzie and the women were stirred into action to hose and scrub the verandah and inside cement floors even more vigorously than usual. The seagrass mats were taken outside to be beaten clean, the curtains and cushions washed, every surface was wiped and polished. The clothes cupboards were emptied and everything was aired before they were re-stacked. The baby's cot was freshly painted; the flyscreen over the top of it was replaced so no insect or creepy crawly could get in. The kitchen and pantry were wiped over with antiseptic and rusty tins of food were tossed out.

The chicken and goat pens were cleaned, and Fitzi was charged with replanting and tidying the garden. The outside walls were washed down as mildew was creeping up them, the rambling vines climbing over the pergola and verandah were trimmed back.

John Monroe kept out of the way. 'Happens every time. Next thing she'll be dusting the bloody fences.'

Sally and the boys washed, swept, dusted and tidied the schoolhouse. Rob was instructed to get the stockmen to tidy up the stables and sheds.

Lorna was an efficient tornado, immaculately dressed in her maternity smock and stretch maternity slacks ordered from the mail-order catalogue, her hair smoothly held back in a French roll as she directed proceedings, making the lubras re-do jobs until they were perfect, as well as doing things herself.

Then everything came to a halt. Lorna sat on the verandah and rarely spoke. Meals were mostly silent. The women retreated to their gundies and campfires. The paddocks, stables, yards and sheds were prepared for the expected deluge. A lethargy settled over the station. The air was moist, oppressive and faintly threatening. The men from the blacks' camp took off on a last walkabout for the season, leaving the women to argue amongst themselves.

It was a hot, red evening. Sally sat with Lorna and Rob, sipping cool drinks in the living room when John came in freshly washed and dressed, waving his glass of rum. 'Come see, Sally. It's on the way.'

'What is? Not rain surely? You've been promising that for weeks.'

'Come and see.'

Sally followed him onto the verandah and caught her breath at the amazing sunset spread across the sky. Against the burning colours stretched exquisite banks of high nimbus clouds, tinged with pale pink and lavender, and behind them in the darker indigo patches of sky, forks of lightning dazzled.

'Bloody marvellous, isn't it? I love this country. I know it's probably tough on softies like you and Lorna but, by golly, I couldn't live anywhere else.' John seemed to be speaking to himself.

The lightning and distant thunder rumbled through dinner.

The boys were reading in bed and Sally washed her face and diligently applied face cream. As she left the bathroom Lorna called to her. 'Sally, can I see you for a moment?'

She went into Lorna's bedroom. It was her private space where Sally rarely ventured, even though it was only separated with a thin partition from the rest of the house.

Lorna was sitting on the edge of the big double bed. She pointed to a small suitcase. 'I've packed my port. I just wanted to talk to you about a few things.'

'Of course, Lorna.' Sally stood there wondering if she should sit in the cane chair beside the cot. Lorna's hands were folded over her belly. 'Are you nervous?' she asked. 'It seems strange to think you'll be coming back here with a new person.'

'I like being pregnant,' admitted Lorna. 'I like being left alone. Though this has been a difficult pregnancy, which is why I'm going so early. And because of the Wet.'

'Don't worry, everything will be fine. The boys and I will keep our heads down. They have an exam coming up. I think they're anxious about going away to school, too.'

'I want you to keep them away from the river, the blacks' camp, the single men's quarters. They are not to go anywhere without you.'

'I understand.'

Lorna looked down at her hands. 'John will drink

too much. Just keep the boys away from him when he's had a skinful. I know what he's like but it upsets Tommy and he fights with Ian.'

'Lorna, don't worry. And Rob will be around.'

'Umm.' She didn't answer.

'Aren't you happy, looking forward to bringing the baby home?' asked Sally, trying to change the conversation.

'I just pray the baby is healthy.' She gave a small smile. 'I'm glad you're here, Sally. You've been really wonderful. I hope we'll always remain friends. The saddest part of all this is that you'll be leaving us in a couple of months.'

It hit Sally how things were changing. Barra Creek had become such a part of her life that it seemed incredible that soon she wouldn't be here. What would she do with herself? Much as she wanted to see her family, New Zealand seemed so far away. Sean was a distant, indistinct memory. She'd go home for a visit, she decided, then return to Barra Creek. Or, perhaps join Rob if he had followed his dream and started his own place. She had found what she'd been looking for when she'd turned her back on the trip to England. There was no way she could settle into her former life at home. She was in her twenties, surely this was a time to live life to the full.

'I'll be back, I'm sure. I have to go home anyway. My sister is getting married and I'm to be chief bridesmaid.'

'Is he an approved fiancé?'

'She's marrying Lachlan, my father's Head Cadet. He's the strong, silent type. Not my cup of tea.' Seeing Lorna's slightly raised eyebrow, she went on to explain, 'Only quality boys are selected for cadetships to train in running a sheep station. Quite a high position, different from a musterer on an Australian station. The head cadets are boys from good homes, good schools. He'll do well, Yvonne's life is mapped out.'

'Sally, I think you should take that trip to England, meet people more suited to your background. You can do much better than a fellow like Rob,' said Lorna earnestly.

Sally looked away, surprised that Lorna recognised the seriousness of their relationship. 'I'm not making any plans. But to be fair to Rob, he comes from a good family and we both love horses.'

'Don't bury yourself in the outback. It's hard work and lonely. There's a lot of things you don't know about. Trust me. I wouldn't want to see you throw your life away. It takes a special kind of woman to feel at peace in a place like this.' She turned her head and Sally got the feeling she'd said more than she intended. 'I just wanted to be sure you understand the responsibility you have while I'm away. Goodnight.'

'Night, Lorna.'

Ian was almost asleep, Tommy's bed was empty.

'Where's Tommy?' asked Sally.

'Gone to get a book. He said he was going to raid Dad's library.'

'I'd better go get him.'

She found Tommy standing on a chair looking at the books on the top two shelves above Monroe's desk.

'What are you up to? If your old man catches you there'll be trouble,' hissed Sally.

'I wanted something to read. How come he tells us not to touch these? You and Mum are always telling us to read.'

'People have private things they don't think young boys should see.'

'You mean like these?' Tommy pulled down some thick notebooks.

Sally recognised Monroe's writing on the front. 'They look like diaries. Leave them. Is there anything you want to read?'

'There are all these old books, I'll just take one.' He pulled out a book and climbed down from the chair. 'Look at this – *Secrets of the Pyramids* – I'm going there one day.'

'Fine. But go and read about ancient Egypt in your bed for now. And ask me if you want a book in future.'

As Tommy settled for the night Sally met Rob at their favourite rendezvous spot at the stables. They went for a quiet walk and Sally was tempted to tell him what Lorna had said, but couldn't think how to do it without hurting his feelings. He sensed something was bothering her.

'What's up? Troubles in the big house?'

'Lorna is worried about going away for so long, leaving the boys, knowing John will probably play up. She says she's going to miss me when I go home.'

Rob gripped her arm. 'She's not the only one.'

Sally stopped and turned to face him and blurted, 'Will I see you again, Rob?'

'God, Sally, that's a hard hit.' He took her hand and tenderly stroked her fingers. 'I've been trying to ignore the whole thing. My mother says I stick my head in the sand when I have to deal with something hard. Now, hearing you say that, well, I can't imagine not having you around. I've stayed here longer than I usually do. I should have gone back out mustering by now.'

'Yeah, John made that point. He said I was exerting too much influence.' Sally gave a slight smile.

'But I don't expect you'd want to stay on here just for me.'

'My time here will soon be up – the boys are off to school. Lorna says I should go to England after my sister's wedding.'

'Is that what you want?'

Sally looked away. 'I don't know what I want.'

Rob wrapped her in his arms. 'Sally, I can't offer you anything at the moment. I have dreams, vague plans. If you could give me a bit of time.'

'Like when I come back from England perhaps . . .'

'Exactly. Would you wait for me a bit?' He bent down and kissed her long and hard.

Sally's fears and the insecurities and doubts that Lorna had planted melted. He was a good man, they had so much in common, there was huge physical attraction between them, and Rob had big plans.

'I have big dreams too,' she said. 'Maybe together we can make something happen. I want to be around horses, not working in a city office.'

'Then can we leave it at that – for the moment? You go back to New Zealand, take that overseas trip and then we'll meet. Or I'll come over there to meet your family. We'll see if I get the stamp of approval.'

'It doesn't matter if you don't,' said Sally. 'Though I bet my mother will fall for you.'

Rob was relieved. 'We'll just keep it between us then. Until we can make it something formal. But in the meantime . . .' He brushed his lips across her ear, murmuring sweet and sexy suggestions, and they turned back towards what Sally thought of as their love nest in the stables.

Back in her own bed, she slept fitfully. Despite Rob's declarations of love, it weighed in her heart that they had not made any definite plans.

She was woken in the early dawn by a clap of thunder crashing overhead. She leapt up and rushed along the verandah, her white nightie spotlit every few feet as lightning flashed on and off. She ran into the garden and felt the sharp sting on her skin and breathed in the smell as the first drops of rain hit the thirsty garden. She'd always remember that smell. It was an overpowering ozoney smell that she realised she had been faintly sniffing for the past forty-eight hours. She lifted her face to the hard drops that were now flowing faster. Then behind the curtain of rain came the wind, pushing great streaming torrents. The noise was deafening as the rain hit the tin roofs, slamming against any solid object, the wind whistling. She was soaked through to her skin and for the first time in weeks felt she could take deep clean breaths.

'You're going to get struck by lightning, get in here,' shouted John Monroe. He was standing on the verandah, looking amused.

'It's fantastic! What a sight!' cried Sally as she ran onto the verandah.

Two figures in striped pyjamas raced to join them. 'Wow, here it is!'

'Why're you wet, Sally?'

'Ooh, it's just so exciting!' She took their hands. 'Quick, pull the beds away from the screens – they're getting wet.'

Lorna, wrapped in her dressing-gown, came out and began calmly issuing instructions. 'All the beds will have to be pulled in towards the centre and the outside doors and louvres closed. Sally, go and get dry clothes on. Boys, get back into bed.'

Their exuberance faded and everyone began hurrying to get things organised.

Dressed in dry pyjamas, her hair wrapped in a towel, Sally sat on her bed watching the light show through the vines and screens. The boys had experienced this every year since they were born, so they soon settled to sleep, oblivious to the cacophony.

'Here's to the Wet.'

Sally hadn't heard John Monroe come along the verandah. He handed her a glass of rum.

'Cheers.' She took a sip. It tasted good, warming her insides that felt rain soaked. 'So what happens in the Wet around here? How does anyone work?'

He chuckled. 'Few do if they can help it. The white blokes will take off for their holidays. We'll do the occasional bore run and make sure no stock are stuck anywhere. This is the time for maintenance on the plant and equipment. The blacks will stay in their gundies, play cards, tell stories. They find it easy to pass time doing nothing.'

They sat quietly. It didn't seem possible but Sally thought the rain was growing even louder, making it hard to talk. Monroe finished his rum and leaned down and touched Sally's head. 'Get that wet towel off your head.' His hand stayed for a moment, then he turned and walked along the verandah.

'Thanks for the rum.' Sally cupped her hands around the tumbler. If he heard her, he didn't answer.

Later that day all the verandah furniture was pulled into the main part of the house. Lorna had flour and sugar bags laid at all the doorways so everyone could step onto them while taking their boots off. It was a house rule that shoes and boots were taken off before going inside and the boys knew better than to put a muddy boot near the verandah.

Sally couldn't believe the intensity of the rain and the fact it had barely stopped. 'It's not going to rain like this for months is it?' she asked at breakfast as John Monroe pulled on his heavy oilskin coat.

'Too right. Why do you think it's called the Wet? We need this. It was a piss-weak one last year, very unusual.'

With the Aboriginal men away and the early start of the wet season, it appeared the deluge had unleased a torrent of fights and passion among the women in the camp. By late morning the rain had eased but it was still steamy. In the schoolhouse the lesson was disrupted by a commotion coming from the kitchen.

'Keep your heads down, kids,' Sally said firmly. 'You too Ginger, Frankie, Alice.'

'Dat be Betsy. Maybe baby come,' said Frankie.

Sally pulled on her gumboots and squelched to the kitchen where Betsy, looking very pregnant indeed, was shouting for Lorna.

'What's up? Are you all right, Betsy?' called Sally.

'Big fight longa Mattie an' Tilla . . . whack 'em good, make 'em big cut, firetick.'

Sally knew Tilla was a big lazy woman and Mattie sometimes hung around Snowy. 'Who are they fighting? What's going on with the fire stick? I'll get Missus.'

Sally raced inside but Lorna was already putting on her shoes. 'Sally, get the first-aid kit, the box and the bag.'

'Is it bad? What is going on? I thought all the men were away.'

'That's when the trouble starts. They argue and fight over a man. When the men are in camp they're too busy lying down or getting in swags to fight each other.'

'Can I help?' Sally couldn't imagine women seriously fighting.

'Maybe, take the small bag.' Lorna picked up a rifle and headed for the Land Rover. 'Tell the boys to stay in the schoolroom.'

Lorna drove through the wet grass and under dripping trees that a day before were dry and dusty. Dogs and small children scattered as they drove into the camp. Some kids were splashing in the rain puddles, chasing each other and throwing mud with great hilarity. A knot of women were standing around the remains of a damped-down campfire. Old chairs, empty tins, drums and rubbish were scattered around. The women were waving and gesticulating, some were holding heavy waddies. Lorna blew the horn and they slowly parted.

Two women were facing each other and to Sally's horror they were holding smouldering fire sticks. Mattie lifted her stick and hit Tilla across the head. Tilla didn't flinch, she just let the hot stick bounce off her frizzled hair. Then as her head cleared, she retaliated, whacking Mattie on the shoulder. Mattie didn't duck or attempt to move.

Lorna sailed in between them and Sally gasped as she saw the dreadful wounds they'd inflicted on each other. Lorna made them sit down and, seeing Lizzie, waved her forward. 'You tell them, all done now.'

Lizzie nodded emphatically and burst into a loud, rapid harangue directed at the wounded women. Then she smiled at Lorna. 'All pinish, done. Dem no more cranky. Dem deaf-adder all done fightin'. Man belong Tilla, come back, longa time. Be down wit Mattie. No more belonga Tilla,' she explained.

'Heavens, they've really bashed into each other,' said Sally. Blood was oozing from the long gashes and some skin had been burnt. 'What's with the deaf-adder?' she asked as Lorna pulled out disinfectant and poured it onto a cloth.

'Death adders, that's what they call gossipy old crones. I'm going to have to stitch some of these.' Matter of factly she took out a needle and nylon thread. 'Lizzie, make up ash paste for these burns.'

'Yes, Miz, make 'em up pix 'em up.'

With two other women Lizzie began scooping ash from the edge of the fire, which they mixed with some dried leaves and bark. The injured women were now cheerfully chattering, honour having been established and some agreement reached over the absent man.

The paste was applied to the burns, Lorna expertly stitched up the wounds and packed away her medical kit. She shook her finger at Lizzie. 'You tell them no more fighting. I'm going away and Miss Mitchell can't fix them up. No sewing up, no medicine.'

Sally shook her head, aghast. 'I can't do any of that. Not me, not at all.' Once again she admired the ever-capable Lorna.

Awkwardly Lorna stood up. 'And you be on time in the kitchen for breakfast tomorrow, Lizzie. No pink-hi, you cook, quick smart.'

'You-hi, Missus. You-hi.'

'She might say yes now, but when there's been a blue like this, it rattles the routine for days,' sighed Lorna.

'Can't you stop them? They looked like they were going to kill each other. Just as well you were a nurse. I couldn't do that.'

'If you have to, you do,' said Lorna calmly. 'As soon as the men come back, those two will be up at the store for new dresses, best mates again. They can be free and easy with their sexual favours but they're still women and silly enough to argue over a man.' She glanced at Sally as she started the Land Rover. 'Men aren't worth it.'

Insects and bugs flourished in the Wet – hairy caterpillars and triangular stink bugs were on everything. The frogs seemed to have multiplied by the thousands and sang through the night, revelling in the sodden ground and pools. The sound was deafening. John warned Sally to look out for snakes and to be careful by the river in case it had flooded a nest of croc eggs and a mad mother crocodile was busy defending them.

Lorna began to worry. 'John, how am I going to get out? Snowy says the runway is a bog.'

'Looks like it's easing off this morning. We might have a break for a couple of days. Fitzi and the boys should come in from walkabout now the Wet's here. They'll know. Let's wait till then.'

By nightfall the rain and lightning strikes were back, the power generator was hit and it felt as if Barra Creek was cut off from the rest of the country.

Monroe got busy on the wireless and returned to tell Lorna, 'There's only one thing for it, love, the milk run. Spoke to Cliff over at Billy Springs, he says he's taking his truck into Croydon, we can still get over the big creek and you can pick up the Gulflander from there into Normanton. Then fly on to Cairns.'

'And how will you get back?'

'I reckon I can pick up a boat or barge heading up river from Karumba to Normanton.'

'Is Cliff sure he can get over the train bridge at the big creek? I suppose that means planking the car over.'

'Yeah, we've done it before.'

The narrow wooden bridge was only a little wider than the width of the train gauge, with no fence on either side. John Monroe turned on his heel as Lorna bit her lip. She had been ready to leave for weeks, but now that arrangements were made, she looked pale, and for the first time since Sally had known her, unsure.

Rob later told Sally not to worry. It was very early in the Wet, the river wouldn't be too high. 'It's washed over that bridge before this. If there was a real emergency the Cairns Aerial Ambulance would pick her up.'

Barra Creek's northern neighbour Cliff Field, from Billy Spring Station, rolled up in his heavy-duty, high-wheel-base Land Rover and Lorna and John Monroe drove off after a lingering goodbye with the boys and Lorna repeating instructions to Sally.

The men tried to make Lorna as comfortable as

possible but the road was pot-holed and sludgy with the rain. They pressed on, though, anxious to get over the river before dark. Late afternoon they arrived at the tributary, which was full and flowing fast but hadn't risen to the bridge or overflowed the banks. The men had brought along six planks, which they laid over the train line on the bridge so the Land Rover could drive over, stop-starting as they carried the planks forward so the vehicle could drive on a little further. Lorna found sitting in the four-wheel drive tedious and uncomfortable and, much as she hated heights, she chose to walk slowly down the middle of the rail line ahead of it. She tried not to look down at the fast-moving water below, and concentrated on the gaps between the sleepers. This was no time to put a foot wrong.

By dark they were in Croydon, once a bustling gold-mining centre, now virtually a ghost town except for a few houses, a small pub and a store that sold fuel and some basic commodities. They spent the night in the hotel where they slept in a mildewy room with a sagging bed.

Lorna couldn't face the greasy breakfast and sipped her tea as John ate heartily.

The railway line that ran the ninety miles between Croydon and Normanton was not connected to any other line. There were plans to link Cloncurry and Normanton, but with the gold find in Croydon the railway was diverted there instead. The Gardner rail motor, known as the Gulflander, carried passengers and supplies to the remote stations between Croydon and Normanton.

John helped Lorna into the red and yellow carriage, settled their bags around them and put his feet up on a seat. 'Not long now, love.'

'For you, but I still have a plane to catch tomorrow.'

'Ah, you can relax in Cairns till it's time. What are you going to do with yourself?'

'The guesthouse isn't far from where Marilyn lives. We nursed together down in Melbourne. It will be nice to see her and the family. And there are tests, doctor's visits . . .'

'Yeah, yeah, well good. You take it easy.'

'John, you will be careful while I'm away, won't you? No boozing. Spend time with the boys, watch Sally and Rob. You know what I mean.'

'Bloody hell, Lorna, you're a broken record.'

Rob, Sally and the boys revelled in having the house to themselves. Sally fantasised that it was their home, the boys their children. They all ate at the big table, and after Lizzie had cleared the dishes they played Monopoly. Rob raided John Monroe's stash of liquor and brought out a brandy and a port. When the boys had gone to bed, Sally and Rob curled up together on the lounge and sipped the good brandy.

The ANA plane took off from Normanton for Cairns with Lorna leaning back in her seat, her eyes closed, hands folded over her buckled seatbelt, a resigned expression on her face. John Monroe knew people everywhere he went so it was no trouble to get a lift into Karumba.

He hit the notorious Animal Bar at the Karumba Lodge, which took him a day to sleep off.

A few mornings later John got up at sunrise. He vaguely remembered the arrangement he'd made for a ride back to Normanton on a barge that was ferrying machinery up the Norman River, and the captain had agreed to drop him off at Barra Creek.

He stepped outside his motel room and noticed a drop in temperature. He glanced up at the sky, above the start of the sunrise, to see the phenomenon of the Morning Glory.

Across the horizon rolled several long pipe-shaped clouds that turned over and over in an unbroken line from one side of the sky to the other. A fast wind was whipping them along and it looked like rain might follow. It could be an uncomfortable trip up river but he stayed and studied the strange cloud that he'd heard only ever appeared in the Gulf of Carpentaria and the Gulf of Mexico.

John stepped on board the barge carrying a box of booze, which received frowns from the other two passengers – a Pentecostal minister and a teetotaller drover called Billy Jumpup. With a bottle of rum in his pocket, John Monroe passed the day drinking and yarning with the captain.

They were still drinking after they had dropped off all the other passengers. By the time they were in the vicinity of Barra Creek it was dark and they were both drunk and found it hard to see the small landing. Finally the captain anchored the barge, stood on the bow and fired three rifle shots into the air. Rob and Sally didn't hear, they were playing records and teaching the boys to dance. But Fitzi heard and ran to the river with a fire stick and waved them in to the landing.

John Monroe was very drunk. He threw his haversack to Fitzi and heaved the box of bottles onto the gunwale, shouting directions to the captain who reversed the barge into the landing, hitting it with a shudder that sent the bottles splashing into the river.

'Bloody hell, that's good rum,' shouted Monroe, and jumped over the side into the mud, sinking to his knees. 'Fitzi, get over here with the light.'

The flame from the fire stick didn't throw much light and Monroe shouted at the captain to shine the torch.

Monroe found the floating box and threw it to Fitzi, then probed the mud with his feet and hands, locating most of the bottles.

'You're bloody mad, mate. I'm not putting a foot in there,' exclaimed the barge captain as he helped pull John Monroe free and watched him scramble onto the landing.

'Take the grog up to the house, Fitzi. Thanks for the lift, mate.' Monroe gave a shaky wave and stumbled after Fitzi, then remembered how far it was to the homestead, sat down by a tree and passed out.

Rob heard the clink of bottles in the kitchen, saw Fitzi looking grim and realised what must have happened.

'Sal, get the boys ready for bed, their dad is home. Not in good shape, I'd say.'

Ian and Tommy were behind Sally.

'Where is he?' asked Tommy.

'Passed out near the river, I reckon,' said Rob. 'We'll drive down and get him before he's croc bait.'

'Silly old bugger. Leave him there,' said Ian and left the room followed by Tommy.

Sally and Rob exchanged a glance and Rob gave her a quick kiss. 'Keep out of Monroe's way. I'd say he hasn't been sober for days.'

Sally and the boys heard John Monroe stumble and crash into his bed but Sally kept reading quietly. While the boys were both competent readers, they still liked Sally to read 'hard' books to them, explaining ideas or words as she went along. Once they had gone to sleep she put the book aside and tiptoed along the verandah and peeped around the partition. John Monroe was sprawled across the bed, a sheet pulled over him, a pile of muddy clothes and boots on the floor, a half-empty bottle of rum beside him.

The rain started again and Sally fell asleep, comforted

by the now familiar sound. But she woke not long before dawn. She rolled over and went rigid. Through her partially closed eyes she could see the floor and not far from her bed were the unmistakable bare, muddy feet of John Monroe. Pretending to still be asleep, she saw through her eyelashes that he was sitting on the empty bed in the row along the verandah staring at her. His hands were on his knees as he watched her. In the pale light she couldn't read his expression but she was unnerved.

Ian coughed and rolled on his side, unknowingly breaking a strange spell.

John Monroe got up and padded silently down the verandah.

Chapter Fifteen

SODDEN DAYS PASSED SLOWLY. John Monroe worked in the machinery shed, and while he seemed a bit quieter than usual it was probably because he was feeling contrite over his binge in Karumba. Rob was breaking in horses, slowly and thoroughly, trying to work in between downpours. Sally was bored. Whenever there was a break in the rain she took the boys out for a ride and occasionally Rob would bring Jasper along to get him used to being around other horses. Ian still longed to ride the big stallion.

Mail was sporadic during the Wet. When Donny couldn't land he dropped the mail bag into the home paddock close to the house. Sally's mother and sister wrote to her about Yvonne's wedding preparations, which seemed to Sally to be getting out of hand. Her parents had taken over and were arranging everything and Yvonne and Lachlan had little say in it. Sally knew that's how it was in her parents' circle – weddings gave the families the opportunity to show off and no expense was spared. That was if the marriage was with an 'approved' groom or bride. Otherwise the wedding was played down, which Sally thought would be the case if she and Rob were to get married. Of course, if Rob suddenly came into some money and settled down on the family property, he'd be embraced by the Mitchell clan. She'd never thought about marriage before but now she could see herself sharing her life with Rob.

Each evening before dinner, John Monroe would raise his glass in a toast to his wife. 'Here's to the old girl.'

Lorna called in daily on the wireless and the boys were always eager to talk to her, their first question was inevitably, 'Has the baby come yet?' Then Sally would speak briefly, reassuring her all was well. Knowing the other stations were listening in, personal detail or emotion was kept to a minimum.

John always ended the conversation with 'Take care of yourself, lass.'

Eventually the torrential downpours started again. Monroe came in before dark, hanging his dripping coat, boots and hat outside the kitchen.

'The river is coming up, might run a banker. Seems something has given way upstream. The spit that divided one of the creeks from the main flow has caved in.'

Rob followed him inside, shrugging off his wet-weather gear. 'Isn't Snowy still out?'

'Yeah. He should've taken someone with him.'

'I offered,' said Rob.

'There's no one else here he could have taken?' asked Sally.

'Couple of lazy old blackfellas down in the camp who didn't go walkabout,' said Monroe. 'Isn't that right, Lizzie?'

Lizzie banged a pot on the stove. 'Dem lazy buggas. Reckon dem medicine men. Clever big pella. No need for 'em go walkabout.'

'They're too old to be much help if he finds bogged cattle or horses,' said Rob.

'We might have to launch the boat into the paddocks,' John said with a grin at Sally. 'We've done that before.'

The next day, as the weather cleared, they went about their work and from the schoolhouse Sally heard John Monroe drive off towards the home paddock. The kids from the camp were disruptive, talking and running around the room.

'Settle down, Frankie. Come on, finish your work.'

'Old men comin' back,' he said. 'All dem walkabout mob, come back.'

'How do you know that?'

Tommy laughed. 'Don't ask him. They always just say they know.'

'And they do,' said Ian. 'Betcha in a couple of hours they'll all come back in.'

At lunchtime they all sat at the big table, as had become their custom with Lorna away, when Lizzie walked in with their meals and announced, 'Dem walkabout pellas in de camp now.'

Tommy looked at Sally. 'See, told you so.'

'Now they'll all sit down and do nothing for weeks, unless the rain eases off for a bit. It's the world's longest card game,' said John Monroe.

They ate in silence and Rob was wondering how he could raise the subject of Jasper. He'd asked Monroe about buying him, riding him while he was working at Barra Creek, but taking the horse with him when he left. Monroe had told Rob he'd think about it.

'He has all it takes for the hard slog mustering,' said Rob eventually.

'Mmm.' John kept eating, then asked, 'How many more horses you got to break?'

'Half a dozen or so. Keep me busy for a bit.'

'Can we go riding this arvo, please?' Ian said to Sally. 'We're sick of being cooped up.'

Sally felt the same. 'Let's finish our school work first.' But she gave the boys a wink.

Rob was repairing a saddle a few hours after lunch when he heard the rifle shots. He ran outside and, realising they were coming from the yards near the home paddock, he ran to his ute and took off as fast as he could. The only person with a rifle was Monroe and the shots were a sure sign he was in trouble. Rob doubted he'd be shooting wildlife at this hour of the day. His heart started pounding when he saw the Land Rover near the yard where Jasper was spelled during the day. As he got closer he saw John Monroe sitting slumped beside the truck's door, the rifle beside him.

The yard was empty, the gate open.

'What's up?'

'Done my back, might've broken my leg. Bastard of a horse.'

Rob looked around, a knot tightening in the pit of his stomach. 'Where's Jasper? What the hell happened?'

'I was looking him over, thought I'd check him out. See if he's as good as you reckon.' Monroe stopped, drawing a painful breath. 'Bastard kicked me, and shot through the gate and took off. I managed to drag myself here and get the rifle.'

Rob was staring at the gate. 'It wasn't shut?' The stupid man, he should know better than to get into the yard with an unfamiliar horse and leave the bloody gate open, Rob thought furiously.

'Christ man, help me will you?' snapped Monroe, holding out his arm.

Rob helped him up and he hobbled around the vehicle

to the passenger side. 'Doesn't look like your leg is broken, bad sprain I'd say.'

'My back and hip are killing me. Maybe I shouldn't be moved.' Monroe winced.

'Too late. I think you'll need a hot bath and a long rest. I'll take you back and get Sally and the boys to look for Jasper.'

They'd just set off when Sally and the boys rode up.

'We heard shots, what's happening?'

'Bit of an accident. Jasper kicked your dad and took off,' Rob said, looking at Ian.

'Where's Jasper?' Ian's face was white.

'Charging across the home paddock somewhere. He's a mean bastard,' snapped John Monroe.

'He's not! You are!' shouted Ian. He wheeled his horse and broke into a gallop, heading into the home paddock.

'You watch your mouth,' screamed John Monroe in pain, anger and some embarrassment.

Sally and Tommy took off after Ian. Sally hoped Rob could deal with John Monroe; judging by his temper he wasn't seriously hurt and her nursing skills were non existent.

'Let's split up. We'll meet at the gate at the western boundary fence.'

They rode off and she soon lost sight of the boys amidst the ant hills and scrubby terrain. What a fool John Monroe was to try to ride a stallion who'd only ever been ridden by the gentle horse breaker. Sally had seen Monroe around horses a few times and he was a rough handler, determined to show he was the big boss. Or bully, she thought.

She was cantering, trusting the sure feet of Dancer as she gazed around hoping to see Jasper grazing quietly and not streaking for the hills. Hearing her name she turned and saw Tommy galloping recklessly after her. She reined in.

'You found him?'

'Ian has. Oh Sally, it's terrible . . .' Tommy was crying and Sally turned Dancer close to his horse and reached out to him.

'What's happened? Where's Ian?'

'With him. Oh poor Jasper,' blubbered Tommy. 'Ian's going to kill Dad . . .'

'Where are they? Quick.' Sally was firm. 'Keep your head, Tommy. Just tell me where they are and then go and get Rob.'

'The start of the western fence, near the gates.'

Sally kicked Dancer before he could say any more. Her heart was in her mouth as she raced to the boundary fence. Against the horizon was etched the proud head and solid outline of Jasper. Ian was crouched a short distance away, holding the reins of his horse who stood motionless behind him. Sally slowed, not wanting to frighten Jasper, and dismounted, and leading Dancer walked towards them. Ian held up his hand, indicating she should stay back. Then she saw why and gasped.

Jasper was against the boundary fence; he'd rushed it hoping to gain freedom and return to the hills, or perhaps to escape the bullying of John Monroe. In his panic he had hit the fence, which, in the soft wet ground, had given way. He must have fallen then regained his feet but in the process strands of barbed wire that were stretched along the lower section of the fence had caught him and were wound around his legs, shredding the flesh to the bone. The more he'd tried to free himself the more entangled he became.

'Oh my God.' Sally let Dancer stand as she walked slowly towards the wounded stallion.

Tears were streaming down Ian's face. 'What'll we do?'

'It looks bad. Rob is coming, he'll know. Just don't frighten him, come away.'

Sally's heart was pounding. The stallion turned towards her, fear and anger showing in his eyes, the tilt of his head, the quivering of his body, the levelled ears.

She spoke softly, whispering and consoling. 'Jas . . . it's all right, I know it hurts, boy. Don't move, you'll make it worse. We're going to get you out, Jasper, don't worry. You're going to be fine.' She repeated the soothing words over and over.

'I wish I could kill my father for this,' Ian hissed in a low voice.

'Don't say that. It was an accident, he'd never hurt the horse,' mumbled Sally.

'He doesn't care. Dad'll be mad 'cause he hurt himself. Sally, please don't let him do anything to Jasper.'

'Don't worry, Ian. Your dad will be more worried about his own injuries. We'll have to get the vet, see what he says.'

Ian swung his attention from the stallion for the first time and stared at Sally in shock. 'Vet! They won't get a vet.'

'Of course they will, a vet will know what to do.'

Ian stood up. 'Listen, we don't get vets out here. Animals live or die.'

This was incomprehensible to Sally; her father was always calling the vet out to treat his animals. But of course the distance of Barra Creek would make it impossible. Her heart sank. She was saved from arguing as the Land Rover raced towards them. Rob jumped out and walked slowly forward, studying the stallion.

'Ian, move back, take the other horses away,' he said quietly.

Ian took Dancer and his own horse and led them away. Sally squatted on her haunches, trying to make

308

herself small, unobtrusive and non threatening.

'Oh Jesus, oh hell . . .' muttered Rob under his breath. 'Hey, boy, you got yourself in a little trouble here. Don't worry, we're going to get you out and you'll be just fine.'

Recognising Rob, Jasper shook his head and whinnied.

'How are we going to get him out of that mess? There's wire embedded in his skin, look at his chest. And the bleeding, you can see the bone in his legs,' said Sally, choking up.

'Wire cutters to start with.' He pulled out a pair from the toolbox in the Land Rover, then crouched by Jasper's fetlocks and quietly began snipping through the tangle of barbed wire.

'Okay, Sally, come and hold him while I unsaddle him and see if I can free his back legs. At least he'll be able to walk then, and we have to keep him on his legs.'

'I hope it's not all the wire holding him up. God, Rob, is he going to make it?' she glanced back at Ian who was watching as he held the horses.

Stiffly and painfully John Monroe got out of the Land Rover, carrying his rifle.

'What're you doing, Dad? No! No!' Ian screamed.

Monroe was slamming bullets into the breech. 'Best thing for it, son. Can't see an animal suffer.' He cocked the rifle.

'No. Don't!' Ian dropped the reins he was holding, rushed forward and flung himself at his father, knocking him off balance. John Monroe fell and the rifle went off, a bullet ricocheting into the Land Rover.

'Shit!'

Jasper jerked, trying to rear, the wire dragging deeper into his skin.

'What the hell?' Rob strode over to Monroe. He grabbed the rifle and expelled the other bullet.

'You little bastard. You nearly killed me.' John Monroe shook his fist at Ian.

Ian's face was white but his eyes burned. In a firm, defiant voice he said, 'You hurt Jasper and I will kill you.'

Rob took control and led Monroe back to the vehicle.

'Put that bloody horse down,' yelled John Monroe.

Rob said quietly, 'I made you an offer for the horse, John. It still stands. I'll buy him off you now, yes or no?'

'What for? Bloody horsemeat?' Monroe turned and got into the driver's seat.

'Jasper is my horse, Rob,' cried Ian, suddenly starting to sob.

Monroe slammed the door. 'Do what you bloody want. You're all mad.'

As he drove away, Rob went to Ian and held him. 'Mate, I'm going to look after him. Make him strong again. And then he'll be your horse, for sure.'

He glanced back at the bleeding horse and wondered how the hell he was going to save him. Then, looking down at the boy clinging to him, he rubbed Ian's head. 'You help me, mate, and we'll do our best. That's all we can do. Then it's up to Jasper.'

Fitzi finally arrived towing the old homemade horse float. Rob had freed Jasper, but strands of wire were still embedded in his legs and he'd lost a lot of blood. Fitzi drove Rob back to his ute then took the horse to the stables where he stood shakily, his head down, the fight gone out of him.

On Rob's request, Sally raced into the house, pulled old clean sheets out of the cupboard and ripped them into bandages.

Rob bathed Jasper's legs in warm salty water and gently cut and picked the last of the wire from the trembling horse. Then he bandaged the animal's legs. Ian and Tommy hung around as he led Jasper into a stall.

'Let's leave him. He needs to be quiet. Let him think about what's happened and decide if he's going to get better or not.'

Keeping the boys away from the stables was hard, but Rob was insistent. John Monroe spent the rest of the day in bed, sipping rum and sleeping.

That evening when Lorna came through on the wireless, Sally gave her a brief rundown of events.

'That horse is jinxed. It's only brought bad luck,' said Lorna. 'If it lives, Rob should sell it.'

Rob, Sally, Ian and Tommy ate dinner in miserable silence. The boys went to get ready for bed and John Monroe, looking pale, wandered into the lounge room where Sally was sitting on her own.

'There's some dinner left for you, John. Would you like me to get it?'

'Don't feel like eating. I still feel crook. Might have a hot bath.' He poured himself another rum.

'Sounds like a good idea. Lorna rang, no news.'

He eased himself into a chair. 'I'm too old for another kid. So's she. Hell, why does Ian have it in for me so much?'

'He loves that horse.'

'He's had it in for me before that.'

'The oldest-son syndrome, I suppose. Maybe you should listen to him a bit more, instead of always telling him you're right and he's wrong.'

'He's just a kid.'

'Did you argue with your father?'

He was silent and sipped his drink. 'He died when I was young. Do you agree with your parents all the time?' he countered.

Sally didn't answer for a moment. 'No. But as my father might say, t'was ever thus. He didn't agree with his parents either.'

'Ah, hell. I'm going to throw my bones in the bath. Bloody lucky that flaming horse didn't break anything.'

As he put his glass on the sideboard, Rob came into the room, pulled a wad of notes from his pocket and slapped them on the table.

'Two hundred quid. As we agreed.'

'I don't want your money.'

'I want you to take it. I'll take responsibility for Jasper. Whatever happens now, it's my horse.'

'Don't waste your money. Forget it.'

'I insist. Don't go back on your word.'

'I never break my word. It's on your head then. When that horse dies, you tell my son. You've given him false hope.'

'I'll take that chance.' Rob glanced at Sally and left the room.

They left Jasper alone for a week. Rob hand fed him occasionally, moving quietly, checking the horse stayed on his feet.

After breakfast one morning Rob took Ian aside. 'I'll need your help today.'

They led Jasper out of the stall. Rob unwound the bandages, which were caked with dried blood and rotting flesh, and had Ian run the hose down the animal's legs. Then they washed them with water and salt.

'We've got to watch that proud flesh doesn't build up, I want to keep the straight line of his leg, make sure it heals from beneath. Pass me that tin.'

'What's in it? Smells like . . . brake oil.'

'It is. Whack it on and throw some sulphur on top.

We're going to do this every day for a week. Then it's up to Jasper to heal himself.'

Ian looked at the horse, who seemed more dejected day by day. The lustre was gone from his coat, and he hung his head, taking no interest in what was going on around, or happening to, him.

'I don't think he cares, Rob. He's not going to fight,' said Ian.

That night sitting on his bed, Ian told Sally he thought Jasper was going to die.

'But he's doing okay, Rob said,' cried Tommy.

'His legs are healing but his head and heart aren't good,' said Ian simply. He rolled on his side, turning his back on them.

Some time later Sally stirred from a restless sleep and sat up. Both boys were asleep. Throwing a jacket over her nightie, she pulled on her boots, picked up a torch and walked through the cool damp night to the stables. Clouds covered the moon, rain threatened.

The kerosene lamp hung from a hook, Rob was sitting on a bale of hay outside Jasper's box. The box door was open and Jasper was standing still, looking disinterested.

Sally was surprised to see Fitzi sitting in the shadows.

'How is he?'

'Physically he's doing okay. Trouble is he seems traumatised. He doesn't want to fight. Look how listless he is.'

'What do you think, Fitzi?' she asked the old man.

'Him spirit gone looking for help. He gotta find good spirit people fix 'im up.'

'So how do we do that?'

'Sing 'em up.'

He threw back his head, began to sway and started to

sing. The wailing turned into a sing-song babble, which rose and fell in a half-chant, half-song. It was hypnotic.

The final notes echoed in the silent stable. Then, softly, the rain fell. Fitzi sat, his eyes shut, mumbling to himself and rocking. Rob rose and stroked behind Jasper's ears, soothing him and murmuring.

Sally pulled her jacket round her. Fitzi's head had dropped to his chest and he seemed to be asleep. Rob continued touching and talking to the horse, whose eyes were closed and his breathing less erratic.

But then Jasper's eyes flew open, his ears twitched. Fitzi looked up. The door to the stable was eased open and a bedraggled figure in sodden pyjamas crept inside.

'How is he?'

'Ian, you're soaked, come here.' Sally picked up an old blanket and pulled it around his shoulders.

'Can you make him better, Fitzi?' asked Ian.

'Not dis old blackfella. Dem spirit fella come, talk 'em good to dat one horse. I reckon he listen longa time.'

Ian nodded and crept closer. Rob drew the boy to him and Ian rested his head against the side of the horse.

The stallion lowered his head slightly, his lips moving over his teeth. Ian patted his mane, his hand moving over Jasper's eyes, closing them as he'd seen Rob do, his fingertips massaging behind the ears. Then the boy lay down, settling himself on the straw at the back of the box. The rain pelted and soon Ian closed his eyes.

He slept for several hours. Sally dozed, her head in Rob's lap, the smell of the horse, the dampness, the straw, the smell of Fitzi's baccy, which hung around his head and beard, all mingled in a comforting potpourri.

Eventually, after Fitzi had left, Rob bent down and kissed her cheek and whispered, 'Go to bed.' She nodded and got to her feet as Rob stepped into the box and scooped up the sleeping boy. The horse reached out and sniffed the bundle in Rob's arms then watched them leave. As the kerosene lamp was extinguished, the stallion tentatively flexed one leg, then another. Satisfied, he shook his head and gave a slight wheezy whinny.

Rob put Ian on his bed and said to Sally, 'When he wakes up tell him Jasper is going to be just fine.'

Lorna was admitted to hospital early, 'as a precaution', the doctor said.

'There's a faint chance I might have diabetes. They're doing tests. To tell you the truth I'd rather be there than hanging around Marilyn's place,' she told John over the wireless.

'Do you want me to come down, love?'

'Is the airstrip dry?'

'Not really. They're saying the rain will ease next week.'

'Then there's not much point. I just hope I'll be able to fly back.'

'Don't worry, pet, we'll get you back one way or another.'

'John, I'll have a newborn baby with me.'

'So you will. Don't worry. Get on the wireless as soon as something happens.'

'I'll try. Check the call sign in case I can only leave a message.'

While the wireless was their lifeline – the first thing John did every morning was turn it on – sometimes it wasn't tuned to their frequency and they had to wait to get through. There was a call button that was reserved for severe emergencies only.

When her labour started Lorna had no way of getting through to Barra Creek, and was preoccupied anyway. Compared to the women in the hospital who were delivering their first babies, Lorna thought she'd feel an old hand after three births. But she found the process draining and tiring, and this baby was not going to hurry. She lost track of time in the blur of pain and anxious faces around her. There was talk of a caesarean section then, through her fogged consciousness and the agonising waves rippling and searing across her abdomen, she learned it would have to be a forceps delivery. She was too tired to push and just wanted the whole thing over. She was groggy when the nurse said softly, 'It's a girl, Mrs Monroe. A sweet little girl.' Lorna burst into tears.

She was handed the small bundle firmly wrapped in a pink blanket. Lorna touched her daughter's cheek and the baby opened her wide blue eyes and stared at her. It was only then that she allowed herself to admit that she'd longed for a girl. No child could replace Marty but a little girl . . . how she'd hoped for this.

On Lorna's behalf the hospital staff contacted Barra Creek with the news and John Monroe broke out the good port after dinner to celebrate.

Sally told Lizzie and her face creased in a broad smile. 'Dat good pella news, eh? Little missy be good for dis place. Mebbe be lot 'em piccaninnies when Betsy baby come.'

Sally nodded but she couldn't imagine that Lorna would allow her child to spend too much time with Betsy's baby. Betsy was still a child herself, and the rest of the lubras would help when her time came and with her baby. They seemed to pass children around, even sharing breastfeeding duties.

The boys were thrilled. A girl, and so much younger, was no threat and might help to partly fill the gap where they still missed Marty. When they told the kids from the camp the next day little Alice started jumping up and down and asked Sally if she could 'Push 'em baby pram.'

'So what's the baby's name?' asked Rob.

'I don't know. We'd better ask Lorna when she calls in.'

Sally and Rob were amused at John Monroe leaving the naming of the baby to Lorna. 'It's like he had nothing to do with the whole thing,' said Sally.

'In John's opinion, a girl isn't going to be much use around the station,' said Rob.

The following morning Lorna was on the wireless sounding relaxed and cheerful. 'What do you think of Jillian?' she asked John Monroe, with half of the Gulf country listening in.

'Jilly for short? Like Jillaroo? She'd better get on a horse soon as she can. Yeah, whatever you want, love. Sounds okay to me.' He looked over his shoulder at the breakfast table and Rob, Sally and the boys gave him the thumbs up. 'Everyone else thinks so too.'

The rain had not set in again and the airstrip was passable. Donny flew over it on his mail run and agreed to fly Lorna in from Mount Isa.

She was pale and exhausted after the trip, but pleased to be home. She proudly sat on the verandah to feed the small baby as the boys hovered nearby, surprised to see their very proper mother breastfeeding just as the lubras did.

Soon, life returned to its routine. Lorna rested a lot, with Jilly sleeping in the cot beside her bed. She was a quiet baby and everyone commented on how good she was. John was relieved his sleep wasn't broken by the sound of a crying baby ripping through the house.

Every afternoon Lorna took a long nap and Lizzie, the very heavily pregnant Betsy and little Alice took Jilly in the old cane pram swathed in mosquito netting for a long walk, bumping over the rough track that rocked the infant to sleep.

Betsy continued to do light household tasks under Lizzie's and Lorna's watchful eyes. There was something about Betsy that touched Sally. Her sweetness, lack of guile and the fact she was so young – sixteen perhaps. She was different from most of the other lubras, who were quick to jump into the whitemen's swags and flirt or fight over them for the reward of a new dress, a few sticks of baccy, some loose change or a trinket. She thought back to the young girls who were handed over to Mr Stinky, and she hoped that Betsy's baby was not fathered by the creepy old 'witch doctor'.

Sally would recall those first weeks when Jilly arrived as the most peaceful she'd known at Barra Creek.

Chapter Sixteen

SALLY STOOD AT THE schoolhouse door watching Frankie, Ginger and Alice change from their clean school clothes into their camp clothes. In the simple process of neatly folding their clean shorts and shirts and placing them on the bench, to pulling on their worn-out old camp clothes, Sally thought how they were sloughing off one skin and slipping into another world – one she'd never encountered before. When she'd arrived at Barra Creek theirs seemed a primitive, deficient world that straddled neither one culture nor another. Its inhabitants were treated as less than second-class citizens in the white environment, their subservience made the whites think they were 'stupid' and 'lazy'. Out in their country, though, they were comfortable. Out there the white men acknowledged their superior wisdom and treated the black stockmen as equals, sharing meals and talk of horses, cattle and droving around the campfire.

Sally was slowly beginning to understand that these people had a complex law and belief system, which had guided them for centuries; a history rich in song, dance, art and languages. Their traditional culture, combined with their modern abilities in a stock camp, around cattle, horses and station life, brought grudging respect from the whites. But there was a boundary, like the fence around the homestead, beyond which each reverted to their own.

As she watched the black children laughing and giggling, happy to exchange their school clothes for whatever came to hand, she wondered what would become of them. Frankie could write his name, read a little and was practising writing the alphabet. They all had startling skills when it came to their art. Sally had never seen anything like the drawings they produced in their simple, stylised outlines.

She also wondered about her other students. Ian – so committed to Barra Creek, passionate about Jasper – dreamed of running the station when he grew up. Tommy, so gentle, so sensitive and such a talented writer, longed to travel and see the world beyond the property, dismissing his natural horse skills. And now, a dear little girl, whom she felt sure Lorna would raise in her own shadow – a refined lady with an appreciation of the arts. While John wanted a daughter who'd ride like the wind and fill the place left by Marty.

In such a short time Sally felt her life had become entwined with this family. She'd also become used to the heat, flies, humidity, rain and mildew. She had come to know the dramas in the lives of the blacks and the visiting white workers. She fell asleep to the sounds of crocodiles grunting and barking, wild dogs howling, the occasional noises from horses and cattle, frogs croaking, geckos squeaking – sounds carried in the stillness. She awoke to soft piccaninny light, screeches of birds, John Monroe in the kitchen arguing with Lizzie about milking the goats.

Then the clang of iron calling the men to breakfast, the lilting murmur of the black stockmen and Fitzi, the boys racing along the verandah.

Life back in the South Island was as calm as the Milford Sound: remote, secluded, isolated, parochial, ordered. Bland, she decided. There were strict protocols, everyone knew their place and what was expected of them. Few broke the rules. Sally felt like an outsider when she thought about her life back home. How was she going to settle back there after living on the property? And then there was Rob. What was to become of them? The sex was wonderful and the more time they spent together the more deeply she felt for him. These feelings worried her. Was she only attracted to him because they were thrown together in this isolated place? Would her feelings be the same if they found themselves together somewhere else, away from Barra Creek?

The weeks were trickling past quickly, and everyone was making plans. Baby Jilly's arrival had made little impact on their daily lives. She never cried and she slept a lot but she was not gaining weight. She was a tiny, pale, wisp of a baby who spent hours in the cot with an electric fan cooling the damp air. Even Lorna seemed wilted, her control of everyone and her constant supervision of the household chores had loosened up.

When she had flown home with the baby Lorna had invited Donny to lunch at the homestead. A few weeks later he called on the wireless to say he would take up the offer, and he was bringing a surprise to add to the menu.

He carried a large wet box into the kitchen and inside, packed with ice, were pounds of pale giant prawns.

'A fellow out of Karumba has a trawler and he and a

couple of mates are doing a survey for the government to see if it'd be worth putting a prawn fishery up there.'

'They're always on about trying to develop the north. If they can hit regular catches of these and supply the market they'll be on a winner,' said John Monroe, holding up one of the prawns.

'He calls them banana prawns,' added Donny. 'Whack them on the fire or throw them in boiling water.'

Everyone wanted to talk to Donny and he diplomatically managed to spend time alone with each of them. He admired Jilly and chatted with Lorna, then talked with John and Rob as they cooked the prawns and thick steaks trimmed in yellow fat. After lunch he drove with Sally and the boys down to see Jasper.

As the boys hung over the railing of the yard calling the stallion, Donny leaned close to Sally.

'Do I owe you a prize?'

'What do you mean?'

'Didn't we have a bet whether you'd stick it out or not?' He grinned.

'If we did, you lost.'

'That's for sure. So, sweet Sal, what have you got out of this experience?'

Sally found she was blushing. The normal smart retort didn't come to her lips. 'A damn sight more than I expected, that's for sure.'

'On the plus side?'

She laughed at his arch tone. 'Yes. For lots of reasons.'

'And a big one would be Rob?'

'You're such a nosy old lady,' she teased. 'You know very well what's been going on.'

'Mmm. But what happens now? Don't forget that I saw how you looked when you came back from Darwin, clutching the orchids from dear Doctor Lee.'

'Donny, don't mention that! There was nothing to it. He was just a nice friend while I was on holiday.'

'Pity. He sounded quite divine. So, what's happening with Rob?'

'We're talking about our future. He thinks I should go to England after I've been home for my sister's wedding. Give him a chance to set himself up a bit.'

'So we haven't seen the last of you?'

'Who knows. Come and meet Jasper.'

During the week, the combination of heat and the wet earth had turned the air into a steamy, clinging, invisible blanket. Lorna had Lizzie pull everything leather out of the cupboards and oil them to wipe away the mildew. Shoes, handbags, wallets and belts were all covered in a faint green powder. Betsy wandered around the house with a duster, flicking idly. At every opportunity she hovered at Lorna's doorway, peering at the cot with its flyscreen covering, the legs standing in tins filled with water to keep ants at bay.

Sally was walking towards the schoolhouse and smiled at Fitzi, who was weeding around the verandah steps. Suddenly Betsy's scream pierced the morning, then she yelled out in her own language, causing Fitzi to drop his trowel and run. Sally realised that it must be something serious for Fitzi to rush inside. She'd never seen him venture past the kitchen before. She and Lorna ran along the verandah to the bedroom. Betsy hung at the doorway as Fitzi reached the room.

Looking inside they each froze for a moment, then Lorna pushed Fitzi forward.

Draped across the top of the cot was a huge snake – a taipan – its markings glittering as if lit by electricity. Sally knew it was poisonous. The jewelled head of the snake was inches away from the sleeping baby. It must have been six feet long. Lorna's voice was low, every word forced through her clenched teeth. 'Get rid of that thing, Fitzi.'

'It's all right, Lorna, it can't get through the mesh,' said Sally, trying to sound calm.

Fitzi moved slowly around the cot behind the snake, which lifted its head, watching him, tongue darting. Then before Sally could register what happened, his arm shot out and he grabbed the snake by the tail, threw it in the air and belted it down on the floor like a stockwhip, breaking its back.

He held the snake up above his head and it touched the floor. 'Him big pella closeup. Good tucker.'

Lorna went straight to the cot, peeling back the netting to find Jilly staring up at her. 'I don't care what you do with it, Fitzi, get it outside. And thank you.'

Sally and Betsy followed him as the boys came rushing in.

'Wow! Where was that?' exclaimed Tommy.

'In your bed,' teased Sally.

'Fair dinkum?' He looked shocked.

'She's joking. Are there any more inside?' asked Ian.

Sally looked serious. 'Oh, heck. I hope not.'

'I'll get the women to start poking around with brooms,' said Lorna. 'In the meantime, fetch one of the dogs in here.'

The cattle dog was shown the dead snake and sent inside to search out any others.

A message came from Donny that he'd spotted a mob of cattle on the high ground above the floodplain in the northwest corner of the property. He said the ground looked pretty firm as it was far from the river and marshy swamp land. Rob knew the area he was talking about, and he and Monroe decided to set out and muster them while the rain was holding off. John would take the Land Rover with supplies, dry wood and gear. Rob would bring the plant – men, packhorses and dogs.

The clouds began to roll in again. Sally decided they should have a small party as the boys had passed their exams with good if not brilliant results and as expected would be going down to Sydney next term after the Christmas holidays. Tommy had done very well in English, Ian in mathematics.

The little party – a fancy picnic at one of their favourite spots on a small rise overlooking the spread of the home paddock, the homestead and the river – was rather melancholy. They hobbled the horses and spread out their choice of chocolate cake, fairy bread and cold sausage sandwiches with lots of tomato sauce. They sat on an old rug and Ian boiled the billy for their tea.

'It won't be the same here without you, Sal,' said Tommy. Lorna's direction that they call their governess Miss Mitchell had long been discarded as the bond between them grew.

'You're going into a new life too – boarding school, new friends, the big smoke. And then home for holidays,' said Sally, trying to sound cheerful. She was also finding the idea of leaving Barra Creek difficult.

'Maybe I don't want to spend every holiday here,' said Tommy.

Ian shot him a furious look. 'But you have to. Where else would you go?'

'Oh, maybe we could go to New Zealand, see Sally one time.'

'Of course you could. Come skiing or see what a sheep farm is like. We could do lots of things.'

'I'd like to go to England too,' said Tommy, warming to the idea of travelling.

'We have to stay and look after this place,' said Ian stubbornly. 'Dad will be too old and he won't change anything.'

Sally laughed. 'Come on, he's not even fifty yet. You fellows have to see the world, have a bit of fun before you settle down.'

Tommy nodded enthusiastically but Ian's face set. 'Not me. I hate cities and stuff. I like it here best.'

Sally decided to shift the conversation. 'School will be exciting. I want you to write to me.'

'Oh yes,' said Tommy. 'But I'm not looking forward to it. Ian will be in the big school so I won't know anyone.'

'Nor will I,' said Ian.

'There are a lot of country boys there, I bet you'll find someone you know, or who you've talked to on the wireless,' said Sally. 'Now come on, let's eat. Then we'll go back and see Rob before they go out after that mob Donny spotted.'

Tommy bit into a sandwich and asked casually, 'Are you going to marry Rob?'

'Goodness! Why do you say that? We like each other, but, well, we both have things to do like I said – travelling, deciding where to settle.'

'Why don't you both stay here then? Work for us?' said Ian.

'That's too far away to think about. You might end up doing something quite different.'

'I'm going to England,' said Tommy. 'And I'll write stories about it.'

'I'm staying here,' said Ian firmly. 'I'll never leave Barra Creek.'

A slight shudder ran through Sally. Marty had said the same thing.

Later that night, lying in Rob's arms, Sally talked about the picnic.

'I feel so sad that I can't watch them grow up. I'm sure Tommy will keep in touch, though. Ian is adamant about taking over here, isn't he?'

'Yeah. I foresee trouble. It's not unusual for fathers and sons to butt heads over running the family farm.' He paused. 'I've had my own confrontation with my dad, but I'm sure we can resolve things eventually. But Ian is so . . . angry.' He shook his head. 'He's got so many issues with John.'

'He blames John for anything that goes wrong,' said Sally, thinking of Marty, of Jasper, of dozens of small incidents.

'Let's not worry about it. We'll both be gone from here soon enough, too soon.' He rolled over and kissed her.

Sally returned the kiss but she was feeling fretful. There seemed no definite plans for their future and the more casual Rob became the more she wanted to hold onto him. She understood that he had to deal with the future of his father's station eventually but he told her he didn't want to talk about it, that he'd sort something out. She sighed and knew she'd have to be content with that for the present.

He felt her sigh and tightened his arms around her. 'Feeling sad about going?'

'Of course. But I was thinking I might stop over in Sydney for a few days.'

'A rest before the wedding chaos.'

'Yes, maybe play a bit. I had a good time in Sydney on the way here, and I still know a few people there.'

'Good idea. Gee, we never did have a holiday together.'

'Bit hard when Lorna and John are watching us like hawks.'

'They feel responsible for you while you're under

their roof. We'll make up for it one day.' He sat up and started to dress. 'I'd better get some sleep. We're leaving early tomorrow.'

At three-thirty the next morning John Monroe decided to repack the Land Rover, and in the dark dropped a box on his foot. His cursing woke Lorna who had to treat the small cut. He then wanted breakfast and decided to cook a full meal as they'd be on the road all day. By that time Rob, Snowy and Fitzi had all come up to the house and joined him for breakfast.

It was sunrise and, smelling chops, bacon and eggs cooking, Ian and Tommy got up and sat with the men in the kitchen, tucking into breakfast too. They woke Sally as they leapt out of bed, so she threw on her clothes and went to help John. It always amused her that Monroe, who saw himself as such a tough bloke, was at home cooking in the huge old kitchen that Lizzie regarded as her domain. It was a happy breakfast, with everyone helping to make toast and tea while John flipped eggs in the frying pan and turned the chops, sausages and bacon in the big pan over the open fire.

Lorna, holding Jilly, appeared in the doorway and frowned at the sight of the boys in their pyjamas shaking tomato sauce all over their eggs. 'Is this a midnight party still going on? You'd better wake those lubras and get them in here to clean up after you.'

They watched the men leave, Lorna standing on the verandah with baby Jilly, Sally and the boys at the front gate. The house lubras stood outside the kitchen while the rest of the mob at the blacks' camp stayed in their gundies still sleeping. Some of the older Aboriginal boys also watched them, waiting for the time they could go along on a muster. Most of them were already competent riders, leaping on horses bareback at every opportunity. But until they'd been trained by Fitzi and the stockmen, John Monroe barred the kids from the stock camps.

Sally kept her eyes on Rob, sitting easily in the saddle, his jacket collar turned up, his hat pulled forward. She noticed that he and John Monroe had polished their boots, a ritual they followed even though their boots would be dirty the first time they hit the ground. Rob gave her a smile and a wink, tipped his hat then wheeled his horse away.

Sally felt a slight lump in her throat. Rob was eating into her heart. She was determined to sort out their future – if they were to be together or not – before she left for New Zealand. She hated the unfamiliar sense of insecurity and being the one on the back foot. Briskly she turned back to the boys. 'School today.'

'But we've finished our exams!' they wailed.

'Come on, we're going to have a lesson on how to write a letter.'

'Tommy knows that stuff,' said Ian.

'Maybe, but you need to know too; how to set out a letter to the bank manager, or say thank you for someone's hospitality. Come on, this will be our last lesson together.'

Subdued, they went to get ready.

They worked on the letter writing for an hour. The other kids did their best drawing and writing before Sally asked what was their favourite school activity. They all yelled, 'Singing!'

Ian, though, dropped his head on his desk in mock despair. 'Oh no.'

Lorna, sitting in the garden with Jilly, smiled as she heard the voices singing, or bellowing, rounds that drifted from the schoolhouse. The school bell clanged and there was a chorus of three cheers. What a treasure Sally was, she thought. A string of governesses had come and gone, and then Sally had arrived – so ladylike, so overdressed and so determined to stick it out.

She looked at the little girl in the bouncinette at her feet. If only Sally would be around when Jilly was older. John had made a rare visit to Lorna's bedroom to chat about Sally. He suggested perhaps they should try to persuade her to stay on, be a nanny for Jilly while the boys were away at school. He even suggested they encourage the relationship with Rob if it would keep her there.

'We couldn't have better staff around than the two of them,' he said.

'Sally isn't staff, John. She comes from a very good family who expect a lot more from her. Would you want Jillian to be a nanny?'

He didn't answer for a moment then said, 'She's a good sport. I like having her around.'

Lorna had become close to Sally and she saw clearly that her husband enjoyed the company of the pretty, bright young woman who loved horses and the open spaces. Sally could give him what she could not. Even if he hadn't admitted it to himself, and Sally was completely unaware of the fact that John Monroe found her attractive. Lorna knew he'd never make any overture towards Sally, though, because that would rock the boat too much. Besides, there were plenty of gins around to meet his needs.

Sally was loyal to the family and as women they shared a bond with the children and each other. Lorna was determined that Sally, whom she thought of as a little sister, a friend or a grown daughter, should move up in life. She couldn't bear the thought of her being trapped as she was. Sally might enjoy life at Barra Creek for the moment, but she was still able to make choices. As an independent, free-spirited girl she should follow her desires. Why should women always be under the thumb of their parents or husbands? From what she was reading, times were changing and if Lorna had her life over again, she'd be like Sally.

No, there was no way she was going to encourage Sally to stay. Leaving Barra Creek, and especially Rob, was the best thing Sally could do.

Following the sing-song, school was dismissed. As the black children began to unbutton their shirts, Sally waved her hand. 'Keep 'em school clothes. No more school.'

They stood there, unsure what to do. 'No go longa school, where 'em go, dis place?'

'Tell you what we're doing,' she announced suddenly. 'River. Swim and fish, eh?'

They broke into huge smiles and shouting to the older and younger kids who didn't go to school they all raced away.

'Are we going swimming?' asked Tommy. It was mid morning.

'Why not? It's so hot and school's over.'

'Yippee! C'mon,' shouted Tommy. And for once even serious Ian raced Tommy to the house.

When they got to the river, all the kids from the camp were jumping off the landing, swinging from the tree, and dropping like quick bombs into the water. The smallest of the piccaninnies giggled and bobbed among the waterlilies. Following Ian and Tommy, Sally dived into the cool water. If there were any crocs around they would have been frightened off by the squealing children.

Sally followed the boys, climbing the huge paperbark and swinging from the branch, then she let go and dropped into the water. They ran down the landing, leaping, hugging knees and banging into the water to make the biggest splash. They shrieked and laughed and shouted, inventing games, having competitions where age, status and culture were immaterial.

Out of breath, Sally collapsed on the bank and lay there, feeling the sun dry her, looking at the clear, bright blue sky. The rains had stopped for the moment. She felt cleansed, not just in her body but in her mind. She would never forget this place, but she was ready to move on to the next phase of her life, whatever it might be.

They walked back from the river, the girls balancing huge pink and blue waterlilies on their heads, the boys nudging, jostling, punching playfully.

Sally was going through the chest of drawers in the governess' room where she'd slept only once, on her first night at Barra Creek. She was dismayed to find she'd have to wash the clothes that had been stored there as they were covered in gecko poo. Lorna appeared in the doorway. 'I have to go down to the camp. Betsy is having trouble. Giving birth is normally no problem for them, those old lubras are excellent midwives, but something is wrong apparently.'

'Can I help?' asked Sally hesitantly.

'Have you ever helped birth a baby?'

'Ah, no. I guess I wouldn't be much help.'

Lorna headed out to the verandah then seemed to change her mind and turned back. 'You'd better come with me. Get an old sheet from the cupboard.'

Lizzie directed them past the blacks' camp to a clump of trees. They could see Betsy, who was sitting naked, leaning against a tree, her knees pulled up; sheets of newspaper were spread between her legs and an old lubra sat cross-legged beside her.

Lorna directed Betsy to lie down and she probed her distended belly efficiently. The old woman twisted her hands.

'Him up down,' explained Lizzie.

'Looks like a breech birth.' She sent Lizzie back to the camp for fat, 'anything greasy – cooking oil, margarine'.

Betsy kept staring from Lorna to Sally with wide frightened eyes, occasionally wincing as her muscles contracted.

When Lizzie returned with a tin of lard, Lorna, in pidgin, directed the two lubras to massage the bulge of the baby using the grease, feeling where the baby's head was, trying to encourage the infant to turn and put its head down into the birth canal.

'I'm going back to the house for some castor oil, it's an old wives' tale they say, but it could bring the baby on,' said Lorna.

'It looks like it's trying to come,' said Sally, watching the writhing in Betsy's belly as she bit her lip and mumbled to herself.

Lorna drove away but before she returned, Lizzie and the midwife began talking excitedly. They sat Betsy up and, with Lizzie holding her under the armpits, they helped her into a kneeling position. With a great expulsion of breath and a long moan, she pushed down and the baby slithered onto the newspaper.

The old midwife pulled the cord and the placenta gushed out. She bit the cord, leaving a length that would later dry and drop off, and be kept as 'lucky string' for the baby's good health. She lifted the baby, coated in a grey film, off the paper and put it in Betsy's lap. Lizzie grabbed the torn sheet and began wiping the baby, crooning a kind of chant.

Sally was mesmerised and was relieved at the sound of the truck returning. She waved to Lorna, 'It's here, it's born.' It suddenly occurred to her to see if the baby was a boy or girl and she stepped closer then stopped in shock.

The white mucus had been wiped off the little girl and Sally saw how pale she was, how light skinned. There was no doubting this child's father was a white man.

Betsy put the child to her breast and smiled down at it, stroking the dark down of hair on her head. The baby's dark eyelashes fluttered closed as the mouth began working at the swollen breast.

Lorna took Lizzie aside and spoke quietly to her, then came back to Sally. 'She'll be all right now. They'll look after her. They have ceremonial business to do. They bury the placenta on this spot and sing and carry on. Leave them be.'

They didn't speak as they drove back but before they reached the homestead Lorna turned off the ignition and sat in silence for a few seconds. Finally she said, 'You saw that baby. It's what they call a yella-fella, a half-caste.'

'Who's the father? One of the stockmen? One of the workers? Does she know, do you think?'

'Oh, she knows all right. Betsy has only ever shared one man's swag,' said Lorna tightly.

'Well, does he know? Does it matter? They all seem to be one big family anyway,' said Sally, thinking of how the kids were cuddled and carried by all the women in the camp. Then a thought struck her. 'They will look after her? I mean they won't kill the baby. I've heard things –'

'No. They know who the father is.' Lorna turned to Sally, her knuckles gripping the steering wheel. 'You should know too.'

Sally stared at her.

'It's Rob. I'm sorry, Sally. I think you should know. It's a good thing you're leaving.'

Sally sat there, her mind refusing to absorb the impossible.

'They all do it. The men say it doesn't mean any-thing. It's just a need, nothing to do with their own white women. I've never understood it, but you'll never change it either.'

Lorna didn't add that many white men who had favourite women and then brought a white wife home were soon back with the women. 'They like sex and don't ask for anything,' John had bluntly told her.

A thought flashed through Sally's mind of the night she woke to find John Monroe watching her sleep. She then remembered the scene in the men's quarters where Rob had passed out and the women were hanging on the men. She'd always wondered why Lorna had sent her down there that night. Now she knew that she'd been trying to tell her, warn her.

With a sob Sally stumbled from the car and ran. She ran till she had no more breath and then she fell down and hit her fists on the ground. She cried with pain and sadness. Then she got angry that she'd been so stupid and not seen what probably everyone else knew. Lorna might accept that this went on, she could not. Hurt and rage spilled from her. No wonder John and Lorna had tried to stop her seeing Rob.

Later, from the verandah, Lorna watched Sally walk slowly back towards the house. Her head was down, her shoulders sagged. She knew Sally would be gone before Rob came back from the muster. And she was glad.

Donny landed the plane at Cloncurry where Sally would make the hop to Townsville to fly TAA to Sydney. He took off his earphones and glanced at Sally's sad face.

'Darling heart, don't feel so bad. You only came for a short time not a good time, an adventure, remember, not to change your life.'

'I really loved him, Donny.'

'Aw shucks, as they say in Yankeeland. Listen, I'm

just a simple bush pilot, but I ferry a lot of people around and I see what happens to them out here. I wouldn't want you to stay out here, Sal. You'd shrivel up. You'd get frustrated you couldn't change things – him, the life, the weather.' He took her hand and squeezed it. 'You deserve someone who'll love you, give you the kind of life you want. Believe me, you don't want this.'

'I don't want my old life in New Zealand any more either.'

'Fair enough. Just give this all a bit of time, a bit of perspective. See how you feel in six months. Travel, find the right bloke and the right place.'

'We talked about being together, making plans. And all the while . . . Why, Donny?'

'I'm the wrong person to ask, love. It's just how it's been since pioneer days, I guess, when there weren't any women out here. It's not often a classy girl like you turns up in the middle of woop woop.' He sighed. 'It can be hard to find someone to love when there aren't many to choose from.'

Sally suddenly looked at the handsome young pilot. 'What about you, Donny? I don't know anything about your life, you're always so busy listening to our troubles.'

He unbuckled his seat. 'It's very dull. Come on, sweet, let's unload your ton of luggage. I'll have a word with the blokes to make sure it all gets down to Sydney in one trip and no extra cost.'

'Donny, you've been such a good friend. Really. I'm going to miss you.'

'Come on, no more tears. I'm a great believer in that old song, "*We'll meet again . . . don't know where . . . don't know when . . .*"' He sang in a falsetto voice and Sally had to smile.

She did a lot of thinking on the flight to Sydney. She

also tried not to think . . . about the painful farewell to the two boys, to Lorna and the baby. The fact she hadn't said goodbye to John. It had been John Monroe who'd told her one time that the blacks didn't have a word for goodbye. They just went away and then they'd turn up again. She had no doubt she'd turn up in John and Lorna's life again sometime. Then there was the note she'd left for Rob, which had been so hard to write: her disappointment and hurt, that she needed time away and would be back in touch when she was ready. She'd added: 'Please don't write to me, just yet. This is my decision, Rob. When I am ready I will contact you and then, perhaps, we can consider our future. Love Sally.' She couldn't bear to mention Betsy or the baby.

Finally she slept.

By the time the taxi pulled up outside The Australia Hotel and the doorman opened the door for her, Sally decided she was going to get on with life. First thing tomorrow she'd look into ships sailing to England, after she'd got through the hoopla of her sister's wedding.

Chapter Seventeen

South Island, New Zealand, 1964

IT WAS THE COLOURS, she decided. White fences around green paddocks; golden hills running up to the alps; icy white peaks. Faded weatherboard. Pastel flowers in a cottage garden; sheep fleece that looked dry cleaned. There was no mud. There was the sound of rounded vowels, footsteps muffled by thick carpet, echoes of wind, and, faintly, her father's hounds.

Her home seemed so different to Sally, as did her family. They were pleased to see her, if mildly put out at her unexpected early arrival. She did not elaborate on why she had come home several weeks earlier than planned, and they did not probe. They listened politely to her descriptions of life at Barra Creek. But it was too different, too far away, not of their world or of immediate interest. Instead, the conversation turned to Yvonne's wedding, which dominated their lives at present.

The letters hadn't exaggerated the importance her

parents were placing on the nuptials. With another fat wool cheque for the year her father was sparing no expense; this was an excuse to show off how well the family was doing. Sally was amused that her parents were not at all concerned that they had taken over the event, and Yvonne and Lachlan were being swept along in the tide of preparations. She sat at the dinner table listening as the minutiae of the big day was discussed and planned. Yvonne nodded and agreed with everything their mother said.

'I have booked the hairdresser for ten and asked her to brush your hair over your tiara, so we must be sure to take along the satin bows for the bridesmaids at the same time. The bows are on combs but I want the girl to put them in when they do the hairsets.'

'Yes, Mummy. Thank you.'

Sally raised an eyebrow. 'Tiara?'

'Very discreet, dear. Small pearls, very pretty. Of course, nothing loud,' Emily Mitchell explained.

'So what have you chosen for the bridesmaids, Yvonne? I hope it's a colour I like.'

Yvonne reached for a slice of bread. 'Mummy thought ice blue would be best, with dark blue sashes and ribbons. The boys are in morning suits.'

Emily frowned. 'Do you need that second slice of bread, Yvonne? We don't want any bulges in the dress.' She turned to Sally. 'I had to step in when it came to the bridal attire. Yvonne had ideas of some elaborate gown with gewgaws all over it. As I said to her, we can't have her going into God's house looking like a Christmas tree!'

Sally glanced at Lachlan, who sat quietly through the dinner, acquiescing when spoken to by Emily, deferential when addressing or answering Garth Mitchell. She couldn't imagine Rob being so intimidated by her father, or caring much about all this 'girly stuff'. The thought of him gave her a pang of emotion so she turned her attention to her mother's plans for a visit to the dressmaker for a fitting for her dress. She groaned inwardly. As soon as they waved the happy couple off on their honeymoon Sally would be making plans for England.

Within two weeks of being home Sally felt she was being stifled. The wedding, the family, the predictable routine of life at Ashford Lodge made her feel as if she was penned in a crowded cattle yard. Lachlan had left to join his own family and Yvonne had finished her job at the bank to devote herself to her glory box, table decorations, flowers and the going-away outfit. Sally decided to stay in the flat in Christchurch for a few days and catch up with friends.

Her mother gave her a stern glance. 'What friends, dear?'

'School friends, girls I know in town. I assume Pru is coming to the wedding?'

It suddenly hit Sally with a guilty blow that she hadn't called Pru since arriving home. They had only exchanged a few brief letters. Pru's pain and shame had dented their friendship. Their lives had dramatically diverged and their light-hearted friendship had wilted beneath the hot breath of real life. Her mother dismissed Pru whom she had never considered in the same class as Sally. She'd tolerated Pru because she and Sally had been friends for so long.

'No, Prudence is not coming. I really don't know what got into her in Australia,' sniffed her mother.

Sally bit her tongue, thinking to herself Pru was 'got into' in New Zealand by one of the sons of the best-known families. She waited for a hint of the story and glanced questioningly at Yvonne.

'There was some gossip –'

'We do not gossip, Yvonne,' interjected Mrs Mitchell. 'We were all very disappointed she threw up such an opportunity to travel. You too, Sally.'

'I travelled! I went places no one ever goes!'

'That's the point, dear. That's not travelling. Anyway, Prudence had ambitions above her station. Boys like Gavin Summers marry their own kind.'

'She had such a crush on him, so when he brushed her off she decided to go to England on the spur of the moment. She had to share a cabin with four girls,' said Yvonne, almost shuddering.

Sally was shocked. 'Pru went anyway? Well, well. Good for her. Maybe I'll see her over there.'

Her mother and sister stared at her as she dropped this bombshell. 'You're not serious, Sally. You just came home.' Her mother, having one daughter successfully engaged, was no doubt going to start casting around for a suitable match for the other. 'Your father won't be buying you another ticket, I'm afraid.'

'I can buy my own. I've saved all my pay.'

Emily's mouth tightened. 'We will discuss this another time. I don't want anything to spoil your sister's wedding.'

As soon as she was settled into the flat Sally picked up the telephone and dialled Sean's number. They had let their relationship sink into limbo. She wasn't sure how she felt about him after meeting Rob and Hal, both of whom had aroused strong feelings in her. Sean was not a letter writer and Sally had been swept up in her relationship with Rob. Also, distance had diluted the excitement of the dashing Sean.

His voice was warm and loving as if they had last spoken only a few days before. 'Was it worth the trip?

It sounded pretty rugged. I'm glad you're back home. When can I see you?'

'Whoa,' said Sally, laughing. 'I'm still adjusting. I feel I have one foot here and one back there. It was a pretty special time,' she added quietly.

'I'm glad you went. I sense a change in you, which is only natural. I missed you.'

'Fibber. I bet you didn't.' Yvonne had mentioned in a letter that she'd seen Sean at a few social events with a glamorous woman his own age. Sally knew very well he wouldn't sit around on his own. They'd had a lovely romance and if it hadn't been for Rob, and even the brief courtship of Hal, she probably would have moped for Sean and felt jealous.

'I'm a woman of the world now,' she said.

Sean gave a low, sexy chuckle. 'You were born that, Sal. So, what are your plans?'

The teasing tone left Sally's voice. 'Honestly, Sean, I have no idea. Except that I don't want to stick around here. It all seems such a small pond now – plush, comfortable, protected, and boring. I'll probably go back to my old job for a bit and save some more money. Then I'll make the trek to England as planned. Without a detour.'

'And see Pru? I hear she's over there. Let's get together and you can tell me all the sordid details.'

'What sordid details?' She wondered what he'd heard. She would never break Pru's confidence. 'You're free? No glamorous women underfoot?'

'I'm always here for you, Sal. You're my number-one girl.'

He came to the flat with roses and wine, and they embraced warmly. They were going out to dinner but from the look in Sean's eye and the ardour of his kisses, she knew he had other ideas in mind first.

As he poured the wine she watched him critically.

He was devilishly good looking, but there was something in him she hadn't seen before. There was a tiredness about him. The beautiful clothes, his charm, humour and manners were worn with aplomb, but where was the man? The substance of him? She tried to imagine Sean galloping with wild brumbies, picking his way along a crocodile-infested river, dealing with the black stockmen, the rough conditions of life on a station property, and she almost laughed aloud. He rode to the hounds with skill and style but this was not a man to rescue you in the rough and tumble of the big world. And it hit her that Barra Creek had been a big world. One station in the middle of nowhere had become a country of its own in her mind. Sprawling, brawling, fighting, singing, big spaces, strong men and women tackling great odds. Oh no, Sean would not fit in, just as she knew she could no longer fit in back here.

Her pain at Rob's deceit, the knowledge he'd fathered a child with a young black woman, the extent of her feelings for him, had all left a deep wound. As well as time to heal, she wanted the unguent of soothing, caring and spoiling. Sean's undemanding attentions might help her. She knew she was using Sean and suspected he knew it too, but neither of them cared. What they had suited them both. This was no great passion or grand affair. Sean would distract her until she moved on to whatever happened next. She tried not to think of Rob.

It was unseasonably hot for the big day. Sally had been amused but then irritated at her father's display. In addition to the white marquee set up on the side lawn for the reception after the formal church wedding, Garth had his finest thoroughbreds and prize-winning rams on show in the white-fenced front paddocks along the driveway. His elegant cream Daimler was the bridal car. The numerous trophies, Hunt paraphernalia, show ribbons and family portraits on display would no doubt be noticed by guests venturing into the main rooms of the house.

The heat and the close proximity of the animals attracted a host of blow flies. So here was Sally, on the morning of the wedding, dressed in her chief bridesmaid's dress, hair set and lacquered so that she felt like she was wearing a helmet secured by a giant blue satin bow at the back, scurrying through the house with the vacuum cleaner sucking the dead flies off the window sills.

Her mother paused on her way upstairs. 'Do you know, Sally, I've never seen you do anything domestic before. I hope Mrs Monroe didn't have you doing domestic duties.'

'Mother, you would really like Lorna. She was very particular and she never treated me like staff. I was part of the family. But I certainly learned a lot. The black house girls had to be shown what to do all the time.'

'Well, I can't imagine what that must be like. Thank goodness we have Mrs Sanderson.' She swept up the carpeted stairs carrying the bridal veil.

Dear old Mrs Sanderson, her mother's housekeeper for the past ten years, would never cope with Lorna's stringent standards under extreme conditions, thought Sally.

Yvonne and Lachlan's lunchtime wedding was duly photographed for the social pages in the newspapers and magazines. The ceremony was held in the nearby Anglican church. The small stone building was a sought-after venue because of its beautiful stained-glass windows and exquisite proportions.

The couple was blessed, showered with confetti and rose petals, and left the church to the strains of a lone piper. They led the entourage of cars to the reception for one hundred and thirty guests at Ashford Lodge, which had never looked better. A team of gardeners had worked for weeks to have everything blooming and clipped to perfection. While the wedding party was photographed in the garden, guests sipped champagne and spirits before sitting down to Bluff oysters and crayfish, rare beef and ham.

At five o'clock the newlyweds reappeared in their going-away outfits – Yvonne in a tailored suit and small neat hat, Lachlan in a lightweight Harris tweed suit. They were spending the night at the Clarendon Hotel in Christchurch and would return to Ashford Lodge for a luncheon party the next day.

Once the newlyweds were waved away in the decorated Daimler, Emily and Garth invited the older guests into the house for a drink for the road. The young set continued milling in the marquee, waiting for the band to arrive.

Sally danced with everyone, long past caring about the state of her hair or her blue satin shoes. She was bored rigid by it all and felt removed from the silly jokes and hearty laughter of the people around her. Most of the young men were very tight after drinking far too much. Sally felt totally sober – the rum drinking with John Monroe had toughened her constitution. Supper was served at 10 pm and the last dance was at midnight. The girls were whisked off to sleep in makeshift beds in the house. The boys slept in sleeping bags in the woolshed, fortified with the grog Garth thought had been locked away in the garage.

In Sally's room there were three fold-away beds and a mattress on the floor for the bridesmaids. They were all asleep and finally the house was silent. She lay in her bed and fingered the pearl drop pendant that the groom had given each of the bridesmaids, and wondered about her own wedding day. It would be difficult to escape a repeat performance of Yvonne's day. She had heard her mother commenting on improvements and changes she would make for the next wedding.

Sally sank into her shell, becoming, for the first time in her life, something of a recluse, unsure of what she wanted to do, where she wanted to be. She kept putting off making a booking to sail to England. She had been welcomed back to her old job but she was finding being in an office, even for a few hours a day, excruciating. It felt claustrophobic. When her father talked of the next sheep muster at their other family property, Mersham Park, she begged to go down and help.

'Sally, this is work, not a hunt or social ride, you know. Five thousand sheep have to be brought off the tops. The ewes have to be crutched and put into their lambing paddocks.'

'Dad, you forget I've been mustering on a cattle station. I can handle myself.'

His eyebrows shot up. 'Really? I thought you were a governess. That sort of mustering is dangerous. I don't know that I approve of that sort of thing.'

She grinned at her father, who looked very much the country squire in his checked cotton shirt, cravat and tweed jacket. 'Bit late now, Dad. Please, ask Uncle Richard if I can go and help.'

Sally proved to be so adept on horseback and working with the sheep – though she decided she'd prefer to work with cattle any day – that her uncle and the Head Musterer, Flynn Boyle were glad to have her on the team. It was arranged that she would work at Mersham Park three days a week and work two days a week at the office in town. Sally spent her spare time with Yvonne and Lachlan and found she enjoyed being with them in their house in the grounds of Mersham Park, sharing farm talk with Lachlan.

'Sally, you've changed,' said Yvonne. 'You seem a lot more sensible.'

'Oh dear, how awful,' said Sally.

'Well, mature then. Not such a rebel.'

'I suppose dead bodies, crocodile attacks, lubras splitting each other's heads open, chasing wild brumbies, stopping drunken brawls does mature one,' she said, archly.

Yvonne stared at her in shock, then decided she was joking and gave a small laugh.

Back in Christchurch Sally couldn't decide whether to sleep with Sean or not. Thankfully he didn't push it – she suspected he was seeing other women – but he was, nonetheless, considerate, caring and generally available. He was especially useful when she needed rescuing from her mother's clutches. If Emily suspected she was seeing the banned Sean she gave no indication of it, and Sally assumed her mother was feeling triumphant in squashing the 'unsuitable' relationship. No doubt Yvonne had told her the rumours that Sean was seeing women his own age.

Her mother lined up a procession of suitable gentlemen for Sally to meet at family functions, social events and through her old school friends. At first it had been amusing, but Sally quickly grew tired of Emily's attempts to matchmake. Her father took her aside one day to extol the virtue of one of his cadets but Sally quickly held up her hand.

'Dad, Yvonne is very happy with Lachlan. But that's not a life for me.'

347

'You love the horses, the Hunt, what we've built here. I don't have a son. I thought you might be the one to carry on with the thoroughbreds. With the right man beside you of course,' he said.

Sally nearly said something about Rob, about his natural gift with horses, what he'd done with Jasper, how horses were his passion. But instead she merely shrugged. 'Dad, please, let me be. I wish Mum wouldn't keep interfering. I'll find my own husband, thanks.'

Her father was silent for a moment. He had told his wife to ease up on the blatant introductions but he couldn't resist adding, 'Well, Sally, your track record of dating suitable young men hasn't been very responsible so far.'

'I'm twenty-one now. You have to cut the apron strings, you know.'

'That may be so, but you are still my daughter.'

She gave her father a quick kiss. 'Trust me. The right man's out there somewhere,' she said lightly, thinking to herself, but probably not around here.

She'd had a long talk with Sean and felt better. She had poured out the story of her great love for Rob and how he'd hurt her and also her attraction to Hal Lee. Now she didn't know what to do with herself. But a trip away to England still seemed the best alternative. She talked to her parents and said she was going to sail to England and work for a year and then come back and settle down.

Her mother looked relieved. 'I do hope so, dear.'

Her father gave her a quizzical look. 'What sort of work?'

'I have a whole range of new talents, Dad. I can muster a mob of cattle, break in a horse, speak pidgin, and at a pinch, stitch up someone's head.'

'Very useful in the Old Dart,' he commented dryly and returned to his newspaper.

Sally wrote a long letter to Lorna outlining her plans. She knew Lorna had been worried about her. She wrote brief letters in which she gave Sally the latest news about the property, little Jilly who was such a quiet baby she was no trouble at all, unlike Betsy's little girl who was an energetic baby named Daisy. She never mentioned Rob other than it was quiet with all the men gone out mustering. Tommy was a good correspondent. Ian would sometimes scrawl a hasty note at the end of his brother's long letters. They were home for the holidays and Ian was glad to be at Barra Creek but Tommy wrote that he missed Sally and Rob, his mother was preoccupied with their little sister, and Ian and his father were 'still fighting'. He begged Sally to stay in England so he could go and visit her over there. 'I really want to see all the places we learn about. I don't want to spend my life at Barra Creek . . . but Dad expects us to be here and help him. Ian says Dad should give it away and hand it over to him when Jilly is ready for school.'

Sally poured over Tommy's letters. How she missed the boys. How she missed the activity, the smells and the vibrancy. How she missed Rob. She shook herself, refusing to mope. Now she must get on with her life.

Sean invited her to lunch at his flat. They thought it safer to meet at his place than at a restaurant in town where they might run into friends of Sally's parents. She had decided to fly to England, her father relenting and agreeing to pay half the airfare. 'I think they think it's a safer bet I'll get there this time,' she said, laughing.

Sean was due to go to Australia for ten days on business, so they were treating this as a farewell lunch. Sally was setting the table when Sean cried out and came into the small dining room with his hand wrapped in a tea towel. 'I've cut my finger. Sliced the top almost right off.' He looked shaken.

'Ooh, let me see.' The tea towel was soaked in blood. 'Gawd, you have done a job on yourself. I'd better drive you to the hospital. Come on.'

They had to wait a short while as an accident victim was trundled in from an ambulance and whisked behind a curtain. Then Sean was attended to by a young Indian doctor, who deftly stitched his finger back together. Sally stayed out in the waiting room of the busy casualty ward. She watched as a patient, hooked up to monitors and machines, was wheeled in on a bed. Next to him a young girl was lying still, her frightened eyes darting between her mother and father, who sat on either side of her holding her hands. A nurse paused by the girl's bed. 'The specialist is on his way down. You're lucky he happened to be in the hospital seeing another patient.'

'There you go, sir. It will be fine now,' said the doctor as he and Sean walked out from the surgery.

'Sorry about all this,' Sean said when he joined Sally. 'It was probably best we came in. I needed five stitches.'

'I'll finish cooking lunch,' she said. 'You can have a drop of something medicinal.'

Sally glanced back at the young girl as a nurse hurried in saying, 'Here is the doctor,' and pulled the curtain around the bed. But not before Sally had seen the caring face of Doctor Hal Lee.

She clutched Sean's bandaged arm, which he was holding upright. He glanced at her. 'It's not that bad. Don't worry.'

'I don't believe it,' she murmured.

'What's up?' He stopped and looked at her shocked expression.

'I just saw Hal Lee. The doctor I met in Darwin.'

'The handsome devil of the Singapore orchids?'

'Yes.' Sally had shared everything with Sean now. 'He must be a specialist here.'

'Let's go back and find out.'

'No. He's with people. I'll ring up.'

'If you say so, but wouldn't it be easier to ask in there? Come on.' Sean swung back through the swing doors marked Emergency Only.

They were immediately accosted by a nurse. 'I'm sorry you can't come in here. Wait outside and you'll be called.'

'I've just been treated in here. We thought we saw Dr Harold Lee. Could we speak to him, please?'

'Dr Lee is with a patient. He doesn't work here, he's a visiting specialist.'

'Oh, I see. But this young lady is a friend of his.'

'Dr Lee has rooms in Papanui Road. You can contact him there.'

Sally turned away murmuring, 'Thank you.' She was still stunned to see him, and in Christchurch of all places.

Sean was about to follow her when the curtain was pulled back from around the girl's bed and Hal was smiling and shaking the father's hand, both parents looking relieved. He walked away and Sean quickly caught up with him.

'Dr Lee. Excuse me, there's an old friend of yours over there, she didn't want to interrupt you.'

Hal turned around, a faint frown creasing his forehead. Seeing Sally his face lit up and he walked straight over to her. He took her hands and smiled. 'Well, this is a surprise. I thought you were still in Australia.'

'I came home for my sister's wedding. My contract is finished. How long have you been here?'

'Just a month. In fact I sent you a note to Barra Creek saying I was moving here. I thought you might be able to recommend some good restaurants and places to go.'

Sean smiled at them both. 'She certainly can. I'm

Sean Flanagan, an old friend of Sally's. She kindly drove me in – I had a slight accident.' He held up his finger but Hal was looking at Sally.

They just had time to exchange phone numbers before he was whisked away by the Registrar.

Sally put her sunglasses on as they stepped into the parking lot and Sean took her arm.

'Your glowing description of the good doctor didn't mention that he is part Chinese. He's a very attractive man.'

'It didn't seem important. Yes, he is nice. What a surprise.'

Sean opened the car door for her. 'Do you mind driving again? My finger is really hurting now. You are going to show him the sights, I hope?'

'Yes, I will. I'm glad you grabbed him. I might not have bothered to track him down.'

'All part of that other life?' Sean asked gently. And as Sally nodded and eased the car out of the parking lot, he touched her arm. 'He might be able to heal that hole in your heart, Sally . . . give it a chance.'

She glanced at him and smiled. 'You're a good friend, Sean.'

'Always will be, me darlin'.' He smiled to himself and wished he could be there when Sally's parents were introduced to Dr Hal Lee, as he felt sure they would be eventually. If they thought him unsuitable because he was Irish, what would they make of the prospect of Asian blood in the family? Good on you, Sally, he thought fondly. It was one of the things he loved about her – she was always unpredictable.

The courtship of Sally by Doctor Harold Lee was swift, subtle and sensitive. Sally was ready for his gentle romancing. She was lonely, her friends and her sister had all moved on in their lives and she was looking for some direction too. Barra Creek had bitten deeply into her heart and soul. While those at home had written it off as 'Sally's little adventure' or 'Sally's bush job in Australia', no one in New Zealand, apart perhaps from Sean, knew how much her time there – and her love affair with Rob – had affected her.

She'd been hurt and the kisses and caresses of Hal helped her heal. He was charming, caring and interesting. His job was demanding, but being a paediatrician was important to him, and Sally understood this.

She liked the fact that they'd shared an experience together in Darwin, that she'd met his aunties, and that, while he hadn't worked in the Australian outback, he knew something about it and the people who lived there. While showing him around her home, she re-discovered the beauty of the South Island. For once she was able to tell her mother that she was dating a suitable man – a doctor. However she delayed the rest of the introduction, that not only was he part Asian but a practising Catholic to boot.

Hal had rented a pretty house on Rolleston Avenue overlooking Hagley Park and the Avon River. He and Sally began hosting Sunday lunches with a new circle of friends. She spent nearly every weekend with him and they became accepted as a couple. Sally felt comfortable and liked the compliments from Hal's friends – mostly other doctors and their families – that they made an attractive and appealing pair. Hal was generous and Sally began to learn more details of how his family had amassed a considerable fortune. Sean was included in their social events as an old friend of Sally's and if Hal ever suspected that she and Sean had been lovers, he never raised it. He was an attentive lover, with an attractive lean, smooth body and he devoted time to satisfying Sally's desires – in and out of bed. There wasn't the wild, electric passion she'd known with Rob, but slowly she was burying those feelings, putting them behind her as part of a particular phase in her life.

While the timing caught her unawares, she wasn't completely surprised when Hal asked her to marry him. He did it beautifully over a candlelit dinner at The Sign of the Takahe restaurant. Their dessert was served with sweet liqueurs and Hal reached over and took Sally's hand and lifted his glass with the other. 'Here's to you, Sally. If I believed in my family superstitions I'd say my being here was planned by the fates.'

She smiled. 'Darwin then Christchurch. The fates send you to some very different places. Where next, do you think?'

He suddenly looked anxious and put his glass down and took both her hands, then said, 'I came over on a twelve-month contract but plans have changed.'

'Oh, you're leaving sooner?' When he nodded, Sally felt her world suddenly fall apart. The thought of not having him around scared her.

'Yes. I've taken a good job in Sydney, partner in a private practice. Fortunately the hospital here has agreed to let me go six months early.'

She looked down at his hands. Sydney, maybe she should move there too. But before she could speak he said softly, 'Sally, I hate the thought of leaving you. So I was hoping you would agree to marry me. Move to Sydney with me. Would you like that? Your family won't be so far away. I mean, not like Darwin or Europe . . .' he stopped, knowing he was rattling on.

Sally almost burst out laughing at the thought she might be concerned at being far from her family. 'Hal, I'd go anywhere with you. Of course I will. Yes, yes, I'll marry you.'

He smiled with relief and gave a huge sigh. 'I'm so

happy.' He leaned across the table and they kissed. Then he reached into his coat pocket and pulled out a small box and a velvet bag. 'I came prepared, just in case.'

She opened the box and a large diamond ring winked in the candlelight. 'Hal, it's fabulous. Just stunning.'

'It belonged to my grandmother. If you don't like the setting we can change it, put more diamonds around it perhaps. You decide.'

'It's so big. It doesn't need anything changed. It's beautiful.' The two-carat stone was bright and clear with a hint of blue.

He pushed the velvet bag towards her. 'I'm not big on my heritage but I think my mother and grandmother would have liked you to wear this, for good fortune.'

'I feel fortunate already,' laughed Sally.

Inside the bag was a brilliant green jade bangle with an ornate gold clasp.

'It's imperial jade. I thought it would suit you.'

'Hal, I don't know what to say.' Sally was thrilled and touched, and she felt very cherished. At the bottom of all these emotions was a deep sense of relief that, finally, she too had a future to follow.

'You've said the most important thing – yes. Come on, let's dance.'

He held her close as they danced cheek to cheek, the lights of Christchurch twinkling like diamonds down below.

She could put it off no longer. Hal was pestering her to meet her family. For months now she'd managed to delay this occasion with all kinds of excuses, but Hal was determined to meet her father and begin planning for the wedding. When Sally broke the news to them and showed off her ring even her mother was impressed.

'But, Sally, why haven't you brought him home before this? I know you said he was busy but we had no idea it was this serious. Well, we've got oodles of time to get to know him. It'll take months to get the wedding planned.'

'Mother, no. We don't want a large wedding. Hal is moving to Sydney soon, that's why he proposed. He wants to buy a house in the eastern suburbs, overlooking Sydney Harbour.' She quickly threw that in to notify her mother that they wouldn't be staying in Christchurch.

'But surely that's no reason not to have a proper wedding, dear.'

Sally took a deep breath and blurted out the next bit of bad news. 'He's Catholic.'

Her mother's hand flew to her mouth. 'Oh, dear me. What about the children? I hope you haven't promised to bring them up Catholic. They always want that, you know.'

'Mother, I'm not even married yet. I'll deal with that much, much later. I don't think it will be a problem. Hal doesn't come from a big family himself, just a couple of old aunties.'

Her father spoke up. 'Well, there goes your big wedding, Emily. I look forward to meeting your Doctor Hal.' He paused, 'By the way what's his surname? Where're his family from?'

'Lee. Harold Albert Lee,' said Sally quietly.

'Lee? You'll be Mrs Lee?' said her mother looking faintly puzzled. 'It sounds . . . foreign.'

'He's part . . .' Sally hesitated, wondering which part to mention first. 'He's English and a little bit of exotic Chinese. His family were wealthy merchants in Darwin.'

'Chinese!' wailed her mother. 'Oh my Lord, you mean with slant eyes?'

'By merchants, do you mean, shopkeepers?' demanded

her father. 'We'd better meet him, I'm not sure if we can approve of this engagement.'

Sally shut herself in her bedroom. She could hear her distressed mother bleating on the phone to Yvonne. The words 'Chinese', 'Catholic' and 'pigtails' were mentioned.

She finally had to sit Hal down and explain that her parents weren't thrilled at the idea of their engagement. 'They wanted me to marry, you know, a sheep farmer. Someone like them.'

Hal laughed gently. 'You mean they hadn't considered an Asian for a son-in-law. Don't fret about it, I'm not. We'll get along, don't worry.'

'I hate to say it but my parents are snobs,' said Sally.

'So were mine,' said Hal, and they both laughed.

Hal charmed Emily and Garth Mitchell, and the knowledge that he was very wealthy helped them to accept him.

Emily had one niggling worry that she finally, awkwardly, whispered to Sally. 'About any children, dear. With his background, they, they don't throw back, do they?'

Sally smothered a laugh and patted her mother's arm. 'Don't worry, Mum, I'm not going to have little coloured babies with squinty eyes. In fact, I believe we'll have beautiful children.'

'I hope so. For their sake, as much as yours,' she added unconvincingly.

For a little while Emily had to endure the whispers about Sally's seemingly hasty wedding but it soon became evident there was no scandal.

Sally and Hal's wedding was very low key compared to Yvonne's. Thirty guests gathered at 6 pm for the nuptials at the Cathedral of the Blessed Sacrament in Moorhouse Avenue. Because it was a 'mixed' marriage they weren't wed at the altar but near the baptismal font at the entrance to the cathedral.

Sally, unpredictable as always, bought her wedding gown from Balentine's – a shell pink georgette, which was soft and slinky, showing off her curves. She wore high silver sandals and flowers in her hair with no veil. She looked gorgeous if, in her mother's mind, inappropriately dressed. A reception was held in a private room at the Clarendon Hotel. For Sally her wedding was a joyful event, made even more so by the presence of Lorna and John Monroe. They were in Sydney with Jilly seeing the boys and had left Jilly with a close friend of Lorna's to fly over for the wedding. Sally was sorry the boys couldn't be there but knew it would be hard for them to take time off school.

Garth Mitchell made a short, formal toast to the bride and groom, the only planned speech. But John Monroe rose to his feet and, grasping his champagne glass, made a warm, funny speech, and claimed responsibility for bringing the two love birds together by sending Sally to Darwin. Lorna had warned John to behave, he wasn't letting rip at some outback gathering, but his cheerful, laconic speech was the hit of the reception.

Sally gave him a hug and he squeezed her to him, whispering in her ear, 'I like the nightie you're wearing.'

Hal pumped John's hand and embraced Lorna and thanked them for the fact they were responsible for their meeting. 'Mr and Mrs Tsouris are thrilled. They're planning a big reception for us when we go to visit my aunties.'

'We'll go up there before we start house hunting,' said Sally.

'Well then, you'd better come to Barra Creek,' exclaimed John Monroe, and Sally and Lorna exchanged a quick glance. They both knew it was far too soon for Sally to return.

Lorna managed to take Sally aside and said quickly, 'Sally, this is right. This is how it should be for you. You made the right choice. I'm truly happy for you.'

Sally nodded, her eyes downcast, her heart full. Seeing Lorna and John had brought back jumbled feelings.

Doctor and Mrs Lee spent their wedding night at the Clarendon and the next day they drove to Picton to catch the inter-island ferry to Wellington. Hal had promised they'd spend the following Christmas in Europe, so Sally decided she'd show her husband the North Island on their honeymoon.

When they went out fishing in Paihia, Hal was dreadfully seasick, but Sally caught a decent swordfish and another tourist on their boat caught a striped marlin that weighed almost 300 pounds. Sally told Hal stories of fishing for barramundi with the Monroe boys.

In Auckland they stayed at the Grand Hotel opposite the gates of Government House and the next few days they went shopping. Sally delighted in taking her husband into Smith & Caughey's on Queen Street, decking him out in a Viyella shirt, tweed sports coat and woven woollen tie. Sally bought herself beautiful nightgowns at Bennett and Bains, a hat with silk petals on it at Kay Marie Millinery and a pair of lizard shoes at David Elman. Pleased with their buys they lunched at the kiosk in Parnell Rose Gardens. Driving down the Waikato, Sally admired the thoroughbred horse studs. After a stop in Wellington they caught the ferry back to the South Island.

The honeymoon was a blissful time for Sally. Hal spoiled her and promised she could go to town decorating their home in Sydney. 'We'll be doing a lot of entertaining, so you should get the best,' he said. 'I will be working long hours, darling, so you'll be in charge of the house. But every year we'll go to Europe, I promise.'

And they did. They led a glamorous social life as a popular couple in Point Piper. As the years passed Barra Creek became a distant memory Sally tried not to dwell on.

Chapter Eighteen

Kiama, New South Wales, 2003

THE ROOM WAS QUIET, outside the winter rain eased but the ocean was rumpled and cross. Sally topped up their cups of tea and Kate passed the milk. Lorna sat stiffly.

Finally, the young Director of Nursing and the former governess sat still and looked expectantly at her.

Lorna moistened her lips and asked, 'Were you happy, Sally? With Hal?'

'For many years, yes,' said Sally and she smiled at Kate. 'I married a lovely doctor and we have two great kids, grown up now, of course. But after ten years of the eastern suburbs social scene and constant entertaining and European holidays, I longed for the simple life.'

'It doesn't sound so bad,' said Kate. 'It's hard to find a nice single bloke these days. All the doctors got snapped up in med school.'

'You're still very young, Kate,' said Lorna. 'Don't rush into anything.' She turned her attention back to

Sally. 'You and Hal didn't have a long courtship.'

Sally stiffened. 'I recall you telling me I had done the right thing at the time. I don't regret my marriage, we just grew apart. We had different interests and finally we divorced. I have a couple of thoroughbreds on acreage in the hinterland, about forty-five minutes from here,' she said to Kate. 'And the gallery is a nice sideline.'

Kate nodded and looked again at Lorna. Where was this small talk heading?

'Kate can explain things better than I can. These days I lose the thread of my thoughts every so often. I suppose I'll lose the plot eventually,' Lorna said. 'But just the same I feel resentful that Ian has shuffled me into a home.'

Sally gave Kate a questioning look.

'Lorna could manage in her own home with some monitoring, someone checking on her regularly. Her son wants to sell her house.'

'Ian wants to sell? Isn't he running Barra Creek? I suppose Tommy is still in England. I'm sorry I lost touch with them,' said Sally.

'Ian is running Barra Creek . . . into the ground. The bank is threatening to foreclose, but he won't discuss it with me. He wants the money from the sale of my house to help cover the overdraft. Thomas is doing very well and doesn't need any money from me, nor does he have any interest in the property; you know that, Sally.'

Sally explained to Kate. 'He went off to England as soon as he finished school, went to Oxford and stayed there. He writes for a magazine and he's also become quite well known on radio, I believe.'

'Does he have a family?' asked Kate.

'A wife and two stepchildren. They came to visit me some time ago,' said Lorna. 'He doesn't get on with Ian so he doesn't care about Barra Creek.'

'It's difficult to believe two brothers could grow apart,

be so different . . .' Sally's voice trailed off. The conversation was bringing up painful and bittersweet memories.

'Why? What happened, why did you lose touch?' asked Kate.

Sally sighed. 'We were all so close but then, as happens, we got on with our lives, got busier, wrote less often, lost contact.'

'You and Hal were there for me when I needed help with Jilly. Hal was wonderful . . .' Lorna stopped and looked down at her hands.

The silence lengthened, then Sally spoke quietly to Kate, 'Lorna's had more than her share of tragedy.'

Kate nodded. She had heard snatches of Lorna's life when the older woman was rambling during her 'lost' times, but they hadn't made much sense to Kate.

Sally looked out of the window at the garden. Poor little Jilly.

When Sally gave birth to their first child, Jeremy, they had moved from the plush home unit into an elegant house with views across Sydney Harbour. Sally's parents had been impressed when they'd visited, although Garth Mitchell thought the fashionable harbour suburbs were too crowded. 'I need a couple of hundred acres round me so I can breathe,' he declared.

Sally had a gardener to tend the walled gardens around the house, a cleaning lady and a babysitter. When Yvonne asked her what she did all day, Sally was embarrassed to confess that the days flew by with preparations for entertaining, giving and going to parties, and social events. Hal worked long hours and when they weren't dashing out to that evening's function, he liked to relax at home.

Jeremy had just started preschool when Sally received a note from Lorna saying that she and John were coming down to see their boys, so she invited them to stay. Lorna wrote to thank her but said they'd prefer to book into a hotel near the hospital as Jilly was going in for tests.

Sally rang her immediately, the days of calling on the old wireless had long gone. 'What kind of tests? What's wrong with her? Can Hal look at her?'

'Thank you, Sally, but I don't want to impose. The doctor in Townsville has referred us to a specialist. We'd love to see you both, though, and little Jeremy of course.'

'I'd love to see Ian and Tommy. Can you bring them over?'

'Ian will be busy with a cricket match and studying, but I'm sure Tommy would love to come.'

Tommy rang Sally occasionally, he was now caught up in his studies and too busy to write long letters. She was happy he'd adjusted so well. Neither boy had deviated from the plans they'd had when they were younger – Ian to go back to the property, Tommy to go to England.

Lorna and John arrived with Tommy, a tall teenager, and five-year-old Jilly. Sally was overjoyed to have them in her home. She'd set the dining table for a formal lunch and Lorna glanced around at the beautiful carpets, rose-wood furniture, silver and glassware and two Chinese screens, which were old, valuable and the only touch of Hal's Chinese heritage.

'You have a lovely home, Sally.'

'Thank you, Lorna. You taught me well.'

Tommy was invited to go for a swim in the pool before lunch, and Jilly walked slowly around the room, touching each piece of furniture before sitting down on the carpet and entertaining herself by tracing her fingers over a woven rose pattern.

John Monroe leaned in the kitchen doorway with a drink in hand and watched Sally take the beef wellington from the oven. He talked about Barra Creek – Fitzi was doing the work of three men, the lubras were still trouble, the goats had eaten the kitchen garden, Betsy's child Daisy was a bright little thing but a handful – Lorna had banned her from the house and gardens. Rob had gone north. 'The bugger took Jasper with him. Both horse and rider are still working bloody hard, I hear. Snowy is still on the piss but manages to bring in enough cleanskins to keep us going. No one wants to hang around and work these days. We're getting city people coming up to fish, shoot pigs and crocs. Times are changing, Sal.'

'And Ian?'

John Monroe waved a hand. 'Full of big ideas for a teenager. How's your young fella? Are you going to bring him up to see us when he's old enough?'

Sally laughed. 'I'd love to take Jeremy up there, but I don't know if Hal would enjoy it, he's a skier.' She refrained from asking about Jilly who looked so frail and pale, and was so quiet it was unnerving.

After lunch Hal joined Lorna and Jilly. Sally and John sat by the pool as Tommy swam and Jeremy thrashed around in the clean blue water.

'Come on in and race me, Sally,' called Tommy.

'Not this afternoon, I have to go out tonight.' She patted her hairdo, which the Double Bay hairdresser had styled that morning.

'Struth, I never thought you'd turn into a social butterfly, Sal,' said John, taking in her red manicured nails, immaculate clothes and expensive jewellery. 'What do you do for fun when you're on your own? Not this social rounds stuff?'

'I was thinking I'd like to get a horse, keep it at Centennial Park. I miss riding,' she said, surprising herself at articulating the idea. Until then it had been a vague thought in the back of her mind. John's question made her think, she didn't do anything that she enjoyed. The fleeting mention of Rob had caused a pang as she recalled their riding adventures. 'What happened to Dancer?'

'Ian has commandeered her, but she's still your horse. She'll be there for you when come back.'

John went inside to join Hal and Lorna, leaving Sally on the patio with Tommy and Jeremy.

'So, you're still on track for England?' she asked Tommy.

'You bet. I'm going to try for a scholarship to Oxford in a couple of years. My English master said he'd help me.'

'Don't you miss your home?'

He shook his head. 'It was a good place to grow up and holidays there are fun. I take friends from school with me, but I don't want to live there any more. Mum doesn't like me to say that. Ian doesn't want me there, he's got his own ideas.'

'Your dad says it's changing up there.'

'Yeah, the black stockmen get proper money now, the old ways are going, that kind of stuff. Ian can have it. 'Course, you know Dad doesn't agree with any new ideas. I hate the way they argue all the time.' His face creased. 'Ian hasn't forgiven him for Jasper . . . lots of things. I'm glad Rob took Jasper with him.'

'He bought him from your father,' said Sally tightly. 'What is Rob doing?'

'He said he wanted to make more money, work for himself. He left when you got married and hasn't come back. Until then I think he thought you were going back to Barra. He said he missed Ian and me. The place isn't the same any more, Sal.'

'Things never stay the same. We have to look back and think we were lucky, we had lots of good times.'

He climbed out of the pool. 'I'll remember that when I'm in England.'

Later, after the Monroes had gone and Hal and Sally were dressing for a cocktail party, Hal said what had been worrying him all afternoon. 'That's one sick little girl, I'm afraid.'

'Jilly? What is it?'

'She has a degenerative mental and physical problem, a form of autism, but her main problem is a hole in the heart. She has a good specialist but –'

'She's not going to die! Oh, poor Lorna, after Marty . . .'

'Put it this way, she might do well for a while, but it requires major surgery and it's a congenital problem. I promised Lorna I'd stay in touch, check out treatments overseas. She needs a lot of emotional support at the moment.'

'John's not very good at that.'

Sally didn't see the Monroes again before they went back north. Lorna was in touch less and less although she occasionally spoke to Hal on the phone at his rooms. A year later Sally and Hal gave Jeremy a sister, Trisha. Sally sent the Monroes a birth announcement and Lorna sent a gift of embroidered linen from David Jones.

Hal and Sally and the children were in Austria on holidays when Sally called their housekeeper to check that everything was okay at home and the message was relayed that 'Mrs Monroe rang to say her daughter had passed away peacefully'. Sally phoned Barra Creek from Austria but Lizzie answered the phone and when she realised it was 'Miz Sally' all she could do was wail 'bout dat piccaninny all pinish'.

Later Sally learned that Jilly was buried beside Marty on the hill, John Monroe was drinking heavily and Lorna had gone to Cairns for a rest.

She next saw the Monroes when they went to Ian's graduation from King's, and she was shocked at how the

367

tragedy of Jilly's death had aged them. Ian refused to go to university, instead he enrolled in a management course by correspondence and returned to Barra Creek. When Tommy left school the following year he was awarded the Oxford scholarship he had hoped for.

Sally had a full life, too full. The children were involved in school activities and the demands of their social life had increased as Hal had been appointed to the hospital board. Sally wondered how she'd come to be trapped in an existence that was neither fulfilling nor stimulating. Hal was considerate and generous but there was little passion between them. This, she supposed, was how married life turned out, but it wasn't how she'd hoped it would be.

Gradually the lifestyle became intolerable. When she discussed it with Hal, he looked baffled and faintly irritated. Sally had thought about her life carefully. She cherished her two children and knew she had a devoted husband even if their interests had diverged. She was finding Sydney claustrophobic and one day she jumped in the car and drove down the south coast. That was when she discovered Kiama, a pretty seaside town nestled around a harbour with a rugged shoreline and dramatic blowhole, cliffs and headlands. She explored the hinterland and decided she would look for a small rural property where she could escape to now and again.

Hal agreed that if it would make her happy, he would give her the money to buy it. In fact money was the least of their worries; there was a waiting list for appointments to Hal's rooms in Macquarie Street.

Sally toured around the Jamberoo and Kiama area until she found a restored old house on one hundred acres that had been a dairy farm. The land was fairly close to the beach and was only a short distance from the main road. She built stables, a barn and fenced in a large paddock, then bought three horses.

She began to spend more and more time down there and Hal started to go to social functions on his own. She attended to her children's needs but she fussed less about her clothes, her weekly hair and manicure appointments, the social things she'd always done, the rush to keep up with the latest plays, music and movies. Sally didn't miss the coffee klutches, fashion shows, bridge parties and charity luncheons. Instead she was spending time with reps from feed and grain outlets, agricultural specialists, horse breeders and trainers, and the small, active business community of Kiama. The only cultural interest she pursued was discovering a network of local artists who hung their work in restaurants and coffee shops in the town. This started her thinking about opening a gallery. Her world began to dramatically split from Hal's. Their common ground was Jeremy and Trisha, but they were locked into their school world and family times were spent on shopping expeditions, catching up with friends or energetic holidays.

It was difficult for Sally to maintain close ties with her old friends, even her family in New Zealand, as they had little in common. When Lachlan and Yvonne and their children came to visit, Sally rushed them around all the tourist attractions in the city, as she found they ran out of things to talk about if they sat at home or lingered over restaurant meals.

She and Hal found some of their old affection for each other when they returned to Darwin for a week for the funeral of Aunt Winifred. But Hal couldn't wait to get back to Sydney, claiming pressure from patients, and refused to visit Barra Creek as Sally had hoped. Their closeness disappeared again and, inevitably, they drifted further and further apart. Eventually they separated, relatively amicably. Sally moved into the south coast farmhouse, the children were in boarding school and Hal stayed in the family home. It was as civilised as these matters could be. Hal was disappointed their relationship had faltered and hoped a short time apart might rejuvenate their marriage. Their friends were shocked, they'd seemed the perfect couple and they were both devoted to the children.

Once Sally was living on her own, struggling with small domestic problems in an old house, having the freedom to make her own mistakes and choices, she realised what she had been missing. She felt alive in a way she hadn't felt in years. Sad as she was at the breakdown of her marriage, she didn't suffer too many pangs of guilt. Her children were healthy and well adjusted. They accepted the division of their parents' lives – it was not an unusual situation among their friends' families – and they appreciated the stability of their father maintaining the home as it had always been.

After an initial coolness, Hal and Sally started to talk again, mostly about the children, in a warm and friendly manner. They established a friendship of sorts, comforted by the knowledge that there had been no ugly scenes, no other people involved, their children had taken matters in their stride and their lives had not been too disrupted.

Sally had no desire to seek a lover or a new relationship; she was happy enjoying her own company. She didn't delve into Hal's life and didn't want to know if he was seeing anyone else. He wasn't a wildly sexual animal; sleep was his number one pleasure and he was always tired at home.

The legal separation period passed before she'd noticed, so Sally was quite shocked to receive a letter in the post one day notifying her of her divorce nisi. Hal had put the wheels in motion and been generous in his settlement. He had a new woman in his life and the kids had accepted her without much fuss, or a lot of interest it seemed. Marianne was divorced, had been a personal assistant to a corporate manager and was very involved in fund raising for charities. Sally felt a pang of jealousy, wondering if she was younger than her, more glamorous and better in bed. Then she saw a photo in the social pages of the *Australian Women's Weekly*, and saw she was a sleek, fashionably groomed blonde woman about Sally's age. She looked like most of the other women in the social pages.

So here she was, a single woman again. It saddened her, yet it also gave her a small sense of elation. She opened a bottle of wine and wondered what she'd do with the rest of her life. It was 1976.

School holidays approached. Hal rang to ask if the kids could spend both weeks of the holidays with her as he and Marianne were taking a cruise. Sally hated the idea of cruising, she thought it would be like being locked in a floating cocktail party, though Hal had always wanted to go on one. They were welcome to it.

'Of course. I'll ask them what they'd like to do. They enjoy it here on the weekends, but they might get bored spending all the holidays here.'

'I think they'd like to go somewhere, do something different. They're at that adventurous age. I'd take them on the cruise but, frankly, I think they'd find that boring.'

Too right, thought Sally. 'Okay, I'll ring a travel agent and make a few enquiries. I hope they're not expecting a trek through Africa or scuba diving on the reef . . .' she paused as a thought hit her. 'What about Barra Creek? I'll take them there!'

Hal sounded dubious. 'They're such urban kids, Sal, do you think they'd cope with the outback? They're not as horse mad as you are.'

'That's precisely the point. It's not only about horses. I think they need to experience a bit of real life, just as I did.'

'Well, you discuss it with them. They have two weeks of holidays.'

Sally's enthusiasm won Jeremy and Trisha over. She made it sound like a cross between an African safari, the wild west and Jungle Man. She rang John and Lorna. Things did not sound so cheerful up there, but they were both extremely keen to see her.

'It'll be a breath of fresh air to have you here, Sal. It's never been the same since you left . . . then the boys, then Rob. Nope, it's not the same as it used to be,' said John Monroe. Then he lowered his voice. 'Lorna hasn't recovered since we lost the little girl. Your visit might perk her up no end.'

'I gather Tommy is doing well in England. And Ian? How's he going?'

Sally could hear the heat and anger in John's voice. 'Christ, Sally, it's war I tell you. That young fella is getting too big for his boots. All this newfangled bloody gear and ideas. Don't know what they teach them in these fancy management courses. All the good black stockmen have gone, since equal pay came in it's impossible to pay 'em all.'

'Are any of the mob left?' Sally couldn't imagine the Monroes running the property without the station blacks. How on earth was Lorna managing?

'Oh yeah, the camp is still there; the girls and Fitzi. But now we get these young white jackeroos – most of 'em know nothing or think they know it all,' he grumbled.

'Oh, dear. You're sure we won't be an imposition?' Sally was beginning to have second thoughts.

'Not on your nelly. Like I say, it will cheer Lorna up no end. And I reckon it'll do those city kids of yours a lot of good.'

'Yes. I'm not sure what they'll think of the outback at first. But they're young and it will be an adventure.'

'Right then. I'll let Lorna and you work out the details between you.'

Donny had gone to work in Townsville taking tourist charter flights out to the Barrier Reef islands and outback destinations up the Cape. There was now a new pilot and a more organised schedule for the mail, passenger and freight run. Jeremy and Trisha were a little scared of the small plane that flew them over the vast landscape. Sally looked down at the rippling sand ridges, the salt pans, the smudges of green around the ribbon of a grey river tributary. It suddenly reminded her of the pictures Frankie and Ginger used to paint in the schoolhouse.

As they dropped down to the airstrip at Barra Creek she was struggling with her emotions. It was all so familiar and yet strange; the changes were startling. The airstrip had an upgraded surface and there was a corrugated-iron shed that served as a depot for freight and passengers. A new four-wheel drive was waiting to collect them. But then she saw John Monroe, looking much as he always had, grinning broadly. He embraced them all and threw their bags into the back of the Toyota. Laughingly he told the children the story of Sally's arrival but they thought he was exaggerating.

'High heels, stockings, pearls, the lot! And her port in the wheelbarrow and the black kids dragging her along,' he said. 'Lorna was impressed though.'

'Where are Frankie and Ginger?' asked Sally.

'You did a good job on those boys, Sal. Would you believe Frankie is working at Gilbert River? He's a bloody good stockman, he comes and does a big muster with us when we need him, and Ginger has a job over at Karumba. Once he saw the sea he took to it. Hangs around the prawn people.'

'And Alice? Lizzie, Betsy?'

'Lizzie is still sloping round the homestead, Alice is working in a shop in Normanton. Betsy's kid Daisy is a card. I've taught her to ride and drive. She's a real champ.'

At the sight of the house, the years melted away and when she saw Lorna standing in a crisp cotton dress by the garden fence, tears came to Sally's eyes. The children were quiet, this was so different from anything they'd seen before. But driving past the goats, they squealed in delight. Hovering in the side garden, wringing her apron and grinning broadly, was Lizzie. Beside her, waving excitedly, was Betsy. Lizzie's hair was grey, her face more creased, and Betsy had grown quite plump. They came forward wailing, crying and laughing, reaching out to Jeremy and Trisha, who looked apprehensive.

Lorna shooed the women into the house to get morning tea and John carried the kids' bags along the verandah to the beds where Sally and the boys had slept. Sally hurried through the house, pleased to see that little had changed. As she stepped into the outdoor dining area she saw Fitzi standing by the door, holding his hat and looking sheepish. She hurried over and pumped his toughened hand.

'You come back, good one, yeah, Mizzie. And you bring young pellas for learning up here. Good, good,' he said, still holding her hand.

'They've got to learn about the outback, Fitzi. Will you take them for a little walkabout round here, show them everything, eh?'

'They go ride far way?'

'They're not riders . . . yet. We'll show them, right, Fitzi?'

374

'We show 'em, for sure.'

There was a lot of catching up to do over tea and scones, reminiscing and laughing. The children were quiet, tucking into the tea and scones while remembering to be on their best behaviour. Sally had laid down the law, telling them how particular Mrs Monroe was about manners. As teacups were being topped up, a motorbike roared up – Ian had arrived.

The moment he came into the dining room Sally sensed the atmosphere change, the tension increase. He was taller and looked much older than his twenty-five years. He tossed his hat on the back of his chair, kissed Sally's cheek, shook hands with Jeremy and little Trisha and leaned back as Lorna poured his tea. Sally couldn't help noticing he was sitting in the chair that had always been John Monroe's place.

After some initial small talk about how the children had enjoyed the trip, John excused himself. 'I've got to see to a few things.'

'What are you doing, Dad?' Ian's question had an undercurrent of criticism, like *Don't do anything without my approval.*

'Just going to the stables to check on Dancer now her boss is back. How about I take the kids for a run around the place after they've changed out of those travelling clothes?'

'That would be great, John, thanks. I can't wait to see Dancer. She'll be a mature lady now.'

'Is that the horse you rode, Mum?' asked Trisha.

'It is. Maybe we can find a little treat to take her, a carrot or something.'

'I'm sure we can and later you can go for a paddle on the river if you like,' suggested Lorna.

'The river?' Jeremy had heard Sally's stories about the crocodiles.

'Would you like to go fishing? There's been some good barra around, the boys tell me,' Lorna said. 'In fact we're having some for dinner.'

'No spare ribs?' teased Sally.

'We'll get a killer tomorrow,' said Ian, standing up. 'Do you think the kids would like to help?'

'I don't think so, Ian, thanks,' said Sally, knowing her children wouldn't be able to face the killing and the butchering. She wondered now how she had coped so well in her first weeks there. Unlike her children, at least she'd come from a farm. Yes, this experience would be good for them.

When Sally took the children along the verandah and showed them the bathroom, Trisha tugged at her hand.

'There're no rooms, Mum. Do we have to sleep out here?'

'Are there snakes up there?' asked Jeremy, pointing to the thick vines that still wound over the lattice on the verandah.

'There's nothing to worry about. You'll hear all kinds of noises at night, but they're just little creatures.' She hoped there were no crocodiles in earshot. 'There's the little governess' room, Trish, but it's too hot for you to sleep in.'

'I want to sleep in there.' So far her children weren't impressed with the living arrangements.

'What about learning to ride? Then we can get you a horse to ride at my place.'

'Maybe,' said Jeremy, more out of politeness than genuine interest. 'I'd rather learn to ride a motorbike like Ian.'

That first afternoon, John Monroe drove the kids around and Sally, back on Dancer, rode out to the home paddock feeling the happiest she had in years. Snowy waved his hat and rode over to meet her.

'Haven't lost your touch, Sally. You look just the same. I hear you have a couple of kids now.'

'I don't feel any different, Snow. It's good to be back. Yes, I've brought my children with me. How're things going?'

The horses walked beside each other and Snowy rubbed the stubble on his chin. 'Don't like to say much, but you'd understand. Things are a bit crook, to tell you the truth. Ian's turned into a right little Hitler if you ask me. He has all these bloody modern ideas like mustering with helicopters and motorbikes. Dunno why John doesn't slap him back in his boots.' He paused then asked candidly, 'Do you suppose he has something on the old man?'

Sally was thoughtful. She wasn't going to gossip with the likes of the boozy old musterer but she had wondered the same thing. 'Maybe John is letting him have a bit of rope, then he'll pull him in when he gets out of hand. Sons always have to test their fathers, especially when they're working in the same business.'

'I reckon things went downhill after Marty got killed. And Ian still hates Monroe for what happened to Jasper. He was madder than a cut snake when Rob took that stallion.'

'He paid for him. So what's Rob doing?' asked Sally as casually as she could.

'Last I heard he'd married and was getting into them Brahman bloody bulls somewhere in the Territory.'

'Oh, I've read a bit about that. They're pretty hardy and carry a lot of meat.' Sally was surprised at how hurt she was to hear Rob had married and no one had told her. 'Well, I'll be seeing you, Snowy.' She turned Dancer and cantered away.

377

Jeremy and Trisha sat in John Monroe's truck and watched Fitzi, Snowy and Sally on horseback round up a mob of cattle with Ian and one of the young jackeroos on motorbikes. Bringing up the rear was a slim, young boy, his Akubra pulled down low, who rode one of the big stockhorses. Sally wondered if he was Chilla or Bluey's son but she didn't see him again.

Fitzi took the kids on a long walk to the billabong and Lorna arranged picnics, let them help with the goats, ride in the billycart pulled by the nanny goat, and collect eggs and vegetables, which was a great novelty for them.

The children were shy around the blacks, though they liked Fitzi and Betsy made them laugh. Lizzie bossed them and kept telling them debil man stories. Sally hoped Mr Stinky was no longer around. She missed the activity in the blacks' camp and having the black stockmen on the property, and felt sad that no one bothered with corroborees any more.

The single men's quarters were quiet. Ian had set up his own place there, knocking three bunk rooms into one. Sally wanted to spend some time with him and have a talk, but an occasion never came about where they could be alone together. She wondered if this was deliberate. He'd always been serious and somewhat sullen, but she thought about the times they all played, fished, rode and told stories together. She thought she'd always be very close to the three Monroe boys. Now one was dead, one was far away and rarely kept in touch, and Ian treated her, if not as a stranger, then as someone who had briefly passed through his life. That was true, of course, but she liked to think that what they'd shared had been special.

One evening sitting on the verandah with a glass of rum, savouring the peace and solitude, it occurred to her that perhaps Ian was avoiding her because she reminded him of the emotional times they had been through. Lorna came and sat beside her as the sky faded from gold to lavender. 'Like old times, isn't it, Sally?'

'Almost. I'm so glad to be here. How are you, Lorna?'

'I miss my little girl. She filled a big hole in my life.'

'Why do you stay here?' asked Sally softly. She'd seen how intolerable Lorna's relationship was with her husband. She was glad she and Hal had separated before becoming bitter and growing to hate each other. But then, they hadn't lost two children.

'Where would I go? What would I do? Despite everything, maybe because of everything, I feel tied to this place. I'd miss it.'

Sally had to agree. Although she was firm and capable, Lorna had always relied on John, the black workers and her sons to help her. She still looked as elegant and immaculate as ever, though she was very thin and her hair was coloured to cover the grey.

'I'm really sorry about you and Hal. I never expected it.'

'Me neither. But I like being on my own. I don't want to stay alone, but for the moment I'm relishing doing exactly what I want. I love my little place down on the south coast. I'm thinking of getting a few more horses, maybe starting some sort of business. Lorna, you know you're welcome to come and stay with me, for as long as you want.'

'Thank you, Sally. Sometime I will. I don't like leaving Ian and John here together. I try to be the buffer between them.'

The children came running along the verandah and the conversation turned to the suggestion they go out to Snowy's stock camp and sleep under the stars.

Sally could understand their excitement. 'Wow, in

swags, around the campfire. That's an adventure,' she said.

They weren't going far, just a couple of hours' drive. Snowy and two jackeroos would bring in a small mob from the trap yards. John would drive the kids, and Sally and Fitzi would ride.

Early one morning before they left, Sally went for a ride on her own, winding up the small rise at the back of the homestead to visit the sad little graves of Marty and Jilly. She dismounted and sat on the ground beside them. She rested her head on her knees and wept quietly, thinking of sweet Marty and dear little Jilly. How would she cope with losing a child? She couldn't imagine. No wonder such a dark cloud covered the homestead.

As the sun rose high she touched each headstone, then remounted Dancer, but when the horse turned she was surprised to see the young boy who'd helped muster the cattle with her and the others a couple of days before. She reined in, wondering if he'd been sent to fetch her. But he stopped his horse and waited, and Sally realised he was also surprised to see her there. He must have been about twelve or thirteen and his easy riding style reminded her so much of Tommy. He swung out of the saddle and Sally saw he was carrying a bunch of fresh gumtips. He came to Sally and took off his hat.

'Morning, Missus.'

Sally stared in surprise at the child who had short curly hair, beautiful eyes and a wide smiling mouth showing gaps between the front teeth. It was a girl, dressed in a boy's shirt, denim jeans and old boots. Her skin was creamy brown and her nose and face fine boned. Sally's heart lurched, this must be Betsy's child. Rob's child. She managed a smile. 'Hello. Are you Daisy?' As the girl nodded Sally asked, 'What are you doing up here?'

'Boss get me put dese one up here every week. Dey be poor babies dere.'

'Boss? You mean Mr Monroe?'

She nodded then looked worried. 'No tell 'um Miz Monroe. She no like me.'

'No, I won't say anything. It's very nice of you to do that, Daisy. Do you go to school?'

She shook her head. 'Me working horses an' cattle. Learnin 'bout dem tings. Fitzi, Snowy, Monroe Boss show me.'

They must be short handed, thought Sally. Then recalling the tales of Betsy's wild child they probably figured this would keep her out of mischief. Sally nodded. 'You do what you have to, goodbye, Daisy.'

'Bye, Missus.'

Plans changed when John Monroe took Sally aside. 'I'm not going out with you. Why don't you drive? Ian has work here and I've got some things to check out. Fitzi will look out for you.'

'As he always did,' said Sally. 'It's only a night and two days, which will probably be long enough for the kids.'

'We have to get them riding, Sal. They can't come up for holidays here if they can't ride.'

'I'm working on it.' Neither mentioned it but Sally assumed John was thinking the same as she was – too bad Rob wasn't here. He'd have them calmly and confidently riding in no time.

In one respect Sally was glad John wasn't going to be with them, he'd dominate the little group, and she was looking forward to sharing this special experience with her children and Fitzi. He'd promised to tell them some legends after supper round the campfire. Jeremy and Trisha had found Barra Creek exciting and unusual, but the novelty was wearing off. They too felt the tension in the house and it made them uncomfortable. They'd talked about it in whispers at bedtime, but Sally had merely told them how sad Mr and Mrs Monroe were because they had lost Marty and Jilly. She spared them the details of Marty's death.

She knew that she wouldn't bring her children back here. They found it strange to think of their mother as a governess or going out mustering on horseback. There was nothing at Barra Creek that bore any connection with their life with their father in Point Piper or their mother's comfortable, elegantly rustic spread on the south coast.

Lorna made sure they packed food the children would like in addition to flour for the damper and beef stew, and she and John waved them off. Sally drove the new Toyota and Fitzi rode behind her. Snowy and the boys had gone ahead.

'Go get 'em, cowboys!' John called out.

The children waved and Sally glanced fondly at him in the rear-vision mirror. Despite all his crassness and bluster, snapping at Ian and his dismissiveness towards Lorna, she felt sorry for John Monroe, and she liked him.

'Where are we going, Mum? There's no road.' Trisha peered at the dusty track ahead of them.

'We're going to catch some cattle where the wild horses live. If you're lucky, you might see some brumbies or the magical spirits who dance around the campfire at night.'

For a brief moment she saw in her mind the dreadful scene of Marty's death. She'd keep these two precious people close to her and she knew Fitzi was there to watch out for them too. Sally loved Barra Creek but she couldn't help feeling it had been cursed.

Chapter Nineteen

JOHN MONROE CLOSED HIS diary and flung it back on the shelf in the small area that served as his library and office. He then went out on the verandah, lit a cigarette and stared across the garden. How different it looked from when he and Lorna had moved here. She'd done a wonderful job trying to make this Godforsaken place look like a suburban garden. If he was honest with himself, he'd never thought she'd stick it out. Christ, they had had their ups and downs, and more than their fair share of bloody tragedy. What had he done to get kicked in the guts so often, he wondered. And now, when he should be sitting back enjoying life, taking it a bit easy, he had this constant friction with Ian. It had been building for years, he could see that now. He could understand some of the reasons why Ian blamed him for what had gone wrong in their lives. Maybe that was why he'd taken his hand off the wheel, looked away, and Ian had got the better of him. He was facing a situation of either giving up running the property and letting

Ian do things his way, or having an all-out blue and taking control again.

He'd stepped back a little and let Ian try out some ideas, but they had only cost them money. Prices were not what they used to be, costs were high and labour was expensive. Tommy was no help, he'd pissed off to England and would never come back. The future of Barra Creek had to stay with Ian whether Monroe liked it or not. The problem was in standing back; it was infuriating to see how cocky Ian was. He was going to come a cropper for sure, but it would be hard to stand aside and watch him ruin years of hard work. Maybe he and Lorna should take off and leave Ian to it, but he was buggered if he'd do that, this place was his life. Lorna would probably like to travel, go and see Tommy. He hated hotels and travelling to strange places. Aw, shit. It was all too damned hard.

He stubbed out his cigarette against the post and flipped the butt into the bushes.

'Lorna! You there?' he bellowed, stepping inside.

'Please, John. I don't feel well.' Lorna's reply was feeble and she sounded cross. 'What is it?'

He glanced into the room where Lorna was lying on her bed under the mosquito net, a damp cloth on her forehead. 'What's up now?' he asked.

'I don't know. What do you want?' Her eyes were closed and he could tell she didn't want to talk.

'Nothing. I've got some things to see to before Sally gets back. I'm taking the old ute, I'll be back in a day, I guess.'

'Please be here when they get back,' she sighed. While she loved having Sally and the children visit, it was draining her energy. John had promised them a big barbecue when they came in from the stock camp. It would be a relief if he went out checking, bores, horses, cattle, or whatever. A day or so on her own was just what she needed. She pressed the cool towel closer.

Monroe put his .303 rifle on the dash of the ute, threw his gear in the back and drove away without anyone paying any attention. He'd kept quiet, not wanting to scare Sally and her kids, but there'd been reports of another huge croc up river, a real big bastard. It had grabbed a calf and there'd been talk of it getting a dog. Snowy had set a snare for it and John had checked it a few times with no luck. The big old croc had outsmarted them so far.

Snowy had placed a chunk of wild pig across the steep mud slide where the croc went up the bank from the river. Around the bait was a thin metal cable forming a noose. Strong rope cord with a five-hundred pound breaking strain ran from the noose, hanging loose above the snare, up a tree, over a branch and was weighted at the end by a heavy log as a counterbalance. It had proved to be an effective snare in the past. A crocodile had to put its head through the loop to get to the bait and when it moved backwards it tripped the wire, which sprang and tightened around its head. It was stopped from going back into the river by the weight of the log that swung up to the branch.

Monroe planned to check the snare on his way to the bore in the western paddock, but he knew it was simply an excuse to be on his own. Time to think about Ian and the increasing tension between them both. Several times recently they had almost come to blows. The language of dissent and conflicting opinions had given way on many occasions to language of abuse. Even hatred. John fought hard to keep his emotions under control, but he knew things could not go on like this much longer. Something, someone, had to give. They'd both been drinking more heavily than usual, despite the presence of the visitors. Poor Sally, he thought. I wonder what she's making of all this. She must see what's happening. Too polite to say anything, that's Sal.

He parked the ute by the tree line of the creek. He didn't pick up the rifle, figuring that, like so many times before, there'd be no need for it. The dry grass crumpled under his feet as he walked quietly towards the snare. The tree was soon in sight and at once he could see that the log had been moved, and the rope cord was hanging slack. 'Well, well,' he muttered. 'Whaddya know.'

He walked cautiously up to the tree and peered around the trunk. Sure enough the croc, all fifteen feet of it, was lying on the steep mud slide, its head caught in the steel noose. It had been fighting to break free, was covered in mud, and the whole area had been churned up from a long struggle. Even though the croc had eventually crawled towards the tree and lowered the imprisoning log, the noose held tight. The slack line was buried in mud. 'You bloody beauty,' hissed Monroe. 'Gotcha! Not so fuckin' smart after all.'

The croc was still and Monroe, with a feeling of triumph dulling his better judgement, stepped from behind the tree and walked towards the croc, raising his hands and clapping them hard to startle the creature. It thrashed viciously and slid back towards the water. In the same instant Monroe fell backwards, slipping on the muddy bank.

The crocodile's panicked dash tightened the long line, whipping loops of it out of the mud. At the same time, Monroe was thrown off balance again and screamed in fear. His left leg caught in several loops of the rope line running between the croc and the log. The line tightened, cutting into his leg. The croc was half in the water, the log rose and jammed up against the high tree branch. Monroe blacked out in shock and pain.

When he came around minutes later, the world

seemed upside down. He was hanging in the air, dangling from the taut line, his head and shoulders in the mud. He slowly took stock and turned his head to look down the bank and found himself staring into the eyes of the half-submerged croc several yards away. It again shook its head and clawed the mud, but nothing happened. It was a bizarre tableau of man and beast. Each counter-balancing the other until one gave way.

Monroe desperately tried to devise a way out of his predicament, but stayed very still. He figured if he didn't move, the croc wouldn't. Even if he could reach up to his trapped leg, there was little chance of being able to undo the tangled line. He wasn't carrying a knife, either. If he did free himself he'd slide down the steep slope towards the croc. And if the croc decided to race up the bank towards him, then what? Sunset was hours away. That's when the croc would be likely to make a move. They came up onto river banks at sunset. Maybe Snowy would come by. No, he wouldn't be in from the stock camp for another day or so. Ian? He knew the snare was set but wasn't sure where, and John hadn't told anyone he was going to check out the scene.

'Oh, Jesus,' he exclaimed softly. For the first time in a long while, John Monroe started to pray.

Years afterwards Ian still wondered, when unbidden thoughts of that day came to him, what had led him along the path he followed to its swift, unplanned con-clusion. Fate? Coincidence? The subconscious fulfilment of a long-held idea? Or was it the voices he sometimes heard in his head telling him what to do?

He had set out on horseback late in the afternoon and seeing the tyre tracks heading towards the river, he followed on an impulse. Two hours later he knew where his father had gone – to check the croc snare. His horse walked slowly. To his left was the broad creek where barramundi lived and the saurians came to feed, make their nests and stake their territory. The tangle of river growth smothered by the Madagascan rubber vine stopped where a bushfire had ripped through. An occasional melaleuca tree dotted the bank amidst all the grass. He stopped the horse, took a swig of rum from his water bottle and gazed as the last of the sunlight spread like butter on black bread.

He'd had a fear of the river ever since the bore runners' woman had been taken. He and his brothers had sneaked away from Sally and seen the bloody body lying on the grass. The times he'd been swimming he'd made sure the others were ahead of and behind him, and they all made lots of noise.

He felt again the deep disquiet that he lived with – a feeling of frustration, of smothered anger, of loneliness and the fear that he'd always feel this way. When could he step from the shadow of his father, be his own man? He'd have to move, make a break. But he couldn't bring himself to do that. He was afraid, even though Rob had said he could work with him any time he wanted a breather. Ian had always felt a very strong attachment to his home. Unlike Tommy he hated going away and he couldn't wait to come back on school holidays. Once Sally had asked why he loved being here so much, and he couldn't answer. He'd always felt this way, and in one respect he believed he owed it to little Marty to carry on. Marty should be here with him. His death should never have happened. So many things had gone wrong. He took another gulp of the rum, feeling it warm his gut, then he moved the horse forward. He wasn't sure where the snare was set so he went on until he spotted the ute parked in open country. He tethered the horse to the bumper, glanced into the cabin, surprised to see his father's rifle, picked it up and walked towards the river following the trodden grass that marked the path to the bank.

In the fading light he thought it was an apparition, a grotesque illustration from some horror comic. He stopped, his breath catching as the full impact of what he saw hit him – his father caught in a trap, suspended and helpless half way down the bank. It was a bizarre, unexpected and frightening scene. He blinked then shut his eyes for a moment, but when he opened them nothing had changed. Ian was as still as the scene before him, but his mind was in turmoil.

Was his father alive? He felt a rush of emotion and a surge of sudden elation that shocked him. The idea that his father was dead pleased him. He shuddered slightly, and cautiously stepped a little closer. He started to shake and was forced to stop. Looking around carefully, he saw for the first time the massive croc with its head in the steel noose, just clear of the rising tidal water. Man and beast both trapped and both still alive.

His head cleared a little and one of the voices he heard so often whispered, 'Save him. Shoot that bloody thing. A dead easy shot.'

But another louder voice echoed from the distant past and stopped any hint of action. 'Remember all those times, you know, those times when you wished he was dead.' And with it came a flood of pictures, like flashes from horror movies – a flood of memories of hurts and threats. Images that had brought pain, anger and promises of retribution. The world around him became a blur.

The man in the wire trap was no longer his father. It was just a figure, a shape, an empty shell as if blood, life and everything that made him live had been drained away like a butchered killer beast.

The real world came back into focus. Ian saw the

scene again so clearly and knew what would be inevitable unless he made a move. But he couldn't. He opened his mouth, it was dry, his tongue thick, he couldn't make a sound. He dropped his head and closed his eyes to again erase the scene, and then a feeling of great calm came over him. 'It is so easy, so simple,' whispered a voice within him.

The solution to all his anguish. He didn't have to do anything. 'Do nothing,' the voice in his head screamed. 'Walk away. Turn and walk away. You did not cause this to happen. John Monroe, fate, God, had brought this to pass. Do not interfere.'

After half a day here Monroe had little strength left. He felt dizzy and knew he would pass out again. He lifted his head, and saw, standing in the shadow of the trees, his eldest son.

'Thank God you're here! Shoot the bloody thing. Quick!'

Ian didn't answer. He couldn't look at the figure of his father again. Deliberately he turned his back and slowly put one foot in front of the other, with each step walking towards a future free of John Monroe.

In many nights to come, he would hear again the hoarse scream echoing over the silent river . . .

'You baaastaaard!'

He did not see the old beast lift its jaws, dig in its claws and make one last effort to drag its massive body up through the mud. With each patch of muddy ground gained, the slackening rope slowly lowered the weight of John Monroe's head and shoulders towards where the dead pig meat had rested.

Sally and the children were grateful Fitzi had been with them on the stock camp. Sally felt safe and Fitzi had entertained the two city kids by taking them out to find bush tucker, hunt a goanna, watch brolgas dance and learn about surviving in the seemingly empty terrain. Around the campfire he told them stories about the area and Snowy had surprised Sally by recounting some exciting adventures that were, thankfully, relatively wholesome. The children enjoyed the novelty of eating their dinner off a tin plate from the camp oven, and rolling into their swags and looking at the night sky, watching for shooting stars to make a wish. Driving back, Trisha and Jeremy said they'd had a good time but wouldn't want to do it for too long.

'Snowy said they sometimes stay out at those camps for weeks and weeks,' said Jeremy. 'That'd be awful.'

For a moment Sally thought back to her time out in the stock camp with the boys and Rob. How precious and romantic it had been with him. Maybe what she and Rob had shared was only meant to be for a short while in this unreal country of campfires, stars, horses, cattle and the vastness encircling them.

'There was plenty to do, you were on the go from sunrise to sundown. Time for a bit of a yarn after dinner and then into your swag, you were so tired,' she said.

'You really liked it out here, didn't you, Mum?' said Jeremy softly.

'I did. But I ended up in the city with your dad and made a different life from maybe what I'd planned. Never plan your life, kids, things have a habit of turning out quite differently.'

'Well, I'm going to uni and staying in the city,' Jeremy said.

'But we're glad we came. Thanks, Mum,' said Trisha, ever the sensitive little girl.

It was lunchtime and Lorna had the table set by the time the children had cleaned up and come in to eat. Sally was surprised that Lorna was the only one joining them.

'Where is everyone?'

'John has gone out to check on a bore or something. He went yesterday, he'll be back in time to cook the barbecue he promised. Ian is with Snowy, Fitzi and the men outside, working out about moving some cattle. So that leaves us and I want to hear how you enjoyed yourselves.'

In the afternoon, while Lorna had a rest and the children played in the goat cart, Sally went for a ride. She came back past the blacks' camp, now one of more permanent-looking gundies and basic one-room houses, though it was a much smaller settlement than the sprawling community she had known. She slowed Dancer as she came across two old women, Lizzie and young Daisy walking back from the river carrying tubers of waterlilies, a coolamon with seed pods and a couple of fish.

'Got your dinner, eh, Lizzie?'

'Bush tucker, good grub. No more chop, for buy 'em baccy, and new dress, eh. All pinish.'

'No more shop? You get rations though, from Mister and Missus?'

Lizzie shrugged. 'Beef, chooga, tea. No more pretty tings.'

'Mista Ian, close 'em up,' said one of the women. 'We gotta buy tings and order 'em. No more sit down rations.'

Sally dismounted and walked with them, leading Dancer. 'What else has changed, Lizzie?'

The woman shrugged and looked a little po-faced. 'Ever 'ting. No more allsame.'

Sally nodded and as they got closer to the camp she pointed to a tree. 'Daisy, see that tree? That's where you were born. I was there.'

Daisy's face lit up. 'You see me born in dis country? Me proper Barra Creek baby. My mutta want me go 'way, learn up proper white school.' She shook her head. 'Daisy work, lotta work here. Me good with cattle, horses, muster.'

'Daisy good ringer,' said Lizzie.

Sally felt a stab of pain. Just like her father. She wondered if Daisy knew Rob was her dad. Had Betsy ever told her? Then she pushed the thought away. It wouldn't have meant much to her anyway, white fathers weren't part of their lives. Daisy was lucky to have her extended Aboriginal family. Betsy's mob had nurtured her and all she cared about was her home country. Rob, it seemed, cared little for the child he'd fathered.

By evening, with no sign of John Monroe, Lorna became annoyed then agitated, then worried. Snowy and Ian cooked the meal outdoors in the garden. John Monroe was loud and sometimes brash but he was also entertaining. It was a lacklustre gathering without him.

Sally put her children to bed then settled in the living room with Lorna. Ian had disappeared with Snowy. No one was unduly worried that Monroe hadn't returned, though Sally thought it odd. But then, she knew how circumstances out here could hinder the best laid plans. She was tired but she relished the private time with Lorna. The two of them sitting together rehashing events around the station, browsing through catalogues, talking about kids, except this time it was Sally's children. For Sally it was like coming home. She could tell Lorna things she couldn't tell her mother.

'Do you miss Hal?' Lorna asked.

'He hasn't dropped out of my life, because of the children. I don't miss the social whirl he's into. But yes, I miss someone around the house. Reading the newspapers together at breakfast, waiting for him to come home, the evening cocktail, and knowing there's a warm body in the bed.' Sally sighed. 'Our interests are so different, though.'

Lorna nodded and didn't have to say anything. Sally had known, better than anyone, Lorna's relationship with John. Lorna looked thoughtful then said, 'The physical side seems so important in the beginning. But really, what lasts, what you want most, are those other things. Someone to talk to, laugh with, who's interested in the same things.'

The two women sat in silence, each lamenting a mistaken marriage, one feeling there would be no changes in her life, she'd hung on so long, the younger woman fretful she'd make the same mistake again. If indeed she found another partner. Sally, at least, was glad that for the moment she was happy sharing her children, building a new life and maybe, hopefully, she'd find someone to share her life with equally rather than her sharing his.

She changed the subject. 'Fitzi was terrific, but I'm afraid I've raised a pair of city slickers.'

'Why would they be otherwise? Still, it's good they've seen the other side of the coin,' said Lorna.

'I saw Lizzie, the old girls and Daisy this afternoon,' said Sally cautiously. 'You said Daisy was out of control. She does seem bright, she said she was keen on working with the cattle and horses.'

'Mmm. She's a bit of a lad. I think it best she stays away from the house. I don't want her getting any big ideas,' said Lorna nervously.

'She doesn't know about her father?' Sally felt her throat tighten.

'What's to know? He's not around. Leave it, Sally.' Lorna stood up. 'I'm going to bed. I'm sure you must be tired too. Hopefully John will be back in the morning. Goodnight. It's lovely to have you here again.'

'It was a really special time of my life.'

'I know,' said Lorna with a sad note in her voice. She rested her hand on Sally's shoulder for a moment before leaving the room.

Sally went into the kitchen and found Snowy sitting alone at the long table smoking a cigarette. His stubble was grey, his beer belly sagged over his belt.

'Thanks for cooking dinner, Snow. Has Ian gone to bed?'

'Probably. He's been on the grog. Doesn't happen too often but. Well, I'll be hitting the sack.'

'Thanks again for letting me bring the kids along. Do you still do big trips or get in contractors?'

'Ian gets the casual ringers in.' He gave a grin. 'I'm getting a bit old for this caper, Sally. Might throw it in soon.'

'And do what?' She knew nothing about Snowy's personal history.

'I've got a sister over in Townsville. My ex is in Cairns and our kids are around the place. Time to do a bit of serious fishing.'

'Still lots of barra around?'

'Fer sure, but I wouldn't get out on the river with the kids. Been a big bugger of a croc around.'

'Really? John didn't say anything.'

'He didn't want to worry you.' Snowy suddenly looked thoughtful. 'I wonder . . . might check that snare we set. Well, g'night, Sally. Good to have you round the place again. Only seems like yesterday you were racing round with the kids.'

'It was thirteen years ago since I first came here, Snow.'

'Struth, time gets away.'

The screen door banged behind him.

395

At breakfast as her sleepy children struggled with their plates of chops, sausages and fried eggs, Sally watched Ian eat in sullen silence. A hangover, she presumed. What had happened to him, she wondered. She thought back to the three neat little boys who ate at the small table in the dining room. Jeremy and Trisha were sitting at the dining table and would have been horrified at being put at a 'kids' table'. They moaned enough at their mother's 'nagging' about table manners. Boarding schools had changed since Sally's day, although Trisha was doing cookery and etiquette classes.

Lorna, at least, stuck to tradition, remaining in bed until breakfast was over and the ringers and stockmen had left the kitchen.

It was after lunch that the world of Barra Creek changed.

Snowy's Land Rover belted towards the homestead with him firing his rifle from the driver's seat into the air. Everyone came running. A stockman, a ringer and one of the jackeroos reached him and he began gesticulating, waving towards the house. Sally rushed through the garden, knowing something was dreadfully wrong by the expression on Snowy's face.

'What is it?'

'Oh Christ, Sally, get to Lorna. You tell her, I can't. Oh Christ almighty,' he put his head in his hands.

An ashen-faced jackeroo looked at Sally. 'It's the boss, Mr Monroe . . . Snowy found him. Dead.'

'What! Are you sure? Snowy, where is he, what's happened? Quick, call the doctor . . .'

Snowy held up a hand, waving vaguely. 'Nah. No good. It's bloody horrible. A croc. Sally . . .'

She gasped. Not again, not another death. Not John, nothing could get him. He was too big, too loud, too much of a bully. 'Quick, find Ian. We'll have to tell Lorna.'

'You do it, Sally.'

Jeremy and Trisha raced up. 'What's going on, Mum?'

Sally tried to take a deep breath and stop herself shaking. 'There's been an accident. I want you both to keep out of the way and be quiet. Please.'

She began to walk towards the house. Why had this happened when she was here? Was she the one to jinx Barra Creek? Along with the joy and light she felt here, darkness had again fallen on the property.

Lorna stood on the front steps watching Sally. She looked composed, her hands folded as if waiting for the inevitable. For Sally everything was happening in slow motion.

She stood at the bottom of the steps and stared up at Lorna. 'It's John. An accident . . . he's dead, Lorna.' Sally wanted to spare her the details, though God knew what the full story was.

Lorna closed her eyes, seemed to sway slightly, compressed her lips then turned away, saying quietly, 'Please find Ian,' before she went inside.

The police and air ambulance had been notified and people were beginning to appear from everywhere. The wailing from the blacks' camp had started.

'We have to get him,' said Ian, but Snowy put a restraining hand on his arm.

'The cops don't want anyone to go there. I just took one look and left. Believe me, son, you don't want to see it.'

Already the ringers and jackeroos were sitting around whispering about the gruesome details.

'Musta got caught in the snare and got strung up. Caught the croc but it came up the bank and reached him.'

'Ate his bloody head and shoulders, they reckon.'

'The boss is still hanging in the tree with half his top missing.'

No one noticed Fitzi ride quietly away.

Later, after the planes had arrived, the neighbours had driven in, the police had taken photos, shot the croc, cut down John Monroe's body and wrapped it up, ready to take it to the morgue in Normanton. Sally and the women began preparing food. As gently as possible the police sergeant took a statement from Lorna.

Automatically now everyone turned to Ian, who, looking grim and pained, answered questions, signed documents and phoned Tommy in England. The conversation was brief but he came to Sally. 'Tommy would like to speak to you.'

'Tommy, yes it's me. I'm so terribly sorry this has happened.'

'How is my mother?'

'Shocked, very calm, though she's got medication. I don't think it's sunk in for any of us.'

'How long have you been there, Sal?'

'I brought my kids up for a visit.'

'You know what, Sally, I'm planning on getting married, to an English girl. I wish I'd told Dad. Do they need me there? Should I come home?'

'Do you want to, Tommy?'

There was a pause. 'If Mum needs me. But truthfully, I'd rather remember things as they used to be. I'm sure Ian will run everything okay. I mean the funeral . . .'

'There're a lot of hands around the place at the moment. You know how it is. I'll get your mum.'

'Sally, wait, if I don't come will people think badly of me?'

'It's up to you and your mother. It's no one else's business.'

'Was it quick, do you think? I hate to think of him

suffering. How's Ian coping? He's probably feeling bad 'cause he was so shitty to Dad.'

'He's being kept busy. He'll have to deal with his own demons later, I suppose.'

'I'm glad you're there, Sal. Say hello to anyone who's still around.'

'Some of the old mob are here, Tommy. I'll put you onto your mother now.'

After the call Sally tapped at the doorway and found Lorna sitting on the little cane chair next to the baby's cot that had held her four children.

'Tommy told me that he is wondering about . . . arrangements, about coming home.'

Lorna's shoulders lifted. 'Yes. I told him it doesn't matter if he doesn't come. Let him do what he wants. I don't blame him.'

'Are you going to come and have something to eat? The police and the doctor will be leaving soon.'

'I don't want to eat. Tell me when they're leaving.' She paused. 'They're taking him away, aren't they?'

'They have to, Lorna.'

'He has to be buried here. He never wanted to leave Barra Creek, that was the trouble.'

'I'll talk to Ian.'

When the vehicles were ready to set off to the airstrip, Lorna walked onto the verandah. Holding his hat, the police sergeant shook her hand as his assistant and the medical examiner mumbled condolences. A tight knot of the blacks, Fitzi, Lizzie, Betsy and Daisy, hovered by the gate, watching them drive the Land Rover that held John Monroe's body. Young Daisy ran forward and touched the side of the vehicle as the black women hid their faces and moaned loudly.

'Get away!' Lorna's sharp retort shocked those watching. 'Get her away!' She flung out her arm, pointing at Daisy.

Fitzi and Lizzie rushed forward and took the girl away.

'Lorna, what is it?' Sally put her arm around Lorna who was rigid, glaring at the child.

Lorna turned on Sally, hissing furiously, 'As if you, of all people had to ask. She's the jinx, she's the one who's broken up our lives.' She marched into the house leaving the nervous flurry of conversation and movement among everyone watching.

Sally caught Fitzi looking at her and wondered at the expression on his face. Poor bugger, she thought. What was going to happen to them all, and to Barra Creek?

The family decided against a big memorial service, the circumstances of John's death were too harrowing. There was an official announcement that he would be buried beside his son and daughter in a private family service.

Once again Sally was leaving under painful circumstances. She hugged Lorna, who straightened and dabbed her eyes before saying quietly, 'Don't come back again, Sally. There is no peace here.'

A week later John Monroe was buried. After the short service and everyone had gone, Lorna walked around the homestead, through the gardens and down to the stables. Ian and Snowy were keeping busy, station life went on, but Lorna was making her own plans.

It was here that Fitzi came to her, holding his big Akubra hat, shuffling his feet and with eyes downcast, told her he was going on a long walkabout. 'Long time, go way.'

And told her why.

Chapter Twenty

Kiama, 2003

'WHY HAVE YOU COME to see me, Lorna?' They all knew that the purpose of this visit was to do more than just rehash old times.

'I sometimes forget things nowadays but there are some things I cannot forget. Before it's too late, I want to put things right. Well, at least let the truth be told.'

'Settling accounts before Judgment Day?' said Sally. 'Why? Surely there is no point now. It's not going to alter anything.' She now wished Lorna hadn't found her. There was more pain than joy in the memories Lorna was dragging up.

'It concerns two people, first my son Ian. He became a difficult man. I've often wondered why he was spared when the good and the sweet were not. We grew apart; he's not easy to love. After John died I bought my house in Sydney and started a new life. Too late perhaps, but I enjoyed going to the theatre and concerts. I travelled,

I saw Tommy and his little family. But I kept to myself most of the time.'

'Did you go back to Barra Creek?' asked Kate.

'Never. I saw Ian when he came to Sydney on occasions. He married a girl from Brisbane. I didn't care for her, although I went to the wedding. They never had children.'

Sally leaned forward. 'Why didn't you contact me, Lorna? You never answered my cards. I gave up in the end.'

Lorna's hands twisted. 'I couldn't face you, not after what I did.'

Kate and Sally exchanged a swift look, neither woman knew what she was talking about.

Kate took Lorna's hand. 'You told me there was something you had to tell Sally. Was it about Ian?'

'Did I tell you that, dear?' Lorna looked suddenly fearful. 'Did I say anything else about Ian?'

'You don't want him to sell your house. You said the trouble he was in was all his own doing,' Kate reminded her gently.

'What exactly is the trouble?' asked Sally.

Kate looked at Lorna, who nodded, so Kate explained. 'As I understand it, and from the inquiries I've made on Lorna's behalf, Barra Creek is unable to meet its financial obligations and the bank that holds the second mortgage is going to foreclose. Ian hoped that the money he'd get from selling his mother's house would help pay the debts.'

'He was irresponsible with money, kept spending to try to make things better. It just dug a deeper hole,' said Lorna.

'So let him face the consequences. Can't Lorna hang onto her house? How come Lorna has no rights?' Sally asked Kate.

'These cases are difficult. Her son had a solicitor give him power of attorney, she was medically assessed . . . on a bad day,' Kate smiled reassuringly at Lorna, 'and was put into what she believed was respite for some tests.'

'I was tricked. That place is a prison.'

'Now, Lorna, it's not so bad. You're in one of the best facilities . . .'

Kate looked at Sally who said, 'But not where you or I want to end up, eh Kate?'

'No, but undoing it all will be difficult. The first thing is to persuade Ian not to sell Lorna's home so she could stay there with community and home care, maybe later a paid carer.'

'Then Ian will lose the property. He's not going to let that happen,' said Sally. 'Again, I don't see how I can help you, Lorna. Ian certainly isn't going to listen to me after all these years.'

Lorna bit her lip. Kate reached over and said softly, 'You said you were going to tell Sally something –'

'I have to tell you, Sally. I want you to know what happened to John.'

'We know what happened to John.' She didn't want to remember this horror. 'No one could have saved him.'

'Yes, they could. Ian could've saved him.'

Sally leaned forward. 'Lorna, what are you saying?'

'It's been dreadful to know this all these years, but I couldn't say anything. He's my son.'

Sally felt a cold knot begin to twist inside her belly. 'What happened, Lorna?'

'Ian found his father first, when he was still alive, but he walked away, turned his back and left him. He could have saved him.'

Kate and Sally caught their breath at the same moment. 'How do you know this?' asked Sally.

'You're sure you're remembering this correctly,

Lorna? Is it clear in your mind? It didn't happen yesterday . . .' said Kate.

Lorna swung on her. 'It seems like yesterday! It has every day of my life. It's not something a mother can forget. But he was my son, I kept quiet. It wouldn't bring John back.'

'Are you sure, Lorna?' insisted Sally.

'Fitzi told me. He went there right after Snowy had found John. He went before the police arrived. He's a tracker, he could read it all, clear as day. He was upset at knowing too.'

'He was a brilliant tracker,' Sally said to Kate. 'I'd take whatever he said as gospel.'

'He said Ian was there on his horse. Tied it up to the ute and went up close, waited, then he walked away. It was the day before. John must have been alive.' Tears began to stream down Lorna's face. 'My son let his father die. What sort of mother am I?'

Kate made sympathetic noises as Sally sat there in shock. 'He hated his father, but that much?' she said.

'Sometimes people do things on impulse that seem like an instant solution, but regret it later,' said Kate. 'Once he'd walked away, for him there was no turning back. He's had to live with it.'

'So have I,' said Lorna sadly.

'You've never confronted him?' asked Sally, knowing as she said it that Lorna never would.

'Who'd believe me? I was ashamed, I didn't want anyone to know.'

'So why are you telling me now? Surely you don't expect me to confront him?'

'No, no, of course not. But someone should know,' she said. 'If I'm going to be incoherent later on . . . no one will take any notice of anything I say.'

'Now, come on, Lorna, one minute you want your

house back and to lead your own life, the next minute you tell me you're going to lose your grip.' Sally wanted to tell her it was grossly unfair to dump this information on her.

'You do believe Lorna, don't you?' asked Kate in a worried tone. She'd broken a few rules to bring her here but had no idea of the shocking information Lorna wanted to share.

'Unfortunately I do,' sighed Sally. It was a burden she didn't want. Yet, in one sense she was strangely flattered. After all these years, Lorna had turned to her. The time they'd shared had meant a lot to her as well.

'That's not all,' muttered Lorna, and Kate and Sally stared at her, wondering what else she could possibly tell them. When Lorna looked up there were tears in her eyes. 'I've never forgiven myself, Sally, but I want you to know that at the time, it was for you. I didn't want you to be trapped as I was. You deserved much better. I was going to tell you when you visited us after your divorce, but with John dying –'

'Tell me what, Lorna?' Sally's voice was tight.

Kate was still holding the old woman's hand. She pressed it gently.

'It's about Rob, I know you and he were very attracted to each other. I didn't want you to do anything silly like marry him . . .'

Sally struggled to keep quiet, but in her head she was shouting, *We loved each other, I wanted to marry him!*

'So when I told you about Rob and Betsy, about the baby, it wasn't true. Daisy is not his baby. It came to me suddenly that it might make you stop and think.' She turned to Kate, speaking in a rush, 'Most of the men did that, you know, slept with the gins . . .'

Sally lost it. 'Except Rob! I was shattered at the idea that he'd do something like that! How dare you interfere!'

she shouted, rising out of her seat. 'I believed you. I left and never gave him a chance to tell me the truth.'

'Would you have believed him? Would it have made your life better?' said Lorna with some spirit.

'Why didn't you find him and ask if it was true?' Kate asked Sally.

'Because it was a different era. You didn't challenge what someone older told you. I came from a sheltered home, I trusted you, Lorna. I loved you!' Sally's fury had a tearful edge to it. 'Of course it would have made a difference. He was the love of my life. Hal came along and it was all very expedient. I was hurt. I've never got over Rob, after all these years. Now, you calmly want to set your mind at rest and you have just told me I've wasted, lost, years and years of my life. How could you?' Her voice was loud, tearful, and echoed around the silent house. There were no sounds from Julian, who undoubtedly was wondering if he should intervene.

Lorna wrung her hands. 'I couldn't stand it any longer. I had to tell you.'

'So you'd feel better,' shouted Sally. 'How do you think I feel?'

'I'm sorry, so sorry.' Lorna was weeping.

Kate was shaking. She rose and put her hand on Lorna's shoulder and looked at Sally with great sympathy. 'I had no idea about this, what she was going to tell you.'

Sally turned away from them, her arms folded, her shoulders stooped. 'I think you'd better leave.'

Kate took a card from her pocket and put it on the coffee table. 'There's my card, if you want to reach me.'

'I don't think so. You've done enough,' said Sally stiffly.

Julian, looking concerned, hovered in the doorway, 'Can I do anything, Sally?'

'Yes, show these ladies out, please.' Sally strode from the room and Julian heard her bedroom door shut.

Lorna leaned against the car window, her usual straight-backed demeanour gone. Now she hunched into her coat, her face pale.

Kate turned on the windscreen wipers. 'Are you all right?'

'No,' she answered in a small voice. 'I shouldn't have come.'

Kate drove to the end of the road then stopped the car. 'Look, Lorna, I didn't know what you were going to tell your ex-governess. I can understand your need to get it off your chest. But you must understand while you've been living with it for decades, this is a big shock for Sally.'

'I loved her like a little sister, a daughter. It's a terrible thing to have regrets. I kept away from her all these years, I couldn't face her. Especially knowing her marriage had broken up. I didn't have an overwhelming passionate love in my life. John got me pregnant and did the decent thing. I like to think I was a good wife. But what Sally and Rob had, I think, was the real thing. And I destroyed it.'

'Maybe in time Sally will feel less bitter. At least now she knows he never did the wrong thing by her. Where is Rob? What happened to him?'

'It's all too late. He married a country girl, they went to Dog Leg Station in the Territory. It belonged to his father. He was one of the first to get in Brahman cattle up there, though his big love was horses. Sally's too.'

'She seems happy enough. I can see why she didn't like the social scene in Sydney. She's a very down-to-earth woman.'

Lorna almost smiled. 'Strong minded and determined.

Sally's never been a pushover, that's for sure.' She sighed. 'Well, what's done is done. What's going to happen to me, Kate?'

Kate looked at her watch. 'It's getting late and it's miserable weather. I don't want to drive back to Sydney in this. Let's find a nice B&B and stay the night.' And I'm hanging out for a strong drink, thought Kate. 'I'm sure things will look different in the morning.'

Lorna merely nodded, she was exhausted. She'd done what she came to do.

As Kate drove towards the main street of town, so many questions, emotions and scenes ran through her mind, but there was one question she had to ask. 'Lorna, if it wasn't Rob, who is Daisy's father? Do you know?'

'Yes, I know. She was fathered by my husband, John. He didn't have to tell me, I knew. I suspect he knew I knew. When I was packing up to move to Sydney I found his diaries. He didn't write many personal things, but he did write a note that Betsy gave birth to his daughter . . . "a rather delicious little creature" was how he described her.'

Kate drove slowly, her head reeling. What a tangled family. No wonder Lorna hated Daisy. She'd lost a daughter and her husband was attached to his illegitimate child. 'Does Daisy know? Does anyone know? Ian?'

'Absolutely not. John gave Daisy a lot of attention but I told Betsy that if she ever told anyone that Daisy belonged to the boss, I'd put a curse on her. That scared her. I'm sure she didn't sleep only with John. Anyway, I think she believed babies came from spirits in the billabong, or some such.' Lorna turned away, her mouth set in an expression Kate recognised. She was retreating and she'd get no more information from her. She might not be very aware of much tomorrow. Today had been a strain.

Just as well, Kate didn't think she wanted to know any more about Barra Creek.

Sally lay on her bed, bitter tears burning her cheeks. At first she'd hugged her pillow, feeling again Rob's arms around her, his kisses, his gentle slow voice as if they had been together only the night before. Then she'd cursed Lorna for breaking the smooth shell of her life and scrambling her emotions. How easily she'd fallen apart at the thought of Rob and the knowledge that she'd wrongly judged him and thrown away years of happiness. The most hurtful thing was that he had no idea why she'd run from him. She'd never contacted him, and he had abided by her wish not to write or call her. How naive and stupid she'd been. How cruel of Lorna, no matter how good her intentions were at the time. Had he been hurt? Did he care about losing her? From all accounts he was happily married and living on the family station. At least he must have made his peace with his father and brothers.

'Damn you, Lorna,' she said aloud and sat up.

The rain had eased, but the sunset was smothered by the heavy grey sky. There was a tap at her door.

'Sally, I'm going now, do you want anything?' Julian sounded worried.

'Come in, Julian.' Sally wiped her face and smoothed her hair as the young assistant opened the door.

'Bad news?' he asked.

'Catching up on old news. It was a bit traumatic.' She smiled weakly.

'Would you like me to do anything? I've locked up the gallery. Jeremy called, he said not to worry, he'd do the horses tonight.'

'Good on him. Thanks.' Jeremy and his two children were staying in the old farmhouse on her property for a week's holiday. He had established a thriving practice as a solicitor in Sydney, but he enjoyed getting out of town with his family.

'I'm fine now. I'll go and open a bottle of good red. I think I need a drink.'

He smiled with relief to see Sally sounding more like herself. 'Okay, see you tomorrow. G'night.'

She washed her face, taking deep slow breaths, then went to the kitchen. She poured herself a glass of shiraz then turned on the CD and sat in front of the fire. Andrea Bocelli's romantic tenor filled the room. She turned it off and sat in silent contemplation of the fire, sipping her wine.

She was always swift to react, flaring like a rocket, exploding and then petering out, she knew that. Now the shower of sparks Lorna had ignited was fading. She felt less angry at the poor woman. God, what a burden she'd carried around all these years. She had protected her son and he had tossed her into an old people's home to be cared for by others. Lorna, with her standards and proprieties – it was sad that she should be reduced to this. My God, could it happen to her, thought Sally. No husband, children busy with their own lives. Trisha was trekking overseas and virtually unreachable. Surely not. Lorna had really rocked her boat. But bugger you, Lorna, I'm not lifting a finger to help you. There's nothing I can do, it's all too late. It doesn't do me any good to dwell on what might have been. Sally put her empty glass down and turned on the TV news.

Kate poured Lorna a small sherry and helped herself to a gin and tonic from the drinks tray in the lounge room of the quaint B&B they'd checked into.

'I'm glad we're stopping overnight,' said Kate.

'I'm sorry I've been so much trouble.'

'I said I'd help you, but I have to take you back to the nursing home, at least for the moment, until something is decided about your house.'

'I'll never get out of there. Sally won't do anything and I don't blame her.'

'We could approach the Guardianship Tribunal to appoint someone to look into your affairs, hire a solicitor,' began Kate.

'No, no, I don't want to make a fuss. I don't want people poking their nose into my business. No one else must know about Ian.'

'I understand but, Lorna, even though he is your son, he hasn't done the right thing by you.'

Lorna leaned back and closed her eyes. 'I'm tired. I'm not going to battle any more.'

Kate didn't like the look of resignation on the old woman's face. She'd seen it before, when people simply gave up and willed themselves to die. She'd heard about it happening in indigenous cultures around the world too – an old man paddling his boat into the sunset, a woman lying under a tree to die. If one could choose the time, place and condition of one's passing how much easier it would be. Kate had got into this profession to improve the quality of the final stage of a fully lived life. Lorna had touched her heart and her professional sensibilities. If she could make things better for someone like Lorna, it was another small step in changing the attitudes to, and treatment of, the elderly.

The owner of the B&B came and made small talk until she served dinner.

Lorna retired early and Kate watched TV for a while but when their hostess came in with a cup of coffee looking ready to start up a conversation again, Kate decided to go for a walk.

'Rug up. The wind is coming off the ocean, it's nippy.'

'Thank you, I will.'

She enjoyed the salty sea air that whipped through her hair, stung her cheeks and forced her to walk briskly. The faster she walked the quicker her mind worked, and by the time she got back to the guesthouse, she had a plan.

But Sally made the first move.

'Hello, Kate, this is Sally Lee, Lorna's governess.'

'Hi, of course, how are you?' Kate was surprised to hear from her. Two weeks had passed since their visit. 'I was going to call you. Do you want to know how Lorna is?'

'Partly. I'm sorry if I exploded at you both. It was all a bit of a shock.'

'I can imagine. Lorna is all right, a little withdrawn, but functioning okay. I was going to ring you but, please, if you'd rather not . . . be involved,' Kate said hesitantly.

'The reason I'm calling you is because I've done a lot of thinking. While I'll never get over her busting up Rob and me, I'm trying to live in the present and I don't like the idea of Lorna being ripped off by Ian, especially after what he did. I have no doubts that he did walk away from his father.'

'I'm glad you feel like that.'

'I want to help Lorna, but I thought I'd discuss it with you first. You're a very dedicated young woman. Are you this hands-on with all your cases?'

'Unfortunately no,' she said. 'But Lorna has a strong personality, and I like her. She got my attention.'

'Yes, she's good at that. Well, I had a couple of ideas. What about you?'

'I hope you don't think I've overstepped the mark here,' said Kate, 'but once I got involved I couldn't just abandon Lorna. She gave me her son's details in England and I rang him.'

'You called Tommy?'

'Yes, I filled him in as much as needed.'

'Did you tell him about Ian?'

'No! I couldn't break Lorna's confidence. But I did tell him about her financial difficulties.'

'Was he pissed off at Ian?'

'Yes, you might say that. He's not prepared to come back because he's busy with his work, but he's being helpful. It appears the bank is going ahead with the foreclosure.'

'Kate, I'm coming up to Sydney. Let's meet and talk further.' Sally sounded efficient and businesslike.

Ten days later Sally had to pinch herself. I can't believe I'm doing this, again. Going back to Barra Creek, she thought.

Huge white floating prawn factories dotted the milky waters of the Gulf of Carpentaria. From the port of Karumba the tentacles of the Norman River coiled inland beneath the small plane as it banked and soon began its descent into Normanton.

Sally stepped into the familiar heat and noticed the breezy casualness of the locals. As she picked up her small bag a man asked, 'Want a ride into town, love?'

'Thanks, to the train station would be good. I've got the right day I hope.'

'For the Gulflander?' He looked at his watch. 'Yep, it's Thursday, leaves in half an hour.' He gave her a second glance. 'Are you a train buff?'

'I'm heading into Croydon.'

413

He had her tagged as another railway afficionado come to ride the unique 'Tin hare' as they called the grand old railmotor. She thanked him as he dropped her at the railway station where tourists were standing on the lawns, being photographed in front of the beautifully restored Victorian building. Others were collecting fat ripe mangoes that had fallen from the trees nearby.

The train arrived in the deserted gold-mining town of Croydon after lunch and, while the tourists wandered around the historic buildings, Sally waited at the small hotel picking at a sandwich and drinking a cold light beer. A Land Cruiser pulled up outside the pub and a young man in a white shirt with sleeves rolled up neatly, dark trousers and a tie got out and, glancing around, came towards the attractive woman sitting at the table facing the dusty street. 'Mrs Lee? I'm James Hynes, from the bank.'

'You're right on the dot. Have you had lunch?'

'No, I'll get a hamburger. I've been out looking at a property. We've got a bit of a drive ahead of us if we want to get there before five. The road's good, though. Bit different from your day, I guess.'

'Yes. I used to fly into Barra Creek, this is a novelty but it's the only way I could get here at short notice. Where's Mr Langton?'

'Meeting us there. He's flying in from Cloncurry to the Barra strip, then going back to head office in Brisbane. He said you could go back with him, unless you want to stay on, of course.'

'I'll see. Do you do much of this?' she asked the well-presented young man whose cheerful demeanour didn't sit well with the task he had to do.

'Yeah, it's been bad. The drought and all, but it's got to be done. This is just a formality, the people fight as long as they can but if they can't come up with the cash,

414

well, business is business, right?' He wasn't expecting her to show him any sympathy. Mr Langton had filled him in on why he had to bring this lady out to Barra Creek.

They talked little on the drive. Sally was feeling nostalgic and there was a tight pain in her chest as memories washed over her together with the knowledge of what she had to do. She wished it hadn't come to this but, as Lorna and Kate agreed, it was the right thing.

Even after all these years, the land was familiar to her. The shadows of the tall trees at the gate were lengthening as they drove onto the dirt road leading to the homestead. It used to be her favourite time of day, when she turned her horse for home. A knot of people were standing in the front garden, near a ute and a heavily laden truck covered with a roped-down tarpaulin. James pulled up and Sally stared at the group, her heart in her mouth. She didn't recognise the white stockmen leaning against the fence, but to one side among the handful of Aboriginal people she saw the unmistakable figure of Fitzi. Stooped and white-haired he was leaning heavily on a tall, strong-looking woman aged about forty in moleskin pants, a blue shirt and her hat hanging down her back. Her hair was brown and as Sally walked towards them they turned. After peering intently at her, Fitzi recognised her. He nudged the woman and spoke.

'Miss Sally?'

'Fitzi, how are you? I can't believe it's you!' Sally was choked up and saw the old man's rheumy eyes also water.

'He's doing good for an old fella in his eighties,' said the woman. 'I'm Daisy. Been a while since you bin back here at Barra, eh?'

'Nineteen seventy-six.'

The woman looked down. 'Yeah, that was a bad time. Poor Boss . . .'

'Why you come back? Dis bad day, no good.' Fitzi began to shake his head. 'Wot goin 'appen poor pella me, now all dis 'appen?'

'Don't you worry, old man, Daisy mob gonna look after you, no matta what, eh.' But she gave Sally a hard look. 'You helpin' the boss?' She inclined her head towards the homestead with some disdain.

Sally looked away from them and for the first time looked at the house. It was almost smothered in creepers that had died back leaving twisted brown vines covering the verandah posts. The old house had never been grand but in its simplicity and tidiness it had always had a welcoming, comfortable air. Now it looked rundown and forlorn. She turned back to Daisy. 'No, I'm here for another reason. What plans do you have, Daisy?'

'I want to stay, we got good workers round here. We kin make dis a good place.' She shook her head. 'We jist wait, eh?'

'Daisy bin running ever 'ting. She good cattle boss,' said Fitzi. 'You tell big boss Daisy good.'

James Hynes touched Sally's arm. 'Best you wait out here. Mr Langton will talk to you later.'

The sun was sinking as Ian came outside. He was alone, as Sally expected. She had found out that his wife had moved back to Brisbane several years ago. He walked with a straight back, holding himself stiffly and Sally was reminded of Lorna. He looked ahead and held a folder of documents in one hand, a small overnight bag in the other. He was followed by Langton, an older man in a navy jacket, grey trousers, shirt and tie.

Ian saw her and he stopped, quite shocked. 'Sally? What are you doing here?' He glanced around, his face closing, a barrier going up. 'Did my mother send you?'

'No. She doesn't know I'm here. Ian, I'm very sorry it's come to this . . .' Sally faltered.

'Why would you care? Who told you to come? Are you making sure I'm really going so you can tell them all?' he said bitterly.

'I am not here to gloat. Tommy asked me to come.'

'What's he care? He never wanted this place. He never offered to help me.'

'Did you ever ask?'

Ian didn't answer, then he shrugged. 'No point. I knew he wouldn't lift a finger. You can tell my mother I'm not walking out of here with nothing. She doesn't need that house in Sydney.'

'She might not need it, but that's her decision. I suggest you make a fresh start and leave her in peace.'

'What's it to you? You were only here for a little while. You were the governess, for God's sake.'

'I had hoped we'd stay friends. Your mother is my friend. She's suffered all these years knowing something that has been painful. She has protected you, Ian.'

Sally thought she saw a faint flush under his tanned face. 'What're you talking about?'

'About your father. Fitzi told her you left your father to die.'

He swung around and glared at the old man. 'Who's going to believe anything he says? It was years ago, you're all full of bullshit.' He brushed past her and wrenched open the door of the truck.

Sally had seen the flash of fear in his eyes. He knew exactly what she was referring to. She watched silently as the two white stockmen stepped forward and awkwardly shook Ian's hand, mumbling good luck.

James Hynes looped a chain over the gate with a shiny new padlock and snapped it shut. Langton, his supervisor, unfolded a sheet of paper and read aloud a short formal statement that the lands and buildings of the holding known as Barra Creek had been foreclosed upon and that Ian Monroe had forfeited all rights in ownership of said property, which was now vested in the bank as mortgagee in possession.

Daisy, Fitzi and the small group of Aborigines stood huddled together, looking worried. Ian avoided looking at them, got behind the wheel and for a moment Sally thought he was going to say something to her. But as she stepped forward, he turned on the engine and gunned the truck, spraying them with dirt and small stones. Silently they watched him drive away from his childhood home for the last time.

One of the stockmen shook his head. 'As easy as that. Drive off and leave everything you've ever known, that you've worked for. Bloody banks.'

'He was running the place down for years, borrowed too much. The drought did him in. Still, it must be tough,' said another.

'What's he going to do?'

'Heading for Yowah, going opal mining. He's going to a place where no one asks any questions.'

Mr Langton looked at Sally and stepped forward. 'I am instructed by the bank that the property is now officially on the market and available for purchase.'

'And I am instructed to ask you to take this with you. It is an offer in writing to purchase this place by Thomas Monroe. I'm acting on his behalf. Here is the proxy authorising me to sign any papers.'

'I have to take this back and put it through all the right channels. I can't agree to anything here, you know that.'

'I was led to believe there wouldn't be any problems.' Sally was feeling shaky.

'That's probably right, but I can't let you onto the premises, Mrs Lee.'

'I understand. I'll drive back to Normanton with

Mr Hynes. I'm booked into the hotel in Croydon for tonight.'

'I can give you a ride to Brisbane, if you like. Take your pick.'

'Thank you, I'd appreciate the ride back to Normanton.' Sally didn't want to spend any time with the officious bank agent. Also she wanted time to come to terms with all this.

When they had spoken on the phone Tommy had said to her, 'There's no way Ian is getting his hands on Mum's house. Please do what you think is best, Sally. I have so many regrets at not following up on what was going on in my mother's life.'

It took several weeks of meetings between Lorna, Sally and the new solicitor Sally had found for her, but now everything was finalised. Sally returned to Barra Creek.

There was no one living in the homestead; the phone went unanswered. She sent a letter to Daisy to tell her that she'd be arriving with good news, wondering if mail would get to them now that it was common knowledge that the place was unoccupied.

As she drove up to the old house, it looked very deserted. She walked onto the verandah, calling, 'Anyone home?'

There was no answer. She got in her hired four-wheel drive and headed towards the camp. The gundis looked tidy, some chairs were outside in the sun, a few old dogs scratched idly. In the distance a couple of Aboriginal stockmen were working on a fence. In one of the gundis Betsy, now frail, was sleeping. Before Sally was out of the car, Fitzi and Daisy came to meet her.

Their delight in seeing her was tempered by the worry she'd come to 'move us mob on'.

'You didn't get my letter?'

'No mail since Ian left,' said Daisy. 'No one has visited either, no one from the bank.'

'Wot gonna 'appen?' asked Fitzi, taking Sally's hand. 'Dis place be my country. Old Pitzi gonna end up in dat old-age place there in Normanton, bloody jail place, one room. How dis old man gonna lib on him own in one room, eh?'

'Don't worry, Fitzi. It's all been fixed up. But first I've got to talk with Daisy.'

Fitzi read something in Sally's smile and in her eyes and was reassured. 'I boil 'em up billy.' He headed into his gundi to make a pot of tea.

Daisy led Sally to two of the sagging chairs. 'What you fix up now, eh? Me and the boys and my old mother got no place to go.'

'You don't have to go anywhere, Daisy. You were born here under that tree over there. I saw you born, me and Mrs Monroe.'

Daisy looked at her. 'That's right, you told me you were there.'

'Did your mother ever talk to you about your father, your true father?'

Daisy shrugged. 'I got plenty father, Fitzi, uncles, lot of family. Not too many round now but.'

'Daisy, your father was John Monroe. Barra Creek belongs to you because you were born on its land and your father owned it. That means you have as much claim to being here as Ian does.'

Daisy struggled with this knowledge, her face a mixture of emotions as the full impact hit her. 'Dat true? Daisy belong t' the big old boss?' Tears began to run down her face as a mature woman cried for her father like a little girl.

'You talk to Betsy, your mum. It's all right for her to tell you the true story now,' said Sally gently.

Daisy nodded but then looked worried. 'I got no money, how me and Fitzi and my mother all stay here?'

'Do you remember Tommy? Ian's brother? Well, he has paid the money for Barra Creek, and he wants you all to share it, run it and look after it for him.'

'Stay here all time? No move away?'

'Tommy suggested that we could advertise in the *Queensland Country Life* for a manager, to help you all run the place if you like. But you and Tommy, you both own it.'

Fitzi came back out and looked fearful as he saw Daisy weeping but as they explained things to him, a huge smile of relief lit up his face. He patted Daisy's hand. 'Dis place be home, longa time fer Barra Crik people. Good, good.'

Sally was starting to cry. 'It is good, Fitzi. Now come on, what about that cuppa?'

Sally still felt emotional when she related the events to Kate. 'I couldn't believe the look on Fitzi's and Daisy's faces. It was beautiful, just beautiful.'

'So Ian just drove away. Are you sure he won't make any trouble?'

'He's got no more fight in him. You know, in a strange way when I told him that his mother knew what he'd done to his father all those years ago, there was almost a look of relief in his eyes.'

'I wonder if he'll ever ask forgiveness.'

'I don't think he'll ask it from his mother,' said Sally, pushing her coffee cup away and glancing round the crowded cafe. 'How are things going with Lorna's case?'

'It's looking good. This whole thing has perked her up. She was all right at the last medical assessment. Tommy wants her to stay in her home as long as she can.

He's offered to pay for the care she needs and he's going to visit her next month. She's looking forward to that. He sounds very nice.'

'You're looking very pleased with yourself, Kate. And so you should. Thanks should go to you for getting this ball rolling. I'd better make a move, I'm heading back down the coast tonight.'

She went to push back her chair but Kate leaned over and put her hand on hers. 'Sally, there's one last loose end. I've become so involved with the family since hearing all this, I decided I'd make a couple more phone calls.'

'What about? There isn't a problem is there? What could possibly be left to sort out?'

'You and Rob.'

'What! That's ancient history now, I'm afraid. He's been out of the picture for years,' said Sally, but seeing Kate's face she felt her heart constrict. 'What do you mean exactly?'

'I tracked him down. Lorna wanted to tell him what she did, what happened.'

'No! The poor man. No, he doesn't need to know any of this, Lorna is causing more pain, disrupting more lives. Don't let her, Kate.'

'It's too late. She talked to him on the phone. Sally, he's coming down, he wants to see you. And her. He reacted like you did, but now he's just grateful she's told him the truth, at last.'

Sally couldn't speak for a minute. 'You mean, he also wondered about what had happened . . . he cared?'

'Of course! He said he never got over you. He couldn't understand why you didn't give him a chance. Then he figured that he and Barra Creek had just been an interlude in your life.'

Sally closed her eyes, feeling the hurt all over again.

She took a deep breath. 'And what about his family, what do they say?'

'No idea,' said Kate briskly. 'He's been divorced for ten years. He's breeding horses, he also said something about Jasper, that you'd understand. Anyway, he can tell you about it.'

'I can't see him. Oh no! This is too much.'

'What do you mean you can't see him? He sounds gorgeous. When he asked if you were still a beautiful redhead, I said you were a knockout.'

Sally didn't know whether to laugh or cry. 'Kate, I'm sixty years old! I can't start acting like a giddy teenager.'

'Then just feel like it, and enjoy it.'

'Oh my God, I don't know whether to hit you and Lorna or hug you.' She dropped her head on her arms on the table.

'You've got a week. He's going to phone you. He said he's very shy and nervous.' Kate patted Sally's head. 'Are you going to be okay driving?'

Sally sat up and grinned. 'Well, you've given me a hell of a lot to think about on the way home. I'll be there before this has sunk in.'

Outside the coffee shop, Sally hugged Kate. 'I'll call you. I don't know how to thank you for all this.'

Kate looked at the beautiful, vivacious woman in front of her. 'You know, Sally, there's one thing I'd really like, to go and see Barra Creek one day.'

Sally grinned and gave her a thumbs up. 'Done.'

Epilogue

'Your mother can still ride like a champion.' Rob leaned over the rails of the yard watching Sally on the young thoroughbred trot around the ring.

Trisha glanced at the handsome man, thinking it was no wonder her mother had fallen for him. 'She's in her element, that's for sure. In every way, I'd say,' laughed Sally's pretty daughter. 'This has been the best coming-home present I could have. I'm really so happy about you two getting together.' She touched his arm gently and he gave a big grin.

'Yeah, it's pretty good, isn't it? These past couple of months have been like a dream. It's funny how life can pan out. It's never too late for some things.'

The words slipped out so easily. If only he'd believed that all along. He'd been so shocked at Sally's sudden departure, her terse letter, Lorna's cool explanation. He was hurt, bewildered, then mad. There'd been some good natured kidding from a few of the blokes.

'Cripes, what'd ya do to Sally? You scared her off for sure, mate.'

'Did you get her up the duff? Why'd she take off so sudden?'

Rob knew he'd been evasive and vague about making any firm commitment to her. He thought Sally understood. He felt so deeply about her that it scared him. He wanted time to adjust to the overwhelming feelings he had for her. He wanted to make things perfect for her. Then he came to realise his hesitancy, though motivated by the best intentions, had been his undoing. He was just a slow, careful country boy and she was used to sophisticated city ways. He resigned himself to his loss. And planned to wait for Sally to make the first move.

Then he heard she'd married. Broken hearted he returned to the Territory, made his peace with his father and brothers and started afresh. Eventually he married a nice country woman and had two terrific kids. But there was never the spark in his heart that Sally had ignited. While he'd never mentioned Sally to his wife, she must have sensed she never had his total love. Like Sally and Hal, they drifted apart. He resigned himself to a single life in old age, drawing joy from his children.

Then came the phone call from Kate. Before he'd even heard the whole story of Lorna, at the mere mention of Sally's name his heart turned over. He was stunned, but secretly not surprised when he heard what Ian had done. And so the meeting between he and Sally was arranged. They spoke briefly on the phone, Sally's laugh was just as he remembered, but he couldn't help wondering what she'd look like now. So many years had passed, she'd had children, their lives had gone in such different directions, except for their love of horses. He was as nervous as a boy on his first date, but decided that it didn't matter what Sally looked like, to renew the friendship, maybe the companionship would be wonderful.

They were both unprepared for the surge of physical and emotional passion that rushed through them at the sight of each other. The years were swept away in an instant.

Trisha's question broke his sweet reverie.

'Are you going to get married?'

He ran his hand through his hair. 'You're your mother's daughter, aren't you? No beating around the bush. Well, I don't know. It seems a bit unnecessary at our age.'

'Have you asked her?'

'I'm thinking about it.'

'Seems to me you hesitated once before,' said Trisha.

'You might be right.'

'It'd be nice while Lorna still knows what's going on,' she said softly. 'And you'll get to meet our New Zealand rellies!'

'Sally's mother sounds formidable, even at her age I'm still nervous about passing muster by Mrs Mitchell.'

Trisha laughed. 'Our dad was the same. Jem and I were terrified of her when we were little. I think she'd like to see my mum made an honest woman.'

Rob straightened up. 'We'll see. I'd have to pick the right moment.'

'Mum's the word. I'm going down to see Lorna. See ya later, Rob.'

He watched her stride across the paddock to the small cottage where Lorna now lived at Sally's farm. Lorna had changed since selling her house in Sydney and moving there. She'd taken a great interest in the small art gallery and loved to chat to the tourists who called by. Sally's children and grandchildren came and went, and Rob hoped his children would do the same. They still lived in the Territory, but Rob had no regrets at leaving.

He and Sally had decided to set up a small thoroughbred training and breeding program combining her property and his select horses that had been sired by Jasper and his progeny. Funny how the years had disappeared, he thought as he ducked under the rail of the fence. The minute he and Sally had seen each other they knew they'd be together, as they were meant to be. Damn, Trisha was right about him hanging back, not wanting to commit himself all those years ago. He'd wanted to wait until he had everything set up. He knew better now.

Sally watched him walk across the ring, he looked just as he did back at Barra Creek – lean, tall, that fluid way he walked. He was as familiar to her as her own shadow. They'd both had full and interesting lives, but now it was their time. About bloody time too, she thought. She pulled up her horse, and Rob rubbed behind its ear and rested his hand on the bridle.

'I was thinking, Sally . . .'

'Thinking what?' She waited for a small criticism, a suggestion about the horse, her riding.

'I was thinking it was about time we got married.'

Sally blinked, flung back her head and burst out laughing. 'Well, heck, why not? Seeing you asked me. Finally . . .'

She swung down into his outstretched arms.

The horse gave a slight flick of its tail and stood patiently, ignored by the man and woman who held each other tightly.

THE END

ALSO AVAILABLE FROM PAN MACMILLAN

Di Morrissey
Monsoon

Sandy Donaldson has been working in Vietnam for a volunteer organisation, HOPE, for four years. Reluctant to return to Australia when her contract is up, she invites her oldest friend Anna to come and explore the popular tourist destination of beautiful Vietnam.

Both have unexplored links to this country, but swept up in their own relationships and ambitions, they are reluctant to pursue them. A chance meeting with an Australian journalist will encourage the girls to reconnect with their past.

Monsoon is a journey into the hearts and memories of those caught in a certain time, in a particular place.

'An intoxicating blend of drama and mystery set in steamy South-East Asia.'
AUSTRALIAN WOMEN'S WEEKLY

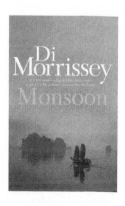

Di Morrissey
The Valley

The Valley is nestled between rugged peaks, divided by a magnificent river. Within its peaceful green contours are held the secrets of generations of tribes, families and loners who have come under its spell.

But some secrets are never shared, never told.

Until one woman returns and begins asking questions . . . and discovers the story of a forgotten valley pioneer whose life becomes entwined with hers. But in looking into her own family's history she uncovers more than she ever expected – and what her mother hoped would always remain a secret . . .

'*The Valley* is a long, juicy page-turner, a generational saga that flows resistlessly.'
THE AGE

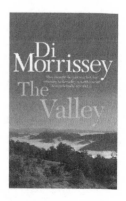

Made in the USA
Lexington, KY
05 April 2015